PENGUIN

NATURE AND SELECTED ESSAYS

RALPH WALDO EMERSON (1803–1882), the son of a Unitarian minister and a chaplain during the American Revolution, was born in 1803 in Boston. He attended the Boston Latin School, and in 1817 entered Harvard, graduating in 1820. Emerson supported himself as a schoolteacher from 1821–1826. In 1826 he was "approbated to preach," and in 1829 became pastor of the Second Church (Unitarian) in Boston. That same year he married Ellen Louise Tucker, who was to die of tuberculosis only seventeen months later. In 1832 Emerson resigned his pastorate and traveled to Europe, where he met Coleridge, Wordsworth, and Carlyle. He settled in Concord, Massachusetts, in 1834, where he began a new career as a public lecturer, and married Lydia Jackson a year later. A group that gathered around Emerson in Concord came to be known as "the Concord School," and included Bronson Alcott, Henry David Thoreau, Nathaniel Hawthorne, and Margaret Fuller. Every year Emerson made a lecture tour; and these lectures were the source of most of his essays. *Nature* (1836), his first published work, contained the essence of his transcendental philosophy, which views the world of phenomena as a sort of symbol of the inner life and emphasizes individual freedom and self-reliance. Emerson's address to the Phi Beta Kappa society of Harvard (1837) and another address to the graduating class of the Harvard Divinity School (1838) applied his doctrine to the scholar and clergyman, provoking sharp controversy. An ardent abolitionist. Emerson lectured and wrote widely against slavery from the 1840s through the Civil War. His principal publications include two volumes of *Essays* (1841, 1844), *Poems* (1847), *Representative Men* (1850), *The Conduct of Life* (1860), and *Society and Solitude* (1870). He died of pneumonia in 1882 and was buried in Concord.

LARZER ZIFF is the author of a number of books on American literary culture, among them *The American 1890s*, winner of the Christian Gauss Award. A member of the American Academy of Arts and Sciences, he is Research Professor of English at Johns Hopkins University.

RALPH WALDO EMERSON

Nature and
Selected Essays

Edited with an Introduction by
LARZER ZIFF

PENGUIN BOOKS

PENGUIN BOOKS

An imprint of Penguin Random House LLC
penguinrandomhouse.com

First published as *Selected Essays* in the United States of America
by The Penguin American Library 1982
Published in Penguin Books 1985
This edition published 2003

ISBN 9780142437629 (paperback)

Library of Congress record available at https://lccn.loc.gov/2003269304

Printed in the United States of America
35th Printing

Set in Sabon MT Pro

Contents

Introduction

Ralph Waldo Emerson occupies the very center of the American intellectual tradition. Reading his works we recognize we are at a great junction point. Puritanism and revolutionary republicanism, their force all but spent, arrive at this junction to be transformed and flow out again, with vigor, as idealism and individualism. The world of nature, battered by the assaults of a burgeoning population, arrives at it to flow out again as spirit rather than matter. The giants of political history, such as Napoleon, who seem to have dominated the lives of thousands, arrive at it to flow out again, not as causes of our destiny, but as effects of the same force that can elevate us all.

From our perspective in the twentieth century, we note this, and yet in order to appreciate the texture of Emerson's achievement we may find it valuable to begin by approaching it from the perspective of the culture in which he lived in his formative years. In the following pages, then, we shall start with the world Emerson found and move from that environment to the world he has left us.

With the publication of *The Sketch Book of Geoffrey Crayon, Gent.* (1819–20), Washington Irving won international fame for himself and some international respect for American culture. The rude American republic of unfinished manners, commercial instincts, and awful art was not, after all, the hopelessly permanent home of aggressively practical mediocrity. Cultivation, Irving demonstrated, was possible. Its previous invisibility had been a matter only of immaturity, not, as English critics would have had it, of the intrinsic nature of American society. Given time for further cultivation, America could be expected to produce more Geoffrey Crayons.

The obstacles to literature around which Irving made his way can be summed up under two headings, history and nature. With regard to history, the United States was of so recent an origin that no significant series of identity-giving events had yet taken place to impart tone to the people or their surroundings. They lacked character because they lacked a common past and therefore lacked common allegiances and a common pattern of reaction to the problems of living the daily life. American conditions were so mutable that uprooting seemed to occur swiftly after each planting: political history was a history of repeated elections and changes of office; family history was marked by the rise and fall of fortunes within two or three generations; intellectual history was punctuated by the ceaseless succession of one religious movement after another—orthodox formalism, moral reform, resurgent pietism.

Nature also seemed opposed to the acculturation of the citizenry despite its promise of abundant prosperity. The brooding weight of the vast, primitive continent stretching beyond the western horizon made the seaboard effort at civilization appear trivial. The task of taming, it seemed, would have to go on for a century at least before a culture, in the traditional sense, would emerge.

The nature that was the staple subject of the romantic artists of Europe bore copious signs of an interchange with everlasting human aspirations. Ruins gave wildflowers their meaning. But American nature was a splendid, empty theater, offering economic promise but suggesting no previous human experience.

At the start of *The Sketch Book*, Geoffrey Crayon tells his reader, "I visited various parts of my own country, and had I been merely a lover of fine scenery I should have felt little desire to seek elsewhere its gratification." But, he complains, all that mighty spectacle—oceanic lakes, lofty mountains, boundless plains— had reference only to itself, while the landscapes of Europe "held forth the charms of storied and poetical associations." Longing for the traces of renowned achievement rather than the exclusive dominance of commonplace reality, longing, that is, for a nurturing marriage of history and nature rather than the exclusive dominance of either the humdrum or unmediated wildness, he went to Europe. When the cry of "Land!" sounded from the watchman on the ship, he sped to the rail to look across the water at a dim form that could be called Europe. With it in his eyes, he experienced the rush of a throng of sensations and exclaimed that he, at last, was gazing on "the land of promise." The needy European, emerging from tradition with an empty stomach, regarded America as the land of promise, but the native son, his stomach full and his imagination starved, reversed the application of the biblical phrase.

Just as European naturalists had hunted down and captured American flora, sketching them and preserving them in notebooks, so Washington Irving conducted a relentless search for those items of the European scene that spoke of the power of the past to dominate the present. As each was located, he described it to bind it in his portfolio. He was avid for everything that resisted mutability and testified, as nothing in America did, to the existence of permanent values.

The enormous popularity of *The Sketch Book* in America indicates how widespread among his compatriots was Irving's longing for stability beyond the shifts of time. They were grateful for the opportunity he provided them to exercise their sense that they shared the sentiments of older peoples despite the shallowness of their history. They were anxious to feel themselves a folk. In the failure of their surroundings to provide the customs that would satisfy this want, they were thankful to be fed with legends they could domesticate and foreign scenes that told them that they were, after all, as tender and as conservative as the people of older cultures.

This yearning for a landscape that spoke of human permanence was in only apparent opposition to everyday American reality. Its fulfillment, as indicated by the popularity of the work of Irving and those who followed in his path—among them Longfellow and also, in some part, Hawthorne—was more a matter of Americans continuing to do what they were doing than otherwise. To be sure, they needed to take greater pains to stabilize their economy and to assure political continuity in order to promote development rather than change. But as settlements continued their steady encroachment on the wildness of the west, and as the older communities of the east proceeded to formalize behavior into customs, so conservative values would control the changing face of American society. The history of the culture would be the history of European man in the new world, bringing to it institutions best fitted to subdue it. American civilization might differ from that of European countries in that it blended people of different stocks and was distinguished by a high degree of mobility, both social and geographical. But classes, or at least distinct social groupings, would stabilize, and the necessarily different American institutions would nevertheless exist to protect the very same elements of human continuity that were protected by the institutions of European civilization.

When Irving spoke of the "storied associations" of the European landscape, he thus attributed the rich suggestiveness he found there to the scene before his eyes rather than to the imagination behind them. In common with many another artist, he affirmed that the "poetic" was a quality that inhered in objective reality and stimulated a responsive feeling commensurate with it in the sensitive observer. With meaning so located, little wonder that American nature could not supply the imagination. If the object had to carry "storied" associations in order to resonate, it had to be connected to a remembered past of human events. The superficiality of the American past meant that it must be assisted by the artist's visiting legends upon the scene until the passage of time provided a memorable body of events. The imagination, that is, was dependent upon, even determined by, history.

Such a view of culture held by thinkers paralleled and reinforced the view of American progress held by their practical countrymen, which assumed that the material advance on natural resources would result in a historical accumulation of cultural resources. American history was the history of the westward movement of European peoples; American culture was the result of their actions upon nature. From the American Revolution to the 1830s these views dominated.

Yet seen from the perspective of the twentieth century, American culture appears to have been shaped far more profoundly by another, much more radical, outlook, one that elevated nature over history, affirmed that the American language was that which nature taught men rather than one that men inflicted upon nature (thereby giving it storied associations), and insisted that facts, which is to say history, were merely apparent and were so far from determining the imagination that they could actually be made to conform to it. Such an outlook inevitably collided with the materialism of the practical view of American progress, as the earlier outlook, represented by Irving, did not. It asserted that the permanence beyond mutability so yearned for was to be located in the ideas which preceded action rather than in the sentiments which were action's leavings. This outlook, one that said that American history must be the history of nature speaking through men, not of men shaping nature, became the single most powerful force in American intellectual life in the nineteenth century and shaped some of America's greatest works of literature, such as *Moby-Dick, Leaves of Grass*, and *Walden*, as well as generating an American school of philosophy, to be furthered by William James and John Dewey. The turnaround from the earlier view to the discovery of a culture rooted in nature, rather than based on the domestication of nature to European manners, was the result of the life and work of one man, Ralph Waldo Emerson. To read his essays is to see a nation discovering its intellectual identity.

When Geoffrey Crayon's *Sketch Book* appeared, Ralph Waldo Emerson was pursuing his decidedly undistinguished undergraduate career at Harvard College. His father, minister of the First Church of Boston, had died when he was eight, and his widowed mother, assisted by friends, struggled successfully to see that, at the least, her boys were educated. Sandwiched between his brilliant older brother, William, and his brilliant younger brothers, Edward and Charles, Ralph dutifully attended college and managed to graduate thirtieth in a class of fifty-nine. His native capacities seemed to fit him for nothing so well as a career as yet another high-minded, if lackluster, New England preacher. By the end of 1829, he was established as minister of the Second Church of Boston, had married, and was beginning to compile a collection of sermons on which he could hope to draw over a long and sedentary career.

The break between the life of this Ralph Waldo Emerson and the life of America's greatest thinker was not sharply dramatic, but it was no less painful for being gradual. Ellen Tucker Emerson died of tuberculosis in February 1831, and in his isolation, her widower increasingly questioned the relation of his convictions to his profession. He concluded that he could not conscientiously administer the Lord's Supper because he did not feel it to have the sacramental meaning given it by his church. His parishioners were patient with the minister in mourning, but after friendly discussions he decided to resign his post. At the time, it was unclear even to him that this was the first public sign of his discontent with the notion of an anthropomorphic god. The concept of the deity that would take its place underlay the first full announcement of his philosophy some five years later. In *Nature* (1836), he would write, "Man is conscious of a universal soul within or behind his individual life, wherein, as in a firmament, the nature of Justice, Truth, Love, Freedom, arise and shine. This universal soul he calls Reason: it is not mine, or thine, or his, but we are its; we are its property and men."

With the assistance of gifts and loans from family and friends, Emerson traveled in Europe from December 1832 to October 1833, visiting, among others, Wordsworth and Coleridge, whose fame was well established, and the then unknown Carlyle, with whom he commenced a lifelong friendship. Soon after his return to America, his wife's estate was settled, and he received a legacy that yielded some $1200 per annum. Far from affluent, he had, nonetheless, thereby become in some part independent, able to choose his opportunities rather than be swayed by them, and he used his independence to purchase time to think what he wished and to experiment with its written expression.

His ministerial background had developed in Emerson the habit of employing oral delivery as an intermediate stage between notebooks and manuscripts, on one hand, and print on the other. Despite resigning his pulpit, therefore, he continued to accept invitations to give guest sermons for some time after his return to America and his move to a home in Concord. A new marketplace for his spoken words, however, was rapidly growing in the American 1830s and soon replaced the pulpit. The lyceum movement which sprang up in communities throughout the Northeast and Middle West (known in those days as the New North) brought secular lectures on literary, philosophical, and scientific topics as well as lighter entertainments to men and women who had grown up habituated to receiving some good part of their learning from the spoken word. The line between instruction and amusement was not a strong one, and as Emerson became active as a lyceum speaker he willingly accepted the need to hold his audience by attracting as well as edifying its members. When they became restive, he blamed his presentation rather than their intelligence, as his journals show, and labored to improve the former as the surest means of affecting the latter. Almost all of his published essays throughout his career received this rigorous form of pretesting.

In September 1835, Emerson married Lydia Jackson and soon thereafter settled into the domestic pattern that was to characterize the remainder of his long life. They were to have four children, the first of whom, Waldo, died at the age of five in 1842, an event that keys the remarkable baritone of "Experience": "Sleep lingers all our lifetime about our eyes, as night hovers all day in the boughs of the fir-tree." But Emerson's Concord life was, in the main, punctuated by the excitement of ideas rather than events. There he was in the midst of friends—Thoreau, Alcott, and Hawthorne were, at various times, his neighbors—and there, as his reputation spread, he received an increasing number of visitors, ranging from pilgrims who wished simply to see him as one wishes to see a monument, to thinkers who wished to sharpen their ideas in conversation with him, to enthusiasts of one or another cause who sought to enlist him in their movements.

When young Henry Adams of Boston, with his flawless social and financial background, pondered his America, he recognized that there was a third force in it apart from the forces of politics and money represented by the two branches of his family. That force he called Concord: it was the influence upon the nation of Emerson's example that man need not be the creature of his circumstances but could rise above his fate and work his way upon the world. "Those men who cannot answer by a superior wisdom these facts or questions of time," Emerson wrote in "History," "serve them. Facts encumber them, tyrannize over them, and make the men of routine, the men of *sense*, in whom a literal obedience to facts has extinguished every spark of that light by which man is truly man. But if the man is true to his better instincts or sentiments, and refuses the dominion of facts, as one that comes of a higher race; remains fast by the soul and sees the principle, then the facts fall aptly and supple into their places; they know their master, and the meanest of them glorifies him."

Fame came to Emerson at a moderate but firm pace. His first major publication, *Nature*, sold five hundred copies within a month, but, more importantly, it reached a consequential readership of American intellectuals conscious that the national mind was mired in a boggy backwater of stale theology. It was reviewed intensely. An audience was thus prepared for his address on The American Scholar at Harvard in the following year, and those who crowded the aisles and perched at the windows to hear him were enthusiastic about his stunning demonstration that the much-lamented shallow past of America was, in fact, a strong enabler, and that nature could teach the American lessons of power unavailable to the European. In 1776, Americans had declared their political independence from Great Britain, but it was not until 1837 that they received from Emerson what Oliver Wendell Holmes called "their intellectual declaration of independence." In the following year, invited to address the graduating class of divinity at Cambridge, Emerson preached pure subversion—a doctrine of perpetual revelation. The storm broke quickly afterward, but none was calmer in the center of its ragings than Emerson. He stood firmly on what he had said, refused to respond to vehement attacks, and coolly administered to himself and all who would listen the reminder that contradiction was not persecution.

Each succeeding book of Emerson's reached a wider audience than the preceding. Although his major essays are commonly considered to be those composed through 1844—a judgment in need of reexamination—his reputation continued to grow beyond that year, and his essays continued to kindle new lights and shape new shadows. After the Civil War, he admitted to himself that his creative powers had indeed waned, but to his death in 1882, some days short of his seventy-ninth birthday, the demand for his public appearance—even if it were but to sit on a platform and be seen—was constant. When *Society and Solitude* was published in 1870, it sold faster than its predecessors, and its shrewd author wrote in his journal: "This is not for its merit, but only shows that old age is a good advertisement. Your name has been seen so often that your book must be worth buying."

Ralph Waldo Emerson turned around Americans' sense of their spatial and temporal location and released the flow of the mainstream of their thought. Surely, patriotic ranters had kept shouting, a land that held such vast natural resources was a land that would breed people to match them. But this was simplistic analogizing, and the more reflective, as has been seen, resigned themselves to the need to domesticate that vast nature because meaning came from human history. Emerson taught a new relation to nature. Once upon a time, man was instinct with nature, as the birds and the beasts are instinct with it, and was an inseparable part of it. But with the growth of his understanding—known mythically as the fall of man—he separated from it and looked on matter as a reality foreign to his soul. He attempts a partial reunion with nature when he searches for its laws so that he can manipulate it, but his thoughts he now regards as one thing and nature's mindless processes as another.

Soul and matter were not so separated, Emerson affirmed. The very language of man, his most human attribute and that which therefore seemed to distinguish him from nature, was a vocabulary that was taught by nature. Man in his fullest state thinks poetically, taking the tropes that furnish his mind from the natural world around him. The spirit that is present behind nature does not act upon us from without but acts within us. "The world proceeds," Emerson says in *Nature*, "from the same spirit as the body of man."

What men commonly call the real, then, is only the apparent. The real, rather, is what they term the ideal—the Idea or Soul of which appearance is but a visible, imperfect termination—and it unites the elements in the natural world to one another and to ourselves. For real, meaning matter, versus ideal, meaning thought, substitute the truer distinction between the real as the idea behind all appearances and the apparent as the mere show of a world apart from us. "As fast as you conform your life to the pure idea in your mind, that will unfold its great proportions," Emerson maintains in *Nature*. A correspondent revolution in things will attend the influx of spirit, "because nature is, as we are, fluid, and moulded by the spirit which we find within ourselves for the looking."

No philosophy is so drenched in the common natural scenes of daily life as is Emerson's, and none has so powerful a sense of these as constant revelations rather than ordinary events. "Crossing a bare common, in snow puddles, at twilight, under a clouded sky, without having in my thoughts any occurrence of special good fortune," he says in *Nature*, "I have enjoyed a perfect exhilaration. I am glad to the brink of fear." This is a dramatization of what elsewhere he calls the perpetual revelation available to us if we remain alert and open. Such nature does not need "storied associations" to affect us, because we are its and it is ours, speakers of the same language. "In this refulgent summer," Emerson begins his message to the divinity students, "it has been a luxury to draw the breath of life. The grass grows, the buds burst, the meadow is spotted with fire and gold in the tint of flowers." He is not providing a pretty pictorial introduction to soften the impact of his revolutionary message. Rather he is validating that message of the divinity of the human soul by describing the effects of the selfsame divinity in the apparent world.

Emerson's theme is flow rather than form, power rather than circumstance. The idealist, he says, sees mind as the only reality and nature, literature, and history as subjective phenomena. We are all natural-born idealists and our disagreements with that philosophy are a measure of our decline into the materialism of appearances. The procession of facts that the materialist calls the world really flows from "an invisible unsounded centre" ("The Transcendentalist") in the self. The exercise of reason relaxes the despotism of the senses and shows us "nature aloof, and, as it were, afloat" (*Nature*), rather than as substantial and resistant to the will.

Experience, one may protest to Emerson, proves otherwise. Things do resist us: ice freezes and fire burns. This, he responds, is only because our higher moments—those in which our reason rather than our sense impression governs—come too infrequently:

"Our faith comes in moments; our vice is habitual. Yet there is a depth in those brief moments which constrains us to ascribe more reality to them than to all other experiences" ("The Over-Soul").

Emerson's ideas of the relation of nature to the self delivered Americans into the custody of America. Instead of regarding their identity as a historically determined consciousness that must impose itself upon the mindless matter of the wild, they were encouraged to see that their land was another expression of the soul centered in themselves, that it beckoned to them to realize their true relation with it. American history could be the history of nature's reassuming alienated man to itself rather than the history of man's warfare with it.

History as conventionally conceived was but an "old chronology of selfishness and pride." Once facts are apprehended as symbols rather than causes, man realizes himself as the maker rather than the effect of his circumstances. "All history," Emerson says in "History," "becomes subjective; in other words there is properly no history, only biography." As a result, his ideas move in an atmosphere in which Plato and Napoleon, Montaigne and Thoreau, Plotinus and Shakespeare share the same immediacy. They appear to be our contemporaries because their writings are not forms but fluxes, are not thoughts but men thinking. Whenever that flow fails to reach us and we feel that we are confronted with words rather than the power of men speaking, we must reject the words regardless of the eminence of their source. Emerson saw this idea to its controversial end: Jesus too must be so regarded.

"But why should you keep your head over your shoulder?" Emerson asks in "Self-Reliance." "Why drag about this corpse of your memory, lest you contradict somewhat you have stated in this or that public place? Suppose you should contradict yourself; what then?" Just as the individual must become rather than be, so history is a lived present rather than a shaping past. It is not a chronology but an instantly available cosmos.

Unlike the views illustrated by Washington Irving, Emerson's ideas set American thought on a course of opposition to American materialism. And although they were opposed to prevailing political and economic beliefs, they were assisted in their career by American events. In 1837, between the opening manifesto,

Nature, and the address on The American Scholar, the United States underwent the greatest crisis in its history, a devastating financial panic. Banks failed, real-estate values plunged, staple foods became scarce, and angry mobs rioted. The material world that seemed so weighty an answer to the idealist collapsed of a sudden and demonstrated the falseness of its seeming solidity. An audience was ripe for the message that we need not submit to facts but can master them.

Another contemporary correlative to Emerson's philosophy was the rise of the American West as a political force. Although he deplored the avarice of the land-hungry speculators and the crass demagoguery of the western politicians, Emerson saw that the West was not just another region adding its voice to those of the North and the South but was an imperfectly articulated idea. It was the spirit of the continent answering back to the Europeanization of the seaboard. Even as he opposed western greed and western rant, Emerson harnessed to his philosophy the power of the brooding plains and silent mountains that put the might of nature in the balance against stock market and legislature.

The political actuality that stimulated Emerson's repeated insistence on self-reliant individualism was the American faith in majority rule. As many a European observer noted, in practice this resulted in a tyranny of public opinion. While it was true that the older hierarchical structures of authority severely limited individual freedom and individual economic opportunity, they did provide some compensation. A man born into a certain class, a certain trade, a certain church, and a certain allegiance to a hereditary ruler knows who he is. What from one side appear as restrictions are, from the other, the sure providers of identity. Once a man has given to Cæsar what is Cæsar's, he is free to think as he pleases and behave as he wishes. He need not fear what others think of him.

This European condition was well epitomized by Goethe when he said: "For myself . . . I have always been a royalist. I have let others babble, and have done as I saw fit." Contrary to the folklore of democracy, such a man experiences a continuity between his acceptance of the autocratic state and his ability to do what pleases him. And surely his iconoclastic theorizing and his free social behavior would have been persecuted in a democratic society in which majority opinion was translated into civil law and, more importantly, where majority morals were translated into the rigorous unwritten laws of acceptable conduct.

In his constant emphasis on the self Emerson was reacting to the social tyranny of the American crowd. He did not for a moment believe that the counter to majority rule should be a return to some form of autocracy. Rather, he pursued the ideal of destroying the mob through bringing to each of its members a sense of himself as a separate person. When he called each man "an infinitely repellent orb," he was expressing a hope: ideally, each of us can develop a sense of self that resists grouping if we follow our reason rather than our understanding. Where others gazed upon a church congregation or a political gathering and saw a mass unified by a purpose or a prejudice, Emerson saw individuals, each with his own integrity, an integrity that was being destroyed by the preacher or party boss who encouraged them to think of themselves as a collectivity.

In May 1839, Emerson returned from attending church to vent in his journal his displeasure with the minister he had heard: "Cease, O thou unauthorized talker, to prate of consolation, and resignation, and spiritual joys, in neat and balanced sentences. For I know these men who sit below, and on the hearing of these words look up. Hush, quickly: for care and calamity are things to them. There is Mr. Tolman, the shoemaker, whose daughter is gone mad, and he is looking up through his spectacles to hear what you can offer for his case. Here is my friend, whose scholars are all leaving him, and he knows not what to turn his hand to next. Here is my wife, who has come to church in hope of being soothed and strengthened after being wounded by the sharp tongue of a slut in her house. Here is the stage-driver who has the jaundice, and cannot get well. Here is B. who failed last week, and he is looking up. O speak things, then, or hold thy tongue." These comments are an example of Emerson's seeing one plus one plus one plus one when he saw a group. For him it was not a trick of perception, it was a moral necessity.

Similarly, in October 1838 Emerson addressed his journal after having observed the local boss of the Democratic party haranguing a group of villagers in a shop: "Here, thought I, is one who loves what I hate." He went on to explain: "I hate numbers. He cares for nothing but numbers and persons. All the qualities of man, all his accomplishments, affections, enterprises, except solely the ticket he votes for, are nothing to this philosopher. Numbers of majorities are all he sees in the newspapers."

European republicans of the day, chafing under the tyranny of one or another monarch and enraged by the cruel division of their native land into parcels, each to be delivered to some petty nobleman in need of a job, opposed such despotism by attempting to rally their countrymen into a sense of their collective self. But in a land in which the tyrant was a collectivity and ruled far more in the mind than in the laws, Emerson reversed the process and attempted to disperse the mob. He writes in his journal in April 1841: "Let there be one man, let there be truth & virtue in one man, in two men, in ten men, then can there be concert: then is concert for the first time possible; now nothing is gained by adding zeroes, but when there is love & truth, these do naturally & necessarily cohabit, cooperate, & bless."

The revolution to which Emerson incites is moral. Each individual must realize that when he exercises his reason he is a majority of one already and insofar as he yields to a merely numerical majority he simply adds zeroes to himself and participates in his own diminishment and in the degradation of democracy.

Although it is not political in its first intent, so severely individualistic a philosophy does have political implications. One who follows it may easily discover that there is no clear line between the disregard of public opinion in favor of reason and the disregard of law in favor of conscience. Emerson's friend and disciple, Thoreau, provided a celebrated illustration when his conscience did not permit him to pay taxes to an unjust state and he spent a night in jail. As a consequence he gave the world his great essay, "On Civil Disobedience," a document soundly Emersonian in its principles. But Emerson did not need to witness Thoreau's disobedience to realize that although ideally the exercise of reason never poses a threat to society, in practice conflicts will occur to the degree that society still proceeds from property rather than character. In such exigencies, he occupied Jefferson's position:

when there is no option but to choose between the anarchy of private excess and the tyranny of public suppression, the former is the lesser evil because natural sanity will quickly temper anarchy whereas suppression once in place cannot readily be removed.

The literary implications of Emerson's teachings were also to be writ large by a disciple. Walt Whitman found in Emerson the central reasons for his poetry. Specifically, Emerson's assertion in "The Poet" that "it is not metres, but a metre-making argument that makes a poem" encouraged Whitman to break with traditional verse forms and seek the form his thought demanded, however far such might be from anything previously regarded as poetry. More broadly, Whitman took from Emerson the idea of the soul as the maker of its world. Just as Adam when he named the beasts completed the creation because until the animals had names they did not exist in the field of thought and thus were unrealized, so Whitman named the objects in his America in completion of the merely political creation of the United States. He did not seek Irving's storied associations but recognized that the meaning resided in the poet rather than in the fact. The act of poetry was the act of naming the parts of his unrealized America. When he dealt, as he often did, with the American crowd, with *en-masse* as he was fond of calling it, Whitman focused on the faces in the crowd, calling them out of their anonymity. Like Emerson, when he saw a gathering he saw individuals. To trace the enormous influence of Whitman on the poets who followed is to recognize what a mighty line is anchored in Emerson.

Orthodox Protestantism was officially outraged by Emerson's ideas, but these ideas drew considerable strength from the protest tradition within *Protest*antism. His idealism was derived from Plato and Plotinus and was modified by Kant and his German and British transcendental followers. It also took hints from Oriental mysticism and the doctrine of the inner light taught by George Fox and his Quaker followers. The assertion that the spirit is above law and is its judge rather than its subject had brought harsh punishment upon those who affirmed it in opposition to the Puritan establishment of seventeenth-century New England, and it scandalized the formalist nineteenth-century descendants of this orthodoxy who held that the days of revelation had ended.

But the Puritan migration to America and the Puritan revolution in England had been fueled by a belief in the vital presence of the spirit and a contempt for the forms of a ritualized church that seemed to have lost the spirit in the canonization of its laws. Such antinomianism lurked in a good number of nineteenth-century Americans, uneasy with both the legalism in conservative churches and the substitution of morality for piety in liberal ones. Emerson struck a note in "Self-Reliance" that they echoed: "There are two confessionals, in one or another of which we must be shriven. You may fulfill your round of duties by clearing yourself in the *direct*, or in the *reflex* way. Consider whether you have satisfied your relations to father, mother, cousin, neighbor, town, cat and dog— whether any of these can upbraid you. But I may also neglect this reflex standard and absolve me to myself. I have my own stern claims and perfect circle. It denies the name of duty to many offices that are called duties. But if I can discharge its debts it enables me to dispense with the popular code. If any one imagines that this law is lax, let him keep its commandment one day."

When Emerson visited in England in 1833, he had done so as a humble searcher hoping to find himself, grateful for those moments spared him by the illustrious. He returned in 1848 as one of the celebrated, invited there to lecture throughout the island. The British wanted not only to hear his specific ideas but to hear an American, and Emerson, they knew, was the foremost embodiment of the best and most characteristic thought of his nation. Emerson's mission was strikingly different from that of the Geoffrey Crayon whom his younger self had partly resembled when he crossed the ocean fifteen years earlier. Still, it was not unfitting that he should undertake this second voyage on a ship called the *Washington Irving*.

The reputation that gained Emerson his English invitation is even wider today. His influence has been great: both directly, in that major writers have had their ideas and their expression shaped by what they learned from him, and indirectly, in that he stands as the representative in thought of American identity and so provides the cornerstone for the words and deeds of many who may not know his work but who when they believe themselves to be influenced by America are actually responding to what Emerson said America meant. Among the former are Thoreau, Whitman, Nietzsche, and Borges. Among the latter are the radical dissenters of the abolition movement and of the movement against the Vietnam War, and writers who insisted on a voice of the American wild more powerful than the murmurs of civilization, writers such as D. H. Lawrence, William Carlos Williams, and Ernest Hemingway.

Emerson insisted on our reading books only to experience those moments in which we hear a voice that we recognize as proceeding from the same center as our own voices. We approach him today as a writer of enormous historical importance, perhaps the single most influential member of the American literary community. The reasons we have for reading him are not, then, the reasons that he gave for reading the classics. And yet were we today to try him by the test he offers, neither he nor we would suffer from the experiment. This is because after all consideration is given, as it should be, to Emerson's philosophy in terms of its consequences for culture, letters, politics, and conduct, the kernel of his appeal is still not reached. This is not public but private. It is not an assertion of victory over the agonies of life but a refusal to knuckle under to them. "Never mind the ridicule, never mind the defeat," Emerson writes in "Experience," "up again, old heart! . . . there is victory yet for all justice; and the true romance which the world exists to realize will be the transformation of genius into practical power." He says that what he writes here is what our inner voice tells us in our sane moments. The kernel of Emerson is that voice.

—LARZER ZIFF

Suggestions for Further Reading

The three major biographies are:

Gay Wilson Allen, *Waldo Emerson: A Biography* (New York, 1981).
Robert D. Richardson, *Emerson: The Mind on Fire* (Berkeley, 1995).
Ralph L. Rusk, *The Life of Ralph Waldo Emerson* (New York, 1949).

An excellent introduction to the riches in Emerson's journals is:

Joel Porte, ed., *Emerson in His Journals* (Cambridge, Mass., 1982).

Among the leading studies of Emerson's thought are:

Jonathan Bishop, *Emerson on the Soul* (Cambridge, Mass., 1964).
John Jay Chapman, *Emerson, and Other Essays* (New York, 1898).
Barbara Packer, *Emerson's Fall* (New York, 1982).
Stephen E. Whicher, *Freedom and Fate: An Inner Life of Ralph Waldo Emerson* (Philadelphia, 1953).

Studies that place Emerson in his literary context are:

F. O. Matthiessen, *American Renaissance* (New York, 1941).
Barbara Packer, "The Transcendentalists," in Sacvan Bercovitch, ed., *The Cambridge History of American Literature, Volume Two* (New York, 1995).
Larzer Ziff, *Literary Democracy* (New York, 1981).

A Note on the Text

All essays in this book are reprinted in their entirety from the standard edition prepared by Emerson's son, Edward Waldo Emerson: *The Complete Works of Ralph Waldo Emerson* (Boston, 1903–4), 12 vols.

Nature and Selected Essays

NATURE

A subtle chain of countless rings
The next unto the farthest brings;
The eye reads omens where it goes,
And speaks all languages the rose;
And, striving to be man, the worm
Mounts through all the spires of form.

INTRODUCTION

Our age is retrospective. It builds the sepulchres of the fathers. It writes biographies, histories, and criticism. The foregoing generations beheld God and nature face to face; we, through their eyes. Why should not we also enjoy an original relation to the universe? Why should not we have a poetry and philosophy of insight and not of tradition, and a religion by revelation to us, and not the history of theirs? Embosomed for a season in nature, whose floods of life stream around and through us, and invite us, by the powers they supply, to action proportioned to nature, why should we grope among the dry bones of the past, or put the living generation into masquerade out of its faded wardrobe? The sun shines to-day also. There is more wool and flax in the fields. There are new lands, new men, new thoughts. Let us demand our own works and laws and worship.

Undoubtedly we have no questions to ask which are unanswerable. We must trust the perfection of the creation so far as to believe that whatever curiosity the order of things has awakened in our minds, the order of things can satisfy. Every man's condition is a solution in hieroglyphic to those inquiries he would put. He acts it as life, before he apprehends it as truth. In like manner, nature is already, in its forms and tendencies, describing its own design. Let us interrogate the great apparition that shines so peacefully around us. Let us inquire, to what end is nature?

All science has one aim, namely, to find a theory of nature. We have theories of races and of functions, but scarcely yet a remote approach to an idea of creation. We are now so far from the road to truth, that religious teachers dispute and hate each other, and speculative men are esteemed unsound and frivolous. But to a sound judgment, the most abstract truth is the most practical. Whenever a true theory appears, it will be its own evidence. Its test is, that it will explain all phenomena. Now many are thought not only unexplained but inexplicable as language, sleep, madness, dreams, beasts, sex.

Philosophically considered, the universe is composed of Nature and the Soul. Strictly speaking, therefore it that is separate from us, all which Philosophy distinguishes as the NOT ME, that is, both nature and art, all other men and my own body, must be ranked under this name, NATURE. In enumerating the values of nature and casting up their sum, I shall use the word in both senses;—in its common and in its philosophical import. In inquiries so general as our present one, the inaccuracy is not material; no confusion of thought will occur. *Nature*, in the common sense, refers to essences unchanged by man; space, the air, the river, the leaf. *Art* is applied to the mixture of his will with the same things, as in a house, a canal, a statue, a picture. But his operations taken together are so insignificant, a little chipping, baking, patching, and washing, that in an impression so grand as that of the world on the human mind, they do not vary the result.

NATURE

I

To go into solitude, a man needs to retire as much from his chamber as from society. I am not solitary whilst I read and write, though nobody is with me. But if a man would be alone, let him look at the stars. The rays that come from those heavenly worlds will separate between him and what he touches. One might think the atmosphere was made transparent with this design, to give man, in the heavenly bodies, the perpetual presence of the sublime. Seen in the streets of cities, how great they are! If the stars should appear one night in a thousand years, how would men believe and adore; and preserve for many generations the remembrance of the city of God which had been shown! But every night come out these envoys of beauty, and light the universe with their admonishing smile.

The stars awaken a certain reverence, because though always present, they are inaccessible; but all natural objects make a kindred impression, when the mind is open to their influence. Nature never wears a mean appearance. Neither does the wisest man extort her secret, and lose his curiosity by finding out all her perfection. Nature never became a toy to a wise spirit. The flowers, the animals, the mountains, reflected the wisdom of his best hour, as much as they had delighted the simplicity of his childhood.

When we speak of nature in this manner, we have a distinct but most poetical sense in the mind. We mean the integrity of impression made by manifold natural objects. It is this which distinguishes the stick of timber of the wood-cutter from the tree of the poet. The charming landscape which I saw this morning is indubitably made up of some twenty or thirty farms. Miller owns this field, Locke that, and Manning the woodland beyond. But none of them owns the landscape. There is a property in the horizon which no man has but he whose eye can integrate all the parts, that is, the poet. This is the best part of these men's farms, yet to this their warranty-deeds give no title.

To speak truly, few adult persons can see nature. Most persons do not see the sun. At least they have a very superficial seeing. The sun illuminates only the eye of the man, but shines into the eye and the heart of the child. The lover of nature is he whose inward and outward senses are still truly adjusted to each other; who has retained the spirit of infancy even into the era of manhood. His intercourse with heaven and earth becomes part of his daily food. In the presence of nature a wild delight runs through the man, in spite of real sorrows. Nature says,—he is my creature, and maugre all his impertinent griefs, he shall be glad with me. Not the sun or the summer alone, but every hour and season yields its tribute of delight; for every hour and change corresponds to and authorizes a different state of the mind, from breathless noon to grimmest midnight. Nature is a setting that fits equally well a comic or a mourning piece. In good health, the air is a cordial of incredible virtue. Crossing a bare common, in snow puddles, at twilight, under a clouded sky, without having in my thoughts any occurrence of special good fortune, I have enjoyed a perfect exhilaration. I am glad to the brink of fear. In the woods, too, a man casts off his years, as the snake his slough, and at what period soever of life is always a child. In the woods is perpetual youth. Within these plantations of God, a decorum and sanctity reign, a perennial festival is dressed, and the guest sees not how he should tire of them in a thousand years. In the woods, we return to reason and faith. There I feel that nothing can befall me in life,—no disgrace, no calamity (leaving me my eyes), which nature cannot repair. Standing on the bare ground,—my head bathed by the blithe air and uplifted into infinite space,—all mean egotism vanishes. I become a transparent eyeball; I am nothing; I see all; the currents of the Universal Being circulate through me; I am part or parcel of God. The name of the nearest friend sounds then foreign and accidental: to be brothers, to be acquaintances, master or servant, is then a trifle and a disturbance. I am the lover of uncontained and immortal beauty. In the wilderness, I find something more dear and connate than in streets or villages. In the tranquil landscape, and especially in the distant line of the horizon, man beholds somewhat as beautiful as his own nature.

The greatest delight which the fields and woods minister is the suggestion of an occult relation between man and the vegetable. I am not alone and unacknowledged. They nod to me, and I to them. The waving of the boughs in the storm is new to me and old. It takes me by surprise, and yet is not unknown. Its effect is like that of a higher thought or a better emotion coming over me, when I deemed I was thinking justly or doing right.

Yet it is certain that the power to produce this delight does not reside in nature, but in man, or in a harmony of both. It is necessary to use these pleasures with great temperance. For nature is not always tricked in holiday attire, but the same scene which yesterday breathed perfume and glittered as for the frolic of the nymphs is overspread with melancholy to-day. Nature always wears the colors of the spirit. To a man laboring under calamity, the heat of his own fire hath sadness in it. Then there is a kind of contempt of the landscape felt by him who has just lost by death a dear friend. The sky is less grand as it shuts down over less worth in the population.

COMMODITY

II

Whoever considers the final cause of the world will discern a multitude of uses that enter as parts into that result. They all admit of being thrown into one of the following classes: Commodity; Beauty; Language; and Discipline.

Under the general name of commodity, I rank all those advantages which our senses owe to nature. This, of course, is a benefit which is temporary and mediate, not ultimate, like its service to the soul. Yet although low, it is perfect in its kind, and is the only use of nature which all men apprehend. The misery of man appears like childish petulance, when we explore the steady and prodigal provision that has been made for his support and delight on this green ball which floats him through the heavens. What angels invented these splendid ornaments, these rich conveniences, this ocean of air above, this ocean of water beneath, this firmament of earth between? this zodiac of lights, this tent of dropping clouds, this striped coat of climates, this fourfold year? Beasts, fire, water, stones, and corn serve him. The field is at once his floor, his work-yard, his play-ground, his garden, and his bed.

> "More servants wait on man
> Than he'll take notice of."[1]

Nature, in its ministry to man, is not only the material, but is also the process and the result. All the parts incessantly work into each other's hands for the profit of man. The wind sows the seed; the sun evaporates the sea; the wind blows the vapor to the field; the ice, on the other side of the planet, condenses rain on this; the rain feeds the plant; the plant feeds the animal; and thus the endless circulations of the divine charity nourish man.

The useful arts are reproductions or new combinations by the wit of man, of the same natural benefactors. He no longer waits for favoring gales, but by means of steam, he realizes the fable of Æolus's bag, and carries the two and thirty winds in the boiler of his boat. To diminish friction, he paves the road with iron bars, and, mounting a coach with a ship-load of men, animals, and merchandise behind him, he darts through the country, from town to town, like an eagle or a swallow through the air. By the aggregate of these aids, how is the face of the world changed, from the era of Noah to that of Napoleon! The private poor man hath cities, ships, canals, bridges, built for him. He goes to the post-office, and the human race run on his errands; to the bookshop, and the human race read and write of all that happens, for him; to the court-house, and nations repair his wrongs. He sets his house upon the road, and the human race go forth every morning, and shovel out the snow, and cut a path for him.

But there is no need of specifying particulars in this class of uses. The catalogue is endless, and the examples so obvious, that I shall leave them to the reader's reflection, with the general remark, that this mercenary benefit is one which has respect to a farther good. A man is fed, not that he may be fed, but that he may work.

BEAUTY

III

A nobler want of man is served by nature, namely, the love of Beauty.

The ancient Greeks called the world κόσμος,[2] beauty. Such is the constitution of all things, or such the plastic power of the human eye, that the primary forms, as the sky, the mountain, the tree, the animal, give us a delight *in and for themselves*; a pleasure arising from outline, color, motion, and grouping. This seems partly owing to the eye itself. The eye is the best of artists. By the mutual action of its structure and of the laws of light, perspective is produced, which integrates every mass of objects, of what character soever, into a well colored and shaded globe, so that where the particular objects are mean and unaffecting, the landscape which they compose is round and symmetrical. And as the eye is the best composer, so light is the first of painters. There is no object so foul that intense light will not make beautiful. And the stimulus it affords to the sense, and a sort of infinitude which it hath, like space and time, make all matter gay. Even the corpse has its own beauty. But besides this general grace diffused over nature, almost all the individual forms are agreeable to the eye, as is proved by our endless imitations of some of them, as the acorn, the grape, the pine-cone, the wheat-ear, the egg, the wings and forms of most birds, the lion's claw, the serpent, the butterfly, sea-shells, flames, clouds, buds, leaves, and the forms of many trees, as the palm.

For better consideration, we may distribute the aspects of Beauty in a threefold manner.

1. First, the simple perception of natural forms is a delight. The influence of the forms and actions in nature is so needful to man, that, in its lowest functions, it seems to lie on the confines of commodity and beauty. To the body and mind which have been cramped by noxious work or company, nature is medicinal and restores their tone. The tradesman, the attorney comes out of the din and craft of the street and sees the sky and the woods, and is a man again. In their eternal calm, he finds himself. The health of the eye seems to demand a horizon. We are never tired, so long as we can see far enough.

But in other hours, Nature satisfies by its loveliness, and without any mixture of corporeal benefit. I see the spectacle of morning from the hilltop over against my house, from daybreak to sunrise, with emotions which an angel might share. The long slender bars of cloud float like fishes in the sea of crimson light.

From the earth, as a shore, I look out into that silent sea. I seem to partake its rapid transformations; the active enchantment reaches my dust, and I dilate and conspire with the morning wind. How does Nature deify us with a few and cheap elements! Give me health and a day, and I will make the pomp of emperors ridiculous. The dawn is my Assyria; the sunset and moonrise my Paphos, and unimaginable realms of faerie; broad noon shall be my England of the senses and the understanding; the night shall be my Germany of mystic philosophy and dreams.

Not less excellent, except for our less susceptibility in the afternoon, was the charm, last evening, of a January sunset. The western clouds divided and subdivided themselves into pink flakes modulated with tints of unspeakable softness, and the air had so much life and sweetness that it was a pain to come within doors. What was it that nature would say? Was there no meaning in the live repose of the valley behind the mill, and which Homer or Shakspeare could not re-form for me in words? The leafless trees become spires of flame in the sunset, with the blue east for their background, and the stars of the dead calices of flowers, and every withered stem and stubble rimed with frost, contribute something to the mute music.

The inhabitants of cities suppose that the country landscape is pleasant only half the year. I please myself with the graces of the winter scenery, and believe that we are as much touched by it as by the genial influences of summer. To the attentive eye, each moment of the year has its own beauty, and in the same field, it beholds, every hour, a picture which was never seen before, and which shall never be seen again. The heavens change every moment, and reflect their glory or gloom on the plains beneath. The state of the crop in the surrounding farms alters the expression of the earth from week to week. The succession of native plants in the pastures and roadsides, which makes the silent clock by which time tells the summer hours, will make even the divisions of the day sensible to a keen observer. The tribes of birds and insects, like the plants punctual to their time, follow each other, and the year has room for all. By water-courses, the variety is greater. In July, the blue pontederia or pickerel-weed blooms in large beds in the shallow parts of our pleasant river, and swarms with yellow butterflies in continual motion. Art cannot rival this pomp of purple and gold. Indeed the river is a perpetual gala, and boasts each month a new ornament.

But this beauty of Nature which is seen and felt as beauty, is the least part. The shows of day, the dewy morning, the rainbow, mountains, orchards in blossom, stars, moonlight, shadows in still water, and the like, if too eagerly hunted, become shows merely, and mock us with their unreality. Go out of the house to see the moon, and 't is mere tinsel; it will not please as when its light shines upon your necessary journey. The beauty that shimmers in the yellow afternoons of October, who ever could clutch it? Go forth to find it, and it is gone; 't is only a mirage as you look from the windows of diligence.

2. The presence of a higher, namely, of the spiritual element is essential to its perfection. The high and divine beauty which can be loved without effeminacy, is that which is found in combination with the human will. Beauty is the mark God sets upon virtue. Every natural action is graceful. Every heroic act is also decent, and causes the place and the bystanders to shine. We are taught by great actions that the universe is the property of every individual in it. Every rational creature has all nature for his dowry and estate. It is his, if he will. He may divest himself of it; he may creep into a corner, and abdicate his kingdom, as most men do, but he is entitled to the world by his constitution. In proportion to the energy of his thought and will, he takes up the world into himself. "All those things for which men plough, build, or sail, obey virtue;" said Sallust 'The winds and waves," said Gibbon, "are always on the side of the ablest navigators." So are the sun and moon and all the stars of heaven. When a noble act is done,—perchance in a scene of great natural beauty; when Leonidas and his three hundred martyrs consume one day in dying, and the sun and moon come each and look at them once in the steep defile of Thermopylæ; when Arnold Winkelried, in the high Alps, under the shadow of the avalanche, gathers in his side a sheaf of Austrian spears to break the line for his comrades; are not these heroes entitled to add the beauty of the scene to the beauty of the

deed? When the bark of Columbus nears the shore of America;—before it the beach lined with savages, fleeing out of all their huts of cane; the sea behind; and the purple mountains of the Indian Archipelago around, can we separate the man from the living picture? Does not the New World clothe his form with her palm-groves and savannahs as fit drapery? Ever does natural beauty steal in like air, and envelope great actions. When Sir Harry Vane was dragged up the Tower-hill, sitting on a sled, to suffer death as the champion of the English laws, one of the multitude cried out to him, "You never sate on so glorious a seat!" Charles II., to intimidate the citizens of London, caused the patriot Lord Russell to be drawn in an open coach through the principal streets of the city on his way to the scaffold. "But," his biographer says, "the multitude imagined they saw liberty and virtue sitting by his side." In private places, among sordid objects, an act of truth or heroism seems at once to draw to itself the sky as its temple, the sun as its candle. Nature stretches out her arms to embrace man, only let his thoughts be of equal greatness. Willingly does she follow his steps with the rose and the violet, and bend her lines of grandeur and grace to the decoration of her darling child. Only let his thoughts be of equal scope, and the frame will suit the picture. A virtuous man is in unison with her works, and makes the central figure of the visible sphere. Homer, Pindar, Socrates, Phocion, associate themselves fitly in our memory with the geography and climate of Greece. The visible heavens and earth sympathize with Jesus. And in common life whosoever has seen a person of powerful character and happy genius, will have remarked how easily he took all things along with him,—the persons, the opinions, and the day, and nature became ancillary to a man.

3. There is still another aspect under which the beauty of the world may be viewed, namely, as it becomes an object of the intellect. Beside the relation of things to virtue, they have a relation to thought. The intellect searches out the absolute order of things as they stand in the mind of God, and without the colors of affection. The intellectual and the active powers seem to succeed each other, and the exclusive activity of the one generates the exclusive activity of the other. There is something unfriendly in each to the other, but they are like the alternate periods of feeding and work-

ing in animals; each prepares and will be followed by the other. Therefore does beauty, which, in relation to actions, as we have seen, comes unsought, and comes because it is unsought, remain for the apprehension and pursuit of the intellect; and then again, in its turn, of the active power. Nothing divine dies. All good is eternally reproductive. The beauty of nature re-forms itself in the mind, and not for barren contemplation, but for new creation.

All men are in some degree impressed by the face of the world; some men even to delight. This love of beauty is Taste. Others have the same love in such excess, that, not content with admiring, they seek to embody it in new forms. The creation of beauty is Art.

The production of a work of art throws a light upon the mystery of humanity. A work of art is an abstract or epitome of the world. It is the result or expression of nature, in miniature. For although the works of nature are innumerable and all different, the result or the expression of them all is similar and single. Nature is a sea of forms radically alike and even unique. A leaf, a sunbeam, a landscape, the ocean, make an analogous impression on the mind. What is common to them all,—that perfectness and harmony, is beauty. The standard of beauty is the entire circuit of natural forms,—the totality of nature; which the Italians expressed by defining beauty "il più nell' uno."[3] Nothing is quite beautiful alone; nothing but is beautiful in the whole. A single object is only so far beautiful as it suggests this universal grace. The poet, the painter, the sculptor, the musician, the architect, seek each to concentrate this radiance of the world on one point, and each in his several work to satisfy the love of beauty which stimulates him to produce. Thus is Art a nature passed through the alembic of man. Thus in art does Nature work through the will of a man filled with the beauty of her first works.

The world thus exists to the soul to satisfy the desire of beauty. This element I call an ultimate end. No reason can be asked or given why the soul seeks beauty. Beauty, in its largest and profoundest sense, is one expression for the universe. God is the all-fair. Truth, and goodness, and beauty, are but different faces of the same All. But beauty in nature is not ultimate. It is the herald of inward and eternal beauty, and is not alone a solid and satisfactory

good. It must stand as a part, and not as yet the last or highest
expression of the final cause of Nature.

LANGUAGE

IV

Language is a third use which Nature subserves to man. Nature is the
vehicle of thought, and in a simple, double, and three-fold degree.

1. Words are signs of natural facts.
2. Particular natural facts are symbols of particular spiritual
    facts.
3. Nature is the symbol of spirit.

1. Words are signs of natural facts. The use of natural history is
to give us aid in supernatural history; the use of the outer creation, to give us language for the beings and changes of the inward
creation. Every word which is used to express a moral or intellectual fact, if traced to its root, is found to be borrowed from some
material appearance. *Right* means *straight*; *wrong* means *twisted*.
Spirit primarily means *wind*; *transgression*, the crossing of a *line*;
supercilious, the *raising of the eyebrow*. We say the *heart* to
express emotion, the *head* to denote thought; and *thought* and
emotion are words borrowed from sensible things, and now
appropriated to spiritual nature. Most of the process by which
this transformation is made, is hidden from us in the remote time
when language was framed; but the same tendency may be daily
observed in children. Children and savages use only nouns or
names of things, which they convert into verbs, and apply to analogous mental acts.

2. But this origin of all words that convey a spiritual import,—
so conspicuous a fact in the history of language,—is our least
debt to nature. It is not words only that are emblematic; it is
things which are emblematic. Every natural fact is a symbol of
some spiritual fact. Every appearance in nature corresponds to
some state of the mind, and that state of the mind can only be

described by presenting that natural appearance as its picture. An enraged man is a lion, a cunning man is a fox, a firm man is a rock, a learned man is a torch. A lamb is innocence; a snake is subtle spite; flowers express to us the delicate affections. Light and darkness are our familiar expression for knowledge and ignorance; and heat for love. Visible distance behind and before us, is respectively our image of memory and hope.

Who looks upon a river in a meditative hour and is not reminded of the flux of all things? Throw a stone into the stream, and the circles that propagate themselves are the beautiful type of all influence. Man is conscious of a universal soul within or behind his individual life, wherein, as in a firmament, the natures of Justice, Truth, Love, Freedom, arise and shine. This universal soul he calls Reason: it is not mine, or thine, or his, but we are its; we are its property and men. And the blue sky in which the private earth is buried, the sky with its eternal calm, and full of everlasting orbs, is the type of Reason. That which intellectually considered we call Reason, considered in relation to nature, we call Spirit. Spirit is the Creator. Spirit hath life in itself. And man in all ages and countries embodies it in his language as the FATHER.

It is easily seen that there is nothing lucky or capricious in these analogies, but that they are constant, and pervade nature. These are not the dreams of a few poets, here and there, but man is an analogist, and studies relations in all objects. He is placed in the centre of beings, and a ray of relation passes from every other being to him. And neither can man be understood without these objects, nor these objects without man. All the facts in natural history taken by themselves, have no value, but are barren, like a single sex. But marry it to human history, and it is full of life. Whole floras, all Linnæus' and Buffon's volumes, are dry catalogues of facts; but the most trivial of these facts, the habit of a plant, the organs, or work, or noise of an insect, applied to the illustration of a fact in intellectual philosophy, or in any way associated to human nature, affects us in the most lively and agreeable manner. The seed of a plant,—to what affecting analogies in the nature of man is that little fruit made use of, in all discourse, up to the voice of Paul, who calls the human corpse a seed,—"It is sown a natural body; it is raised a spiritual body." The motion of the earth round its axis and round the sun, makes the day and the year. These are certain amounts of brute light and heat. But is there no intent of an analogy between man's life and the seasons? And do the seasons gain no grandeur or pathos from that analogy? The instincts of the ant are very unimportant considered as the ant's; but the moment a ray of relation is seen to extend from it to man, and the little drudge is seen to be a monitor, a little body with a mighty heart, then all its habits, even that said to be recently observed, that it never sleeps, become sublime.

Because of this radical correspondence between visible things and human thoughts, savages, who have only what is necessary, converse in figures. As we go back in history, language becomes more picturesque, until its infancy, when it is all poetry; or all spiritual facts are represented by natural symbols. The same symbols are found to make the original elements of all languages. It has moreover been observed, that the idioms of all languages approach each other in passages of the greatest eloquence and power. And as this is the first language, so is it the last. This immediate dependence of language upon nature, this conversion of an outward phenomenon into a type of somewhat in human life, never loses its power to affect us. It is this which gives that piquancy to the conversation of a strong-natured farmer or backwoodsman, which all men relish.

A man's power to connect his thought with its proper symbol, and so to utter it, depends on the simplicity of his character, that is, upon his love of truth and his desire to communicate it without loss. The corruption of man is followed by the corruption of language. When simplicity of character and the sovereignty of ideas is broken up by the prevalence of secondary desires,—the desire of riches, of pleasure, of power, and of praise,—and duplicity and falsehood take place of simplicity and truth, the power over nature as an interpreter of the will is in a degree lost; new imagery ceases to be created, and old words are perverted to stand for things which are not; a paper currency is employed, when there is no bullion in the vaults. In due time the fraud is manifest, and words lose all power to stimulate the understanding or the affections. Hundreds of writers may be found in every long-civilized nation who for a short time believe and make others believe that they see and utter truths, who do not of themselves clothe one thought in its natural garment, but who feed unconsciously on the language created by the primary writers of the country, those, namely, who hold primarily on nature.

But wise men pierce this rotten diction and fasten words again to visible things; so that picturesque language is at once a commanding certificate that he who employs it is a man in alliance with truth and God. The moment our discourse rises above the ground line of familiar facts and is inflamed with passion or exalted by thought, it clothes itself in images. A man conversing in earnest, if he watch his intellectual processes, will find that a material image more or less luminous arises in his mind, contemporaneous with every thought, which furnishes the vestment of the thought. Hence, good writing and. brilliant discourse are perpetual allegories. This imagery is spontaneous. It is the blending of experience with the present action of the mind. It is proper creation. It is the working of the Original Cause through the instruments he has already made.

These facts may suggest the advantage which the country-life possesses, for a powerful mind, over the artificial and curtailed life of cities. We know more from nature than we can at will communicate. Its light flows into the mind evermore, and we forget its presence. The poet, the orator, bred in the woods, whose senses have been nourished by their fair and appeasing changes, year after year, without design and without heed,—shall not lose their lesson altogether, in the roar of cities or the broil of politics. Long hereafter, amidst agitation and terror in national councils,—in the hour of revolution,—these solemn images shall reappear in their morning lustre, as fit symbols and words of the thoughts which the passing events shall awaken. At the call of a noble sentiment, again the woods wave, the pines murmur, the river rolls and shines, and the cattle low upon the mountains, as he saw and heard them in his infancy. And with these forms, the spells of persuasion, the keys of power are put into his hands.

3. We are thus assisted by natural objects in the expression of particular meanings. But how great a language to convey such pepper-corn informations! Did it need such noble races of creatures, this profusion of forms, this host of orbs in heaven, to furnish

man with the dictionary and grammar of his municipal speech? Whilst we use this grand cipher to expedite the affairs of our pot and kettle, we feel that we have not yet put it to its use, neither are able. We are like travellers using the cinders of a volcano to roast their eggs. Whilst we see that it always stands ready to clothe what we would say, we cannot avoid the question whether the characters are not significant of themselves. Have mountains, and waves, and skies, no significance but what we consciously give them when we employ them as emblems of our thoughts? The world is emblematic. Parts of speech are metaphors, because the whole of nature is a metaphor of the human mind. The laws of moral nature answer to those of matter as face to face in a glass. "The visible world and the relation of its parts, is the dial plate of the invisible." The axioms of physics translate the laws of ethics. Thus, "the whole is greater than its part;" "reaction is equal to action;" "the smallest weight may be made to lift the greatest, the difference of weight being compensated by time;" and many the like propositions, which have an ethical as well as physical sense. These propositions have a much more extensive and universal sense when applied to human life, than when confined to technical use.

In like manner, the memorable words of history and the proverbs of nations consist usually of a natural fact, selected as a picture or parable of a moral truth. Thus; A rolling stone gathers no moss; A bird in the hand is worth two in the bush; A cripple in the right way will beat a racer in the wrong; Make hay while the sun shines; 'T is hard to carry a full cup even; Vinegar is the son of wine; The last ounce broke the camel's back; Long-lived trees make roots first;—and the like. In their primary sense these are trivial facts, but we repeat them for the value of their analogical import. What is true of proverbs, is true of all fables, parables, and allegories.

This relation between the mind and matter is not fancied by some poet, but stands in the will of God, and so is free to be known by all men. It appears to men, or it does not appear. When in fortunate hours we ponder this miracle, the wise man doubts if at all other times he is not blind and deaf;

> "Can such things be,
> And overcome us like a summer's cloud,
> Without our special wonder?"[4]

for the universe becomes transparent, and the light of higher laws than its own shines through it. It is the standing problem which has exercised the wonder and the study of every fine genius since the world began; from the era of the Egyptians and the Brahmins to that of Pythagoras, of Plato, of Bacon, of Leibnitz, of Swedenborg. There sits the Sphinx at the road-side, and from age to age, as each prophet comes by, he tries his fortune at reading her riddle. There seems to be a necessity in spirit to manifest itself in material forms; and day and night, river and storm, beast and bird, acid and alkali, preëxist in necessary Ideas in the mind of God, and are what they are by virtue of preceding affections in the world of spirit. A Fact is the end or last issue of spirit. The visible creation is the terminus or the circumference of the invisible world. "Material objects," said a French philosopher, "are necessarily kinds of *scoriæ* of the substantial thoughts of the Creator, which must always preserve an exact relation to their first origin; in other words, visible nature must have a spiritual and moral side."

This doctrine is abstruse, and though the images of "garment," "scoriæ," "mirror," etc., may stimulate the fancy, we must summon the aid of subtler and more vital expositors to make it plain. "Every scripture is to be interpreted by the same spirit which gave it forth,"—is the fundamental law of criticism. A life in harmony with Nature, the love of truth and of virtue, will purge the eyes to understand her text. By degrees we may come to know the primitive sense of the permanent objects of nature, so that the world shall be to us an open book, and every form significant of its hidden life and final cause.

A new interest surprises us, whilst, under the view now suggested, we contemplate the fearful extent and multitude of objects; since "every object rightly seen, unlocks a new faculty of the soul." That which was unconscious truth, becomes, when interpreted and defined in an object, a part of the domain of knowledge,— a new weapon in the magazine of power.

DISCIPLINE

V

In view of the significance of nature, we arrive at once at a new fact, that nature is a discipline. This use of the world includes the preceding uses, as parts of itself.

Space, time, society, labor, climate, food, locomotion, the animals, the mechanical forces, give us sincerest lessons, day by day, whose meaning is unlimited. They educate both the Understanding and the Reason. Every property of matter is a school for the understanding,—its solidity or resistance, its inertia, its extension, its figure, its divisibility. The understanding adds, divides, combines, measures, and finds nutriment and room for its activity in this worthy scene. Meantime, Reason transfers all these lessons into its own world of thought, by perceiving the analogy that marries Matter and Mind.

1. Nature is a discipline of the understanding in intellectual truths. Our dealing with sensible objects is a constant exercise in the necessary lessons of difference, of likeness, of order, of being and seeming, of progressive arrangement; of ascent from particular to general; of combination to one end of manifold forces. Proportioned to the importance of the organ to be formed, is the extreme care with which its tuition is provided,—a care pretermitted in no single case. What tedious training, day after day, year after year, never ending, to form the common sense; what continual reproduction of annoyances, inconveniences, dilemmas; what rejoicing over us of little men; what disputing of prices, what reckonings of interest,—and all to form the Hand of the mind;—to instruct us that "good thoughts are no better than good dreams, unless they be executed!"

The same good office is performed by Property and its filial systems of debt and credit. Debt, grinding debt, whose iron face the widow, the orphan, and the sons of genius fear and hate;—debt, which consumes so much time, which so cripples and disheartens a great spirit with cares that seem so base, is a preceptor whose lessons cannot be foregone, and is needed most by those who suffer from it most. Moreover, property, which has been well compared to snow,—"if it fall level to-day, it will be blown into drifts to-morrow,"—is the surface action of internal machinery, like the index on the face of a clock. Whilst now it is the gymnastics of the understanding, it is hiving, in the foresight of the spirit, experience in profounder laws.

The whole character and fortune of the individual are affected by the least inequalities in the culture of the understanding; for example, in the perception of differences. Therefore is Space, and therefore Time, that man may know that things are not huddled and lumped, but sundered and individual. A bell and a plough have each their use, and neither can do the office of the other. Water is good to drink, coal to burn, wool to wear; but wool cannot be drunk, nor water spun, nor coal eaten. The wise man shows his wisdom in separation, in gradation, and his scale of creatures and of merits is as wide as nature. The foolish have no range in their scale, but suppose every man is as every other man. What is not good they call the worst, and what is not hateful, they call the best.

In like manner, what good heed Nature forms in us! She pardons no mistakes. Her yea is yea, and her nay, nay.

The first steps in Agriculture, Astronomy, Zoölogy (those first steps which the farmer, the hunter, and the sailor take), teach that Nature's dice are always loaded; that in her heaps and rubbish are concealed sure and useful results.

How calmly and genially the mind apprehends one after another the laws of physics! What noble emotions dilate the mortal as he enters into the councils of the creation, and feels by knowledge the privilege to BE! His insight refines him. The beauty of nature shines in his own breast. Man is greater that he can see this, and the universe less, because Time and Space relations vanish as laws are known.

Here again we are impressed and even daunted by the immense Universe to be explored. "What we know is a point to what we do not know." Open any recent journal of science, and weigh the problems suggested concerning Light, Heat, Electricity, Magnetism, Physiology, Geology, and judge whether the interest of natural science is likely to be soon exhausted.

Passing by many particulars of the discipline of nature, we must not omit to specify two.

The exercise of the Will, or the lesson of power, is taught in every event. From the child's successive possession of his several senses up to the hour when he saith, "Thy will be done!" he is learning the secret that he can reduce under his will not only particular events but great classes, nay, the whole series of events, and so conform all facts to his character. Nature is thoroughly mediate. It is made to serve. It receives the dominion of man as meekly as the ass on which the Saviour rode. It offers all its kingdoms to man as the raw material which he may mould into what is useful. Man is never weary of working it up. He forges the subtile and delicate air into wise and melodious words, and gives them wing as angels of persuasion and command. One after another his victorious thought comes up with and reduces all things, until the world becomes at last only a realized will,—the double of the man.

2. Sensible objects conform to the premonitions of Reason and reflect the conscience. All things are moral; and in their boundless changes have an unceasing reference to spiritual nature. Therefore is nature glorious with form, color, and motion; that every globe in the remotest heaven, every chemical change from the rudest crystal up to the laws of life, every change of vegetation from the first principle of growth in the eye of a leaf, to the tropical forest and antediluvian coal-mine, every animal function from the sponge up to Hercules, shall hint or thunder to man the laws of right and wrong, and echo the Ten Commandments. Therefore is Nature ever the ally of Religion: lends all her pomp and riches to the religious sentiment. Prophet and priest, David, Isaiah, Jesus, have drawn deeply from this source. This ethical character so penetrates the bone and marrow of nature, as to seem the end for which it was made. Whatever private purpose is answered by any member or part, this is its public and universal function, and is never omitted. Nothing in nature is exhausted in its first use. When a thing has served an end to the uttermost, it is wholly new for an ulterior service. In God, every end is converted into a new means. Thus the use of commodity, regarded by itself, is mean and squalid. But it is to the mind an education in the doctrine of Use, namely, that a thing is good only so far as it serves; that a conspiring of parts and efforts to the production of an end is

essential to any being. The first and gross manifestation of this truth is our inevitable and hated training in values and wants, in corn and meat.

It has already been illustrated, that every natural process is a version of a moral sentence. The moral law lies at the centre of nature and radiates to the circumference. It is the pith and marrow of every substance, every relation, and every process. All things with which we deal, preach to us. What is a farm but a mute gospel? The chaff and the wheat, weeds and plants, blight, rain, insects, sun,—it is a sacred emblem from the first furrow of spring to the last stack which the snow of winter overtakes in the fields. But the sailor, the shepherd, the miner, the merchant, in their several resorts, have each an experience precisely parallel, and leading to the same conclusion: because all organizations are radically alike. Nor can it be doubted that this moral sentiment which thus scents the air, grows in the grain, and impregnates the waters of the world, is caught by man and sinks into his soul. The moral influence of nature upon every individual is that amount of truth which it illustrates to him. Who can estimate this? Who can guess how much firmness the sea-beaten rock has taught the fisherman? how much tranquillity has been reflected to man from the azure sky, over whose unspotted deeps the winds forevermore drive flocks of stormy clouds, and leave no wrinkle or stain? how much industry and providence and affection we have caught from the pantomime of brutes? What a searching preacher of self-command is the varying phenomenon of Health!

Herein is especially apprehended the unity of Nature,—the unity in variety,—which meets us everywhere. All the endless variety of things make an identical impression. Xenophanes complained in his old age, that, look where he would, all things hastened back to Unity. He was weary of seeing the same entity in the tedious variety of forms. The fable of Proteus has a cordial truth. A leaf, a drop, a crystal, a moment of time, is related to the whole, and partakes of the perfection of the whole. Each particle is a microcosm, and faithfully renders the likeness of the world.

Not only resemblances exist in things whose analogy is obvious, as when we detect the type of the human hand in the flipper of the fossil saurus, but also in objects wherein there is great superficial unlikeness. Thus architecture is called "frozen music," by De Staël and Goethe. Vitruvius thought an architect should be a musician. "A Gothic church," said Coleridge, "is a petrified religion." Michael Angelo maintained, that, to an architect, a knowledge of anatomy is essential. In Haydn's oratorios, the notes present to the imagination not only motions, as of the snake, the stag, and the elephant, but colors also; as the green grass. The law of harmonic sounds reappears in the harmonic colors. The granite is differenced in its laws only by the more or less of heat from the river that wears it away. The river, as it flows, resembles the air that flows over it; the air resembles the light which traverses it with more subtile currents; the light resembles the heat which rides with it through Space. Each creature is only a modification of the other; the likeness in them is more than the difference, and their radical law is one and the same. A rule of one art, or a law of one organization, holds true throughout nature. So intimate is this Unity, that, it is easily seen, it lies under the undermost garment of Nature, and betrays its source in Universal Spirit. For it pervades Thought also. Every universal truth which we express in words, implies or supposes every other truth. *Omne verum vero consonat.*[5] It is like a great circle on a sphere, comprising all possible circles; which, however, may be drawn and comprise it in like manner. Every such truth is the absolute Ens seen from one side. But it has innumerable sides.

The central Unity is still more conspicuous in actions. Words are finite organs of the infinite mind. They cannot cover the dimensions of what is in truth. They break, chop, and impoverish it. An action is the perfection and publication of thought. A right action seems to fill the eye, and to be related to all nature. "The wise man, in doing one thing, does all; or, in the one thing he does rightly, he sees the likeness of all which is done rightly."

Words and actions are not the attributes of brute nature. They introduce us to the human form, of which all other organizations appear to be degradations. When this appears among so many that surround it, the spirit prefers it to all others. It says, "From such as this have I drawn joy and knowledge; in such as this have I found and beheld myself; I will speak to it; it can speak again; it can yield me thought already formed and alive." In fact, the eye,—the mind,—is always accompanied by these forms, male and female; and these are incomparably the richest informations of the power and order that lie at the heart of things. Unfortunately every one of them bears the marks as of some injury; is marred and superficially defective. Nevertheless, far different from all deaf and dumb nature around them, these all rest like fountain-pipes on the unfathomed sea of thought, and virtue whereto they alone, of all organizations, are the entrances.

It were a pleasant inquiry to follow into detail their ministry to our education, but where would it stop? We are associated in adolescent and adult life with some friends, who, like skies and waters, are coextensive with our idea; who, answering each to a certain affection of the soul, satisfy our desire on that side; whom we lack power to put at such focal distance from us, that we can mend or even analyze them. We cannot choose but love them. When much intercourse with a friend has supplied us with a standard of excellence, and has increased our respect for the resources of God who thus sends a real person to outgo our ideal; when he has, moreover, become an object of thought, and, whilst his character retains all its unconscious effect, is converted in the mind into solid and sweet wisdom,—it is a sign to us that his office is closing, and he is commonly withdrawn from our sight in a short time.

IDEALISM

VI

Thus is the unspeakable but intelligible and practicable meaning of the world conveyed to man, the immortal pupil, in every object of sense. To this one end of Discipline, all parts of nature conspire.

A noble doubt perpetually suggests itself,—whether this end be not the Final Cause of the Universe; and whether nature outwardly exists. It is a sufficient account of that Appearance we call the World, that God will teach a human mind, and so makes it the receiver of a certain number of congruent sensations, which we call sun and moon, man and woman, house and trade. In my utter impotence to test the authenticity of the report of my senses, to know whether the impressions they make on me correspond with outlying objects, what difference does it make, whether Orion is up there in heaven, or some god paints the image in the firmament of the soul? The relations of parts and the end of the whole remaining the same, what is the difference, whether land and sea interact, and worlds revolve and intermingle without number or end,—deep yawning under deep, and galaxy balancing galaxy, throughout absolute space,—or whether, without relations of time and space, the same appearances are inscribed in the constant faith of man? Whether nature enjoy a substantial existence without, or is only in the apocalypse of the mind, it is alike useful and alike venerable to me. Be it what it may, it is ideal to me so long as I cannot try the accuracy of my senses.

The frivolous make themselves merry with the Ideal theory, as if its consequences were burlesque; as if it affected the stability of nature. It surely does not. God never jests with us, and will not compromise the end of nature by permitting any inconsequence in its procession. Any distrust of the permanence of laws would paralyze the faculties of man. Their permanence is sacredly respected, and his faith therein is perfect. The wheels and springs of man are all set to the hypothesis of the permanence of nature. We are not built like a ship to be tossed, but like a house to stand. It is a natural consequence of this structure, that so long as the active powers predominate over the reflective, we resist with indignation any hint that nature is more short-lived or mutable than spirit. The broker, the wheelwright, the carpenter, the tollman, are much displeased at the intimation.

But whilst we acquiesce entirely in the permanence of natural laws, the question of the absolute existence of nature still remains open. It is the uniform effect of culture on the human mind, not to shake our faith in the stability of particular phenomena, as of heat, water, azote; but to lead us to regard nature as phenomenon, not a substance; to attribute necessary existence to spirit; to esteem nature as an accident and an effect.

To the senses and the unrenewed understanding, belongs a sort of instinctive belief in the absolute existence of nature. In their view man and nature are indissolubly joined. Things are ultimates, and they never look beyond their sphere. The presence of Reason mars this faith. The first effort of thought tends to relax this despotism of the senses which binds us to nature as if we were a part of it, and shows us nature aloof, and, as it were, afloat. Until this higher agency intervened, the animal eye sees, with wonderful accuracy, sharp outlines and colored surfaces. When the eye of Reason opens, to outline and surface are at once added grace and expression. These proceed from imagination and affection, and abate somewhat of the angular distinctness of objects. If the Reason be stimulated to more earnest vision, outlines and surfaces become transparent, and are no longer seen; causes and spirits are seen through them. The best moments of life are these delicious awakenings of the higher powers, and the reverential withdrawing of nature before its God.

Let us proceed to indicate the effects of culture.

1. Our first institution in the Ideal philosophy is a hint from Nature herself.

Nature is made to conspire with spirit to emancipate us. Certain mechanical changes, a small alteration in our local position, apprizes us of a dualism. We are strangely affected by seeing the shore from a moving ship, from a balloon, or through the tints of an unusual sky. The least change in our point of view gives the whole world a pictorial air. A man who seldom rides, needs only to get into a coach and traverse his own town, to turn the street into a puppet-show. The men, the women,—talking, running, bartering, fighting,—the earnest mechanic, the lounger, the beggar, the boys, the dogs, are unrealized at once, or, at least, wholly detached from all relation to the observer, and seen as apparent, not substantial beings. What new thoughts are suggested by seeing a face of country quite familiar, in the rapid movement of the railroad car! Nay, the most wonted objects, (make a very slight change in the point of vision,) please us most. In a camera obscura, the butcher's cart, and the figure of one of our own family amuse us. So a portrait of a well-known face gratifies us. Turn the eyes upside down, by looking at the landscape through your legs, and how agreeable is the picture, though you have seen it any time these twenty years!

In these cases, by mechanical means, is suggested the difference between the observer and the spectacle—between man and nature. Hence arises a pleasure mixed with awe; I may say, a low degree of the sublime is felt, from the fact, probably, that man is hereby apprized that whilst the world is a spectacle, something in himself is stable.

2. In a higher manner the poet communicates the same pleasure. By a few strokes he delineates, as on air, the sun, the mountain, the camp, the city, the hero, the maiden, not different from what we know them, but only lifted from the ground and afloat before the eye. He unfixes the land and the sea, makes them revolve around the axis of his primary thought, and disposes them anew. Possessed himself by a heroic passion, he uses matter as symbols of it. The sensual man conforms thoughts to things; the poet conforms things to his thoughts. The one esteems nature as rooted and fast; the other, as fluid, and impresses his being thereon. To him, the refractory world is ductile and flexible; he invests dust and stones with humanity, and makes them the words of the Reason. The Imagination may be defined to be the use which the Reason makes of the material world. Shakspeare possesses the power of subordinating nature for the purposes of expression, beyond all poets. His imperial muse tosses the creation like a bauble from hand to hand, and uses it to embody any caprice of thought that is uppermost in his mind. The remotest spaces of nature are visited, and the farthest sundered things are brought together, by a subtile spiritual connection. We are made aware that magnitude of material things is relative, and all objects shrink and expand to serve the passion of the poet. Thus in his sonnets, the lays of birds, the scents and dyes of flowers he finds to be the *shadow* of his beloved; time, which keeps her from him, is his *chest*; the suspicion she has awakened, is her *ornament*;

> The ornament of beauty is Suspect,
> A crow which flies in heaven's sweetest air.[6]

His passion is not the fruit of chance; it swells, as he speaks, to a city, or a state.

> No, it was builded far from accident;
> It suffers not in smiling pomp, nor falls
> Under the brow of thralling discontent;
> It fears not policy, that heretic,
> That works on leases of short numbered hours,
> But all alone stands hugely politic.[7]

In the strength of his constancy, the Pyramids seem to him recent and transitory. The freshness of youth and love dazzles him with its resemblance to morning;

> Take those lips away
> Which so sweetly were forsworn;
> And those eyes,—the break of day,
> Lights that do mislead the morn.[8]

The wild beauty of this hyperbole, I may say in passing, it would not be easy to match in literature.

This transfiguration which all material objects undergo through the passion of the poet,—this power which he exerts to dwarf the great, to magnify the small,—might be illustrated by a thousand examples from his Plays. I have before me the Tempest, and will cite only these few lines.

> ARIEL. The strong based promontory
> Have I made shake, and by the spurs plucked up
> The pine and cedar.

Prospero calls for music to soothe the frantic Alonzo, and his companions;

> A solemn air, and the best comforter
> To an unsettled fancy, cure thy brains
> Now useless, boiled within thy skull.

Again;

> The charm dissolves apace,
> And, as the morning steals upon the night,
> Melting the darkness, so their rising senses
> Begin to chase the ignorant fumes that mantle
> Their clearer reason.

> Their understanding
> Begins to swell: and the approaching tide
> Will shortly fill the reasonable shores
> That now lie foul and muddy.

The perception of real affinities between events (that is to say, of *ideal* affinities, for those only are real), enables the poet thus to make free with the most imposing forms and phenomena of the world, and to assert the predominance of the soul.

3. Whilst thus the poet animates nature with his own thoughts, he differs from the philosopher only herein, that the one proposes Beauty as his main end; the other Truth. But the philosopher, not less than the poet, postpones the apparent order and relations of things to the empire of thought. "The problem of philosophy," according to Plato, "is, for all that exists conditionally, to find a ground unconditioned and absolute." It proceeds on the faith that a law determines all phenomena, which being known, the phenomena can be predicted. That law, when in the mind, is an idea. Its beauty is infinite. The true philosopher and the true poet are one, and a beauty, which is truth, and a truth, which is beauty, is the aim of both. Is not the charm of one of Plato's or Aristotle's definitions strictly like that of the Antigone of Sophocles? It is, in both cases, that a spiritual life has been imparted to nature; that the solid seeming block of matter has been pervaded and dissolved by a thought; that this feeble human being has penetrated the vast masses of nature with an informing soul, and recognized itself in their harmony, that is, seized their law. In physics, when this is attained, the memory disburthens itself of its cumbrous catalogues of particulars, and carries centuries of observation in a single formula.

Thus even in physics, the material is degraded before the spiritual. The astronomer, the geometer, rely on their irrefragable analysis, and disdain the results of observation. The sublime remark of Euler on his law of arches, "This will be found contrary to all experience, yet is true;" had already transferred nature into the mind, and left matter like an outcast corpse.

4. Intellectual science has been observed to beget invariably a doubt of the existence of matter. Turgot said, "He that has never doubted the existence of matter, may be assured he has no aptitude for metaphysical inquiries." It fastens the attention upon immortal necessary uncreated natures, that is, upon Ideas; and in their presence we feel that the outward circumstance is a dream and a shade. Whilst we wait in this Olympus of gods, we think of nature as an appendix to the soul. We ascend into their region, and know that these are the thoughts of the Supreme Being. "These are they who were set up from everlasting, from the beginning, or ever the earth was. When he prepared the heavens, they were there; when he established the clouds above, when he strengthened the fountains of the deep. Then they were by him, as one brought up with him. Of them took he counsel."[9]

Their influence is proportionate. As objects of science they are accessible to few men. Yet all men are capable of being raised by piety or by passion, into their region. And no man touches these divine natures, without becoming, in some degree, himself divine. Like a new soul, they renew the body. We become physically nimble and lightsome; we tread on air; life is no longer irksome, and we think it will never be so. No man fears age or misfortune or death in their serene company, for he is transported out of the district of change. Whilst we behold unveiled the nature of Justice and Truth, we learn the difference between the absolute and the conditional or relative. We apprehend the absolute. As it were, for the first time, *we exist*. We become immortal, for we learn that time and space are relations of matter; that with a perception of truth or a virtuous will they have no affinity.

5. Finally, religion and ethics, which may be fitly called the practice of ideas, or the introduction of ideas into life, have an analogous effect with all lower culture, in degrading nature and suggesting its dependence on spirit. Ethics and religion differ

herein; that the one is the system of human duties commencing
from man; the other, from God. Religion includes the personality
of God; Ethics does not. They are one to our present design. They
both put nature under foot. The first and last lesson of religion is,
"The things that are seen, are temporal; the things that are
unseen, are eternal." It puts an affront upon nature. It does that
for the unschooled, which philosophy does for Berkeley and
Viasa. The uniform language that may be heard in the churches
of the most ignorant sects is—"Contemn the unsubstantial shows
of the world; they are vanities, dreams, shadows, unrealities; seek
the realities of religion." The devotee flouts nature. Some theoso-
phists have arrived at a certain hostility and indignation towards
matter, as the Manichean and Plotinus. They distrusted in themselves any looking back to these flesh-pots of Egypt. Plotinus was
ashamed of his body. In short, they might all say of matter, what
Michael Angelo said of external beauty, "It is the frail and weary
weed, in which God dresses the soul which he has called into
time."

It appears that motion, poetry, physical and intellectual science, and religion, all tend to affect our convictions of the reality
of the external world. But I own there is something ungrateful in
expanding too curiously the particulars of the general proposition, that all culture tends to imbue us with idealism. I have no
hostility to nature, but a child's love to it. I expand and live in the
warm day like corn and melons. Let us speak her fair. I do not
wish to fling stones at my beautiful mother, nor soil my gentle
nest. I only wish to indicate the true position of nature in regard
to man, wherein to establish man all right education tends; as the
ground which to attain is the object of human life, that is, of
man's connection with nature. Culture inverts the vulgar views of
nature, and brings the mind to call that apparent which it uses to
call real, and that real which it uses to call visionary. Children, it
is true, believe in the external world. The belief that it appears
only, is an afterthought, but with culture this faith will as surely
arise on the mind as did the first.

The advantage of the ideal theory over the popular faith is this,
that it presents the world in precisely that view which is most
desirable to the mind. It is, in fact, the view which Reason, both

speculative and practical, that is, philosophy and virtue, take. For seen in the light of thought, the world always is phenomenal; and virtue subordinates it to the mind. Idealism sees the world in God. It beholds the whole circle of persons and things, of actions and events, of country and religion, not as painfully accumulated, atom after atom, act after act, in an aged creeping Past, but as one vast picture which God paints on the instant eternity for the contemplation of the soul. Therefore the soul holds itself off from a too trivial and microscopic study of the universal tablet. It respects the end too much to immerse itself in the means. It sees something more important in Christianity than the scandals of ecclesiastical history or the niceties of criticism; and, very incurious concerning persons or miracles, and not at all disturbed by chasms of historical evidence, it accepts from God the phenomenon, as it finds it, as the pure and awful form of religion in the world. It is not hot and passionate at the appearance of what it calls its own good or bad fortune, at the union or opposition of other persons. No man is its enemy. It accepts whatsoever befalls, as part of its lesson. It is a watcher more than a doer, and it is a doer, only that it may the better watch.

SPIRIT

VII

It is essential to a true theory of nature and of man, that it should contain somewhat progressive. Uses that are exhausted or that may be, and facts that end in the statement, cannot be all that is true of this brave lodging wherein man is harbored, and wherein all his faculties find appropriate and endless exercise. And all the uses of nature admit of being summed in one, which yields the activity of man an infinite scope. Through all its kingdoms, to the suburbs and outskirts of things, it is faithful to the cause whence it had its origin. It always speaks of Spirit. It suggests the absolute. It is a perpetual effect. It is a great shadow pointing always to the sun behind us.

The aspect of Nature is devout. Like the figure of Jesus, she stands with bended head, and hands folded upon the breast. The happiest man is he who learns from nature the lesson of worship.

Of that ineffable essence which we call Spirit, he that thinks most, will say least. We can foresee God in the coarse, and, as it were, distant phenomena of matter; but when we try to define and describe himself, both language and thought desert us, and we are as helpless as fools and savages. That essence refuses to be recorded in propositions, but when man has worshipped him intellectually, the noblest ministry of nature is to stand as the apparition of God. It is the organ through which the universal spirit speaks to the individual, and strives to lead back the individual to it.

When we consider Spirit, we see that the views already presented do not include the whole circumference of man. We must add some related thoughts.

Three problems are put by nature to the mind: What is matter? Whence is it? and Whereto? The first of these questions only, the ideal theory answers. Idealism saith: matter is a phenomenon, not a substance. Idealism acquaints us with the total disparity between the evidence of our own being and the evidence of the world's being. The one is perfect; the other, incapable of any assurance; the mind is a part of the nature of things; the world is a divine dream, from which we may presently awake to the glories and certainties of day. Idealism is a hypothesis to account for nature by other principles than those of carpentry and chemistry. Yet, if it only deny the existence of matter, it does not satisfy the demands of the spirit. It leaves God out of me. It leaves me in the splendid labyrinth of my perceptions, to wander without end. Then the heart resists it, because it balks the affections in denying substantive being to men and women. Nature is so pervaded with human life that there is something of humanity in all and in every particular. But this theory makes nature foreign to me, and does not account for that consanguinity which we acknowledge to it.

Let it stand then, in the present state of our knowledge, merely as a useful introductory hypothesis, serving to apprize us of the eternal distinction between the soul and the world.

But when, following the invisible steps of thought, we come to inquire, Whence is matter? and Whereto? many truths arise to us out of the recesses of consciousness. We learn that the highest is present to the soul of man; that the dread universal essence, which is not wisdom, or love, or beauty, or power, but all in one, and each entirely, is that for which all things exist, and that by which they are; that spirit creates; that behind nature, throughout nature, spirit is present; one and not compound it does not act upon us from without, that is, in space and time, but spiritually, or through ourselves: therefore, that spirit, that is, the Supreme Being, does not build up nature around us, but puts it forth through us, as the life of the tree puts forth new branches and leaves through the pores of the old. As a plant upon the earth, so a man rests upon the bosom of God; he is nourished by unfailing fountains, and draws at his need inexhaustible power. Who can set bounds to the possibilities of man? Once inhale the upper air, being admitted to behold the absolute natures of justice and truth, and we learn that man has access to the entire mind of the Creator, is himself the creator in the finite. This view, which admonishes me where the sources of wisdom and power lie, and points to virtue as to

> "The golden key
> Which opes the palace of eternity,"[10]

carries upon its face the highest certificate of truth, because it animates me to create my own world through the purification of my soul.

The world proceeds from the same spirit as the body of man. It is a remoter and inferior incarnation of God, a projection of God in the unconscious. But it differs from the body in one important respect. It is not, like that, now subjected to the human will. Its serene order is inviolable by us. It is, therefore, to us, the present expositor of the divine mind. It is a fixed point whereby we may measure our departure. As we degenerate, the contrast between us and our house is more evident. We are as much strangers in nature as we are aliens from God. We do not understand the notes of birds. The fox and the deer run away from us; the bear and tiger rend us. We do not know the uses of more than a few plants, as corn and the apple, the potato and the vine. Is not the landscape, every glimpse of which hath a grandeur, a face of him? Yet this may show us what discord is between man and nature, for you cannot freely admire a noble landscape if laborers are digging in the field hard by. The poet finds something ridiculous in his delight until he is out of the sight of men.

PROSPECTS

VIII

In inquiries respecting the laws of the world and the frame of things, the highest reason is always the truest. That which seems faintly possible, it is so refined, is often faint and dim because it is deepest seated in the mind among the eternal verities. Empirical science is apt to cloud the sight, and by the very knowledge of functions and processes to bereave the student of the manly contemplation of the whole. The savant becomes unpoetic. But the best read naturalist who lends an entire and devout attention to truth, will see that there remains much to learn of his relation to the world, and that it is not to be learned by any addition or subtraction or other comparison of known quantities, but is arrived at by untaught sallies of the spirit, by a continual self-recovery, and by entire humility. He will perceive that there are far more excellent qualities in the student than preciseness and infallibility; that a guess is often more fruitful than an indisputable affirmation, and that a dream may let us deeper into the secret of nature than a hundred concerted experiments.

For the problems to be solved are precisely those which the physiologist and the naturalist omit to state. It is not so pertinent to man to know all the individuals of the animal kingdom, as it is to know whence and whereto is this tyrannizing unity in his constitution, which evermore separates and classifies things, endeavoring to reduce the most diverse to one form. When I behold a rich landscape, it is less to my purpose to recite correctly the order and superposition of the strata, than to know why all thought of multitude is lost in a tranquil sense of unity. I cannot greatly honor minuteness in details, so long as there is no hint to explain the relation between things and thoughts; no ray upon the *meta-*

physics of conchology, of botany, of the arts, to show the relation of the forms of flowers, shells, animals, architecture, to the mind, and build science upon ideas. In a cabinet of natural history, we become sensible of a certain occult recognition and sympathy in regard to the most unwieldy and eccentric forms of beast, fish, and insect. The American who has been confined, in his own country, to the sight of buildings designed after foreign models, is surprised on entering York Minister or St. Peter's at Rome, by the feeling that these structures are imitations also,—faint copies of an invisible archetype. Nor has science sufficient humanity, so long as the naturalist overlooks that wonderful congruity which subsists between man and the world; of which he is lord, not because he is the most subtile inhabitant, but because he is its head and heart, and finds something of himself in every great and small thing, in every mountain stratum, in every new law of color, fact of astronomy, or atmospheric influence which observation or analysis lays open. A perception of this mystery inspires the muse of George Herbert, the beautiful psalmist of the seven-teenth century. The following lines are part of his little poem on Man.

> Man is all symmetry,
> Full of proportions, one limb to another,
>   And all to all the world besides.
>   Each part may call the farthest, brother;
> For head with foot hath private amity,
>   And both with moons and tides.
>
> Nothing hath got so far
> But man hath caught and kept it as his prey;
>   His eyes dismount the highest star:
>   He is in little all the sphere.
> Herbs gladly cure our flesh, because that they
>   Find their acquaintance there.
>
> For us, the winds do blow,
> The earth doth rest, heaven move, and fountains flow;
>   Nothing we see, but means our good,
>   As our delight, or as our treasure;

The whole is either our cupboard of food,
   Or cabinet of pleasure.

   The stars have us to bed:
Night draws the curtain; which the sun withdraws.
   Music and light attend our head.
   All things unto our flesh are kind,
In their descent and being; to our mind,
   In their ascent and cause.

   More servants wait on man
Than he'll take notice of. In every path,
   He treads down that which doth befriend him
   When sickness makes him pale and wan.
Oh mighty love! Man is one world, and hath
   Another to attend him.

The perception of this class of truths makes the attraction which draws men to science, but the end is lost sight of in attention to the means. In view of this half-sight of science, we accept the sentence of Plato, that "poetry comes nearer to vital truth than history." Every surmise and vaticination of the mind is entitled to a certain respect, and we learn to prefer imperfect theories, and sentences which contain glimpses of truth, to digested systems which have no one valuable suggestion. A wise writer will feel that the ends of study and composition are best answered by announcing undiscovered regions of thought, and so communicating, through hope, new activity to the torpid spirit.

I shall therefore conclude this essay with some traditions of man and nature, which a certain poet sang to me; and which, as they have always been in the world, and perhaps reappear to every bard, may be both history and prophecy.[11]

'The foundations of man are not in matter, but in spirit. But the element of spirit is eternity. To it, therefore, the longest series of events, the oldest chronologies are young and recent. In the cycle of the universal man, from whom the known individuals proceed, centuries are points, and all history is but the epoch of one degradation.

'We distrust and deny inwardly our sympathy with nature. We own and disown our relation to it, by turns. We are like Nebuchadnezzar, dethroned, bereft of reason, and eating grass like an ox. But who can set limits to the remedial force of spirit?

'A man is a god in ruins. When men are innocent, life shall be longer, and shall pass into the immortal as gently as we awake from dreams. Now, the world would be insane and rabid, if these disorganizations should last for hundreds of years. It is kept in check by death and infancy. Infancy is the perpetual Messiah, which comes into the arms of fallen men, and pleads with them to return to paradise.

'Man is the dwarf of himself. Once he was permeated and dissolved by spirit. He filled nature with his overflowing currents. Out from him sprang the sun and moon; from man the sun, from woman the moon. The laws of his mind, the periods of his actions externized themselves into day and night, into the year and the seasons. But, having made for himself this huge shell, his waters retired; he no longer fills the veins and veinlets; he is shrunk to a drop. He sees that the structure still fits him, but fits him colossally. Say, rather, once it fitted him, now it corresponds to him from far and on high. He adores timidly his own work. Now is man the follower of the sun, and woman the follower of the moon. Yet sometimes he starts in his slumber, and wonders at himself and his house, and muses strangely at the resemblance betwixt him and it. He perceives that if his law is still paramount, if still he have elemental power, if his word is sterling yet in nature, it is not conscious power, it is not inferior but superior to his will. It is instinct.' Thus my Orphic poet sang.

At present, man applies to nature but half his force. He works on the world with his understanding alone. He lives in it and masters it by a penny-wisdom; and he that works most in it is but a half-man, and whilst his arms are strong and his digestion good, his mind is imbruted, and he is a selfish savage. His relation to nature, his power over it, is through the understanding, as by manure; the economic use of fire, wind, water, and the mariner's needle; steam, coal, chemical agriculture; the repairs of the human body by the dentist and the surgeon. This is such a resumption of power as if a banished king should buy his territories inch by inch,

instead of vaulting at once into his throne. Meantime, in the thick
darkness, there are not wanting gleams of a better light,—occasional
examples of the action of man upon nature with his entire force,—
with reason as well as understanding. Such examples are, the traditions of miracles in the earliest antiquity of all nations; the
history of Jesus Christ; the achievements of a principle, as in religious and political revolutions, and in the abolition of the slave-
trade; the miracles of enthusiasm, as those reported of Swedenborg,
Hohenlohe, and the Shakers; many obscure and yet contested
facts, now arranged under the name of Animal Magnetism; prayer;
eloquence; self-healing; and the wisdom of children. These are
examples of Reason's momentary grasp of the sceptre; the exertions of a power which exists not in time or space, but an instan-
taneous in-streaming causing power. The difference between the
actual and the ideal force of man is happily figured by the school-
men, in saying, that the knowledge of man is an evening knowledge, *vespertina cognitio*, but that of God is a morning knowledge,
matutina cognitio.

The problem of restoring to the world original and eternal
beauty is solved by the redemption of the soul. The ruin or the
blank that we see when we look at nature, is in our own eye. The
axis of vision is not coincident with the axis of things, and so they
appear not transparent but opaque. The reason why the world
lacks unity, and lies broken and in heaps, is because man is dis-
united with himself. He cannot be a naturalist until he satisfies all
the demands of the spirit. Love is as much its demand as perception. Indeed, neither can be perfect without the other. In the uttermost meaning of the words, thought is devout, and devotion is
thought. Deep calls unto deep. But in actual life, the marriage is
not celebrated. There are innocent men who worship God after
the tradition of their fathers, but their sense of duty has not yet
extended to the use of all their faculties. And there are patient
naturalists, but they freeze their subject under the wintry light of
the understanding. Is not prayer also a study of truth,—a sally of
the soul into the unfound infinite? No man ever prayed heartily
without learning something. But when a faithful thinker, resolute
to detach every object from personal relations and see it in the
light of thought, shall, at the same time, kindle science with the

fire of the holiest affections, then will God go forth anew into the creation.

It will not need, when the mind is prepared for study, to search for objects. The invariable mark of wisdom is to see the miraculous in the common. What is a day? What is a year? What is summer? What is woman? What is a child? What is sleep? To our blindness, these things seem unaffecting. We make fables to hide the baldness of the fact and conform it, as we say, to the higher law of the mind. But when the fact is seen under the light of an idea, the gaudy fable fades and shrivels. We behold the real higher law. To the wise, therefore, a fact is true poetry, and the most beautiful of fables. These wonders are brought to our own door. You also are a man. Man and woman and their social life, poverty, labor, sleep, fear, fortune, are known to you. Learn that none of these things is superficial, but that each phenomenon has its roots in the faculties and affections of the mind. Whilst the abstract question occupies your intellect, nature brings it in the concrete to be solved by your hands. It were a wise inquiry for the closet, to compare, point by point, especially at remarkable crises in life, our daily history with the rise and progress of ideas in the mind.

So shall we come to look at the world with new eyes. It shall answer the endless inquiry of the intellect,—What is truth? and of the affections,—What is good? by yielding itself passive to the educated Will. Then shall come to pass what my poet said: 'Nature is not fixed but fluid. Spirit alters, moulds, makes it. The immobility or bruteness of nature is the absence of spirit; to pure spirit it is fluid, it is volatile, it is obedient. Every spirit builds itself a house, and beyond its house a world, and beyond its world a heaven. Know then that the world exists for you. For you is the phenomenon perfect. What we are, that only can we see. All that Adam had, all that Cæsar could, you have and can do. Adam called his house, heaven and earth; Cæsar called his house, Rome; you perhaps call yours, a cobbler's trade; a hundred acres of ploughed land; or a scholar's garret. Yet line for line and point for point your dominion is as great as theirs, though without fine names. Build therefore your own world. As fast as you conform your life to the pure idea in your mind, that will unfold its great proportions. A correspondent revolution in things will attend the influx of the spirit. So fast will disagreeable appearances, swine, spiders, snakes, pests, mad-houses, prisons, enemies, vanish; they are temporary and shall be no more seen. The sordor and filths of nature, the sun shall dry up and the wind exhale. As when the summer comes from the south the snow-banks melt and the face of the earth becomes green before it, so shall the advancing spirit create its ornaments along its path, and carry with it the beauty it visits and the song which enchants it; it shall draw beautiful faces, warm hearts, wise discourse, and heroic acts, around its way, until evil is no more seen. The kingdom of man over nature, which cometh not with observation,—a dominion such as now is beyond his dream of God,—he shall enter without more wonder than the blind man feels who is gradually restored to perfect sight.'

NOTES

1. George Herbert, "Man."
2. *Kosmos.*
3. "The many in the one."
4. Shakespeare, *Macbeth.*
5. "All truth accords with truth."
6. Sonnet LXX.
7. Sonnet CXXIV.
8. *Measure for Measure.*
9. Proverbs 8.
10. Milton, *Comus.*
11. Although the orphic arrangement of the thoughts is the result of a number of influences, such as that of Bronson Alcott, the "certain poet" is Emerson himself. One of his sources, Proclus, wrote, "He who desires to signify divine concerns through symbols is orphic."

THE AMERICAN SCHOLAR

AN ORATION DELIVERED BEFORE THE
PHI BETA KAPPA SOCIETY, AT CAMBRIDGE,
AUGUST 31, 1837.

MR. PRESIDENT AND GENTLEMEN:

I greet you on the recommencement of our literary year. Our anniversary is one of hope, and, perhaps, not enough of labor. We do not meet for games of strength or skill, for the recitation of histories, tragedies, and odes, like the ancient Greeks; for parliaments of love and poesy, like the Troubadours; nor for the advancement of science, like our contemporaries in the British and European capitals. Thus far, our holiday has been simply a friendly sign of the survival of the love of letters amongst a people too busy to give to letters any more. As such it is precious as the sign of an indestructible instinct. Perhaps the time is already come when it ought to be, and will be, something else; when the sluggard intellect of this continent will look from under its iron lids and fill the postponed expectation of the world with something better than the exertions of mechanical skill. Our day of dependence, our long apprenticeship to the learning of other lands, draws to a close. The millions that around us are rushing into life, cannot always be fed on the sere remains of foreign harvests. Events, actions arise, that must be sung, that will sing themselves. Who can doubt that poetry will revive and lead in a new age, as the star in the constellation Harp, which now flames in our zenith, astronomers announce, shall one day be the pole-star for a thousand years?

In this hope I accept the topic which not only usage but the nature of our association seem to prescribe to this day,—the AMERICAN SCHOLAR. Year by year we come up hither to read one more chapter of his biography. Let us inquire what light new days and events have thrown on his character and his hopes.

It is one of those fables which out of an unknown antiquity convey an unlooked-for wisdom, that the gods, in the beginning, divided Man into men, that he might be more helpful to himself; just as the hand was divided into fingers, the better to answer its end.

The old fable covers a doctrine ever new and sublime; that there is One Man,—present to all particular men only partially, or through one faculty; and that you must take the whole society to find the whole man. Man is not a farmer, or a professor, or an engineer, but he is all. Man is priest, and scholar, and statesman, and producer, and soldier. In the *divided* or social state these functions are parcelled out to individuals, each of whom aims to do his stint of the joint work, whilst each other performs his. The fable implies that the individual, to possess himself, must sometimes return from his own labor to embrace all the other laborers. But, unfortunately, this original unit, this fountain of power, has been so distributed to multitudes, has been so minutely subdivided and peddled out, that it is spilled into drops, and cannot be gathered. The state of society is one in which the members have suffered amputation from the trunk, and strut about so many walking monsters,—a good finger, a neck, a stomach, an elbow, but never a man.

Man is thus metamorphosed into a thing, into many things. The planter, who is Man sent out into the field to gather food, is seldom cheered by any idea of the true dignity of his ministry. He sees his bushel and his cart, and nothing beyond, and sinks into the farmer, instead of Man on the farm. The tradesman scarcely ever gives an ideal worth to his work, but is ridden by the routine of his craft, and the soul is subject to dollars. The priest becomes a form; the attorney a statute-book; the mechanic a machine; the sailor a rope of the ship.

In this distribution of functions the scholar is the delegated intellect. In the right state he is *Man Thinking*. In the degenerate state, when the victim of society, he tends to become a mere thinker, or still worse, the parrot of other men's thinking.

In this view of him, as Man Thinking, the theory of his office is contained. Him Nature solicits with all her placid, all her monitory pictures; him the past instructs; him the future invites. Is not indeed every man a student, and do not all things exist for the student's behoof? And, finally, is not the true scholar the only true master? But the old oracle said, "All things have two handles: beware of the wrong one." In life, too often, the scholar errs with mankind and forfeits his privilege. Let us see him in his school, and consider him in reference to the main influences he receives.

I. The first in time and the first in importance of the influences upon the mind is that of nature. Every day, the sun; and, after sunset, Night and her stars. Ever the winds blow; ever the grass grows. Every day, men and women, conversing—beholding and beholden. The scholar is he of all men whom this spectacle most engages. He must settle its value in his mind. What is nature to him? There is never a beginning, there is never an end, to the inexplicable continuity of this web of God, but always circular power returning into itself. Therein it resembles his own spirit, whose beginning, whose ending, he never can find,—so entire, so boundless. Far too as her splendors shine, system on system shooting like rays, upward, downward, without centre, without circumference,—in the mass and in the particle, Nature hastens to render account of herself to the mind. Classification begins. To the young mind every thing is individual, stands by itself. By and by, it finds how to join two things and see in them one nature; then three, then three thousand; and so, tyrannized over by its own unifying instinct, it goes on tying things together, diminishing anomalies, discovering roots running under ground whereby contrary and remote things cohere and flower out from one stem. It presently learns that since the dawn of history there has been a constant accumulation and classifying of facts. But what is classification but the perceiving that these objects are not chaotic, and are not foreign, but have a law which is also a law of the human mind?

The astronomer discovers that geometry, a pure abstraction of the human mind, is the measure of planetary motion. The chemist finds proportions and intelligible method throughout matter; and science is nothing but the finding of analogy, identity, in the most remote parts. The ambitious soul sits down before each refractory fact; one after another reduces all strange constitutions, all new powers, to their class and their law, and goes on forever to animate the last fibre of organization, the outskirts of nature, by insight.

Thus to him, to this schoolboy under the bending dome of day, is suggested that he and it proceed from one root; one is leaf and one is flower; relation, sympathy, stirring in every vein. And what is that root? Is not that the soul of his soul? A thought too bold; a dream too wild. Yet when this spiritual light shall have revealed the law of more earthly natures,—when he has learned to worship the soul, and to see that the natural philosophy that now is, is only the first gropings of its gigantic hand, he shall look forward to an ever expanding knowledge as to a becoming creator. He shall see that nature is the opposite of the soul, answering to it part for part. One is seal and one is print. Its beauty is the beauty of his own mind. Its laws are the laws of his own mind. Nature then becomes to him the measure of his attainments. So much of nature as he is ignorant of, so much of his own mind does he not yet possess. And, in fine, the ancient precept, "Know thyself," and the modern precept, "Study nature," become at last one maxim.

II. The next great influence into the spirit of the scholar is the mind of the Past,—in whatever form, whether of literature, of art, of institutions, that mind is inscribed. Books are the best type of the influence of the past, and perhaps we shall get at the truth,— learn the amount of this influence more conveniently,—by considering their value alone.

The theory of books is noble. The scholar of the first age received into him the world around; brooded thereon; gave it the new arrangement of his own mind, and uttered it again. It came into him life; it went out from him truth. It came to him shortlived actions; it went out from him immortal thoughts. It came to him business, it went from him poetry. It was dead fact; now, it is quick thought. It can stand, and it can go. It now endures, it now flies, it now inspires. Precisely in proportion to the depth of mind from which it issued, so high does it soar, so long does it sing.

Or, I might say, it depends on how far the process has gone, of transmuting life into truth. In proportion to the completeness of the distillation, so will the purity and imperishableness of the product be. But none is quite perfect. As no air-pump can by any means make a perfect vacuum, so neither can any artist entirely exclude the conventional, the local, the perishable from his book, or write a book of pure thought, that shall be as efficient, in all respects, to a remote posterity, as to contemporaries, or rather to the second age. Each age, it is found, must write its own books; or rather, each generation for the next succeeding. The books of an older period will not fit this.

Yet hence arises a grave mischief. The sacredness which attaches to the act of creation, the act of thought, is transferred to the record. The poet chanting was felt to be a divine man: henceforth the chant is divine also. The writer was a just and wise spirit: henceforward it is settled the book is perfect; as love of the hero corrupts into worship of his statue. Instantly the book becomes noxious: the guide is a tyrant. The sluggish and perverted mind of the multitude, slow to open to the incursions of Reason, having once so opened, having once received this book, stands upon it, and makes an outcry if it is disparaged. Colleges are built on it. Books are written on it by thinkers, not by Man Thinking; by men of talent, that is, who start wrong, who set out from accepted dogmas, not from their own sight of principles. Meek young men grow up in libraries, believing it their duty to accept the views which Cicero, which Locke, which Bacon, have given; forgetful that Cicero, Locke, and Bacon were only young men in libraries when they wrote these books.

Hence, instead of Man Thinking, we have the bookworm. Hence the book-learned class, who value books, as such; not as related to nature and the human constitution, but as making a sort of Third Estate with the world and the soul. Hence the restorers of readings, the emendators, the bibliomaniacs of all degrees.

Books are the best of things, well used; abused, among the worst. What is the right use? What is the one end which all means go to effect? They are for nothing but to inspire. I had better never see a book than to be warped by its attraction clean out of my own orbit, and made a satellite instead of a system. The one thing in the world, of value, is the active soul. This every man is entitled to; this every man contains within him, although in almost all men obstructed and as yet unborn. The soul active sees absolute truth and utters truth, or creates. In this action it is genius; not the privilege of here and there a favorite, but the sound estate of every man. In its essence it is progressive. The book, the college, the school of art, the institution of any kind, stop with some past utterance of genius. This is good, say they,—let us hold by this. They pin me down. They look backward and not forward. But genius looks forward: the eyes of man are set in his forehead, not in his hindhead: man hopes: genius creates. Whatever talents may be, if the man create not, the pure efflux of the Deity is not his;— cinders and smoke there may be, but not yet flame. There are creative manners, there are creative actions, and creative words; manners, actions, words, that is, indicative of no custom or authority, but springing spontaneous from the mind's own sense of good and fair.

On the other part, instead of being its own seer, let it receive from another mind its truth, though it were in torrents of light, without periods of solitude, inquest, and self-recovery, and a fatal disservice is done. Genius is always sufficiently the enemy of genius by over-influence. The literature of every nation bears me witness. The English dramatic poets have Shakspearized now for two hundred years.

Undoubtedly there is a right way of reading, so it be sternly subordinated. Man Thinking must not be subdued by his instruments. Books are for the scholar's idle times. When he can read God directly, the hour is too precious to be wasted in other men's transcripts of their readings. But when the intervals of darkness come, as come they must,—when the sun is hid and the stars withdraw their shining,—we repair to the lamps which were kindled by their ray, to guide our steps to the East again, where the dawn is. We hear, that we may speak. The Arabian proverb says, "A fig tree, looking on a fig tree, becometh fruitful."

It is remarkable, the character of the pleasure we derive from the best books. They impress us with the conviction that one nature wrote and the same reads. We read the verses of one of the great English poets, of Chaucer, of Marvell, of Dryden, with the most modern joy,—with a pleasure, I mean, which is in great part caused by the abstraction of all *time* from their verses. There is some awe mixed with the joy of our surprise, when this poet, who lived in some past world, two or three hundred years ago, says that which lies close to my own soul, that which I also had well-nigh thought and said. But for the evidence thence afforded to the philosophical doctrine of the identity of all minds, we should suppose some preëstablished harmony, some foresight of souls that were to be, and some preparation of stores for their future wants, like the fact observed in insects, who lay up food before death for the young grub they shall never see.

I would not be hurried by any love of system, by any exaggeration of instincts, to underrate the Book. We all know, that as the human body can be nourished on any food, though it were boiled grass and the broth of shoes, so the human mind can be fed by any knowledge. And great and heroic men have existed who had almost no other information than by the printed page. I only would say that it needs a strong head to bear that diet. One must be an inventor to read well. As the proverb says, "He that would bring home the wealth of the Indies, must carry out the wealth of the Indies." There is then creative reading as well as creative writing. When the mind is braced by labor and invention, the page of whatever book we read becomes luminous with manifold allusion. Every sentence is doubly significant, and the sense of our author is as broad as the world. We then see, what is always true, that as the seer's hour of vision is short and rare among heavy days and months, so is its record, perchance, the least part of his volume. The discerning will read, in his Plato or Shakspeare, only the least part,—only the authentic utterances of the oracle;—all the rest he rejects, were it never so many times Plato's and Shakspeare's.

Of course there is a portion of reading quite indispensable to a wise man. History and exact science he must learn by laborious reading. Colleges, in like manner, have their indispensable office,—to teach elements. But they can only highly serve us when they aim not to drill, but to create; when they gather from far every ray of various genius to their hospitable halls, and by the concentrated fires, set the hearts of their youth on flame. Thought and knowledge are natures in which apparatus and pretension avail nothing. Gowns and pecuniary foundations, though of towns of gold, can never countervail the least sentence or syllable of wit. Forget this, and our American colleges will recede in their public importance, whilst they grow richer every year.

III. There goes in the world a notion that the scholar should be a recluse, a valetudinarian,—as unfit for any handiwork or public labor as a penknife for an axe. The so-called "practical men" sneer at speculative men, as if, because they speculate or *see*, they could do nothing. I have heard it said that the clergy,—who are always, more universally than any other class, the scholars of their day,—are addressed as women; that the rough, spontaneous conversation of men they do not hear, but only a mincing and diluted speech. They are often virtually disfranchised; and indeed there are advocates for their celibacy. As far as this is true of the studious classes, it is not just and wise. Action is with the scholar subordinate, but it is essential. Without it he is not yet man. Without it thought can never ripen into truth. Whilst the world hangs before the eye as a cloud of beauty, we cannot even see its beauty. Inaction is cowardice, but there can be no scholar without the heroic mind. The preamble of thought, the transition through which it passes from the unconscious to the conscious, is action. Only so much do I know, as I have lived. Instantly we know whose words are loaded with life, and whose not.

The world,—this shadow of the soul, or *other me*,—lies wide around. Its attractions are the keys which unlock my thoughts and make me acquainted with myself. I run eagerly into this resounding tumult. I grasp the hands of those next me, and take my place in the ring to suffer and to work, taught by an instinct that so shall the dumb abyss be vocal with speech. I pierce its order; I dissipate its fear; I dispose of it within the circuit of my expanding life. So much only of life as I know by experience, so much of the wilderness have I vanquished and planted, or so far have I extended my being, my dominion. I do not see how any man can afford, for the sake of his nerves and his nap, to spare any action in which he can partake. It is pearls and rubies to his

discourse. Drudgery, calamity, exasperation, want, are instruc-
tors in eloquence and wisdom. The true scholar grudges every
opportunity of action past by, as a loss of power. It is the raw
material out of which the intellect moulds her splendid products.
A strange process too, this by which experience is converted into
thought, as a mulberry leaf is converted into satin. The manufacture goes forward at all hours.

The actions and events of our childhood and youth are now
matters of calmest observation. They lie like fair pictures in the
air. Not so with our recent actions,—with the business which we
now have in hand. On this we are quite unable to speculate. Our
affections as yet circulate through it. We no more feel or know it
than we feel the feet, or the hand, or the brain of our body. The
new deed is yet a part of life,—remains for a time immersed in
our unconscious life. In some contemplative hour it detaches itself
from the life like a ripe fruit, to become a thought of the mind.
Instantly it is raised, transfigured; the corruptible has put on
incorruption. Henceforth it is an object of beauty, however base
its origin and neighborhood. Observe too the impossibility of
antedating this act. In its grub state, it cannot fly, it cannot shine,
it is a dull grub. But suddenly, without observation, the selfsame
thing unfurls beautiful wings, and is an angel of wisdom. So is
there no fact, no event, in our private history, which shall not,
sooner or later, lose its adhesive, inert form, and astonish us by
soaring from our body into the empyrean. Cradle and infancy,
school and playground, the fear of boys, and dogs, and ferules,
the love of little maids and berries, and many another fact that
once filled the whole sky, are gone already; friend and relative,
profession and party, town and country, nation and world, must
also soar and sing.

Of course, he who has put forth his total strength in fit actions
has the richest return of wisdom. I will not shut myself out of this
globe of action, and transplant an oak into a flower-pot, there to
hunger and pine; nor trust the revenue of some single faculty, and
exhaust one vein of thought, much like those Savoyards, who, getting their livelihood by carving shepherds, shepherdesses, and
smoking Dutchmen, for all Europe, went out one day to the
mountain to find stock, and discovered that they had whittled up

the last of their pine trees. Authors we have, in numbers, who have written out their vein, and who, moved by a commendable prudence, sail for Greece or Palestine, follow the trapper into the prairie, or ramble round Algiers, to replenish their merchantable stock.

If it were only for a vocabulary, the scholar would be covetous of action. Life is our dictionary. Years are well spent in country labors; in town; in the insight into trades and manufactures; in frank intercourse with many men and women; in science; in art; to the one end of mastering in all their facts a language by which to illustrate and embody our perceptions. I learn immediately from any speaker how much he has already lived, through the poverty or the splendor of his speech. Life lies behind us as the quarry from whence we get tiles and copestones for the masonry of to-day. This is the way to learn grammar. Colleges and books only copy the language which the field and the work-yard made.

But the final value of action, like that of books, and better than books, is that it is a resource. That great principle of Undulation in nature, that shows itself in the inspiring and expiring of the breath; in desire and satiety; in the ebb and flow of the sea; in day and night; in heat and cold; and, as yet more deeply ingrained in every atom and every fluid, is known to us under the name of Polarity,—these "fits of easy transmission and reflection," as Newton called them, are the law of nature because they are the law of spirit.

The mind now thinks, now acts, and each fit reproduces the other. When the artist has exhausted his materials, when the fancy no longer paints, when thoughts are no longer apprehended and books are a weariness,—he has always the resource to *live*. Character is higher than intellect. Thinking is the function. Living is the functionary. The stream retreats to its source. A great soul will be strong to live, as well as strong to think. Does he lack organ or medium to impart his truths? He can still fall back on this elemental force of living them. This is a total act. Thinking is a partial act. Let the grandeur of justice shine in his affairs. Let the beauty of affection cheer his lowly roof. Those "far from fame," who dwell and act with him, will feel the force of his constitution in the doings and passages of the day better than it can be measured by any public and designed display. Time shall teach him that the scholar loses no hour which the man lives. Herein he unfolds the sacred germ of his instinct, screened from influence. What is lost in seemliness is gained in strength. Not out of those on whom systems of education have exhausted their culture, comes the helpful giant to destroy the old or to build the new, but out of unhandselled savage nature; out of terrible Druids and Berserkers come at last Alfred and Shakspeare.

I hear therefore with joy whatever is beginning to be said of the dignity and necessity of labor to every citizen. There is virtue yet in the hoe and the spade, for learned as well as for unlearned hands. And labor is everywhere welcome; always we are invited to work; only be this limitation observed, that a man shall not for the sake of wider activity sacrifice any opinion to the popular judgments and modes of action.

I have now spoken of the education of the scholar by nature, by books, and by action. It remains to say somewhat of his duties.

They are such as become Man Thinking. They may all be comprised in self-trust. The office of the scholar is to cheer, to raise, and to guide men by showing them facts amidst appearances. He plies the slow, unhonored, and unpaid task of observation. Flamsteed and Herschel, in their glazed observatories, may catalogue the stars with the praise of all men, and the results being splendid and useful, honor is sure. But he, in his private observatory, cataloguing obscure and nebulous stars of the human mind, which as yet no man has thought of as such,—watching days and months sometimes for a few facts; correcting still his old records;—must relinquish display and immediate fame. In the long period of his preparation he must betray often an ignorance and shiftlessness in popular arts, incurring the disdain of the able who shoulder him aside. Long he must stammer in his speech; often forego the living for the dead. Worse yet, he must accept—how often!—poverty and solitude. For the ease and pleasure of treading the old road, accepting the fashions, the education, the religion of society, he takes the cross of making his own, and, of course, the self-accusation, the faint heart, the frequent uncertainty and loss of time, which are the nettles and tangling vines in the way of the self-relying and self-directed; and the state of virtual hostility in which he seems to stand to society, and especially to educated society. For all this loss and scorn, what offset? He is to find consolation in exercising the highest functions of human nature. He is one who raises himself from private considerations and breathes and lives on public and illustrious thoughts. He is the world's eye. He is the world's heart. He is to resist the vulgar prosperity that retrogrades ever to barbarism, by preserving and communicating heroic sentiments, noble biographies, melodious verse, and the conclusions of history. Whatsoever oracles the human heart, in all emergencies, in all solemn hours, has uttered as its commentary on the world of actions,—these he shall receive and impart. And whatsoever new verdict Reason from her inviolable seat pronounces on the passing men and events of to-day,—this he shall hear and promulgate.

These being his functions, it becomes him to feel all confidence in himself, and to defer never to the popular cry. He and he only knows the world. The world of any moment is the merest appearance. Some great decorum, some fetish of a government, some ephemeral trade, or war, or man, is cried up by half mankind and cried down by the other half, as if all depended on this particular up or down. The odds are that the whole question is not worth the poorest thought which the scholar has lost in listening to the controversy. Let him not quit his belief that a popgun is a popgun, though the ancient and honorable of the earth affirm it to be the crack of doom. In silence, in steadiness, in severe abstraction, let him hold by himself; add observation to observation, patient of neglect, patient of reproach, and bide his own time,—happy enough if he can satisfy himself alone that this day he has seen something truly. Success treads on every right step. For the instinct is sure, that prompts him to tell his brother what he thinks. He then learns that in going down into the secrets of his own mind he has descended into the secrets of all minds. He learns that he who has mastered any law in his private thoughts, is master to that extent of all men whose language he speaks, and of all into whose language his own can be translated. The poet, in utter solitude remembering his spontaneous thoughts and recording them, is found to have recorded that which men in crowded cities find true for them also. The orator distrusts at first the fitness of his frank confessions, his want of knowledge of the persons he addresses, until he finds that he is the complement of his hearers;—that they drink his words because he fulfils for them their own nature; the deeper he dives into his privatest, secretest presentiment, to his wonder he finds this is the most acceptable, most public, and universally true. The people delight in it; the better part of every man feels, This is my music; this is myself.

In self-trust all the virtues are comprehended. Free should the scholar be,—free and brave. Free even to the definition of freedom, "without any hindrance that does not arise out of his own constitution." Brave; for fear is a thing which a scholar by his very function puts behind him. Fear always springs from ignorance. It is a shame to him if his tranquillity, amid dangerous times, arise from the presumption that like children and women his is a protected class; or if he seek a temporary peace by the diversion of his thoughts from politics or vexed questions, hiding his head like an ostrich in the flowering bushes, peeping into microscopes, and turning rhymes, as a boy whistles to keep his courage up. So is the danger a danger still; so is the fear worse. Manlike let him turn and face it. Let him look into its eye and search its nature, inspect its origin,—see the whelping of this lion,—which lies no great way back; he will then find in himself a perfect comprehension of its nature and extent; he will have made his hands meet on the other side, and can henceforth defy it and pass on superior. The world is his who can see through its pretension. What deafness, what stone-blind custom, what over-grown error you behold is there only by sufferance,—by your sufferance. See it to be a lie, and you have already dealt it its mortal blow.

Yes, we are the cowed,—we the trustless. It is a mischievous notion that we are come late into nature; that the world was finished a long time ago. As the world was plastic and fluid in the hands of God, so it is ever to so much of his attributes as we bring to it. To ignorance and sin, it is flint. They adapt themselves to it as they may; but in proportion as a man has any thing in him divine, the firmament flows before him and takes his signet and form. Not he is great who can alter matter, but he who can alter my state of mind. They are the kings of the world who give the color of their present thought to all nature and all art, and persuade men by the cheerful serenity of their carrying the matter, that this thing which they do is the apple which the ages have desired to pluck, now at last ripe, and inviting nations to the harvest. The great man makes the great thing. Wherever Macdonald sits, there is the head of the table. Linnæus makes botany the most alluring of studies, and wins it from the farmer and the herb-woman; Davy, chemistry; and Cuvier, fossils. The day is always his who works in it with serenity and great aims. The unstable estimates of men crowd to him whose mind is filled with a truth, as the heaped waves of the Atlantic follow the moon.

For this self-trust, the reason is deeper than can be fathomed,—darker than can be enlightened. I might not carry with me the feeling of my audience in stating my own belief. But I have already shown the ground of my hope, in adverting to the doctrine that man is one. I believe man has been wronged; he has wronged himself. He has almost lost the light that can lead him back to his prerogatives. Men are become of no account. Men in history, men in the world of to-day, are bugs, are spawn, and are called "the mass" and "the herd." In a century, in a millennium, one or two men; that is to say, one or two approximations to the right state of every man. All the rest behold in the hero or the poet their own green and crude being,—ripened; yes, and are content to be less, so *that* may attain to its full stature. What a testimony, full of grandeur, full of pity, is borne to the demands of his own nature, by the poor clansman, the poor partisan, who rejoices in the glory of his chief. The poor and the low find some amends to their immense moral capacity, for their acquiescence in a political and social inferiority. They are content to be brushed like flies from the path of a great person, so that justice shall be done by him to that common nature which it is the dearest desire of all to see enlarged and glorified. They sun themselves in the great man's light, and feel it to be their own element. They cast the dignity of man from their down-trod selves upon the shoulders of a hero, and will perish to add one drop of blood to make that great heart beat, those giant sinews combat and conquer. He lives for us, and we live in him.

Men, such as they are, very naturally seek money or power; and power because it is as good as money,—the "spoils," so called, "of office." And why not? for they aspire to the highest, and this, in their sleep-walking, they dream is highest. Wake them and they shall quit the false good and leap to the true, and leave governments to clerks and desks. This revolution is to be wrought by the gradual domestication of the idea of Culture. The main enterprise of the world for splendor, for extent, is the upbuilding of a man. Here are the materials strewn along the ground. The private life of one man shall be a more illustrious monarchy, more formidable to its enemy, more sweet and serene in its influence to its friend, than any kingdom in history. For a man, rightly viewed, comprehendeth the particular natures of all men. Each philosopher, each bard, each actor has only done for me, as by a delegate, what one day I can do for myself. The books which once we valued more than the apple of the eye, we have quite exhausted. What is that but saying that we have come up with the point of view which the universal mind took through the eyes of one scribe; we have been that man, and have passed on. First, one, then another, we drain all cisterns, and waxing greater by all these supplies, we crave a better and more abundant food. The man has never lived that can feed us ever. The human mind cannot be enshrined in a person who shall set a barrier on any one side to this unbounded, unboundable empire. It is one central fire, which, flaming now out of the lips of Etna, lightens the capes of Sicily, and now out of the throat of Vesuvius, illuminates the towers and vineyards of Naples. It is one light which beams out of a thousand stars. It is one soul which animates all men.

But I have dwelt perhaps tediously upon this abstraction of the Scholar. I ought not to delay longer to add what I have to say of nearer reference to the time and to this country.

Historically, there is thought to be a difference in the ideas which predominate over successive epochs, and there are data for marking the genius of the Classic, of the Romantic, and now of the Reflective or Philosophical age. With the views I have intimated of the oneness or the identity of the mind through all individuals, I do not much dwell on these differences. In fact, I believe each individual passes through all three. The boy is a Greek; the youth, romantic; the adult, reflective. I deny not, however, that a revolution in the leading idea may be distinctly enough traced.

Our age is bewailed as the age of Introversion. Must that needs be evil? We, it seems, are critical; we are embarrassed with second thoughts; we cannot enjoy any thing for hankering to know whereof the pleasure consists; we are lined with eyes; we see with our feet; the time is infected with Hamlet's unhappiness,—

"Sicklied o'er with the pale cast of thought."

It is so bad then? Sight is the last thing to be pitied. Would we be blind? Do we fear lest we should outsee nature and God, and drink truth dry? I look upon the discontent of the literary class as a mere announcement of the fact that they find themselves not in the state of mind of their fathers, and regret the coming state as untried; as a boy dreads the water before he has learned that he can swim. If there is any period one would desire to be born in, is it not the age of Revolution; when the old and the new stand side by side and admit of being compared; when the energies of all men are searched by fear and by hope; when the historic glories of the old can be compensated by the rich possibilities of the new era? This time, like all times, is a very good one, if we but know what to do with it.

I read with some joy of the auspicious signs of the coming days, as they glimmer already through poetry and art, through philosophy and science, through church and state.

One of these signs is the fact that the same movement which effected the elevation of what was called the lowest class in the state, assumed in literature a very marked and as benign an aspect. Instead of the sublime and beautiful, the near, the low, the common, was explored and poetized. That which had been negligently trodden under foot by those who were harnessing and provisioning themselves for long journeys into far countries, is suddenly found to be richer than all foreign parts. The literature of the poor, the feelings of the child, the philosophy of the street, the meaning of household life, are the topics of the time. It is a great stride. It is a sign—is it not?—of new vigor when the extremities are made active, when currents of warm life run into the hands and the feet. I ask not for the great, the remote, the romantic; what is doing in Italy or Arabia; what is Greek art, or Provençal minstrelsy; I embrace the common, I explore and sit at the feet of the familiar, the low. Give me insight into to-day, and you may have the antique and future worlds. What would we really know the meaning of? The meal in the firkin; the milk in the pan; the ballad in the street; the news of the boat; the glance of the eye; the form and the gait of the body;—show me the ultimate reason of these matters; show me the sublime presence of the highest spiritual cause lurking, as always it does lurk, in these suburbs and extremities of nature; let me see every trifle bristling with the polarity that ranges it instantly on an eternal law; and the shop, the plough, and the ledger referred to the like cause by which light undulates and poets sing;—and the world lies no longer a dull miscellany and lumber-room, but has form and order; there is no trifle, there is no puzzle, but one design unites and animates the farthest pinnacle and the lowest trench.

This idea has inspired the genius of Goldsmith, Burns, Cowper, and, in a newer time, of Goethe, Wordsworth, and Carlyle. This idea they have differently followed and with various success. In contrast with their writing, the style of Pope, of Johnson, of Gibbon, looks cold and pedantic. This writing is blood-warm. Man is surprised to find that things near are not less beautiful and wondrous than things remote. The near explains the far. The drop is a small ocean. A man is related to all nature. This perception of the worth of the vulgar is fruitful in discoveries. Goethe, in this very thing the most modern of the moderns, has shown us, as none ever did, the genius of the ancients.

There is one man of genius who has done much for this philosophy of life, whose literary value has never yet been rightly estimated;— I mean Emanuel Swedenborg. The most imaginative of men, yet writing with the precision of a mathematician, he endeavored to engraft a purely philosophical Ethics on the popular Christianity of his time. Such an attempt of course must have difficulty which no genius could surmount. But he saw and showed the connection between nature and the affections of the soul. He pierced the emblematic or spiritual character of the visible, audible, tangible world. Especially did his shade-loving muse hover over and interpret the lower parts of nature; he showed the mysterious bond that allies moral evil to the foul material forms, and has given in epical parables a theory of insanity, of beasts, of unclean and fearful things.

Another sign of our times, also marked by an analogous political movement, is the new importance given to the single person. Every thing that tends to insulate the individual,—to surrround him with barriers of natural respect, so that each man shall feel the world is his, and man shall treat with man as a sovereign state with a sovereign state,—tends to true union as well as greatness. "I learned," said the melancholy Pestalozzi, "that no man in God's wide earth is either willing or able to help any other man." Help must come from the bosom alone. The scholar is that man who must take up into himself all the ability of the time, all the contributions of the past, all the hopes of the future. He must be an university of knowledges. If there be one lesson more than another which should pierce his ear, it is, The world is nothing, the man is all; in yourself is the law of all nature, and you know not yet how a globule of sap ascends; in yourself slumbers the whole of Reason; it is for you to know all; it is for you to dare all. Mr. President and Gentlemen, this confidence in the unsearched might of man belongs, by all motives, by all prophecy, by all preparation, to the American Scholar. We have listened too long to the courtly muses of Europe. The spirit of the American freeman is already suspected to be timid, imitative, tame. Public and private avarice make the air we breathe thick and fat. The scholar is decent, indolent, complaisant. See already the tragic consequence. The mind of this country, taught to aim at low objects, eats upon itself. There is no work for any but the decorous and the complaisant. Young men of the fairest promise, who begin life upon our shores, inflated by the mountain winds, shined upon by all the stars of God, find the earth below not in unison with these, but are hindered from action by the disgust which the principles on which business is managed inspire, and turn drudges, or die of disgust, some of them suicides. What is the remedy? They did not yet see, and thousands of young men as hopeful now crowding to the barriers for the career do not yet see, that if the single man plant himself indomitably on his instincts, and there abide, the huge world will come round to him. Patience,—patience; with the shades of all the good and great for company; and for solace the perspective of your own infinite life; and for work the study and the communication of principles, the making those instincts prevalent, the conversion of the world. Is it not the chief disgrace in the world, not to be an unit;—not to be reckoned one character;—not to yield that peculiar fruit which each man was created to bear, but to be reckoned in the gross, in the hundred, or the thousand, of the party, the section, to which we belong; and our opinion predicted geographically, as the north, or the south? Not so, brothers and friends—please God, ours shall not be so. We will walk on our own feet; we will work with our own hands; we will speak our own minds. The study of letters shall be no longer a name for pity, for doubt, and for sensual indulgence. The dread of man and the love of man shall be a wall of defence and a wreath of joy around all. A nation of men will for the first time exist, because each believes himself inspired by the Divine Soul which also inspires all men.

AN ADDRESS DELIVERED BEFORE THE SENIOR CLASS IN DIVINITY COLLEGE, CAMBRIDGE

SUNDAY EVENING, JULY 15, 1838.

In this refulgent summer, it has been a luxury to draw the breath of life. The grass grows, the buds burst, the meadow is spotted with fire and gold in the tint of flowers. The air is full of birds, and sweet with the breath of the pine, the balm-of-Gilead, and the new hay. Night brings no gloom to the heart with its welcome shade. Through the transparent darkness the stars pour their almost spiritual rays. Man under them seems a young child, and his huge globe a toy. The cool night bathes the world as with a river, and prepares his eyes again for the crimson dawn. The mystery of nature was never displayed more happily. The corn and the wine have been freely dealt to all creatures, and the never-broken silence with which the old bounty goes forward has not yielded yet one word of explanation. One is constrained to respect the perfection of this world in which our senses converse. How wide; how rich; what invitation from every property it gives to every faculty of man! In its fruitful soils; in its navigable sea; in its mountains of metal and stone; in its forests of all woods; in its animals; in its chemical ingredients; in the powers and path of light, heat, attraction and life, it is well worth the pith and heart of great men to subdue and enjoy it. The planters, the mechanics, the inventors, the astronomers, the builders of cities, and the captains, history delights to honor.

But when the mind opens and reveals the laws which traverse the universe and make things what they are, then shrinks the great world at once into a mere illustration and fable of this mind. What am I? and What is? asks the human spirit with a curiosity new-kindled, but never to be quenched. Behold these out-running laws, which our imperfect apprehension can see tend this way and that, but not come full circle. Behold these infinite relations, so like, so unlike; many, yet one. I would study, I would know, I would admire forever. These works of thought have been the entertainments of the human spirit in all ages.

A more secret, sweet, and overpowering beauty appears to man when his heart and mind open to the sentiment of virtue. Then he is instructed in what is above him. He learns that his being is without bound; that to the good, to the perfect, he is born, low as he now lies in evil and weakness. That which he venerates is still his own, though he has not realized it yet. *He ought.* He knows the sense of that grand word, though his analysis fails to render account of it. When in innocency or when by intellectual perception he attains to say,—"I love the Right; Truth is beautiful within and without for evermore. Virtue, I am thine; save me; use me; thee will I serve, day and night, in great, in small, that I may be not virtuous, but virtue;"—then is the end of the creation answered, and God is well pleased.

The sentiment of virtue is a reverence and delight in the presence of certain divine laws. It perceives that this homely game of life we play, covers, under what seem foolish details, principles that astonish. The child amidst his baubles is learning the action of light, motion, gravity, muscular force; and in the game of human life, love, fear, justice, appetite, man, and God, interact. These laws refuse to be adequately stated. They will not be written out on paper, or spoken by the tongue. They elude our persevering thought; yet we read them hourly in each other's faces, in each other's actions, in our own remorse. The moral traits which are all globed into every virtuous act and thought,—in speech we must sever, and describe or suggest by painful enumeration of many particulars. Yet, as this sentiment is the essence of all religion, let me guide your eye to the precise objects of the sentiment, by an enumeration of some of those classes of facts in which this element is conspicuous.

The intuition of the moral sentiment is an insight of the perfection of the laws of the soul. These laws execute themselves. They are out of time, out of space, and not subject to circumstance. Thus in the soul of man there is a justice whose retributions are instant and entire. He who does a good deed is instantly ennobled. He who does a mean deed is by the action itself contracted. He who puts off impurity, thereby puts on purity. If a man is at heart just, then in so far is he God; the safety of God, the immortality of God, the majesty of God do enter into that man with justice. If a man dissemble, deceive, he deceives himself, and goes out of acquaintance with his own being. A man in the view of absolute goodness, adores, with total humility. Every step so downward, is a step upward. The man who renounces himself, comes to himself.

See how this rapid intrinsic energy worketh everywhere, righting wrongs, correcting appearances, and bringing up facts to a harmony with thoughts. Its operation in life, though slow to the senses, is at last as sure as in the soul. By it a man is made the Providence to himself, dispensing good to his goodness, and evil to his sin. Character is always known. Thefts never enrich; alms never impoverish; murder will speak out of stone walls. The least admixture of a lie,—for example, the taint of vanity, any attempt to make a good impression, a favorable appearance,—will instantly vitiate the effect. But speak the truth, and all nature and all spirits help you with unexpected furtherance. Speak the truth, and all things alive or brute are vouchers, and the very roots of the grass underground there do seem to stir and move to bear you witness. See again the perfection of the Law as it applies itself to the affections, and becomes the law of society. As we are, so we associate. The good, by affinity, seek the good; the vile, by affinity, the vile. Thus of their own volition, souls proceed into heaven, into hell.

These facts have always suggested to man the sublime creed that the world is not the product of manifold power, but of one will, of one mind; and that one mind is everywhere active, in each ray of the star, in each wavelet of the pool; and whatever opposes that will is everywhere balked and baffled, because things are made so, and not otherwise. Good is positive. Evil is merely privative, not absolute: it is like cold, which is the privation of heat. All evil is so much death or nonentity. Benevolence is absolute and real. So much benevolence as a man hath, so much life hath he. For all things proceed out of this same spirit, which is differently named love, justice, temperance, in its different applications, just as the ocean receives different names on the several shores which it washes. All things proceed out of the same spirit, and all things conspire with it. Whilst a man seeks good ends, he is strong by the whole strength of nature. In so far as he roves from these ends, he bereaves himself of power, or auxiliaries; his being shrinks out of all remote channels, he becomes less and less, a mote, a point, until absolute badness is absolute death.

The perception of this law of laws awakens in the mind a sentiment which we call the religious sentiment, and which makes our highest happiness. Wonderful is its power to charm and to command. It is a mountain air. It is the embalmer of the world. It is myrrh and storax, and chlorine and rosemary. It makes the sky and the hills sublime, and the silent song of the stars is it. By it is the universe made safe and habitable, not by science or power. Thought may work cold and intransitive in things, and find no end or unity; but the dawn of the sentiment of virtue on the heart, gives and is the assurance that Law is sovereign over all natures; and the worlds, time, space, eternity, do seem to break out into joy.

This sentiment is divine and deifying. It is the beatitude of man. It makes him illimitable. Through it, the soul first knows itself. It corrects the capital mistake of the infant man, who seeks to be great by following the great, and hopes to derive advantages *from another*,—by showing the fountain of all good to be in himself, and that he, equally with every man, is an inlet into the deeps of Reason. When he says, "I ought;" when love warms him; when he chooses, warned from on high, the good and great deed; then, deep melodies wander through his soul from Supreme Wisdom.— Then he can worship, and be enlarged by his worship; for he can never go behind this sentiment. In the sublimest flights of the soul, rectitude is never surmounted, love is never outgrown.

This sentiment lies at the foundation of society, and successively creates all forms of worship. The principle of veneration never dies out. Man fallen into superstition, into sensuality, is never quite without the visions of the moral sentiment. In like manner, all the expressions of this sentiment are sacred and permanent in proportion to their purity. The expressions of this sentiment affect us more than all other compositions. The sentences of the oldest time, which ejaculate this piety, are still fresh and fragrant. This thought dwelled always deepest in the minds of men in the devout and contemplative East; not alone in Palestine, where it reached its purest expression, but in Egypt, in Persia, in India, in China. Europe has always owed to oriental genius its divine impulses. What these holy bards said, all sane men found agreeable and true. And the unique impression of Jesus upon mankind, whose name is not so much written as ploughed into the history of this world, is proof of the subtle virtue of this infusion.

Meantime, whilst the doors of the temple stand open, night and day, before every man, and the oracles of this truth cease never, it is guarded by one stern condition; this, namely: it is an intuition. It cannot be received at second hand. Truly speaking, it is not instruction, but provocation, that I can receive from another soul. What he announces, I must find true in me, or reject; and on his word, or as his second, be he who he may, I can accept nothing. On the contrary, the absence of this primary faith is the presence of degradation. As is the flood, so is the ebb. Let this faith depart, and the very words it spake and the things it made become false and hurtful. Then falls the church, the state, art, letters, life. The doctrine of the divine nature being forgotten, a sickness infects and dwarfs the constitution. Once man was all; now he is an appendage, a nuisance. And because the indwelling Supreme Spirit cannot wholly be got rid of, the doctrine of it suffers this perversion, that the divine nature is attributed to one or two persons, and denied to all the rest, and denied with fury. The doctrine of inspiration is lost; the base doctrine of the majority of voices usurps the place of the doctrine of the soul. Miracles, prophecy, poetry, the ideal life, the holy life, exist as ancient history merely; they are not in the belief, nor in the aspiration of society; but, when suggested, seem ridiculous. Life is comic or pitiful as soon as the high ends of being fade out of sight, and man becomes nearsighted, and can only attend to what addresses the senses.

These general views, which, whilst they are general, none will contest, find abundant illustration in the history of religion, and especially in the history of the Christian church. In that, all of us have had our birth and nurture. The truth contained in that, you, my young friends, are now setting forth to teach. As the Cultus, or established worship of the civilized world, it has great historical interest for us. Of its blessed words, which have been the consolation of humanity, you need not that I should speak. I shall endeavor to discharge my duty to you on this occasion, by pointing out two errors in its administration, which daily appear more gross from the point of view we have just now taken.

Jesus Christ belonged to the true race of prophets. He saw with open eye the mystery of the soul. Drawn by its severe harmony, ravished with its beauty, he lived in it, and had his being there. Alone in all history he estimated the greatness of man. One man was true to what is in you and me. He saw that God incarnates himself in man, and evermore goes forth anew to take possession of his World. He said, in this jubilee of sublime emotion, 'I am divine. Through me, God acts; through me, speaks. Would you see God, see me; or see thee, when thou also thinkest as I now think.' But what a distortion did his doctrine and memory suffer in the same, in the next, and the following ages! There is no doctrine of the Reason which will bear to be taught by the Understanding. The understanding caught this high chant from the poet's lips, and said, in the next age, 'This was Jehovah come down out of heaven. I will kill you, if you say he was a man.' The idioms of his language and the figures of his rhetoric have usurped the place of his truth; and churches are not built on his principles, but on his tropes. Christianity became a Mythus, as the poetic teaching of Greece and of Egypt, before. He spoke of miracles; for he felt that man's life was a miracle, and all that man doth, and he knew that this daily miracle shines as the character ascends. But the word Miracle, as pronounced by Christian churches, gives a false impression; it is Monster. It is not one with the blowing clover and the falling rain.

He felt respect for Moses and the prophets, but no unfit tenderness at postponing their initial revelations to the hour and the man that now is; to the eternal revelation in the heart. Thus was he a true man. Having seen that the law in us is commanding, he would not suffer it to be commanded. Boldly, with hand, and heart, and life, he declared it was God. Thus is he, as I think, the only soul in history who has appreciated the worth of man.

1. In this point of view we become sensible of the first defect of historical Christianity. Historical Christianity has fallen into the error that corrupts all attempts to communicate religion. As it appears to us, and as it has appeared for ages, it is not the doctrine of the soul, but an exaggeration of the personal, the positive, the ritual. It has dwelt, it dwells, with noxious exaggeration about the *person* of Jesus. The soul knows no persons. It invites every man to expand to the full circle of the universe, and will have no preferences but those of spontaneous love. But by this eastern monarchy of a Christianity, which indolence and fear have built, the friend of man is made the injurer of man. The manner in which his name is surrounded with expressions which were once sallies of admiration and love, but are now petrified into official titles, kills all generous sympathy and liking. All who hear me, feel that the language that describes Christ to Europe and America is not the style of friendship and enthusiasm to a good and noble heart, but is appropriated and formal,—paints a demigod, as the Orientals or the Greeks would describe Osiris or Apollo. Accept the injurious impositions of our early catechetical instruction, and even honesty and self-denial were but splendid sins, if they did not wear the Christian name. One would rather be

"A pagan, suckled in a creed outworn,"[1]

than to be defrauded of his manly right in coming into nature and finding not names and places, not land and professions, but even virtue and truth foreclosed and monopolized. You shall not be a man even. You shall not own the world; you shall not dare and live after the infinite Law that is in you, and in company with the infinite Beauty which heaven and earth reflect to you in all lovely forms; but you must subordinate your nature to Christ's nature;

you must accept our interpretations, and take his portrait as the vulgar draw it.

That is always best which gives me to myself. The sublime is excited in me by the great stoical doctrine, Obey thyself. That which shows God in me, fortifies me. That which shows God out of me, makes me a wart and a wen. There is no longer a necessary reason for my being. Already the long shadows of untimely oblivion creep over me, and I shall decease forever.

The divine bards are the friends of my virtue, of my intellect, of my strength. They admonish me that the gleams which flash across my mind are not mine, but God's; that they had the like, and were not disobedient to the heavenly vision. So I love them. Noble provocations go out from them, inviting me to resist evil; to subdue the world; and to Be. And thus, by his holy thoughts, Jesus serves us, and thus only. To aim to convert a man by miracles is a profanation of the soul. A true conversion, a true Christ, is now, as always, to be made by the reception of beautiful sentiments. It is true that a great and rich soul, like his, falling among the simple, does so preponderate, that, as his did, it names the world. The world seems to them to exist for him, and they have not yet drunk so deeply of his sense as to see that only by coming again to themselves, or to God in themselves, can they grow forevermore. It is a low benefit to give me something; it is a high benefit to enable me to do somewhat of myself. The time is coming when all men will see that the gift of God to the soul is not a vaunting, overpowering, excluding sanctity, but a sweet, natural goodness, a goodness like thine and mine, and that so invites thine and mine to be and to grow.

The injustice of the vulgar tone of preaching is not less flagrant to Jesus than to the souls which it profanes. The preachers do not see that they make his gospel not glad, and shear him of the locks of beauty and the attributes of heaven. When I see a majestic Epaminondas, or Washington; when I see among my contemporaries a true orator, an upright judge, a dear friend; when I vibrate to the melody and fancy of a poem; I see beauty that is to be desired. And so lovely, and with yet more entire consent of my human being, sounds in my ear the severe music of the bards that have sung of the true God in all ages. Now do not degrade the life and dialogues of Christ out of the circle of this charm, by insulation and peculiarity. Let them lie as they befell, alive and warm, part of human life and of the landscape and of the cheerful day.

2. The second defect of the traditionary and limited way of using the mind of Christ is a consequence of the first; this, namely; that the Moral Nature, that Law of laws whose revelations introduce greatness—yea, God himself—into the open soul, is not explored as the fountain of the established teaching in society. Men have come to speak of the revelation as somewhat long ago given and done, as if God were dead. The injury to faith throttles the preacher; and the goodliest of institutions becomes an uncertain and inarticulate voice.

It is very certain that it is the effect of conversation with the beauty of the soul, to beget a desire and need to impart to others the same knowledge and love. If utterance is denied, the thought lies like a burden on the man. Always the seer is a sayer. Somehow his dream is told; somehow he publishes it with solemn joy: sometimes with pencil on canvas, sometimes with chisel on stone, sometimes in towers and aisles of granite, his soul's worship is builded; sometimes in anthems of indefinite music, but clearest and most permanent, in words.

The man enamored of this excellency becomes its priest or poet. The office is coeval with the world. But observe the condition, the spiritual limitation of the office. The spirit only can teach. Not any profane man, not any sensual, not any liar, not any slave can teach, but only he can give, who has; he only can create, who is. The man on whom the soul descends, through whom the soul speaks, alone can teach. Courage, piety, love, wisdom, can teach; and every man can open his door to these angels, and they shall bring him the gift of tongues. But the man who aims to speak as books enable, as synods use, as the fashion guides, and as interest commands, babbles. Let him hush.

To this holy office you propose to devote yourselves. I wish you may feel your call in throbs of desire and hope. The office is the first in the world. It is of that reality that it cannot suffer the deduction of any falsehood. And it is my duty to say to you that the need was never greater of new revelation than now. From the views I have already expressed, you will infer the sad conviction, which I share, I believe, with numbers, of the universal decay and now almost death of faith in society. The soul is not preached. The Church seems to totter to its fall, almost all life extinct. On this occasion, any complaisance would be criminal which told you, whose hope and commission it is to preach the faith of Christ, that the faith of Christ is preached.

It is time that this ill-suppressed murmur of all thoughtful men against the famine of our churches;—this moaning of the heart because it is bereaved of the consolation, the hope, the grandeur that come alone out of the culture of the moral nature,—should be heard through the sleep of indolence, and over the din of routine. This great and perpetual office of the preacher is not discharged. Preaching is the expression of the moral sentiment in application to the duties of life. In how many churches, by how many prophets, tell me, is man made sensible that he is an infinite Soul; that the earth and heavens are passing into his mind; that he is drinking forever the soul of God? Where now sounds the persuasion, that by its very melody imparadises my heart, and so affirms its own origin in heaven? Where shall I hear words such as in elder ages drew men to leave all and follow,—father and mother, house and land, wife and child? Where shall I hear these august laws of moral being so pronounced as to fill my ear, and I feel ennobled by the offer of my uttermost action and passion? The test of the true faith, certainly, should be its power to charm and command the soul, as the laws of nature control the activity of the hands,—so commanding that we find pleasure and honor in obeying. The faith should blend with the light of rising and of setting suns, with the flying cloud, the singing bird, and the breath of flowers. But now the priest's Sabbath has lost the splendor of nature; it is unlovely; we are glad when it is done; we can make, we do make, even sitting in our pews, a far better, holier, sweeter, for ourselves.

Whenever the pulpit is usurped by a formalist, then is the worshipper defrauded and disconsolate. We shrink as soon as the prayers begin, which do not uplift, but smite and offend us. We are fain to wrap our cloaks about us, and secure, as best we can, a solitude that hears not. I once heard a preacher who sorely tempted me to say I would go to church no more. Men go, thought

I, where they are wont to go, else had no soul entered the temple
in the afternoon. A snow-storm was falling around us. The snow-
storm was real, the preacher merely spectral, and the eye felt the
sad contrast in looking at him, and then out of the window behind
him into the beautiful meteor of the snow. He had lived in vain.
He had no one word intimating that he had laughed or wept, was
married or in love, had been commended, or cheated, or cha-
grined. If he had ever lived and acted, we were none the wiser for
it. The capital secret of his profession, namely, to convert life into
truth, he had not learned. Not one fact in all his experience had
he yet imported into his doctrine. This man had ploughed and
planted and talked and bought and sold; he had read books; he
had eaten and drunken; his head aches, his heart throbs; he smiles
and suffers; yet was there not a surmise, a hint, in all the discourse, that he had ever lived at all. Not a line did he draw out of
real history. The true preacher can be known by this, that he deals
out to the people his life,—life passed through the fire of thought.
But of the bad preacher, it could not be told from his sermon what
age of the world he fell in; whether he had a father or a child;
whether he was a freeholder or a pauper; whether he was a citizen
or a countryman; or any other fact of his biography. It seemed
strange that the people should come to church. It seemed as if
their houses were very unentertaining, that they should prefer this
thoughtless clamor. It shows that there is a commanding attraction in the moral sentiment, that can lend a faint tint of light to
dulness and ignorance coming in its name and place. The good
hearer is sure he has been touched sometimes; is sure there is
somewhat to be reached, and some word that can reach it. When
he listens to these vain words, he comforts himself by their relation to his remembrance of better hours, and so they clatter and
echo unchallenged.

I am not ignorant that when we preach unworthily, it is not
always quite in vain. There is a good ear, in some men, that draws
supplies to virtue out of very indifferent nutriment. There is
poetic truth concealed in all the commonplaces of prayer and of
sermons, and though foolishly spoken, they may be wisely heard;
for each is some select expression that broke out in a moment of
piety from some stricken or jubilant soul, and its excellency made

it remembered. The prayers and even the dogmas of our church are like the zodiac of Denderah and the astronomical monuments of the Hindoos, wholly insulated from anything now extant in the life and business of the people. They mark the height to which the waters once rose. But this docility is a check upon the mischief from the good and devout. In a large portion of the community, the religious service gives rise to quite other thoughts and emotions. We need not chide the negligent servant. We are struck with pity, rather, at the swift retribution of his sloth. Alas for the unhappy man that is called to stand in the pulpit, and *not* give bread of life. Everything that befalls, accuses him. Would he ask contributions for the missions, foreign or domestic? Instantly his face is suffused with shame, to propose to his parish that they should send money a hundred or a thousand miles, to furnish such poor fare as they have at home and would do well to go the hundred or the thousand miles to escape. Would he urge people to a godly way of living;— and can he ask a fellow-creature to come to Sabbath meetings, when he and they all know what is the poor uttermost they can hope for therein? Will he invite them privately to the Lord's Supper? He dares not. If no heart warm this rite, the hollow, dry, creaking formality is too plain, than that he can face a man of wit and energy and put the invitation without terror. In the street, what has he to say to the bold village blasphemer? The village blasphemer sees fear in the face, form, and gait of the minister.

Let me not taint the sincerity of this plea by any oversight of the claims of good men. I know and honor the purity and strict conscience of numbers of the clergy. What life the public worship retains, it owes to the scattered company of pious men, who minister here and there in the churches, and who, sometimes accepting with too great tenderness the tenet of the elders, have not accepted from others, but from their own heart, the genuine impulses of virtue, and so still command our love and awe, to the sanctity of character. Moreover, the exceptions are not so much to be found in a few eminent preachers, as in the better hours, the truer inspirations of all,—nay, in the sincere moments of every man. But, with whatever exception, it is still true that tradition characterizes the preaching of this country; that it comes out of the memory, and not out of the soul; that it aims at what is usual, and not at what is necessary and eternal; that thus historical Christianity destroys the power of preaching, by withdrawing it from the exploration of the moral nature of man; where the sublime is, where are the resources of astonishment and power. What a cruel injustice it is to that Law, the joy of the whole earth, which alone can make thought dear and rich; that Law whose fatal sureness the astronomical orbits poorly emulate;—that it is travestied and depreciated, that it is behooted and behowled, and not a trait, not a word of it articulated. The pulpit in losing sight of this Law, loses its reason, and gropes after it knows not what. And for want of this culture the soul of the community is sick and faithless. It wants nothing so much as a stern, high, stoical, Christian discipline, to make it know itself and the divinity that speaks through it. Now man is ashamed of himself; he skulks and sneaks through the world, to be tolerated, to be pitied, and scarcely in a thousand years does any man dare to be wise and good, and so draw after him the tears and blessings of his kind.

Certainly there have been periods when, from the inactivity of the intellect on certain truths, a greater faith was possible in names and persons. The Puritans in England and America found in the Christ of the Catholic Church and in the dogmas inherited from Rome, scope for their austere piety and their longings for civil freedom. But their creed is passing away, and none arises in its room. I think no man can go with his thoughts about him into one of our churches, without feeling that what hold the public worship had on men is gone, or going. It has lost its grasp on the affection of the good and the fear of the bad. In the country, neighborhoods, half parishes are *signing off*, to use the local term. It is already beginning to indicate character and religion to withdraw from the religious meetings. I have heard a devout person, who prized the Sabbath, say in bitterness of heart, "On Sundays, it seems wicked to go to church." And the motive that holds the best there is now only a hope and a waiting. What was once a mere circumstance, that the best and the worst men in the parish, the poor and the rich, the learned and the ignorant, young and old, should meet one day as fellows in one house, in sign of an equal right in the soul, has come to be a paramount motive for going thither.

My friends, in these two errors, I think, I find the causes of a decaying church and a wasting unbelief. And what greater calamity can fall upon a nation than the loss of worship? Then all things go to decay. Genius leaves the temple to haunt the senate or the market. Literature becomes frivolous. Science is cold. The eye of youth is not lighted by the hope of other worlds, and age is without honor. Society lives to trifles, and when men die we do not mention them.

And now, my brothers, you will ask, What in these desponding days can be done by us? The remedy is already declared in the ground of our complaint of the Church. We have contrasted the Church with the Soul. In the soul then let the redemption be sought. Wherever a man comes, there comes revolution. The old is for slaves. When a man comes, all books are legible, all things transparent, all religions are forms. He is religious. Man is the wonderworker. He is seen amid miracles. All men bless and curse. He saith yea and nay, only. The stationariness of religion; the assumption that the age of inspiration is past, that the Bible is closed; the fear of degrading the character of Jesus by representing him as a man;—indicate with sufficient clearness the falsehood of our theology. It is the office of a true teacher to show us that God is, not was; that He speaketh, not spake. The true Christianity,—a faith like Christ's in the infinitude of man,—is lost. None believeth in the soul of man, but only in some man or person old and departed. Ah me! no man goeth alone. All men go in flocks to this saint or that poet, avoiding the God who seeth in secret. They cannot see in secret; they love to be blind in public. They think society wiser than their soul, and know not that one soul, and their soul, is wiser than the whole world. See how nations and races flit by on the sea of time and leave no ripple to tell where they floated or sunk, and one good soul shall make the name of Moses, or of Zeno, or of Zoroaster, reverend forever. None assayeth the stern ambition to be the Self of the nation and of nature, but each would be an easy secondary to some Christian scheme, or sectarian connection, or some eminent man. Once leave your own knowledge of God, your own sentiment, and take secondary knowledge, as St. Paul's, or George Fox's, or Swedenborg's, and you get wide from God with every year this secondary form lasts, and if, as now, for centuries,—the chasm yawns to that breadth, that men can scarcely be convinced there is in them anything divine.

Let me admonish you, first of all, to go alone; to refuse the good models, even those which are sacred in the imagination of men, and dare to love God without mediator or veil. Friends enough you shall find who will hold up to your emulation Wesleys and Oberlins, Saints and Prophets. Thank God for these good men, but say, 'I also am a man.' Imitation cannot go above its model. The imitator dooms himself to hopeless mediocrity. The inventor did it because it was natural to him, and so in him it has a charm. In the imitator something else is natural, and he bereaves himself of his own beauty, to come short of another man's.

Yourself a newborn bard of the Holy Ghost, cast behind you all conformity, and acquaint men at first hand with Deity. Look to it first and only, that fashion, custom, authority, pleasure, and money, are nothing to you,—are not bandages over your eyes, that you cannot see,—but live with the privilege of the immeasurable mind. Not too anxious to visit periodically all families and each family in your parish connection,—when you meet one of these men or women, be to them a divine man; be to them thought and virtue; let their timid aspirations find in you a friend; let their trampled instincts be genially tempted out in your atmosphere; let their doubts know that you have doubted, and their wonder feel that you have wondered. By trusting your own heart, you shall gain more confidence in other men. For all our penny-wisdom, for all our soul-destroying slavery to habit, it is not to be doubted that all men have sublime thoughts; that all men value the few real hours of life; they love to be heard; they love to be caught up into the vision of principles. We mark with light in the memory the few interviews we have had, in the dreary years of routine and of sin, with souls that made our souls wiser; that spoke what we thought; that told us what we knew; that gave us leave to be what we inly were. Discharge to men the priestly office, and, present or absent, you shall be followed with their love as by an angel.

And, to this end, let us not aim at common degrees of merit. Can we not leave, to such as love it, the virtue that glitters for the commendation of society, and ourselves pierce the deep solitudes of absolute ability and worth? We easily come up to the standard of goodness in society. Society's praise can be cheaply secured, and almost all men are content with those easy merits; but the instant effect of conversing with God will be to put them away. There are persons who are not actors, not speakers, but influences; persons too great for fame, for display; who disdain eloquence; to whom all we call art and artist, seems too nearly allied to show and by-ends, to the exaggeration of the finite and selfish, and loss of the universal. The orators, the poets, the commanders encroach on us only as fair women do, by our allowance and homage. Slight them by preoccupation of mind, slight them, as you can well afford to do, by high and universal aims, and they instantly feel that you have right, and that it is in lower places that they must shine. They also feel your right; for they with you are open to the influx of the all-knowing Spirit, which annihilates before its broad noon the little shades and gradations of intelligence in the compositions we call wiser and wisest.

In such high communion let us study the grand strokes of rectitude: a bold benevolence, an independence of friends, so that not the unjust wishes of those who love us shall impair our freedom, but we shall resist for truth's sake the freest flow of kindness, and appeal to sympathies far in advance; and,—what is the highest form in which we know this beautiful element,—a certain solidity of merit, that has nothing to do with opinion, and which is so essentially and manifestly virtue, that it is taken for granted that the right, the brave, the generous step will be taken by it, and nobody thinks of commending it. You would compliment a coxcomb doing a good act, but you would not praise an angel. The silence that accepts merit as the most natural thing in the world, is the highest applause. Such souls, when they appear, are the Imperial Guard of Virtue, the perpetual reserve, the dictators of fortune. One needs not praise their courage,—they are the heart and soul of nature. O my friends, there are resources in us on which we have not drawn. There are men who rise refreshed on hearing a threat; men to whom a crisis which intimidates and paralyzes the majority,—demanding not the faculties of prudence and thrift, but comprehension, immovableness, the readiness of sacrifice,—comes graceful and beloved as a bride. Napoleon said of Massena, that he was not himself until the battle began to go against him; then, when the dead began to fall in ranks around him, awoke his powers of combination, and he put on terror and victory as a robe. So it is in rugged crises, in unweariable endurance, and in aims which put sympathy out of question, that the angel is shown. But these are heights that we can scarce remember and look up to without contrition and shame. Let us thank God that such things exist.

And now let us do what we can to rekindle the smouldering, nigh quenched fire on the altar. The evils of the church that now is are manifest. The question returns, What shall we do? I confess, all attempts to project and establish a Cultus with new rites and forms, seem to me vain. Faith makes us, and not we it, and faith makes its own forms. All attempts to contrive a system are as cold as the new worship introduced by the French to the goddess of Reason,—to-day, pasteboard and filigree, and ending to-morrow in madness and murder. Rather let the breath of new life be breathed by you through the forms already existing. For if once you are alive, you shall find they shall become plastic and new. The remedy to their deformity is first, soul, and second, soul, and evermore, soul. A whole popedom of forms one pulsation of virtue can uplift and vivify. Two inestimable advantages Christianity has given us; first the Sabbath, the jubilee of the whole world, whose light dawns welcome alike into the closet of the philosopher, into the garret of toil, and into prison-cells, and everywhere suggests, even to the vile, the dignity of spiritual being. Let it stand forevermore, a temple, which new love, new faith, new sight shall restore to more than its first splendor to mankind. And secondly, the institution of preaching,—the speech of man to men,—essentially the most flexible of all organs, of all forms. What hinders that now, everywhere, in pulpits, in lecture-rooms, in houses, in fields, wherever the invitation of men or your own occasions lead you, you speak the very truth, as your life and conscience teach it, and cheer the waiting, fainting hearts of men with new hope and new revelation?

I look for the hour when that supreme Beauty which ravished the souls of those Eastern men, and chiefly of those Hebrews, and through their lips spoke oracles to all time, shall speak in the

West also. The Hebrew and Greek Scriptures contain immortal sentences, that have been bread of life to millions. But they have no epical integrity; are fragmentary; are not shown in their order to the intellect. I look for the new Teacher that shall follow so far those shining laws that he shall see them come full circle; shall see their rounding complete grace; shall see the world to be the mirror of the soul; shall see the identity of the law of gravitation with purity of heart; and shall show that the Ought, that Duty, is one thing with Science, with Beauty, and with Joy.

NOTES

1. Wordsworth, "The world is too much with us."

MAN THE REFORMER

A LECTURE READ BEFORE THE MECHANICS'
APPRENTICES' LIBRARY ASSOCIATION,
BOSTON, JANUARY 25, 1841.

MR. PRESIDENT, AND GENTLEMEN:

I wish to offer to your consideration some thoughts on the particular and general relations of man as a reformer. I shall assume
that the aim of each young man in this association is the very
highest that belongs to a rational mind. Let it be granted that our
life, as we lead it, is common and mean; that some of those offices
and functions for which we were mainly created are grown so
rare in society that the memory of them is only kept alive in old
books and in dim traditions; that prophets and poets, that beautiful and perfect men we are not now, no, nor have even seen such;
that some sources of human instruction are almost unnamed and
unknown among us; that the community in which we live will
hardly bear to be told that every man should be open to ecstacy or
a divine illumination, and his daily walk elevated by intercourse
with the spiritual world. Grant all this, as we must, yet I suppose
none of my auditors will deny that we ought to seek to establish
ourselves in such disciplines and courses as will deserve that guidance and clearer communication with the spiritual nature. And
further, I will not dissemble my hope that each person whom I
address has felt his own call to cast aside all evil customs, timidi-
ties, and limitations, and to be in his place a free and helpful man,
a reformer, a benefactor, not content to slip along through the
world like a footman or a spy, escaping by his nimbleness and

apologies as many knocks as he can, but a brave and upright man, who must find or cut a straight road to everything excellent in the earth, and not only go honorably himself, but make it easier for all who follow him to go in honor and with benefit.

In the history of the world the doctrine of Reform had never such scope as at the present hour. Lutherans, Herrnhutters, Jesuits, Monks, Quakers, Knox, Wesley, Swedenborg, Bentham, in their accusations of society, all respected something,—church or state, literature or history, domestic usages, the market town, the dinner table, coined money. But now all these and all things else hear the trumpet, and must rush to judgment,—Christianity, the laws, commerce, schools, the farm, the laboratory; and not a kingdom, town, statute, rite, calling, man, or woman, but is threatened by the new spirit.

What if some of the objections whereby our institutions are assailed are extreme and speculative, and the reformers tend to idealism? That only shows the extravagance of the abuses which have driven the mind into the opposite extreme. It is when your facts and persons grow unreal and fantastic by too much falsehood, that the scholar flies for refuge to the world of ideas, and aims to recruit and replenish nature from that source. Let ideas establish their legitimate sway again in society, let life be fair and poetic, and the scholars will gladly be lovers, citizens, and philanthropists.

It will afford no security from the new ideas, that the old nations, the laws of centuries, the property and institutions of a hundred cities, are built on other foundations. The demon of reform has a secret door into the heart of every lawmaker, of every inhabitant of every city. The fact that a new thought and hope have dawned in your breast, should apprize you that in the same hour a new light broke in upon a thousand private hearts. That secret which you would fain keep,—as soon as you go abroad, lo! there is one standing on the doorstep to tell you the same. There is not the most bronzed and sharpened money-catcher who does not, to your consternation almost, quail and shake the moment he hears a question prompted by the new ideas. We thought he had some semblance of ground to stand upon, that such as he at least would die hard; but he trembles and flees. Then

the scholar says, 'Cities and coaches shall never impose on me
again; for behold every solitary dream of mine is rushing to fulfil-
ment. That fancy I had, and hesitated to utter because you would
laugh,—the broker, the attorney, the market-man are saying the
same thing. Had I waited a day longer to speak, I had been too
late. Behold, State Street thinks, and Wall Street doubts, and
begins to prophesy!'

It cannot be wondered at that this general inquest into abuses
should arise in the bosom of society, when one considers the practical impediments that stand in the way of virtuous young men.
The young man, on entering life, finds the way to lucrative
employments blocked with abuses. The ways of trade are grown
selfish to the borders of theft, and supple to the borders (if not
beyond the borders) of fraud. The employments of commerce are
not intrinsically unfit for a man, or less genial to his faculties; but
these are now in their general course so vitiated by derelictions
and abuses at which all connive, that it requires more vigor and
resources than can be expected of every young man, to right himself in them; he is lost in them; he cannot move hand or foot in
them. Has he genius and virtue? the less does he find them fit for
him to grow in, and if he would thrive in them, he must sacrifice
all the brilliant dreams of boyhood and youth as dreams; he must
forget the prayers of his childhood and must take on him the har-
ness of routine and obsequiousness. If not so minded, nothing is
left him but to begin the world anew, as he does who puts the
spade into the ground for food. We are all implicated of course in
this charge; it is only necessary to ask a few questions as to the
progress of the articles of commerce from the fields where they
grew, to our houses, to become aware that we eat and drink and
wear perjury and fraud in a hundred commodities. How many
articles of daily consumption are furnished us from the West
Indies; yet it is said that in the Spanish islands the venality of the
officers of the government has passed into usage, and that no article passes into our ships which has not been fraudulently cheap-
ened. In the Spanish islands, every agent or factor of the Americans,
unless he be a consul, has taken oath that he is a Catholic, or has
caused a priest to make that declaration for him. The abolitionist
has shown us our dreadful debt to the southern negro. In the

island of Cuba, in addition to the ordinary abominations of slavery, it appears only men are bought for the plantations, and one dies in ten every year, of these miserable bachelors, to yield us sugar. I leave for those who have the knowledge the part of sifting the oaths of our custom-houses; I will not inquire into the oppression of the sailors; I will not pry into the usages of our retail trade. I content myself with the fact that the general system of our trade (apart from the blacker traits, which, I hope, are exceptions denounced and unshared by all reputable men) is a system of selfishness; is not dictated by the high sentiments of human nature; is not measured by the exact law of reciprocity, much less by the sentiments of love and heroism, but is a system of distrust, of concealment, of superior keenness, not of giving but of taking advantage. It is not that which a man delights to unlock to a noble friend; which he meditates on with joy and self-approval in his hour of love and aspiration; but rather what he then puts out of sight, only showing the brilliant result, and atoning for the manner of acquiring, by the manner of expending it. I do not charge the merchant or the manufacturer. The sins of our trade belong to no class, to no individual. One plucks, one distributes, one eats. Every body partakes, every body confesses,—with cap and knee volunteers his confession, yet none feels himself accountable. He did not create the abuse; he cannot alter it. What is he? an obscure private person who must get his bread. That is the vice,—that no one feels himself called to act for man, but only as a fraction of man. It happens therefore that all such ingenuous souls as feel within themselves the irrepressible strivings of a noble aim, who by the law of their nature must act simply, find these ways of trade unfit for them, and they come forth from it. Such cases are becoming more numerous every year.

But by coming out of trade you have not cleared yourself. The trail of the serpent reaches into all the lucrative professions and practices of man. Each has its own wrongs. Each finds a tender and very intelligent conscience a disqualification for success. Each requires of the practitioner a certain shutting of the eyes, a certain dapperness and compliance, an acceptance of customs, a sequestration from the sentiments of generosity and love, a compromise of private opinion and lofty integrity. Nay, the evil custom reaches into the whole institution of property, until our laws which establish and protect it seem not to be the issue of love and reason, but of selfishness. Suppose a man is so unhappy as to be born a saint, with keen perceptions but with the conscience and love of an angel, and he is to get his living in the world; he finds himself excluded from all lucrative works; he has no farm, and he cannot get one; for to earn money enough to buy one requires a sort of concentration toward money, which is the selling himself for a number of years, and to him the present hour is as sacred and inviolable as any future honor. Of course, whilst another man has no land, my title to mine, your title to yours, is at once vitiated. Inextricable seem to be the twinings and tendrils of this evil, and we all involve ourselves in it the deeper by forming connections, by wives and children, by benefits and debts.

Considerations of this kind have turned the attention of many philanthropic and intelligent persons to the claims of manual labor, as a part of the education of every young man. If the accumulated wealth of the past generation is thus tainted,—no matter how much of it is offered to us,—we must begin to consider if it were not the nobler part to renounce it, and to put ourselves into primary relations with the soil and nature, and abstaining from whatever is dishonest and unclean, to take each of us bravely his part, with his own hands, in the manual labor of the world.

But it is said, 'What! will you give up the immense advantages reaped from the division of labor, and set every man to make his own shoes, bureau, knife, wagon, sails, and needle? This would be to put men back into barbarism by their own act.' I see no instant prospect of a virtuous revolution; yet I confess I should not be pained at a change which threatened a loss of some of the luxuries or conveniences of society, if it proceeded from a preference of the agricultural life out of the belief that our primary duties as men could be better discharged in that calling. Who could regret to see a high conscience and a purer taste exercising a sensible effect on young men in their choice of occupation, and thinning the ranks of competition in the labors of commerce, of law, and of state? It is easy to see that the inconvenience would last but a short time. This would be great action, which always opens the eyes of men. When many persons shall have done this, when the majority shall admit the necessity of reform in all these institutions, their abuses will be redressed, and the way will be open again to the advantages which arise from the division of labor, and a man may select the fittest employment for his peculiar talent again, without compromise.[1]

But quite apart from the emphasis which the times give to the doctrine that the manual labor of society ought to be shared among all the members, there are reasons proper to every individual why he should not be deprived of it. The use of manual labor is one which never grows obsolete, and which is inapplicable to no person. A man should have a farm or a mechanical craft for his culture. We must have a basis for our higher accomplishments, our delicate entertainments of poetry and philosophy, in the work of our hands. We must have an antagonism in the tough world for all the variety of our spiritual faculties, or they will not be born. Manual labor is the study of the external world. The advantage of riches remains with him who procured them, not with the heir. When I go into my garden with a spade, and dig a bed, I feel such an exhilaration and health that I discover that I have been defrauding myself all this time in letting others do for me what I should have done with my own hands. But not only health, but education is in the work. Is it possible that I, who get indefinite quantities of sugar, hominy, cotton, buckets, crockery-ware, and letter-paper, by simply signing my name once in three months to a cheque in favor of John Smith & Co. traders, get the fair share of exercise to my faculties by that act which nature intended for me in making all these far-fetched matters important to my comfort? It is Smith himself, and his carriers, and dealers, and manufacturers; it is the sailor, the hide-drogher, the butcher, the negro, the hunter, and the planter, who have intercepted the sugar of the sugar, and the cotton of the cotton. They have got the education, I only the commodity. This were all very well if I were necessarily absent, being detained by work of my own, like theirs, work of the same faculties; then should I be sure of my hands and feet; but now I feel some shame before my wood-chopper, my ploughman, and my cook, for they have some sort of self-sufficiency, they can contrive without my aid to bring the day and year round, but I depend on them, and have not earned by use a right to my arms and feet.

Consider further the difference between the first and second owner of property. Every species of property is preyed on by its own enemies, as iron by rust; timber by rot; cloth by moths; provisions by mould, putridity, or vermin; money by thieves; an orchard by insects; a planted field by weeds and the inroad of cattle; a stock of cattle by hunger; a road by rain and frost; a bridge by freshets. And whoever takes any of these things into his possession, takes the charge of defending them from this troop of enemies, or of keeping them in repair. A man who supplies his own want, who builds a raft or a boat to go a-fishing, finds it easy to caulk it, or put in a tholepin, or mend the rudder. What he gets only as fast as he wants for his own ends, does not embarrass him, or take away his sleep with looking after. But when he comes to give all the goods he has year after year collected, in one estate to his son,—house, orchard, ploughed land, cattle, bridges, hardware, wooden-ware, carpets, cloths, provisions, books, money,— and cannot give him the skill and experience which made or collected these, and the method and place they have in his own life, the son finds his hands full,—not to use these things, but to look after them and defend them from their natural enemies. To him they are not means, but masters. Their enemies will not remit; rust, mould, vermin, rain, sun, freshet, fire, all seize their own, fill him with vexation, and he is converted from the owner into a watchman or a watch-dog to this magazine of old and new chattels. What a change! Instead of the masterly good humor and sense of power and fertility of resource in himself; instead of those strong and learned hands, those piercing and learned eyes, that supple body, and that mighty and prevailing heart which the father had, whom nature loved and feared, whom snow and rain, water and land, beast and fish seemed all to know and to serve,— we have now a puny, protected person, guarded by walls and curtains, stoves and down beds, coaches, and men-servants and women-servants from the earth and the sky, and who, bred to depend on all these, is made anxious by all that endangers those possessions, and is forced to spend so much time in guarding them, that he has quite lost sight of their original use, namely, to help him to his ends,—to the prosecution of his love; to the helping of his friend, to the worship of his God, to the enlargement of his knowledge, to the serving of his country, to the indulgence of his sentiment; and he is now what is called a rich man,—the menial and runner of his riches.

Hence it happens that the whole interest of history lies in the fortunes of the poor. Knowledge, Virtue, Power are the victories of man over his necessities, his march to the dominion of the world. Every man ought to have this opportunity to conquer the world for himself. Only such persons interest us, Spartans, Romans, Saracens, English, Americans, who have stood in the jaws of need, and have by their own wit and might extricated themselves, and made man victorious.

I do not wish to overstate this doctrine of labor, or insist that every man should be a farmer, any more than that every man should be a lexicographer. In general one may say that the husbandman's is the oldest and most universal profession, and that where a man does not yet discover in himself any fitness for one work more than another, this may be preferred. But the doctrine of the Farm is merely this, that every man ought to stand in primary relations with the work of the world; ought to do it himself, and not to suffer the accident of his having a purse in his pocket, or his having been bred to some dishonorable and injurious craft, to sever him from those duties; and for this reason, that labor is God's education; that he only is a sincere learner, he only can become a master, who learns the secrets of labor, and who by real cunning extorts from nature its sceptre.

Neither would I shut my ears to the plea of the learned professions, of the poet, the priest, the lawgiver, and men of study generally; namely, that in the experience of all men of that class, the amount of manual labor which is necessary to the maintenance of a family, indisposes and disqualifies for intellectual exertion. I know it often, perhaps usually, happens that where there is a fine organization, apt for poetry and philosophy, that individual finds himself compelled to wait on his thoughts; to waste several days that he may enhance and glorify one; and is better taught by a moderate and dainty exercise, such as rambling in the fields, rowing, skating, hunting, than by the downright drudgery of the farmer and the smith. I would not quite forget the venerable counsel of the Egyptian mysteries, which declared that "there were

two pairs of eyes in man, and it is requisite that the pair which are
beneath should be closed, when the pair that are above them perceive, and that when the pair above them are closed, those which
are beneath should be opened." Yet I will suggest that no separation from labor can be without some loss of power and of truth to
the seer himself; that, I doubt not, the faults and vices of our literature and philosophy, their too great fineness, effeminacy, and
melancholy, are attributable to the enervated and sickly habits of
the literary class. Better that the book should not be quite so
good, and the book-maker abler and better, and not himself often
a ludicrous contrast to all that he has written.

But granting that for ends so sacred and dear some relaxation
must be had, I think that if a man find in himself any strong bias
to poetry, to art, to the contemplative life, drawing him to these
things with a devotion incompatible with good husbandry, that
man ought to reckon early with himself, and, respecting the com-
pensations of the Universe, ought to ransom himself from the
duties of economy by a certain rigor and privation in his habits.
For privileges so rare and grand, let him not stint to pay a great
tax. Let him be a cænobite, a pauper, and if need be, celibate also.
Let him learn to eat his meals standing, and to relish the taste of
fair water and black bread. He may leave to others the costly conveniences of housekeeping, and large hospitality, and the possession of works of art. Let him feel that genius is a hospitality, and
that he who can create works of art needs not collect them. He
must live in a chamber, and postpone his self-indulgence, fore-
warned and forearmed against that frequent misfortune of men of
genius,—the taste for luxury. This is the tragedy of genius;—
attempting to drive along the ecliptic with one horse of the heavens and one horse of the earth, there is only discord and ruin and
downfall to chariot and charioteer.

The duty that every man should assume his own vows, should
call the institutions of society to account, and examine their fitness to him, gains in emphasis if we look at our modes of living. Is
our housekeeping sacred and honorable? Does it raise and inspire
us, or does it cripple us instead? I ought to be armed by every part
and function of my household, by all my social function, by my
economy, by my feasting, by my voting, by my traffic. Yet I am

almost no party to any of these things. Custom does it for me, gives me no power therefrom, and runs me in debt to boot. We spend our incomes for paint and paper, for a hundred trifles, I know not what, and not for the things of a man. Our expense is almost all for conformity. It is for cake that we run in debt; it is not the intellect, not the heart, not beauty, not worship, that costs so much. Why needs any man be rich? Why must he have horses, fine garments, handsome apartments, access to public houses and places of amusement? Only for want of thought. Give his mind a new image, and he flees into a solitary garden or garret to enjoy it, and is richer with that dream than the fee of a county could make him. But we are first thoughtless, and then find that we are moneyless. We are first sensual, and then must be rich. We dare not trust our wit for making our house pleasant to our friend, and so we buy ice-creams. He is accustomed to carpets, and we have not sufficient character to put floor cloths out of his mind whilst he stays in the house, and so we pile the floor with carpets. Let the house rather be a temple of the Furies of Lacedæmon, formidable and holy to all, which none but a Spartan may enter or so much as behold. As soon as there is faith, as soon as there is society, comfits and cushions will be left to slaves. Expense will be inventive and heroic. We shall eat hard and lie hard, we shall dwell like the ancient Romans in narrow tenements, whilst our public edifices, like theirs, will be worthy for their proportion of the landscape in which we set them, for conversation, for art, for music, for worship. We shall be rich to great purposes; poor only for selfish ones.

Now what help for these evils? How can the man who has learned but one art, procure all the conveniences of life honestly? Shall we say all we think?—Perhaps with his own hands. Suppose he collects or makes them ill;—yet he has learned their lesson. If he cannot do that?—Then perhaps he can go without. Immense wisdom and riches are in that. It is better to go without, than to have them at too great a cost. Let us learn the meaning of economy. Economy is a high, humane office, a sacrament, when its aim is grand; when it is the prudence of simple tastes, when it is practised for freedom, or love, or devotion. Much of the economy which we see in houses is of a base origin, and is best kept out of sight. Parched corn eaten to-day, that I may have roast fowl to my dinner Sunday, is a baseness; but parched corn and a house with one apartment, that I may be free of all perturbations, that I may be serene and docile to what the mind shall speak, and girt and road-ready for the lowest mission of knowledge or goodwill, is frugality for gods and heroes.

Can we not learn the lesson of self-help? Society is full of infirm people, who incessantly summon others to serve them. They contrive everywhere to exhaust for their single comfort the entire means and appliances of that luxury to which our invention has yet attained. Sofas, ottomans, stoves, wine, game-fowl, spices, perfumes, rides, the theatre, entertainments,—all these they want, they need, and whatever can be suggested more than these they crave also, as if it was the bread which should keep them from starving; and if they miss any one, they represent themselves as the most wronged and most wretched persons on earth. One must have been born and bred with them to know how to prepare a meal for their learned stomach. Meantime they never bestir themselves to serve another person; not they! they have a great deal more to do for themselves than they can possibly perform, nor do they once perceive the cruel joke of their lives, but the more odious they grow, the sharper is the tone of their complaining and craving. Can anything be so elegant as to have few wants and to serve them one's self, so as to have somewhat left to give, instead of being always prompt to grab? It is more elegant to answer one's own needs than to be richly served; inelegant perhaps it may look to-day, and to a few, but it is an elegance forever and to all.

I do not wish to be absurd and pedantic in reform. I do not wish to push my criticism on the state of things around me to that extravagant mark that shall compel me to suicide, or to an absolute isolation from the advantages of civil society. If we suddenly plant our foot and say,—I will neither eat nor drink nor wear nor touch any food or fabric which I do not know to be innocent, or deal with any person whose whole manner of life is not clear and rational, we shall stand still. Whose is so? Not mine; not thine; not his. But I think we must clear ourselves each one by the interrogation, whether we have earned our bread to-day by the hearty contribution of our energies to the common benefit; and we must not cease to *tend* to the correction of flagrant wrongs, by laying one stone aright every day.

But the idea which now begins to agitate society has a wider scope than our daily employments, our households, and the institutions of property. We are to revise the whole of our social structure, the State, the school, religion, marriage, trade, science, and explore their foundations in our own nature; we are to see that the world not only fitted the former men, but fits us, and to clear ourselves of every usage which has not its roots in our own mind. What is a man born for but to be a Reformer, a Re-maker of what man has made; a renouncer of lies; a restorer of truth and good, imitating that great Nature which embosoms us all, and which sleeps no moment on an old past, but every hour repairs herself, yielding us every morning a new day, and with every pulsation a new life? Let him renounce everything which is not true to him, and put all his practices back on their first thoughts, and do nothing for which he has not the whole world for his reason. If there are inconveniences and what is called ruin in the way, because we have so enervated and maimed ourselves, yet it would be like dying of perfumes to sink in the effort to re-attach the deeds of every day to the holy and mysterious recesses of life.

The power which is at once spring and regulator in all efforts of reform is the conviction that there is an infinite worthiness in man, which will appear at the call of worth, and that all particular reforms are the removing of some impediment. Is it not the highest duty that man should be honored in us? I ought not to allow any man, because he has broad lands, to feel that he is rich in my presence. I ought to make him feel that I can do without his riches, that I cannot be bought,—neither by comfort, neither by pride,—and though I be utterly penniless, and receiving bread from him, that he is the poor man beside me. And if, at the same time, a woman or a child discovers a sentiment of piety, or a juster way of thinking than mine, I ought to confess it by my respect and obedience, though it go to alter my whole way of life.

The Americans have many virtues, but they have not Faith and Hope. I know no two words whose meaning is more lost sight of. We use these words as if they were as obsolete as Selah and Amen.

And yet they have the broadest meaning and the most cogent application to Boston in this year. The Americans have little faith. They rely on the power of a dollar; they are deaf to a sentiment. They think you may talk the north wind down as easily as raise society; and no class more faithless than the scholars or intellectual men. Now if I talk with a sincere wise man, and my friend, with a poet, with a conscientious youth who is still under the dominion of his own wild thoughts, and not yet harnessed in the team of society to drag with us all in the ruts of custom, I see at once how paltry is all this generation of unbelievers, and what a house of cards their institutions are, and I see what our brave man, what one great thought executed might effect. I see that the reason of the distrust of the practical man in all theory, is his inability to perceive the means whereby we work. Look, he says, at the tools with which this world of yours is to be built. As we cannot make a planet, with atmosphere, rivers, and forests, by means of the best carpenters' or engineers' tools, with chemist's laboratory and smith's forge to boot,—so neither can we ever construct that heavenly society you prate of out of foolish, sick, selfish men and women, such as we know them to be. But the believer not only beholds his heaven to be possible, but already to begin to exist,—not by the men or materials the statesman uses, but by men transfigured and raised above themselves by the power of principles. To principles something else is possible that transcends all the power of expedients.

Every great and commanding moment in the annals of the world is the triumph of some enthusiasm. The victories of the Arabs after Mahomet, who, in a few years, from a small and mean beginning, established a larger empire than that of Rome, is an example. They did they knew not what The naked Derar, horsed on an idea, was found an overmatch for a troop of Roman cavalry. The women fought like men, and conquered the Roman men. They were miserably equipped, miserably fed. They were Temperance troops. There was neither brandy nor flesh needed to feed them. They conquered Asia, and Africa, and Spain, on barley. The Caliph Omar's walking-stick struck more terror into those who saw it than another man's sword. His diet was barley bread; his sauce was salt; and oftentimes by way of abstinence he ate his bread without salt. His drink was water. His palace was built of mud; and when he left Medina to go to the conquest of Jerusalem, he rode on a red camel, with a wooden platter hanging at his saddle, with a bottle of water and two sacks, one holding barley and the other dried fruits.

But there will dawn ere long on our politics, on our modes of living, a nobler morning than that Arabian faith, in the sentiment of love. This is the one remedy for all ills, the panacea of nature. We must be lovers, and at once the impossible becomes possible. Our age and history, for these thousand years, has not been the history of kindness, but of selfishness. Our distrust is very expensive. The money we spend for courts and prisons is very ill laid out. We make, by distrust, the thief, and burglar, and incendiary, and by our court and jail we keep him so. An acceptance of the sentiment of love throughout Christendom for a season would bring the felon and the outcast to our side in tears, with the devotion of his faculties to our service. See this wide society of laboring men and women. We allow ourselves to be served by them, we live apart from them, and meet them without a salute in the streets. We do not greet their talents, nor rejoice in their good fortune, nor foster their hopes, nor in the assembly of the people vote for what is dear to them. Thus we enact the part of the selfish noble and king from the foundation of the world. See, this tree always bears one fruit. In every household, the peace of a pair is poisoned by the malice, slyness, indolence, and alienation of domestics. Let any two matrons meet, and observe how soon their conversation turns on the troubles from their "*help*," as our phrase is. In every knot of laborers the rich man does not feel himself among his friends,—and at the polls he finds them arrayed in a mass in distinct opposition to him. We complain that the politics of masses of the people are controlled by designing men, and led in opposition to manifest justice and the common weal, and to their own interest. But the people do not wish to be represented or ruled by the ignorant and base. They only vote for these, because they were asked with the voice and semblance of kindness. They will not vote for them long. They inevitably prefer wit and probity. To use an Egyptian metaphor, it is not their will for any long time "to raise the nails of wild beasts, and to depress the heads of the sacred birds." Let our affection flow out to our fellows; it would operate in a day the greatest of all revolutions. It is better to work on institutions by the sun than by the wind. The State must consider the poor man, and all voices must speak for him. Every child that is born must have a just chance for his bread. Let the amelioration in our laws of property proceed from the concession of the rich, not from the grasping of the poor. Let us begin by habitual imparting. Let us understand that the equitable rule is, that no one should take more than his share, let him be ever so rich. Let me feel that I am to be a lover. I am to see to it that the world is the better for me, and to find my reward in the act. Love would put a new face on this weary old world in which we dwell as pagans and enemies too long, and it would warm the heart to see how fast the vain diplomacy of statesmen, the impotence of armies, and navies, and lines of defence, would be superseded by this unarmed child. Love will creep where it cannot go, will accomplish that by imperceptible methods,—being its own lever, fulcrum, and power,—which force could never achieve. Have you not seen in the woods, in a late autumn morning, a poor fungus or mushroom,—a plant without any solidity, nay, that seemed nothing but a soft mush or jelly,—by its constant, total, and inconceivably gentle pushing, manage to break its way up through the frosty ground, and actually to lift a hard crust on its head? It is the symbol of the power of kindness. The virtue of this principle in human society in application to great interests is obsolete and forgotten. Once or twice in history it has been tried in illustrious instances, with signal success. This great, overgrown, dead Christendom of ours still keeps alive at least the name of a lover of mankind. But one day all men will be lovers; and every calamity will be dissolved in the universal sunshine.

Will you suffer me to add one trait more to this portrait of man the reformer? The mediator between the spiritual and the actual world should have a great prospective prudence. An Arabian poet describes his hero by saying,

> Sunshine was he
> In the winter day;
> And in the midsummer
> Coolness and shade.

He who would help himself and others should not be a subject of irregular and interrupted impulses of virtue, but a continent, persisting, immovable person,—such as we have seen a few scattered up and down in time for the blessing of the world; men who have in the gravity of their nature a quality which answers to the fly-wheel in a mill, which distributes the motion equably over all the wheels and hinders it from falling unequally and suddenly in destructive shocks. It is better that joy should be spread over all the day in the form of strength, than that it should be concentrated into ecstasies, full of danger and followed by reactions. There is a sublime prudence which is the very highest that we know of man, which, believing in a vast future,—sure of more to come than is yet seen,—postpones always the present hour to the whole life; postpones talent to genius, and special results to character. As the merchant gladly takes money from his income to add to his capital, so is the great man very willing to lose particular powers and talents, so that he gain in the elevation of his life. The opening of the spiritual senses disposes men ever to greater sacrifices, to leave their signal talents, their best means and skill of procuring a present success, their power and their fame,—to cast all things behind, in the insatiable thirst for divine communications. A purer fame, a greater power rewards the sacrifice. It is the conversion of our harvest into seed. As the farmer casts into the ground the finest ears of his grain, the time will come when we too shall hold nothing back, but shall eagerly convert more than we now possess into means and powers, when we shall be willing to sow the sun and the moon for seeds.

NOTES

1. This lecture was delivered several months after the founding of the Brook Farm community.

HISTORY

There is no great and no small
To the Soul that maketh all:
And where it cometh, all things are;
And it cometh everywhere.

I am owner of the sphere,
Of the seven stars and the solar year,
Of Cæsar's hand, and Plato's brain,
Of Lord Christ's heart, and Shakspeare's strain.

There is one mind common to all individual men. Every man is an
inlet to the same and to all of the same. He that is once admitted
to the right of reason is made a freeman of the whole estate. What
Plato has thought, he may think; what a saint has felt, he may feel;
what at any time has befallen any man, he can understand. Who
hath access to this universal mind is a party to all that is or can be
done, for this is the only and sovereign agent.

Of the works of this mind history is the record. Its genius is
illustrated by the entire series of days. Man is explicable by nothing less than all his history. Without hurry, without rest, the
human spirit goes forth from the beginning to embody every faculty, every thought, every emotion which belongs to it, in appropriate events. But the thought is always prior to the fact; all the
facts of history preëxist in the mind as laws. Each law in turn is
made by circumstances predominant, and the limits of nature
give power to but one at a time. A man is the whole encyclopædia
of facts. The creation of a thousand forests is in one acorn, and

Egypt, Greece, Rome, Gaul, Britain, America, lie folded already in the first man. Epoch after epoch, camp, kingdom, empire, republic, democracy, are merely the application of his manifold spirit to the manifold world.

This human mind wrote history, and this must read it. The Sphinx must solve her own riddle. If the whole of history is in one man, it is all to be explained from individual experience. There is a relation between the hours of our life and the centuries of time. As the air I breathe is drawn from the great repositories of nature, as the light on my book is yielded by a star a hundred millions of miles distant, as the poise of my body depends on the equilibrium of centrifugal and centripetal forces, so the hours should be instructed by the ages and the ages explained by the hours. Of the universal mind each individual man is one more incarnation. All its properties consist in him. Each new fact in his private experience flashes a light on what great bodies of men have done, and the crises of his life refer to national crises. Every revolution was first a thought in one man's mind, and when the same thought occurs to another man, it is the key to that era. Every reform was once a private opinion, and when it shall be a private opinion again it will solve the problem of the age. The fact narrated must correspond to something in me to be credible or intelligible. We, as we read, must become Greeks, Romans, Turks, priest and king, martyr and executioner; must fasten these images to some reality in our secret experience, or we shall learn nothing rightly. What befell Asdrubal or Cæsar Borgia is as much an illustration of the mind's powers and depravations as what has befallen us. Each new law and political movement has a meaning for you. Stand before each of its tablets and say, 'Under this mask did my Proteus nature hide itself.' This remedies the defect of our too great nearness to ourselves. This throws our actions into perspective,—and as crabs, goats, scorpions, the balance and the waterpot lose their meanness when hung as signs in the zodiac, so I can see my own vices without heat in the distant persons of Solomon, Alcibiades, and Catiline.

It is the universal nature which gives worth to particular men and things. Human life, as containing this, is mysterious and inviolable, and we hedge it round with penalties and laws. All laws derive hence their ultimate reason; all express more or less distinctly some command of this supreme, illimitable essence. Property also holds of the soul, covers great spiritual facts, and instinctively we at first hold to it with swords and laws and wide and complex combinations. The obscure consciousness of this fact is the light of all our day, the claim of claims; the plea for education, for justice, for charity; the foundation of friendship and love and of the heroism and grandeur which belong to acts of self-reliance. It is remarkable that involuntarily we always read as superior beings. Universal history, the poets, the romancers, do not in their stateliest pictures,—in the sacerdotal, the imperial palaces, in the triumphs of will or of genius,—anywhere lose our ear, anywhere make us feel that we intrude, that this is for better men; but rather is it true that in their grandest strokes we feel most at home. All that Shakspeare says of the king, yonder slip of a boy that reads in the corner feels to be true of himself. We sympathize in the great moments of history, in the great discoveries, the great resistances, the great prosperities of men;—because there law was enacted, the sea was searched, the land was found, or the blow was struck, *for us*, as we ourselves in that place would have done or applauded.

We have the same interest in condition and character. We honor the rich because they have externally the freedom, power, and grace which we feel to be proper to man, proper to us. So all that is said of the wise man by Stoic or Oriental or modern essayist, describes to each reader his own idea, describes his unattained but attainable self. All literature writes the character of the wise man. Books, monuments, pictures, conversation, are portraits in which he finds the lineaments he is forming. The silent and the eloquent praise him and accost him, and he is stimulated wherever he moves, as by personal allusions. A true aspirant therefore never needs look for allusions personal and laudatory in discourse. He hears the commendation, not of himself, but, more sweet, of that character he seeks, in every word that is said concerning character, yea further in every fact and circumstance,—in the running river and the rustling corn. Praise is looked, homage tendered, love flows, from mute nature, from the mountains and the lights of the firmament.

These hints, dropped as it were from sleep and night, let us use in broad day. The student is to read history actively and not passively; to esteem his own life the text, and books the commentary. Thus compelled, the Muse of history will utter oracles, as never to those who do not respect themselves. I have no expectation that any man will read history aright who thinks that what was done in a remote age, by men whose names have resounded far, has any deeper sense than what he is doing to-day.

The world exists for the education of each man. There is no age or state of society or mode of action in history to which there is not somewhat corresponding in his life. Every thing tends in a wonderful manner to abbreviate itself and yield its own virtue to him. He should see that he can live all history in his own person. He must sit solidly at home, and not suffer himself to be bullied by kings or empires, but know that he is greater than all the geography and all the government of the world; he must transfer the point of view from which history is commonly read, from Rome and Athens and London, to himself, and not deny his conviction that he is the court, and if England or Egypt have anything to say to him he will try the case; if not, let them forever be silent. He must attain and maintain that lofty sight where facts yield their secret sense, and poetry and annals are alike. The instinct of the mind, the purpose of nature, betrays itself in the use we make of the signal narrations of history. Time dissipates to shining ether the solid angularity of facts. No anchor, no cable, no fences avail to keep a fact a fact. Babylon, Troy, Tyre, Palestine, and even early Rome are passing already into fiction. The Garden of Eden, the sun standing still in Gibeon, is poetry thenceforward to all nations. Who cares what the fact was, when we have made a constellation of it to hang in heaven an immortal sign? London and Paris and New York must go the same way. "What is history," said Napoleon, "but a fable agreed upon?" This life of ours is stuck round with Egypt, Greece, Gaul, England, War, Colonization, Church, Court and Commerce, as with so many flowers and wild ornaments grave and gay. I will not make more account of them. I believe in Eternity. I can find Greece, Asia, Italy, Spain and the Islands,—the genius and creative principle of each and of all eras, in my own mind.

We are always coming up with the emphatic facts of history in our private experience and verifying them here. All history becomes subjective; in other words there is properly no history, only biography. Every mind must know the whole lesson for itself,—must go over the whole ground. What it does not see, what it does not live, it will not know. What the former age has epitomized into a formula or rule for manipular convenience, it will lose all the good of verifying for itself, by means of the wall of that rule. Somewhere, sometime, it will demand and find compensation for that loss, by doing the work itself. Ferguson discovered many things in astronomy which had long been known. The better for him.

History must be this or it is nothing. Every law which the state enacts indicates a fact in human nature; that is all. We must in ourselves see the necessary reason of every fact,—see how it could and must be. So stand before every public and private work; before an oration of Burke, before a victory of Napoleon, before a martyrdom of Sir Thomas More, of Sidney, of Marmaduke Robinson;[1] before a French Reign of Terror, and a Salem hanging of witches; before a fanatic Revival and the Animal Magnetism in Paris, or in Providence. We assume that we under like influence should be alike affected, and should achieve the like; and we aim to master intellectually the steps and reach the same height or the same degradation that our fellow, our proxy has done.

All inquiry into antiquity, all curiosity respecting the Pyramids, the excavated cities, Stonehenge, the Ohio Circles, Mexico, Memphis,—is the desire to do away this wild, savage, and preposterous There or Then, and introduce in its place the Here and the Now. Belzoni digs and measures in the mummy-pits and pyramids of Thebes until he can see the end of the difference between the monstrous work and himself. When he has satisfied himself, in general and in detail, that it was made by such a person as he, so armed and so motived, and to ends to which he himself should also have worked, the problem is solved; his thought lives along the whole line of temples and sphinxes and catacombs, passes through them all with satisfaction, and they live again to the mind, or are *now*.

A Gothic cathedral affirms that it was done by us and not done by us. Surely it was by man, but we find it not in our man. But we apply ourselves to the history of its production. We put ourselves into the place and state of the builder. We remember the forest-dwellers, the first temples, the adherence to the first type, and the decoration of it as the wealth of the nation increased; the value which is given to wood by carving led to the carving over the whole mountain of stone of a cathedral. When we have gone through this process, and added thereto the Catholic Church, its cross, its music, its processions, its Saints' days and image-worship, we have as it were been the man that made the minster; we have seen how it could and must be. We have the sufficient reason.

The difference between men is in their principle of association. Some men classify objects by color and size and other accidents of appearance; others by intrinsic likeness, or by the relation of cause and effect. The progress of the intellect is to the clearer vision of causes, which neglects surface differences. To the poet, to the philosopher, to the saint, all things are friendly and sacred, all events profitable, all days holy, all men divine. For the eye is fastened on the life, and slights the circumstance. Every chemical substance, every plant, every animal in its growth, teaches the unity of cause, the variety of appearance.

Upborne and surrounded as we are by this all-creating nature, soft and fluid as a cloud or the air, why should we be such hard pedants, and magnify a few forms? Why should we make account of time, or of magnitude, or of figure? The soul knows them not, and genius, obeying its law, knows how to play with them as a young child plays with graybeards and in churches. Genius studies the causal thought, and far back in the womb of things sees the rays parting from one orb, that diverge, ere they fall, by infinite diameters. Genius watches the monad through all his masks as he performs the metempsychosis of nature. Genius detects through the fly, through the caterpillar, through the grub, through the egg, the constant individual; through countless individuals the fixed species; through many species the genus; through all genera the steadfast type; through all the kingdoms of organized life the eternal unity. Nature is a mutable cloud which is always and never the same. She casts the same thought into troops of forms, as a poet makes twenty fables with one moral. Through the bruteness and toughness of matter, a subtle spirit bends all things to its own will. The adamant streams into soft but precise form before it, and whilst I look at it its outline and texture are changed again. Nothing is so fleeting as form; yet never does it quite deny itself. In man we still trace the remains or hints of all that we esteem badges of servitude in the lower races; yet in him they enhance his nobleness and grace; as Io, in Æschylus, transformed to a cow, offends the imagination; but how changed when as Isis in Egypt she meets Osiris-Jove, a beautiful woman with nothing of the metamorphosis left but the lunar horns as the splendid ornament of her brows!

The identity of history is equally intrinsic, the diversity equally obvious. There is, at the surface, infinite variety of things; at the centre there is simplicity of cause. How many are the acts of one man in which we recognize the same character! Observe the sources of our information in respect to the Greek genius. We have the *civil history* of that people, as Herodotus, Thucydides, Xenophon, and Plutarch have given it; a very sufficient account of what manner of persons they were and what they did. We have the same national mind expressed for us again in their *literature*, in epic and lyric poems, drama, and philosophy; a very complete form. Then we have it once more in their *architecture*, a beauty as of temperance itself, limited to the straight line and the square,—a builded geometry. Then we have it once again in *sculpture*, the "tongue on the balance of expression," a multitude of forms in the utmost freedom of action and never transgressing the ideal serenity; like votaries performing some religious dance before the gods, and, though in convulsive pain or mortal combat, never daring to break the figure and decorum of their dance. Thus of the genius of one remarkable people we have a fourfold representation: and to the senses what more unlike than an ode of Pindar, a marble centaur, the peristyle of the Parthenon, and the last actions of Phocion?

Every one must have observed faces and forms which, without any resembling feature, make a like impression on the beholder. A particular picture or copy of verses, if it do not awaken the same train of images, will yet superinduce the same sentiment as some

wild mountain walk, although the resemblance is nowise obvious
to the senses, but is occult and out of the reach of the understanding. Nature is an endless combination and repetition of a very few
laws. She hums the old well-known air through innumerable vari-
ations.

Nature is full of a sublime family likeness throughout her
works, and delights in startling us with resemblances in the most
unexpected quarters. I have seen the head of an old sachem of the
forest which at once reminded the eye of a bald mountain sum-
mit, and the furrows of the brow suggested the strata of the rock.
There are men whose manners have the same essential splendor
as the simple and awful sculpture on the friezes of the Parthenon
and the remains of the earliest Greek art. And there are compositions of the same strain to be found in the books of all ages. What
is Guido's Rospigliosi Aurora but a morning thought, as the
horses in it are only a morning cloud? If any one will but take
pains to observe the variety of actions to which he is equally
inclined in certain moods of mind, and those to which he is averse,
he will see how deep is the chain of affinity.

A painter told me that nobody could draw a tree without in
some sort becoming a tree; or draw a child by studying the outlines of its form merely,—but by watching for a time his motions
and plays, the painter enters into his nature and can then draw
him at will in every attitude. So Roos "entered into the inmost
nature of a sheep." I knew a draughtsman employed in a public
survey who found that he could not sketch the rocks until their
geological structure was first explained to him. In a certain state
of thought is the common origin of very diverse works. It is the
spirit and not the fact that is identical. By a deeper apprehension,
and not primarily by a painful acquisition of many manual skills,
the artist attains the power of awakening other souls to a given
activity.

It has been said that "common souls pay with what they do,
nobler souls with that which they are." And why? Because a profound nature awakens in us by its actions and words, by its very
looks and manners, the same power and beauty that a gallery of
sculpture or of pictures addresses.

Civil and natural history, the history of art and of literature, must be explained from individual history, or must remain words. There is nothing but is related to us, nothing that does not interest us,—kingdom, college, tree, horse, or iron shoe,—the roots of all things are in man. Santa Croce and the Dome of St. Peter's are lame copies after a divine model. Strasburg Cathedral is a material counterpart of the soul of Erwin of Steinbach. The true poem is the poet's mind; the true ship is the ship-builder. In the man, could we lay him open, we should see the reason for the last flourish and tendril of his work; as every spine and tint in the sea-shell preëxists in the secreting organs of the fish. The whole of heraldry and of chivalry is in courtesy. A man of fine manners shall pronounce your name with all the ornament that titles of nobility could ever add.

The trivial experience of every day is always verifying some old prediction to us and converting into things the words and signs which we had heard and seen without heed. A lady with whom I was riding in the forest said to me that the woods always seemed to her *to wait*, as if the genii who inhabit them suspended their deeds until the wayfarer had passed onward; a thought which poetry has celebrated in the dance of the fairies, which breaks off on the approach of human feet. The man who has seen the rising moon break out of the clouds at midnight, has been present like an archangel at the creation of light and of the world. I remember one summer day in the fields my companion pointed out to me a broad cloud, which might extend a quarter of a mile parallel to the horizon, quite accurately in the form of a cherub as painted over churches,—a round block in the centre, which it was easy to animate with eyes and mouth, supported on either side by wide-stretched symmetrical wings. What appears once in the atmosphere may appear often, and it was undoubtedly the archetype of that familiar ornament. I have seen in the sky a chain of summer lightning which at once showed to me that the Greeks drew from nature when they painted the thunderbolt in the hand of Jove. I have seen a snow-drift along the sides of the stone wall which obviously gave the idea of the common architectural scroll to abut a tower.

By surrounding ourselves with the original circumstances we invent anew the orders and the ornaments of architecture, as we see how each people merely decorated its primitive abodes. The Doric temple preserves the semblance of the wooden cabin in which the Dorian dwelt. The Chinese pagoda is plainly a Tartar tent. The Indian and Egyptian temples still betray the mounds and subterranean houses of their forefathers. "The custom of making houses and tombs in the living rock," says Heeren in his Researches on the Ethiopians, "determined very naturally the principal character of the Nubian Egyptian architecture to the colossal form which it assumed. In these caverns, already prepared by nature, the eye was accustomed to dwell on huge shapes and masses, so that when art came to the assistance of nature it could not move on a small scale without degrading itself. What would statues of the usual size, or neat porches and wings have been, associated with those gigantic halls before which only Colossi could sit as watchmen or lean on the pillars of the interior?"

The Gothic church plainly originated in a rude adaptation of the forest trees, with all their boughs, to a festal or solemn arcade; as the bands about the cleft pillars still indicate the green withes that tied them. No one can walk in a road cut through pine woods, without being struck with the architectural appearance of the grove, especially in winter, when the barrenness of all other trees shows the low arch of the Saxons. In the woods in a winter afternoon one will see as readily the origin of the stained glass window, with which the Gothic cathedrals are adorned, in the colors of the western sky seen through the bare and crossing branches of the forest. Nor can any lover of nature enter the old piles of Oxford and the English cathedrals, without feeling that the forest overpowered the mind of the builder, and that his chisel, his saw and plane still reproduced its ferns, its spikes of flowers, its locust, elm, oak, pine, fir and spruce.

The Gothic cathedral is a blossoming in stone subdued by the insatiable demand of harmony in man. The mountain of granite blooms into an eternal flower, with the lightness and delicate finish as well as the aerial proportions and perspective of vegetable beauty.

In like manner all public facts are to be individualized, all private facts are to be generalized. Then at once History becomes fluid and true, and Biography deep and sublime. As the Persian imitated in the slender shafts and capitals of his architecture the stem and flower of the lotus and palm, so the Persian court in its magnificent era never gave over the nomadism of its barbarous tribes, but travelled from Ecbatana, where the spring was spent, to Susa in summer and to Babylon for the winter.

In the early history of Asia and Africa, Nomadism and Agriculture are the two antagonist facts. The geography of Asia and of Africa necessitated a nomadic life. But the nomads were the terror of all those whom the soil or the advantages of a market had induced to build towns. Agriculture therefore was a religious injunction, because of the perils of the state from nomadism. And in these late and civil countries of England and America these propensities still fight out the old battle, in the nation and in the individual. The nomads of Africa were constrained to wander, by the attacks of the gad-fly, which drives the cattle mad, and so compels the tribe to emigrate in the rainy season and to drive off the cattle to the higher sandy regions. The nomads of Asia follow the pasturage from month to month. In America and Europe the nomadism is of trade and curiosity; a progress, certainly, from the gad-fly of Astaboras to the Anglo- and Italo-mania of Boston Bay. Sacred cities, to which a periodical religious pilgrimage was enjoined, or stringent laws and customs tending to invigorate the national bond, were the check on the old rovers; and the cumulative values of long residence are the restraints on the itinerancy of the present day. The antagonism of the two tendencies is not less active in individuals, as the love of adventure or the love of repose happens to predominate. A man of rude health and flowing spirits has the faculty of rapid domestication, lives in his wagon and roams through all latitudes as easily as a Calmuc. At sea, or in the forest, or in the snow, he sleeps as warm, dines with as good appetite, and associates as happily as beside his own chimneys. Or perhaps his facility is deeper seated, in the increased range of his faculties of observation, which yield him points of interest wherever fresh objects meet his eyes. The pastoral nations were needy and hungry to desperation; and this intellectual nomadism, in its excess, bankrupts the mind through the dissipation of power on a miscellany of objects. The home-keeping wit, on the other hand, is that continence or content which finds all the elements of life in its own soil; and which has its own perils of monotony and deterioration, if not stimulated by foreign infusions.

Every thing the individual sees without him corresponds to his states of mind, and every thing is in turn intelligible to him, as his onward thinking leads him into the truth to which that fact or series belongs.

The primeval world,—the Fore-World, as the Germans say,—I can dive to it in myself as well as grope for it with researching fingers in catacombs, libraries, and the broken reliefs and torsos of ruined villas.

What is the foundation of that interest all men feel in Greek history, letters, art and poetry, in all its periods from the Heroic or Homeric age down to the domestic life of the Athenians and Spartans, four or five centuries later? What but this, that every man passes personally through a Grecian period. The Grecian state is the era of the bodily nature, the perfection of the senses,— of the spiritual nature unfolded in strict unity with the body. In it existed those human forms which supplied the sculptor with his models of Hercules, Phoebus, and Jove; not like the forms abounding in the streets of modern cities, wherein the face is a confused blur of features, but composed of incorrupt, sharply defined and symmetrical features, whose eye-sockets are so formed that it would be impossible for such eyes to squint and take furtive glances on this side and on that, but they must turn the whole head. The manners of that period are plain and fierce. The reverence exhibited is for personal qualities; courage, address, self-command, justice, strength, swiftness, a loud voice, a broad chest. Luxury and elegance are not known. A sparse population and want make every man his own valet, cook, butcher and soldier, and the habit of supplying his own needs educates the body to wonderful performances. Such are the Agamemnon and Diomed of Homer, and not far different is the picture Xenophon gives of himself and his compatriots in the Retreat of the Ten Thousand. "After the army had crossed the river Teleboas in Armenia, there fell much snow, and the troops lay miserably on the ground covered with it. But Xenophon arose naked, and taking an axe, began to split wood; whereupon others rose and did the like." Throughout his army exists a boundless liberty of speech. They quarrel for plunder, they wrangle with the generals on each new order, and Xenophon is as sharp-tongued as any and sharper-tongued than most, and so gives as good as he gets. Who does not see that this is a gang of great boys, with such a code of honor and such lax discipline as great boys have?

The costly charm of the ancient tragedy, and indeed of all the old literature, is that the persons speak simply,—speak as persons who have great good sense without knowing it, before yet the reflective habit has become the predominant habit of the mind. Our admiration of the antique is not admiration of the old, but of the natural. The Greeks are not reflective, but perfect in their senses and in their health, with the finest physical organization in the world. Adults acted with the simplicity and grace of children. They made vases, tragedies and statues, such as healthy senses should,—that is, in good taste. Such things have continued to be made in all ages, and are now, wherever a healthy physique exists; but, as a class, from their superior organization, they have surpassed all. They combine the energy of manhood with the engaging unconsciousness of childhood. The attraction of these manners is that they belong to man, and are known to every man in virtue of his being once a child; besides that there are always individuals who retain these characteristics. A person of childlike genius and inborn energy is still a Greek, and revives our love of the Muse of Hellas. I admire the love of nature in the Philoctetes. In reading those fine apostrophes to sleep, to the stars, rocks, mountains and waves, I feel time passing away as an ebbing sea. I feel the eternity of man, the identity of his thought. The Greek had, it seems, the same fellow-beings as I. The sun and moon, water and fire, met his heart precisely as they meet mine. Then the vaunted distinction between Greek and English, between Classic and Romantic schools, seems superficial and pedantic. When a thought of Plato becomes a thought to me,—when a truth that fired the soul of Pindar fires mine, time is no more. When I feel that we two meet in a perception, that our two souls are tinged with the same hue, and do as it were run into one, why should I measure degrees of latitude, why should I count Egyptian years?

The student interprets the age of chivalry by his own age of chivalry, and the days of maritime adventure and circumnavigation by quite parallel miniature experiences of his own. To the sacred history of the world he has the same key. When the voice of a prophet out of the deeps of antiquity merely echoes to him a sentiment of his infancy, a prayer of his youth, he then pierces to the truth through all the confusion of tradition and the caricature of institutions.

Rare, extravagant spirits come by us at intervals, who disclose to us new facts in nature. I see that men of God have from time to time walked among men and made their commission felt in the heart and soul of the commonest hearer. Hence evidently the tripod, the priest, the priestess inspired by the divine afflatus.

Jesus astonishes and overpowers sensual people. They cannot unite him to history, or reconcile him with themselves. As they come to revere their intuitions and aspire to live holily, their own piety explains every fact, every word.

How easily these old worships of Moses, of Zoroaster, of Menu, of Socrates, domesticate themselves in the mind. I cannot find any antiquity in them. They are mine as much as theirs.

I have seen the first monks and anchorets, without crossing seas or centuries. More than once some individual has appeared to me with such negligence of labor and such commanding contemplation, a haughty beneficiary begging in the name of God, as made good to the nineteenth century Simeon the Stylite, the Thebais, and the first Capuchins.

The priestcraft of the East and West, of the Magian, Brahmin, Druid, and Inca, is expounded in the individual's private life. The cramping influence of a hard formalist on a young child, in repressing his spirits and courage, paralyzing the understanding, and that without producing indignation, but only fear and obedience, and even much sympathy with the tyranny,—is a familiar fact, explained to the child when he becomes a man, only by seeing that the oppressor of his youth is himself a child tyrannized over by those names and words and forms of whose influence he was merely the organ to the youth. The fact teaches him how Belus was worshipped and how the Pyramids were built, better than the discovery by Champollion of the names of all the workmen and the cost of every tile. He finds Assyria and the Mounds of Cholula at his door, and himself has laid the courses.

Again, in that protest which each considerate person makes against the superstition of his times, he repeats step for step the part of old reformers, and in the search after truth finds, like them, new perils to virtue. He learns again what moral vigor is needed to supply the girdle of a superstition. A great licentiousness treads on the heels of a reformation. How many times in the history of the world has the Luther of the day had to lament the decay of piety in his own household! "Doctor," said his wife to Martin Luther, one day, "how is it that whilst subject to papacy we prayed so often and with such fervor, whilst now we pray with the utmost coldness and very seldom?"

The advancing man discovers how deep a property he has in literature,—in all fable as well as in all history. He finds that the poet was no odd fellow who described strange and impossible situations, but that universal man wrote by his pen a confession true for one and true for all. His own secret biography he finds in lines wonderfully intelligible to him, dotted down before he was born. One after another he comes up in his private adventures with every fable of Æsop, of Homer, of Hafiz, of Ariosto, of Chaucer, of Scott, and verifies them with his own head and hands.

The beautiful fables of the Greeks, being proper creations of the imagination and not of the fancy, are universal verities. What a range of meanings and what perpetual pertinence has the story of Prometheus! Beside its primary value as the first chapter of the history of Europe, (the mythology thinly veiling authentic facts, the invention of the mechanic arts and the migration of colonies,) it gives the history of religion, with some closeness to the faith of later ages. Prometheus is the Jesus of the old mythology. He is the friend of man; stands between the unjust "justice" of the Eternal Father and the race of mortals, and readily suffers all things on their account. But where it departs from the Calvinistic Christianity and exhibits him as the defier of Jove, it represents a state of mind which readily appears wherever the doctrine of Theism is taught in a crude, objective form, and which seems the self-defence of man against this untruth, namely a discontent with the believed fact that a God exists, and a feeling that the obligation of

reverence is onerous. It would steal if it could the fire of the Creator, and live apart from him and independent of him. The Prometheus Vinctus is the romance of skepticism. Not less true to all
time are the details of that stately apologue. Apollo kept the flocks
of Admetus, said the poets. When the gods come among men,
they are not known. Jesus was not; Socrates and Shakspeare were
not. Antæus was suffocated by the gripe of Hercules, but every
time he touched his mother-earth his strength was renewed. Man
is the broken giant, and in all his weakness both his body and his
mind are invigorated by habits of conversation with nature. The
power of music, the power of poetry, to unfix and as it were clap
wings to solid nature, interprets the riddle of Orpheus. The philosophical perception of identity through endless mutations of form
makes him know the Proteus. What else am I who laughed or
wept yesterday, who slept last night like a corpse, and this morning stood and ran? And what see I on any side but the transmigra-
tions of Proteus? I can symbolize my thought by using the name of
any creature, of any fact, because every creature is man agent or
patient. Tantalus is but a name for you and me. Tantalus means
the impossibility of drinking the waters of thought which are
always gleaming and waving within sight of the soul. The trans-
migration of souls is no fable. I would it were; but men and women
are only half human. Every animal of the barn-yard, the field and
the forest, of the earth and of the waters that are under the earth,
has contrived to get a footing and to leave the print of its features
and form in some one or other of these upright, heaven-facing
speakers. Ah! brother, stop the ebb of thy soul,—ebbing downward into the forms into whose habits thou hast now for many
years slid. As near and proper to us is also that old fable of the
Sphinx, who was said to sit in the road-side and put riddles to
every passenger. If the man could not answer, she swallowed him
alive. If he could solve the riddle, the Sphinx was slain. What is
our life but an endless flight of winged facts or events? In splendid
variety these changes come, all putting questions to the human
spirit. Those men who cannot answer by a superior wisdom these
facts or questions of time, serve them. Facts encumber them, tyrannize over them, and make the men of routine, the men of *sense*,

in whom a literal obedience to facts has extinguished every spark of that light by which man is truly man. But if the man is true to his better instincts or sentiments, and refuses the dominion of facts, as one that comes of a higher race; remains fast by the soul and sees the principle, then the facts fall aptly and supple into their places; they know their master, and the meanest of them glorifies him.

See in Goethe's Helena the same desire that every word should be a thing. These figures, he would say, these Chirons, Griffins, Phorkyas, Helen and Leda, are somewhat, and do exert a specific influence on the mind. So far then are they eternal entities, as real to-day as in the first Olympiad. Much revolving them he writes out freely his humor, and gives them body to his own imagination. And although that poem be as vague and fantastic as a dream, yet is it much more attractive than the more regular dramatic pieces of the same author, for the reason that it operates a wonderful relief to the mind from the routine of customary images,—awakens the reader's invention and fancy by the wild freedom of the design, and by the unceasing succession of brisk shocks of surprise.

The universal nature, too strong for the petty nature of the bard, sits on his neck and writes through his hand; so that when he seems to vent a mere caprice and wild romance, the issue is an exact allegory. Hence Plato said that "poets utter great and wise things which they do not themselves understand." All the fictions of the Middle Age explain themselves as a masked or frolic expression of that which in grave earnest the mind of that period toiled to achieve. Magic and all that is ascribed to it is a deep presentiment of the powers of science. The shoes of swiftness, the sword of sharpness, the power of subduing the elements, of using the secret virtues of minerals, of understanding the voices of birds, are the obscure efforts of the mind in a right direction. The preternatural prowess of the hero, the gift of perpetual youth, and the like, are alike the endeavor of the human spirit "to bend the shows of things to the desires of the mind."

In Perceforest and Amadis de Gaul a garland and a rose bloom on the head of her who is faithful, and fade on the brow of the inconstant. In the story of the Boy and the Mantle even a mature reader may be surprised with a glow of virtuous pleasure at the triumph of the gentle Venelas; and indeed all the postulates of elfin annals,—that the fairies do not like to be named; that their gifts are capricious and not to be trusted; that who seeks a treasure must not speak; and the like,—I find true in Concord, however they might be in Cornwall or Bretagne.

Is it otherwise in the newest romance? I read the Bride of Lammermoor. Sir William Ashton is a mask for a vulgar temptation, Ravenswood Castle a fine name for proud poverty, and the foreign mission of state only a Bunyan disguise for honest industry. We may all shoot a wild bull that would toss the good and beautiful, by fighting down the unjust and sensual. Lucy Ashton is another name for fidelity, which is always beautiful and always liable to calamity in this world.

But along with the civil and metaphysical history of man, another history goes daily forward,—that of the external world,—in which he is not less strictly implicated. He is the compend of time; he is also the correlative of nature. His power consists in the multitude of his affinities, in the fact that his life is intertwined with the whole chain of organic and inorganic being. In old Rome the public roads beginning at the Forum proceeded north, south, east, west, to the centre of every province of the empire, making each market-town of Persia, Spain and Britain pervious to the soldiers of the capital: so out of the human heart go as it were highways to the heart of every object in nature, to reduce it under the dominion of man. A man is a bundle of relations, a knot of roots, whose flower and fruitage is the world. His faculties refer to natures out of him and predict the world he is to inhabit, as the fins of the fish foreshow that water exists, or the wings of an eagle in the egg presuppose air. He cannot live without a world. Put Napoleon in an island prison, let his faculties find no men to act on, no Alps to climb, no stake to play for, and he would beat the air, and appear stupid. Transport him to large countries, dense population, complex interests and antagonist power, and you shall see that the man Napoleon, bounded that is by such a profile and outline, is not the virtual Napoleon. This is but Talbot's shadow;—

> "His substance is not here.
> For what you see is but the smallest part
> And least proportion of humanity;
> But were the whole frame here,
> It is of such a spacious, lofty pitch,
> Your roof were not sufficient to contain it."[2]

Columbus needs a planet to shape his course upon. Newton and Laplace need myriads of age and thick-strewn celestial areas. One may say a gravitating solar system is already prophesied in the nature of Newton's mind. Not less does the brain of Davy or of Gay-Lussac, from childhood exploring the affinities and repulsions of particles, anticipate the laws of organization. Does not the eye of the human embryo predict the light? the ear of Handel predict the witchcraft of harmonic sound? Do not the constructive fingers of Watt, Fulton, Whittemore, Arkwright, predict the fusible, hard, and temperable texture of metals, the properties of stone, water, and wood? Do not the lovely attributes of the maiden child predict the refinements and decorations of civil society? Here also we are reminded of the action of man on man. A mind might ponder its thoughts for ages and not gain so much self-knowledge as the passion of love shall teach it in a day. Who knows himself before he has been thrilled with indignation at an outrage, or has heard an eloquent tongue, or has shared the throb of thousands in a national exultation or alarm? No man can ante-date his experience, or guess what faculty or feeling a new object shall unlock, any more than he can draw to-day the face of a person whom he shall see to-morrow for the first time.

I will not now go behind the general statement to explore the reason of this correspondency. Let it suffice that in the light of these two facts, namely, that the mind is One, and that nature is its correlative, history is to be read and written.

Thus in all ways does the soul concentrate and reproduce its treasures for each pupil. He too shall pass through the whole cycle of experience. He shall collect into a focus the rays of nature. History no longer shall be a dull book. It shall walk incarnate in every just and wise man. You shall not tell me by languages and titles a catalogue of the volumes you have read. You shall make me feel what periods you have lived. A man shall be the Temple of Fame. He shall walk, as the poets have described that goddess, in a robe painted all over with wonderful events and experiences;—his own form and features by their exalted intelligence shall be that variegated vest. I shall find in him the Foreworld; in his childhood the Age of Gold, the Apples of Knowledge, the Argonautic Expedition, the calling of Abraham, the building of the Temple, the Advent of Christ, Dark Ages, the Revival of Letters, the Reformation, the discovery of new lands, the opening of new sciences and new regions in man. He shall be the priest of Pan, and bring with him into humble cottages the blessing of the morning stars, and all the recorded benefits of heaven and earth.

Is there somewhat overweening in this claim? Then I reject all I have written, for what is the use of pretending to know what we know not? But it is the fault of our rhetoric that we cannot strongly state one fact without seeming to belie some other. I hold our actual knowledge very cheap. Hear the rats in the wall, see the lizard on the fence, the fungus under foot, the lichen on the log. What do I know sympathetically, morally, of either of these worlds of life? As old as the Caucasian man,—perhaps older,—these creatures have kept their counsel beside him, and there is no record of any word or sign that has passed from one to the other. What connection do the books show between the fifty or sixty chemical elements and the historical eras? Nay, what does history yet record of the metaphysical annals of man? What light does it shed on those mysteries which we hide under the names Death and Immortality? Yet every history should be written in a wisdom which divined the range of our affinities and looked at facts as symbols. I am ashamed to see what a shallow village tale our so-called History is. How many times we must say Rome, and Paris, and Constantinople! What does Rome know of rat and lizard? What are Olympiads and Consulates to these neighboring systems of being? Nay, what food or experience or succor have they for the Esquimaux seal-hunter, for the Kanàka in his canoe, for the fisherman, the stevedore, the porter?

Broader and deeper we must write our annals,—from an ethical reformation, from an influx of the ever new, ever sanative conscience,—if we would trulier express our central and wide-related nature, instead of this old chronology of selfishness and pride to which we have too long lent our eyes. Already that day exists for us, shines in on us at unawares, but the path of science and of letters is not the way into nature. The idiot, the Indian, the child and unschooled farmer's boy stand nearer to the light by which nature is to be read, than the dissector or the antiquary.

NOTES

1. Emerson seems unconsciously to have compounded into one the names of the two Quakers executed in Boston in 1659, Marmaduke Stevenson and William Robinson.
2. Adapted from Shakespeare, *Henry VI,* Part 1.

SELF-RELIANCE

Man is his own star; and the soul that can
Render an honest and a perfect man,
Commands all light, all influence, all fate;
Nothing to him falls early or too late.
Our acts our angels are, or good or ill,
Our fatal shadows that walk by us still.

Epilogue to Beaumont and Fletcher's
Honest Man's Fortune

Cast the bantling on the rocks,
Suckle him with the she-wolf's teat,
Wintered with the hawk and fox,
Power and speed be hands and feet.

I read the other day some verses written by an eminent painter which were original and not conventional. The soul always hears an admonition in such lines, let the subject be what it may. The sentiment they instil is of more value than any thought they may contain. To believe your own thought, to believe that what is true for you in your private heart is true for all men,—that is genius. Speak your latent conviction, and it shall be the universal sense; for the inmost in due time becomes the outmost, and our first thought is rendered back to us by the trumpets of the Last Judgment. Familiar as the voice of the mind is to each, the highest merit we ascribe to Moses, Plato and Milton is that they set at naught books and traditions, and spoke not what men, but what *they* thought. A man should learn to detect and watch that gleam of light which flashes across his mind from within, more than the lustre of the firmament of bards and sages. Yet he dismisses without notice his thought, because it is his. In every work of genius we recognize our own rejected thoughts; they come back to us with a certain alienated majesty. Great works of art have no more affecting lesson for us than this. They teach us to abide by our spontaneous impression with good-humored inflexibility then most when the whole cry of voices is on the other side. Else to-morrow a stranger will say with masterly good sense precisely what we have thought and felt all the time, and we shall be forced to take with shame our own opinion from another.

There is a time in every man's education when he arrives at the conviction that envy is ignorance; that imitation is suicide; that he must take himself for better for worse as his portion; that though the wide universe is full of good, no kernel of nourishing corn can come to him but through his toil bestowed on that plot of ground which is given to him to till. The power which resides in him is new in nature, and none but he knows what that is which he can do, nor does he know until he has tried. Not for nothing one face, one character, one fact, makes much impression on him, and another none. This sculpture in the memory is not without preëstablished harmony. The eye was placed where one ray should fall, that it might testify of that particular ray. We but half express ourselves, and are ashamed of that divine idea which each of us represents. It may be safely trusted as proportionate and of good issues, so it be faithfully imparted, but God will not have his work made manifest by cowards. A man is relieved and gay when he has put his heart into his work and done his best; but what he has said or done otherwise shall give him no peace. It is a deliverance which does not deliver. In the attempt his genius deserts him; no muse befriends; no invention, no hope.

Trust thyself: every heart vibrates to that iron string. Accept the place the divine providence has found for you, the society of your contemporaries, the connection of events. Great men have always done so, and confided themselves childlike to the genius of their age, betraying their perception that the absolutely trustworthy was seated at their heart, working through their hands, pre-dominating in all their being. And we are now men, and must accept in the highest mind the same transcendent destiny; and not minors and invalids in a protected corner, not cowards fleeing before a revolution, but guides, redeemers and benefactors, obeying the Almighty effort and advancing on Chaos and the Dark.

What pretty oracles nature yields us on this text in the face and behavior of children, babes, and even brutes! That divided and rebel mind, that distrust of a sentiment because our arithmetic has computed the strength and means opposed to our purpose, these have not. Their mind being whole, their eye is as yet unconquered, and when we look in their faces we are disconcerted. Infancy conforms to nobody; all conform to it; so that one babe commonly makes four or five out of the adults who prattle and play to it. So God has armed youth and puberty and manhood no less with its own piquancy and charm, and made it enviable and gracious and its claims not to be put by, if it will stand by itself. Do not think the youth has no force, because he cannot speak to you and me. Hark! in the next room his voice is sufficiently clear and emphatic. It seems he knows how to speak to his contemporaries. Bashful or bold then, he will know how to make us seniors very unnecessary.

The nonchalance of boys who are sure of a dinner, and would disdain as much as a lord to do or say aught to conciliate one, is the healthy attitude of human nature. A boy is in the parlor what the pit is in the playhouse; independent, irresponsible, looking out from his corner on such people and facts as pass by, he tries and sentences them on their merits, in the swift, summary way of boys, as good, bad, interesting, silly, eloquent, troublesome. He cumbers himself never about consequences, about interests; he gives an independent, genuine verdict. You must court him; he does not court you. But the man is as it were clapped into jail by his consciousness. As soon as he has once acted or spoken with *éclat* he is a committed person, watched by the sympathy or the hatred of hundreds, whose affections must now enter into his account. There is no Lethe for this. Ah, that he could pass again into his neutrality! Who can thus avoid all pledges and, having observed, observe again from the same unaffected, unbiased, unbribable, unaffrighted innocence,—must always be formidable. He would utter opinions on all passing affairs, which being seen to be not private but necessary, would sink like darts into the ear of men, and put them in fear.

These are the voices which we hear in solitude, but they grow faint and inaudible as we enter into the world. Society everywhere is in conspiracy against the manhood of every one of its members. Society is a joint-stock company, in which the members agree, for the better securing of his bread to each shareholder, to surrender the liberty and culture of the eater. The virtue in most request is conformity. Self-reliance is its aversion. It loves not realities and creators, but names and customs.

Whoso would be a man, must be a nonconformist. He who would gather immortal palms must not be hindered by the name of goodness, but must explore if it be goodness. Nothing is at last sacred but the integrity of your own mind. Absolve you to yourself, and you shall have the suffrage of the world. I remember an answer which when quite young I was prompted to make to a valued adviser who was wont to importune me with the dear old doctrines of the church. On my saying, "What have I to do with the sacredness of traditions, if I live wholly from within?" my friend suggested,—"But these impulses may be from below, not from above." I replied, "They do not seem to me to be such; but if I am the Devil's child, I will live then from the Devil." No law can be sacred to me but that of my nature. Good and bad are but names very readily transferable to that or this; the only right is what is after my constitution; the only wrong what is against it. A man is to carry himself in the presence of all opposition as if every thing were titular and ephemeral but he. I am ashamed to think how easily we capitulate to badges and names, to large societies and dead institutions. Every decent and well-spoken individual affects and sways me more than is right. I ought to go upright and vital, and speak the rude truth in all ways. If malice and vanity wear the coat of philanthropy, shall that pass? If an angry bigot assumes this bountiful cause of Abolition, and comes to me with his last news from Barbadoes, why should I not say to him, 'Go love thy infant; love thy wood-chopper; be good-natured and modest; have that grace; and never varnish your hard, uncharitable ambition with this incredible tenderness for black folk a thousand miles off. Thy love afar is spite at home.' Rough and graceless would be such greeting, but truth is handsomer than the affectation of love. Your goodness must have some edge to it,—else it is none. The doctrine of hatred must be preached, as the counteraction of the doctrine of love, when that pules and whines. I shun father and mother and wife and brother when my genius calls me. I would write on the lintels of the door-post, *Whim*. I hope it is somewhat better than whim at last, but we cannot spend the day in explanation. Expect me not to show cause why I seek or why I exclude company. Then again, do not tell me, as a good man did to-day, of my obligation to put all poor men in good situations. Are they *my* poor? I tell thee, thou foolish philanthropist, that I grudge the dollar, the dime, the cent I give to such men as do not belong to me and to whom I do not belong. There is a class of persons to whom by all spiritual affinity I am bought and sold; for them I will go to prison if need be; but your miscellaneous popular charities; the education at college of fools; the building of meeting-houses to the vain end to which many now stand; alms to sots, and the thousand-fold Relief Societies;—though I confess with shame I sometimes succumb and give the dollar, it is a wicked dollar, which by and by I shall have the manhood to withhold.

Virtues are, in the popular estimate, rather the exception than the rule. There is the man *and* his virtues. Men do what is called a good action, as some piece of courage or charity, much as they would pay a fine in expiation of daily non-appearance on parade. Their works are done as an apology or extenuation of their living in the world,—as invalids and the insane pay a high board. Their virtues are penances. I do not wish to expiate, but to live. My life is for itself and not for a spectacle. I much prefer that it should be of a lower strain, so it be genuine and equal, than that it should be glittering and unsteady. I wish it to be sound and sweet, and not to need diet and bleeding. I ask primary evidence that you are a man, and refuse this appeal from the man to his actions. I know that for myself it makes no difference whether I do or forbear those actions which are reckoned excellent. I cannot consent to pay for a privilege where I have intrinsic right. Few and mean as my gifts may be, I actually am, and do not need for my own assurance or the assurance of my fellows any secondary testimony.

What I must do is all that concerns me, not what the people think. This rule, equally arduous in actual and in intellectual life, may serve for the whole distinction between greatness and meanness. It is the harder because you will always find those who think they know what is your duty better than you know it. It is easy in the world to live after the world's opinion; it is easy in solitude to live after our own; but the great man is he who in the midst of the crowd keeps with perfect sweetness the independence of solitude.

The objection to conforming to usages that have become dead to you is that it scatters your force. It loses your time and blurs the impression of your character. If you maintain a dead church, contribute to a dead Bible-society, vote with a great party either for the government or against it, spread your table like base housekeepers,—under all these screens I have difficulty to detect the precise man you are: and of course so much force is withdrawn from your proper life. But do your work, and I shall know you. Do your work, and you shall reinforce yourself. A man must consider what a blind-man's-bluff is this game of conformity. If I know your sect I anticipate your argument. I hear a preacher announce for his text and topic the expediency of one of the institutions of his church. Do I not know beforehand that not possibly can he say a new and spontaneous word? Do I not know that with all this ostentation of examining the grounds of the institution he will do no such thing? Do I not know that he is pledged to himself not to look but at one side, the permitted side, not as a man, but as a parish minister? He is a retained attorney, and these airs of the bench are the emptiest affectation. Well, most men have bound their eyes with one or another handkerchief, and attached themselves to some one of these communities of opinion. This conformity makes them not false in a few particulars, authors of a few lies, but false in all particulars. Their every truth is not quite true. Their two is not the real two, their four not the real four; so that every word they say chagrins us and we know not where to begin to set them right. Meantime nature is not slow to equip us in the prison-uniform of the party to which we adhere. We come to wear one cut of face and figure, and acquire by degrees the gentlest asinine expression. There is a mortifying experience in particular, which does not fail to wreak itself also in the general history; I mean "the foolish face of praise," the forced smile which we put on in company where we do not feel at ease, in answer to conversation which does not interest us. The muscles, not spontaneously moved but moved by a low usurping wilfulness, grow tight about the outline of the face, with the most disagreeable sensation.

For nonconformity the world whips you with its displeasure. And therefore a man must know how to estimate a sour face. The by-standers look askance on him in the public street or in the friend's parlor. If this aversion had its origin in contempt and resistance like his own he might well go home with a sad countenance; but the sour faces of the multitude, like their sweet faces, have no deep cause, but are put on and off as the wind blows and a newspaper directs. Yet is the discontent of the multitude more formidable than that of the senate and the college. It is easy enough for a firm man who knows the world to brook the rage of the cultivated classes. Their rage is decorous and prudent, for they are timid, as being very vulnerable themselves. But when to their feminine rage the indignation of the people is added, when the ignorant and the poor are aroused, when the unintelligent brute force that lies at the bottom of society is made to growl and mow, it needs the habit of magnanimity and religion to treat it godlike as a trifle of no concernment.

The other terror that scares us from self-trust is our consistency; a reverence for our past act or word because the eyes of others have no other data for computing our orbit than our past acts, and we are loth to disappoint them.

But why should you keep your head over your shoulder? Why drag about this corpse of your memory, lest you contradict somewhat you have stated in this or that public place? Suppose you should contradict yourself; what then? It seems to be a rule of wisdom never to rely on your memory alone, scarcely even in acts of pure memory, but to bring the past for judgment into the thousand-eyed present, and live ever in a new day. In your metaphysics you have denied personality to the Deity, yet when the devout motions of the soul come, yield to them heart and life, though they should clothe God with shape and color. Leave your theory, as Joseph his coat in the hand of the harlot, and flee.

A foolish consistency is the hobgoblin of little minds, adored by little statesmen and philosophers and divines. With consistency a great soul has simply nothing to do. He may as well concern himself with his shadow on the wall. Speak what you think now in hard words and tomorrow speak what to-morrow thinks in hard words again, though it contradict every thing you said today.— 'Ah, so you shall be sure to be misunderstood.'—Is it so bad then to be misunderstood? Pythagoras was misunderstood, and Socrates, and Jesus, and Luther, and Copernicus, and Galileo, and Newton, and every pure and wise spirit that ever took flesh. To be great is to be misunderstood.

I suppose no man can violate his nature. All the sallies of his will are rounded in by the law of his being, as the inequalities of Andes and Himmaleh are insignificant in the curve of the sphere. Nor does it matter how you gauge and try him. A character is like an acrostic or Alexandrian stanza;—read it forward, backward, or across, it still spells the same thing. In this pleasing contrite wood-life which God allows me, let me record day by day my honest thought without prospect or retrospect, and, I cannot doubt, it will be found symmetrical, though I mean it not and see it not. My book should smell of pines and resound with the hum of insects. The swallow over my window should interweave that thread or straw he carries in his bill into my web also. We pass for what we are. Character teaches above our wills. Men imagine that they communicate their virtue or vice only by overt actions, and do not see that virtue or vice emit a breath every moment.

There will be an agreement in whatever variety of actions, so they be each honest and natural in their hour. For of one will, the actions will be harmonious, however unlike they seem. These varieties are lost sight of at a little distance, at a little height of thought. One tendency unites them all. The voyage of the best ship is a zigzag line of a hundred tacks. See the line from a sufficient distance, and it straightens itself to the average tendency. Your genuine action will explain itself and will explain your other genuine actions. Your conformity explains nothing. Act singly, and what you have already done singly will justify you now.

Greatness appeals to the future. If I can be firm enough to-day to do right and scorn eyes, I must have done so much right before as to defend me now. Be it how it will, do right now. Always scorn appearances and you always may. The force of character is cumulative. All the foregone days of virtue work their health into this. What makes the majesty of the heroes of the senate and the field, which so fills the imagination? The consciousness of a train of great days and victories behind. They shed a united light on the advancing actor. He is attended as by a visible escort of angels. That is it which throws thunder into Chatham's voice, and dignity into Washington's port, and America into Adams's eye. Honor is venerable to us because it is no ephemera. It is always ancient virtue. We worship it to-day because it is not of to-day. We love it and pay it homage because it is not a trap for our love and homage, but is self-dependent, self-derived, and therefore of an old immaculate pedigree, even if shown in a young person.

I hope in these days we have heard the last of conformity and consistency. Let the words be gazetted and ridiculous henceforward. Instead of the gong for dinner, let us hear a whistle from the Spartan fife. Let us never bow and apologize more. A great man is coming to eat at my house. I do not wish to please him; I wish that he should wish to please me. I will stand here for humanity, and though I would make it kind, I would make it true. Let us affront and reprimand the smooth mediocrity and squalid contentment of the times, and hurl in the face of custom and trade and office, the fact which is the upshot of all history, that there is a great responsible Thinker and Actor working wherever a man works; that a true man belongs to no other time or place, but is the centre of things. Where he is, there is nature. He measures you and all men and all events. Ordinarily, every body in society reminds us of somewhat else, or of some other person. Character, reality, reminds you of nothing else; it takes place of the whole creation. The man must be so much that he must make all circumstances indifferent. Every true man is a cause, a country, and an age; requires infinite spaces and numbers and time fully to accomplish his design;—and posterity seem to follow his steps as a train of clients. A man Cæsar is born, and for ages after we have a Roman Empire. Christ is born, and millions of minds so grow and cleave to his genius that he is confounded with virtue and the possible of man. An institution is the lengthened shadow of one man; as, Monachism, of the Hermit Antony; the Reformation, of Luther; Quakerism, of Fox; Methodism, of Wesley; Abolition, of Clarkson. Scipio, Milton called "the height of Rome;" and all history resolves itself very easily into the biography of a few stout and earnest persons.

Let a man then know his worth, and keep things under his feet. Let him not peep or steal, or skulk up and down with the air of a charity-boy, a bastard, or an interloper in the world which exists for him. But the man in the street, finding no worth in himself which corresponds to the force which built a tower or sculptured a marble god, feels poor when he looks on these. To him a palace, a statue, or a costly book have an alien and forbidding air, much like a gay equipage, and seem to say like that, "Who are you, Sir?" Yet they all are his, suitors for his notice, petitioners to his faculties that they will come out and take possession. The picture waits for my verdict; it is not to command me, but I am to settle its claims to praise. That popular fable of the sot who was picked up dead-drunk in the street, carried to the duke's house, washed and dressed and laid in the duke's bed, and, on his waking, treated with all obsequious ceremony like the duke, and assured that he had been insane, owes its popularity to the fact that it symbolizes so well the state of man, who is in the world a sort of sot, but now and then wakes up, exercises his reason and finds himself a true prince.

Our reading is mendicant and sycophantic. In history our imagination plays us false. Kingdom and lordship, power and estate, are a gaudier vocabulary than private John and Edward in a small house and common day's work; but the things of life are the same to both; the sum total of both is the same. Why all this deference to Alfred and Scanderbeg and Gustavus? Suppose they were virtuous; did they wear out virtue? As great a stake depends on your private act to-day as followed their public and renowned steps. When private men shall act with original views, the lustre will be transferred from the actions of kings to those of gentlemen.

The world has been instructed by its kings, who have so magnetized the eyes of nations. It has been taught by this colossal symbol the mutual reverence that is due from man to man. The joyful loyalty with which men have everywhere suffered the king, the noble, or the great proprietor to walk among them by a law of his own, make his own scale of men and things and reverse theirs, pay for benefits not with money but with honor, and represent the law in his person, was the hieroglyphic by which they obscurely signified their consciousness of their own right and comeliness, the right of every man.

The magnetism which all original action exerts is explained when we inquire the reason of self-trust. Who is the Trustee? What is the aboriginal Self, on which a universal reliance may be grounded? What is the nature and power of that science-baffling star, without parallax, without calculable elements, which shoots a ray of beauty even into trivial and impure actions, if the least mark of independence appear? The inquiry leads us to that source, at once the essence of genius, of virtue, and of life, which we call Spontaneity or Instinct. We denote this primary wisdom as Intuition, whilst all later teachings are tuitions. In that deep force, the last fact behind which analysis cannot go, all things find their common origin. For the sense of being which in calm hours rises, we know not how, in the soul, is not diverse from things, from space, from light, from time, from man, but one with them and proceeds obviously from the same source whence their life and being also proceed. We first share the life by which things exist and afterwards see them as appearances in nature and forget that we have shared their cause. Here is the fountain of action and of thought. Here are the lungs of that inspiration which giveth man wisdom and which cannot be denied without impiety and atheism. We lie in the lap of immense intelligence, which makes us receivers of its truth and organs of its activity. When we discern justice, when we discern truth, we do nothing of ourselves, but allow a passage to its beams. If we ask whence this comes, if we seek to pry into the soul that causes, all philosophy is at fault. Its presence or its absence is all we can affirm. Every man discriminates between the voluntary acts of his mind and his involuntary perceptions, and knows that to his involuntary perceptions a perfect faith is due. He may err in the expression of them, but he

knows that these things are so, like day and night, not to be disputed. My wilful actions and acquisitions are but roving;—the
idlest reverie, the faintest native emotion, command my curiosity
and respect. Thoughtless people contradict as readily the statement of perceptions as of opinions, or rather much more readily;
for they do not distinguish between perception and notion. They
fancy that I choose to see this or that thing. But perception is not
whimsical, but fatal. If I see a trait, my children will see it after
me, and in course of time all mankind,—although it may chance
that no one has seen it before me. For my perception of it is as
much a fact as the sun.

The relations of the soul to the divine spirit are so pure that it is
profane to seek to interpose helps. It must be that when God speaketh he should communicate, not one thing, but all things; should
fill the world with his voice; should scatter forth light, nature,
time, souls, from the centre of the present thought; and new date
and new create the whole. Whenever a mind is simple and receives
a divine wisdom, old things pass away,—means, teachers, texts,
temples fall; it lives now, and absorbs past and future into the
present hour. All things are made sacred by relation to it,—one as
much as another. All things are dissolved to their centre by their
cause, and in the universal miracle petty and particular miracles
disappear. If therefore a man claims to know and speak of God
and carries you backward to the phraseology of some old mould-
ered nation in another country, in another world, believe him not.
Is the acorn better than the oak which is its fulness and completion? Is the parent better than the child into whom he has cast his
ripened being? Whence then this worship of the past? The centuries are conspirators against the sanity and authority of the soul.
Time and space are but physiological colors which the eye makes,
but the soul is light: where it is, is day; where it was, is night; and
history is an impertinence and an injury if it be any thing more
than a cheerful apologue or parable of my being and becoming.

Man is timid and apologetic; he is no longer upright; he dares
not say 'I think,' 'I am,' but quotes some saint or sage. He is
ashamed before the blade of grass or the blowing rose. These
roses under my window make no reference to former roses or to
better ones; they are for what they are; they exist with God to-day.

There is no time to them. There is simply the rose; it is perfect in every moment of its existence. Before a leaf-bud has burst, its whole life acts; in the full-blown flower there is no more; in the leafless root there is no less. Its nature is satisfied and it satisfies nature in all moments alike. But man postpones or remembers; he does not live in the present, but with reverted eye laments the past, or, heedless of the riches that surround him, stands on tiptoe to foresee the future. He cannot be happy and strong until he too lives with nature in the present, above time.

This should be plain enough. Yet see what strong intellects dare not yet hear God himself unless he speak the phraseology of I know not what David, or Jeremiah, or Paul. We shall not always set so great a price on a few texts, on a few lives. We are like children who repeat by rote the sentences of grandames and tutors, and, as they grow older, of the men of talents and character the chance to see,—painfully recollecting the exact word they spoke; afterwards, when they come into the point of view which those had who uttered these sayings, they understand them and are willing to let the words go; for at any time they can use words as good when occasion comes. If we live truly, we shall see truly. It is as easy for the strong man to be strong, as it is for the weak to be weak. When we have new perception, we shall gladly disburden the memory of its hoarded treasures as old rubbish. When a man lives with God, his voice shall be as sweet as the murmur of the brook and the rustle of the corn.

And now at last the highest truth on this subject remains unsaid; probably cannot be said; for all that we say is the far-off remembering of the intuition. That thought by what I can now nearest approach to say it, is this. When good is near you, when you have life in yourself, it is not by any known or accustomed way; you shall not discern the footprints of any other; you shall not see the face of man; you shall not hear any name;—the way, the thought, the good, shall be wholly strange and new. It shall exclude example and experience. You take the way from man, not to man. All persons that ever existed are its forgotten ministers. Fear and hope are alike beneath it. There is somewhat low even in hope. In the hour of vision there is nothing that can be called gratitude, nor properly joy. The soul raised over passion beholds identity and eternal causation, perceives the self-existence of Truth and Right, and calms itself with knowing that all things go well. Vast spaces of nature, the Atlantic Ocean, the South Sea; long intervals of time, years, centuries, are of no account. This which I think and feel underlay every former state of life and circumstances, as it does underlie my present, and what is called life and what is called death.

Life only avails, not the having lived. Power ceases in the instant of repose; it resides in the moment of transition from a past to a new state, in the shooting of the gulf, in the darting to an aim. This one fact the world hates; that the soul *becomes*; for that forever degrades the past, turns all riches to poverty, all reputation to a shame, confounds the saint with the rogue, shoves Jesus and Judas equally aside. Why then do we prate of self-reliance? Inasmuch as the soul is present there will be power not confident but agent. To talk of reliance is a poor external way of speaking. Speak rather of that which relies because it works and is. Who has more obedience than I masters me, though he should not raise his finger. Round him I must revolve by the gravitation of spirits. We fancy it rhetoric when we speak of eminent virtue. We do not yet see that virtue is Height, and that a man or a company of men, plastic and permeable to principles, by the law of nature must overpower and ride all cities, nations, kings, rich men, poets, who are not.

This is the ultimate fact which we so quickly reach on this, as on every topic, the resolution of all into the ever-blessed ONE. Self-existence is the attribute of the Supreme Cause, and it constitutes the measure of good by the degree in which it enters into all lower forms. All things real are so by so much virtue as they contain. Commerce, husbandry, hunting, whaling, war, eloquence, personal weight, are somewhat, and engage my respect as examples of its presence and impure action. I see the same law working in nature for conservation and growth. Power is, in nature, the essential measure of right. Nature suffers nothing to remain in her kingdoms which cannot help itself. The genesis and maturation of a planet, its poise and orbit, the bended tree recovering itself from the strong wind, the vital resources of every animal and vegetable, are demonstrations of the self-sufficing and there-fore self-relying soul.

Thus all concentrates: let us not rove; let us sit at home with the cause. Let us stun and astonish the intruding rabble of men and books and institutions by a simple declaration of the divine fact. Bid the invaders take the shoes from off their feet, for God is here within. Let our simplicity judge them, and our docility to our own law demonstrate the poverty of nature and fortune beside our native riches.

But now we are a mob. Man does not stand in awe of man, nor is his genius admonished to stay at home, to put itself in commu-nication with the internal ocean, but it goes abroad to beg a cup of water of the urns of other men. We must go alone. I like the silent church before the service begins, better than any preaching. How far off, how cool, how chaste the persons look, begirt each one with a precinct or sanctuary! So let us always sit. Why should we assume the faults of our friend, or wife, or father, or child, because they sit around our hearth, or are said to have the same blood? All men have my blood and I all men's. Not for that will I adopt their petulance or folly, even to the extent of being ashamed of it. But your isolation must not be mechanical, but spiritual, that is, must be elevation. At times the whole world seems to be in conspiracy to importune you with emphatic trifles. Friend, client, child, sickness, fear, want, charity, all knock at once at thy closet door and say,—'Come out unto us.' But keep thy state; come not into their confusion. The power men possess to annoy me I give them by a weak curiosity. No man can come near me but through my act. "What we love that we have, but by desire we bereave our-selves of the love."

If we cannot at once rise to the sanctities of obedience and faith, let us at least resist our temptations; let us enter into the state of war and wake Thor and Woden, courage and constancy, in our Saxon breasts. This is to be done in our smooth times by speaking the truth. Check this lying hospitality and lying affec-tion. Live no longer to the expectation of these deceived and deceiving people with whom we converse. Say to them, 'O father, O mother, O wife, O brother, O friend, I have lived with you after appearances hitherto. Henceforward I am the truth's. Be it known unto you that henceforward I obey no law less than the eternal law. I will have no covenants but proximities. I shall endeavor to nourish my parents, to support my family, to be the chaste husband of one wife,—but these relations I must fill after a new and unprecedented way. I appeal from your customs. I must be myself. I cannot break myself any longer for you, or you. If you can love me for what I am, we shall be the happier. If you cannot, I will still seek to deserve that you should. I will not hide my tastes or aversions. I will so trust that what is deep is holy, that I will do strongly before the sun and moon whatever inly rejoices me and the heart appoints. If you are noble, I will love you; if you are not, I will not hurt you and myself by hypocritical attentions. If you are true, but not in the same truth with me, cleave to your companions; I will seek my own. I do this not selfishly but humbly and truly. It is alike your interest, and mine, and all men's, however long we have dwelt in lies, to live in truth. Does this sound harsh to-day? You will soon love what is dictated by your nature as well as mine, and if we follow the truth it will bring us out safe at last.'—But so may you give these friends pain. Yes, but I cannot sell my liberty and my power, to save their sensibility. Besides, all persons have their moments of reason, when they look out into the region of absolute truth; then will they justify me and do the same thing.

The populace think that your rejection of popular standards is a rejection of all standard, and mere antinomianism; and the bold sensualist will use the name of philosophy to gild his crimes. But the law of consciousness abides. There are two confessionals, in one or the other of which we must be shriven. You may fulfil your round of duties by clearing yourself in the *direct*, or in the *reflex* way. Consider whether you have satisfied your relations to father, mother, cousin, neighbor, town, cat and dog—whether any of these can upbraid you. But I may also neglect this reflex standard and absolve me to myself. I have my own stern claims and perfect circle. It denies the name of duty to many offices that are called duties. But if I can discharge its debts it enables me to dispense with the popular code. If any one imagines that this law is lax, let him keep its commandment one day.

And truly it demands something godlike in him who has cast off the common motives of humanity and has ventured to trust himself for a taskmaster. High be his heart, faithful his will, clear his sight, that he may in good earnest be doctrine, society, law, to himself, that a simple purpose may be to him as strong as iron necessity is to others!

If any man consider the present aspects of what is called by distinction *society*, he will see the need of these ethics. The sinew and heart of man seem to be drawn out, and we are become timorous, desponding whimperers. We are afraid of truth, afraid of fortune, afraid of death, and afraid of each other. Our age yields no great and perfect persons. We want men and women who shall renovate life and our social state, but we see that most natures are insolvent, cannot satisfy their own wants, have an ambition out of all proportion to their practical force and do lean and beg day and night continually. Our housekeeping is mendicant, our arts, our occupations, our marriages, our religion we have not chosen, but society has chosen for us. We are parlor soldiers. We shun the rugged battle of fate, where strength is born.

If our young men miscarry in their first enterprises they lose all heart. If the young merchant fails, men say he is *ruined*. If the finest genius studies at one of our colleges and is not installed in an office within one year afterwards in the cities or suburbs of Boston or New York, it seems to his friends and to himself that he is right in being disheartened and in complaining the rest of his life. A sturdy lad from New Hampshire or Vermont, who in turn tries all the professions, who *teams it, farms it, peddles*, keeps a school, preaches, edits a newspaper, goes to Congress, buys a township, and so forth, in successive years, and always like a cat falls on his feet, is worth a hundred of these city dolls. He walks abreast with his days and feels no shame in not 'studying a profession,' for he does not postpone his life, but lives already. He has not one chance, but a hundred chances. Let a Stoic open the resources of man and tell men they are not leaning willows, but can and must detach themselves; that with the exercise of self-trust, new powers shall appear; that a man is the word made flesh, born to shed healing to the nations; that he should be ashamed of our compassion, and that the moment he acts from himself, tossing the laws, the books, idolatries and customs out of the window, we pity him no more but thank and revere him;—and that teacher shall restore the life of man to splendor and make his name dear to all history.

It is easy to see that a greater self-reliance must work a revolution in all the offices and relations of men; in their religion; in their education; in their pursuits; their modes of living; their association; in their property; in their speculative views.

1. In what prayers do men allow themselves! That which they call a holy office is not so much as brave and manly. Prayer looks abroad and asks for some foreign addition to come through some foreign virtue, and loses itself in endless mazes of natural and supernatural, and mediatorial and miraculous. Prayer that craves a particular commodity, anything less than all good, is vicious. Prayer is the contemplation of the facts of life from the highest point of view. It is the soliloquy of a beholding and jubilant soul. It is the spirit of God pronouncing his works good. But prayer as a means to effect a private end is meanness and theft. It supposes dualism and not unity in nature and consciousness. As soon as the man is at one with God, he will not beg. He will then see prayer in all action. The prayer of the farmer kneeling in his field to weed it, the prayer of the rower kneeling with the stroke of his oar, are true prayers heard throughout nature, though for cheap ends. Caratach, in Fletcher's "Bonduca," when admonished to inquire the mind of the god Audate, replies,—

> His hidden meaning lies in our endeavors;
> Our valors are our best gods.

Another sort of false prayers are our regrets. Discontent is the want of self-reliance: it is infirmity of will. Regret calamities if you can thereby help the sufferer; if not, attend your own work and already the evil begins to be repaired. Our sympathy is just as base. We come to them who weep foolishly and sit down and cry for company, instead of imparting to them truth and health in rough electric shocks, putting them once more in communication with their own reason. The secret of fortune is joy in our hands. Welcome evermore to gods and men is the self-helping man. For him all doors are flung wide; him all tongues greet, all honors crown, all eyes follow with desire. Our love goes out to him and embraces him because he did not need it. We solicitously and apologetically caress and celebrate him because he held on his way and scorned our disapprobation. The gods love him because men hated him. "To the persevering mortal," said Zoroaster, "the blessed Immortals are swift."

As men's prayers are a disease of the will, so are their creeds a disease of the intellect. They say with those foolish Israelites, 'Let not God speak to us, lest we die. Speak thou, speak any man with us, and we will obey.' Everywhere I am hindered of meeting God in my brother, because he has shut his own temple doors and recites fables merely of his brother's, or his brother's brother's God. Every new mind is a new classification. If it prove a mind of uncommon activity and power, a Locke, a Lavoisier, a Hutton, a Bentham, a Fourier, it imposes its classification on other men, and lo! a new system. In proportion to the depth of the thought, and so to the number of the objects it touches and brings within reach of the pupil, is his complacency. But chiefly is this apparent in creeds and churches, which are also classifications of some powerful mind acting on the elemental thought of duty and man's relation to the Highest. Such is Calvinism, Quakerism, Swedenborgism. The pupil takes the same delight in subordinating every thing to the new terminology as a girl who has just learned botany in seeing a new earth and new seasons thereby. It will happen for a time that the pupil will find his intellectual power has grown by the study of his master's mind. But in all unbalanced minds the classification is idolized, passes for the end and not for a speedily exhaustible means, so that the walls of the system blend to their eye in the remote horizon with the walls of the universe; the luminaries of heaven seem to them hung on the arch their master built. They cannot imagine how you aliens have any right to see,—how you can see; 'It must be somehow that you stole the light from us.' They do not yet perceive that light, unsystematic, indomitable, will break into any cabin, even into theirs. Let them chirp awhile and call it their own. If they are honest and do well, presently their neat new pinfold will be too strait and low, will crack, will lean, will rot and vanish, and the immortal light, all young and joyful, million-orbed, million-colored, will beam over the universe as on the first morning.

2. It is for want of self-culture that the superstition of Travelling, whose idols are Italy, England, Egypt, retains its fascination for all educated Americans. They who made England, Italy, or Greece venerable in the imagination, did so by sticking fast where they were, like an axis of the earth. In manly hours we feel that duty is our place. The soul is no traveller; the wise man stays at home, and when his necessities, his duties, on any occasion call him from his house, or into foreign lands, he is at home still and shall make men sensible by the expression of his countenance that he goes, the missionary of wisdom and virtue, and visits cities and men like a sovereign and not like an interloper or a valet.

I have no churlish objection to the circumnavigation of the globe for the purposes of art, of study, and benevolence, so that the man is first domesticated, or does not go abroad with the hope of finding somewhat greater than he knows. He who travels to be amused, or to get somewhat which he does not carry, travels away from himself, and grows old even in youth among old things. In Thebes, in Palmyra, his will and mind have become old and dilapidated as they. He carries ruins to ruins.

Travelling is a fool's paradise. Our first journeys discover to us the indifference of places. At home I dream that at Naples, at Rome, I can be intoxicated with beauty and lose my sadness. I pack my trunk, embrace my friends, embark on the sea and at last wake up in Naples, and there beside me is the stern fact, the sad self, unrelenting, identical, that I fled from. I see the Vatican and the palaces. I affect to be intoxicated with sights and suggestions, but I am not intoxicated. My giant goes with me wherever I go.

3. But the rage of travelling is a symptom of a deeper unsoundness affecting the whole intellectual action. The intellect is vagabond, and our system of education fosters restlessness. Our minds travel when our bodies are forced to stay at home. We imitate; and what is imitation but the travelling of the mind? Our houses are built with foreign taste; our shelves are garnished with foreign ornaments; our opinions, our tastes, our faculties, lean, and follow the Past and the Distant. The soul created the arts wherever

they have flourished. It was in his own mind that the artist sought his model. It was an application of his own thought to the thing to be done and the conditions to be observed. And why need we copy the Doric or the Gothic model? Beauty, convenience, grandeur of thought and quaint expression are as near to us as to any, and if the American artist will study with hope and love the precise thing to be done by him, considering the climate, the soil, the length of the day, the wants of the people, the habit and form of the government, he will create a house in which all these will find themselves fitted, and taste and sentiment will be satisfied also.

Insist on yourself; never imitate. Your own gift you can present every moment with the cumulative force of a whole life's cultivation; but of the adopted talent of another you have only an extemporaneous half possession. That which each can do best, none but his Maker can teach him. No man yet knows what it is, nor can, till that person has exhibited it. Where is the master who could have taught Shakspeare? Where is the master who could have instructed Franklin, or Washington, or Bacon, or Newton? Every great man is a unique. The Scipionism of Scipio is precisely that part he could not borrow. Shakspeare will never be made by the study of Shakspeare. Do that which is assigned you, and you cannot hope too much or dare too much. There is at this moment for you an utterance brave and grand as that of the colossal chisel of Phidias, or trowel of the Egyptians, or the pen of Moses or Dante, but different from all these. Not possibly will the soul, all rich, all eloquent, with thousand-cloven tongue, deign to repeat itself; but if you can hear what these patriarchs say, surely you can reply to them in the same pitch of voice; for the ear and the tongue are two organs of one nature. Abide in the simple and noble regions of thy life, obey thy heart, and thou shalt reproduce the Foreworld again.

4. As our Religion, our Education, our Art look abroad, so does our spirit of society. All men plume themselves on the improvement of society, and no man improves.

Society never advances. It recedes as fast on one side as it gains on the other. It undergoes continual changes; it is barbarous, it is civilized, it is christianized, it is rich, it is scientific; but this change is not amelioration. For every thing that is given something is taken. Society acquires new arts and loses old instincts. What a contrast between the well-clad, reading, writing, thinking American, with a watch, a pencil and a bill of exchange in his pocket, and the naked New Zealander, whose property is a club, a spear, a mat and an undivided twentieth of a shed to sleep under! But compare the health of the two men and you shall see that the white man has lost his aboriginal strength. If the traveller tell us truly, strike the savage with a broad-axe and in a day or two the flesh shall unite and heal as if you struck the blow into soft pitch, and the same blow shall send the white to his grave.

The civilized man has built a coach, but has lost the use of his feet. He is supported on crutches, but lacks so much support of muscle. He has a fine Geneva watch, but he fails of the skill to tell the hour by the sun. A Greenwich nautical almanac he has, and so being sure of the information when he wants it, the man in the street does not know a star in the sky. The solstice he does not observe; the equinox he knows as little; and the whole bright calendar of the year is without a dial in his mind. His note-books impair his memory; his libraries overload his wit; the insurance-office increases the number of accidents; and it may be a question whether machinery does not encumber; whether we have not lost by refinement some energy, by a Christianity, entrenched in establishments and forms, some vigor of wild virtue. For every Stoic was a Stoic; but in Christendom where is the Christian?

There is no more deviation in the moral standard than in the standard of height or bulk. No greater men are now than ever were. A singular equality may be observed between the great men of the first and of the last ages; nor can all the science, art, religion, and philosophy of the nineteenth century avail to educate greater men than Plutarch's heroes, three or four and twenty centuries ago. Not in time is the race progressive. Phocion, Socrates, Anaxagoras, Diogenes, are great men, but they leave no class. He who is really of their class will not be called by their name, but will be his own man, and in his turn the founder of a sect. The arts and inventions of each period are only its costume and do not invigorate men. The harm of the improved machinery may compensate its good. Hudson and Behring accomplished so much in their fishing-boats as to astonish Parry and Franklin, whose equipment exhausted the resources of science and art. Galileo, with an

opera-glass, discovered a more splendid series of celestial phenomena than any one since. Columbus found the New World in
an undecked boat. It is curious to see the periodical disuse and
perishing of means and machinery which were introduced with
loud laudation a few years or centuries before. The great genius
returns to essential man. We reckoned the improvements of the
art of war among the triumphs of science, and yet Napoleon conquered Europe by the bivouac, which consisted of falling back on
naked valor and disencumbering it of all aids. The Emperor held
it impossible to make a perfect army, says Las Casas, "without
abolishing our arms, magazines, commissaries and carriages,
until, in imitation of the Roman custom, the soldier should receive
his supply of corn, grind it in his hand-mill and bake his bread
himself."

Society is a wave. The wave moves onward, but the water of
which it is composed does not. The same particle does not rise
from the valley to the ridge. Its unity is only phenomenal. The
persons who make up a nation to-day, next year die, and their
experience dies with them.

And so the reliance on Property, including the reliance on governments which protect it, is the want of self-reliance. Men have
looked away from themselves and at things so long that they have
come to esteem the religious, learned and civil institutions as
guards of property, and they deprecate assaults on these, because
they feel them to be assaults on property. They measure their
esteem of each other by what each has, and not by what each is.
But a cultivated man becomes ashamed of his property, out of
new respect for his nature. Especially he hates what he has if he
see that it is accidental,—came to him by inheritance, or gift, or
crime; then he feels that it is not having; it does not belong to him,
has no root in him and merely lies there because no revolution or
no robber takes it away. But that which a man is, does always by
necessity acquire; and what the man acquires, is living property,
which does not wait the beck of rulers, or mobs, or revolutions, or
fire, or storm, or bankruptcies, but perpetually renews itself
wherever the man breathes. "Thy lot or portion of life," said the
Caliph Ali, "is seeking after thee; therefore be at rest from seeking
after it." Our dependence on these foreign goods leads us to our

slavish respect for numbers. The political parties meet in numerous conventions; the greater the concourse and with each new uproar of announcement, The delegation from Essex! The Democrats from New Hampshire! The Whigs of Maine! the young patriot feels himself stronger than before by a new thousand of eyes and arms. In like manner the reformers summon conventions and vote and resolve in multitude. Not so, O friends! will the God deign to enter and inhabit you, but by a method precisely the reverse. It is only as a man puts off all foreign support and stands alone that I see him to be strong and to prevail. He is weaker by every recruit to his banner. Is not a man better than a town? Ask nothing of men, and, in the endless mutation, thou only firm column must presently appear the upholder of all that surrounds thee. He who knows that power is inborn, that he is weak because he has looked for good out of him and elsewhere, and, so perceiving throws himself unhesitatingly on his thought, instantly rights himself, stands in the erect position, commands his limbs, works miracles; just as a man who stands on his feet is stronger than a man who stands on his head.

So use all that is called Fortune. Most men gamble with her, and gain all, and lose all, as her wheel rolls. But do thou leave as unlawful these winnings, and deal with Cause and Effect, the chancellors of God. In the Will work and acquire, and thou hast chained the wheel of Chance, and shall sit hereafter out of fear from her rotations. A political victory, a rise of rents, the recovery of your sick or the return of your absent friend, or some other favorable event raises your spirits, and you think good days are preparing for you. Do not believe it. Nothing can bring you peace but yourself. Nothing can bring you peace but the triumph of principles.

NOTES

1. "Do not seek yourself outside yourself."

THE OVER-SOUL

"But souls that of his own good life partake,
He loves as his own self; dear as his eye
They are to Him: He'll never them forsake:
When they shall die, then God himself shall die:
They live, they live in blest eternity."

Henry More.

Space is ample, east and west,
But two cannot go abreast,
Cannot travel in it two:
Yonder masterful cuckoo
Crowds every egg out of the nest,
Quick or dead, except its own;
A spell is laid on sod and stone,
Night and Day've been tampered with,
Every quality and pith
Surcharged and sultry with a power
That works its will on age and hour.

There is a difference between one and another hour of life in their authority and subsequent effect. Our faith comes in moments; our vice is habitual. Yet there is a depth in those brief moments which constrains us to ascribe more reality to them than to all other experiences. For this reason the argument which is always forthcoming to silence those who conceive extraordinary hopes of man, namely the appeal to experience, is for ever invalid and vain. We give up the past to the objector, and yet we hope. He must explain this hope. We grant that human life is mean, but how did we find out that it was mean? What is the ground of this uneasiness of ours; of this old discontent? What is the universal sense of want and ignorance, but the fine innuendo by which the soul makes its enormous claim? Why do men feel that the natural history of man has never been written, but he is always leaving behind what you have said of him, and it becomes old, and books of metaphysics worthless? The philosophy of six thousand years has not searched the chambers and magazines of the soul. In its experiments there has always remained, in the last analysis, a residuum it could not resolve. Man is a stream whose source is hidden. Our being is descending into us from we know not whence. The most exact calculator has no prescience that somewhat incalculable may not balk the very next moment. I am constrained every moment to acknowledge a higher origin for events than the will I call mine.

As with events, so is it with thoughts. When I watch that flowing river, which, out of regions I see not, pours for a season its streams into me, I see that I am a pensioner; not a cause but a surprised spectator of this ethereal water; that I desire and look up and put myself in the attitude of reception, but from some alien energy the visions come.

The Supreme Critic on the errors of the past and the present, and the only prophet of that which must be, is that great nature in which we rest as the earth lies in the soft arms of the atmosphere; that Unity, that Over-Soul, within which every man's particular being is contained and made one with all other; that common heart of which all sincere conversation is the worship, to which all right action is submission; that overpowering reality which confutes our tricks and talents, and constrains every one to pass for what he is, and to speak from his character and not from his tongue, and which evermore tends to pass into our thought and hand and become wisdom and virtue and power and beauty. We live in succession, in division, in parts, in particles. Meantime within man is the soul of the whole; the wise silence; the universal beauty, to which every part and particle is equally related; the eternal ONE. And this deep power in which we exist and whose beatitude is all accessible to us, is not only self-sufficing and perfect in every hour, but the act of seeing and the thing seen, the seer

and the spectacle, the subject and the object, are one. We see the
world piece by piece, as the sun, the moon, the animal, the tree;
but the whole, of which these are the shining parts, is the soul.
Only by the vision of that Wisdom can the horoscope of the ages
be read, and by falling back on our better thoughts, by yielding to
the spirit of prophecy which is innate in every man, we can know
what it saith. Every man's words who speaks from that life must
sound vain to those who do not dwell in the same thought on their
own part. I dare not speak for it. My words do not carry its august
sense; they fall short and cold. Only itself can inspire whom it
will, and behold! their speech shall be lyrical, and sweet, and universal as the rising of the wind. Yet I desire, even by profane
words, if I may not use sacred, to indicate the heaven of this deity
and to report what hints I have collected of the transcendent simplicity and energy of the Highest Law.

If we consider what happens in conversation, in reveries, in
remorse, in times of passion, in surprises, in the instructions of
dreams, wherein often we see ourselves in masquerade,—the
droll disguises only magnifying and enhancing a real element and
forcing it on our distant notice,—we shall catch many hints that
will broaden and lighten into knowledge of the secret of nature.
All goes to show that the soul in man is not an organ, but animates and exercises all the organs; is not a function, like the
power of memory, of calculation, of comparison, but uses these as
hands and feet; is not a faculty, but a light; is not the intellect or
the will, but the master of the intellect and the will; is the background of our being, in which they lie,—an immensity not possessed and that cannot be possessed. From within or from behind,
a light shines through us upon things and makes us aware that we
are nothing, but the light is all. A man is the façade of a temple
wherein all wisdom and all good abide. What we commonly call
man, the eating, drinking, planting, counting man, does not, as
we know him, represent himself, but misrepresents himself. Him
we do not respect, but the soul, whose organ he is, would he let it
appear through his action, would make our knees bend. When it
breathes through his intellect, it is genius; when it breathes through
his will, it is virtue; when it flows through his affection, it is love.
And the blindness of the intellect begins when it would be something

of itself. The weakness of the will begins when the individual would be something of himself. All reform aims in some one particular to let the soul have its way through us; in other words, to engage us to obey.

Of this pure nature every man is at some time sensible. Language cannot paint it with his colors. It is too subtile. It is undefinable, unmeasurable; but we know that it pervades and contains us. We know that all spiritual being is in man. A wise old proverb says, "God comes to see us without bell;" that is, as there is no screen or ceiling between our heads and the infinite heavens, so is there no bar or wall in the soul, where man, the effect, ceases, and God, the cause, begins. The walls are taken away. We lie open on one side to the deeps of spiritual nature, to the attributes of God. Justice we see and know, Love, Freedom, Power. These natures no man ever got above, but they tower over us, and most in the moment when our interests tempt us to wound them.

The sovereignty of this nature whereof we speak is made known by its independency of those limitations which circumscribe us on every hand. The soul circumscribes all things. As I have said, it contradicts all experience. In like manner it abolishes time and space. The influence of the senses has in most men overpowered the mind to that degree that the walls of time and space have come to look real and insurmountable; and to speak with levity of these limits is, in the world, the sign of insanity. Yet time and space are but inverse measures of the force of the soul. The spirit sports with time,—

> "Can crowd eternity into an hour,
>   Or stretch an hour to eternity."

We are often made to feel that there is another youth and age than that which is measured from the year of our natural birth. Some thoughts always find us young, and keep us so. Such a thought is the love of the universal and eternal beauty. Every man parts from that contemplation with the feeling that it rather belongs to ages than to mortal life. The least activity of the intellectual powers redeems us in a degree from the conditions of time. In sickness, in languor, give us a strain of poetry or a profound sentence, and we are refreshed; or produce a volume of Plato or Shakspeare, or remind us of their names, and instantly we come into a feeling of longevity. See how the deep divine thought reduces centuries and millenniums, and makes itself present through all ages. Is the teaching of Christ less effective now than it was when first his mouth was opened? The emphasis of facts and persons in my thought has nothing to do with time. And so always the soul's scale is one, the scale of the senses and the understanding is another. Before the revelations of the soul, Time, Space and Nature shrink away. In common speech we refer all things to time, as we habitually refer the immensely sundered stars to one concave sphere. And so we say that the Judgment is distant or near, that the Millennium approaches, that a day of certain political, moral, social reforms is at hand, and the like, when we mean that in the nature of things one of the facts we contemplate is external and fugitive, and the other is permanent and connate with the soul. The things we now esteem fixed shall, one by one, detach themselves like ripe fruit from our experience, and fall. The wind shall blow them none knows whither. The landscape, the figures, Boston, London, are facts as fugitive as any institution past, or any whiff of mist or smoke, and so is society, and so is the world. The soul looketh steadily forwards, creating a world before her, leaving worlds behind her. She has no dates, nor rites, nor persons, nor specialties nor men. The soul knows only the soul; the web of events is the flowing robe in which she is clothed.

After its own law and not by arithmetic is the rate of its progress to be computed. The soul's advances are not made by gradation, such as can be represented by motion in a straight line, but rather by ascension of state, such as can be represented by metamorphosis,—from the egg to the worm, from the worm to the fly. The growths of genius are of a certain *total* character, that does not advance the elect individual first over John, then Adam, then Richard, and give to each the pain of discovered inferiority,—but by every throe of growth the man expands there where he works, passing at each pulsation, classes, populations, of men. With each divine impulse the mind rends the thin rinds of the visible and finite, and comes out into eternity, and inspires and expires its air. It converses with truths that have always been spoken in the world, and becomes conscious of a closer sympathy with Zeno and Arrian than with persons in the house.

This is the law of moral and of mental gain. The simple rise as by specific levity not into a particular virtue, but into the region of all the virtues. They are in the spirit which contains them all. The soul requires purity, but purity is not it; requires justice, but justice is not that; requires beneficence, but is somewhat better; so that there is a kind of descent and accommodation felt when we leave speaking of moral nature to urge a virtue which it enjoins. To the well-born child all the virtues are natural, and not painfully acquired. Speak to his heart, and the man becomes suddenly virtuous.

Within the same sentiment is the germ of intellectual growth, which obeys the same law. Those who are capable of humility, of justice, of love, of aspiration, stand already on a platform that commands the sciences and arts, speech and poetry, action and grace. For whoso dwells in this moral beatitude already anticipates those special powers which men prize so highly. The lover has no talent, no skill, which passes for quite nothing with his enamored maiden, however little she may possess of related faculty; and the heart which abandons itself to the Supreme Mind finds itself related to all its works, and will travel a royal road to particular knowledges and powers. In ascending to this primary and aboriginal sentiment we have come from our remote station on the circumference instantaneously to the centre of the world, where, as in the closet of God, we see causes, and anticipate the universe, which is but a slow effect.

One mode of the divine teaching is the incarnation of the spirit in a form,—in forms, like my own. I live in society; with persons who answer to thoughts in my own mind, or express a certain obedience to the great instincts to which I live. I see its presence to them. I am certified of a common nature; and these other souls, these separated selves, draw me as nothing else can. They stir in me the new emotions we call passion; of love, hatred, fear, admiration, pity; thence come conversation, competition, persuasion, cities and war. Persons are supplementary to the primary teaching of the soul. In youth we are mad for persons. Childhood and youth see all the world in them. But the larger experience of man discovers the identical nature appearing through them all. Persons themselves acquaint us with the impersonal. In all conversation between two persons tacit reference is made, as to a third party, to a common nature. That third party or common nature is not social; it is impersonal; is God. And so in groups where debate is earnest, and especially on high questions, the company become aware that the thought rises to an equal level in all bosoms, that all have a spiritual property in what was said, as well as the sayer. They all become wiser than they were. It arches over them like a temple, this unity of thought in which every heart beats with nobler sense of power and duty, and thinks and acts with unusual solemnity. All are conscious of attaining to a higher self-possession. It shines for all. There is a certain wisdom of humanity which is common to the greatest men with the lowest, and which our ordinary education often labors to silence and obstruct. The mind is one, and the best minds, who love truth for its own sake, think much less of property in truth. They accept it thankfully everywhere, and do not label or stamp it with any man's name, for it is theirs long beforehand, and from eternity. The learned and the studious of thought have no monopoly of wisdom. Their violence of direction in some degree disqualifies them to think truly. We owe many valuable observations to people who are not very acute or profound, and who say the thing without effort which we want and have long been hunting in vain. The action of the soul is oftener in that which is felt and left unsaid than in that which is said in any conversation. It broods over every society, and they unconsciously seek for it in each other. We know better than we do. We do not yet possess ourselves, and we know at the same time that we are much more. I feel the same truth how often in my trivial conversation with my neighbors, that somewhat higher in each of us overlooks this by-play, and Jove nods to Jove from behind each of us.

Men descend to meet. In their habitual and mean service to the world, for which they forsake their native nobleness, they resemble those Arabian sheiks who dwell in mean houses and affect an external poverty, to escape the rapacity of the Pacha, and reserve all their display of wealth for their interior and guarded retirements.

As it is present in all persons, so it is in every period of life. It is adult already in the infant man. In my dealing with my child, my Latin and Greek, my accomplishments and my money stead me nothing; but as much soul as I have avails. If I am wilful, he sets his will against mine, one for one, and leaves me, if I please, the degradation of beating him by my superiority of strength. But if I renounce my will and act for the soul, setting that up as umpire between us two, out of his young eyes looks the same soul; he reveres and loves with me.

The soul is the perceiver and revealer of truth. We know truth when we see it, let sceptic and scoffer say what they choose. Foolish people ask you, when you have spoken what they do not wish to hear, 'How do you know it is truth, and not an error of your own?' We know truth when we see it, from opinion, as we know when we are awake that we are awake. It was a grand sentence of Emanuel Swedenborg, which would alone indicate the greatness of that man's perception,—"It is no proof of a man's understanding to be able to affirm whatever he pleases; but to be able to discern that what is true is true, and that what is false is false,—this is the mark and character of intelligence." In the book I read, the good thought returns to me, as every truth will, the image of the whole soul. To the bad thought which I find in it, the same soul becomes a discerning, separating sword, and lops it away. We are wiser than we know. If we will not interfere with our thought, but will act entirely, or see how the thing stands in God, we know the particular thing, and every thing, and every man. For the Maker of all things and all persons stands behind us and casts his dread omniscience through us over things.

But beyond this recognition of its own in particular passages of the individual's experience, it also reveals truth. And here we should seek to reinforce ourselves by its very presence, and to speak with a worthier, loftier strain of that advent. For the soul's communication of truth is the highest event in nature, since it then does not give somewhat from itself, but it gives itself, or passes into and becomes that man whom it enlightens; or in proportion to that truth he receives, it takes him to itself.

We distinguish the announcements of the soul, its manifestations of its own nature, by the term *Revelation*. These are always attended by the emotion of the sublime. For this communication is an influx of the Divine mind into our mind. It is an ebb of the individual rivulet before the flowing surges of the sea of life. Every distinct apprehension of this central commandment agitates men with awe and delight. A thrill passes through all men at the reception of new truth, or at the performance of a great action, which comes out of the heart of nature. In these communications the power to see is not separated from the will to do, but the insight proceeds from obedience, and the obedience proceeds from a joyful perception. Every moment when the individual feels himself invaded by it is memorable. By the necessity of our constitution a certain enthusiasm attends the individual's consciousness of that divine presence. The character and duration of this enthusiasm vary with the state of the individual, from an ecstasy and trance and prophetic inspiration,—which is its rarer appearance,—to the faintest glow of virtuous emotion, in which form it warms, like our household fires, all the families and associations of men, and makes society possible. A certain tendency to insanity has always attended the opening of the religious sense in men, as if they had been "blasted with excess of light." The trances of Socrates, the "union" of Plotinus, the vision of Porphyry, the conversion of Paul, the aurora of Behmen, the convulsions of George Fox and his Quakers, the illumination of Swedenborg, are of this kind. What was in the case of these remarkable persons a ravishment, has, in innumerable instances in common life, been exhibited in less striking manner. Everywhere the history of religion betrays a tendency to enthusiasm. The rapture of the Moravian and Quietist; the opening of the eternal sense of the Word, in the language of the New Jerusalem Church; the *revival* of the Calvinistic churches; the *experiences* of the Methodists, are varying forms of that shudder of awe and delight with which the individual soul always mingles with the universal soul.

The nature of these revelations is the same; they are perceptions of the absolute law. They are solutions of the soul's own questions. They do not answer the questions which the understanding asks. The soul answers never by words, but by the thing itself that is inquired after.

Revelation is the disclosure of the soul. The popular notion of a revelation is that it is a telling of fortunes. In past oracles of the soul the understanding seeks to find answers to sensual questions, and undertakes to tell from God how long men shall exist, what their hands shall do and who shall be their company, adding names and dates and places. But we must pick no locks. We must check this low curiosity. An answer in words is delusive; it is really no answer to the questions you ask. Do not require a description of the countries towards which you sail. The description does not describe them to you, and to-morrow you arrive there and know them by inhabiting them. Men ask concerning the immortality of the soul, the employments of heaven, the state of the sinner, and so forth. They even dream that Jesus has left replies to precisely these interrogatories. Never a moment did that sublime spirit speak in their *patois*. To truth, justice, love, the attributes of the soul, the idea of immutableness is essentially associated. Jesus, living in these moral sentiments, heedless of sensual fortunes, heeding only the manifestations of these, never made the separation of the idea of duration from the essence of these attributes, nor uttered a syllable concerning the duration of the soul. It was left to his disciples to sever duration from the moral elements, and to teach the immortality of the soul as a doctrine, and maintain it by evidences. The moment the doctrine of the immortality is separately taught, man is already fallen. In the flowing of love, in the adoration of humility, there is no question of continuance. No inspired man ever asks this question or condescends to these evidences. For the soul is true to itself, and the man in whom it is shed abroad cannot wander from the present, which is infinite, to a future which would be finite.

These questions which we lust to ask about the future are a confession of sin. God has no answer for them. No answer in words can reply to a question of things. It is not in an arbitrary "decree of God," but in the nature of man, that a veil shuts down on the facts of to-morrow; for the soul will not have us read any other cipher than that of cause and effect. By this veil which curtains events it instructs the children of men to live in to-day. The only mode of obtaining an answer to these questions of the senses is to forego all low curiosity, and, accepting the tide of being which floats us into the secret of nature, work and live, work and live, and all unawares the advancing soul has built and forged for itself a new condition, and the question and the answer are one.

By the same fire, vital, consecrating, celestial, which burns until it shall dissolve all things into the waves and surges of an ocean of light, we see and know each other, and what spirit each is of. Who can tell the grounds of his knowledge of the character of the several individuals in his circle of friends? No man. Yet their acts and words do not disappoint him. In that man, though he knew no ill of him, he put no trust. In that other, though they had seldom met, authentic signs had yet passed, to signify that he might be trusted as one who had an interest in his own character. We know each other very well,—which of us has been just to himself and whether that which we teach or behold is only an aspiration or is our honest effort also.

We are all discerners of spirits. That diagnosis lies aloft in our life or unconscious power. The intercourse of society, its trade, its religion, its friendships, its quarrels, is one wide judicial investigation of character. In full court, or in small committee, or confronted face to face, accuser and accused, men offer themselves to be judged. Against their will they exhibit those decisive trifles by which character is read. But who judges? and what? Not our understanding. We do not read them by learning or craft. No; the wisdom of the wise man consists herein, that he does not judge them; he lets them judge themselves and merely reads and records their own verdict.

By virtue of this inevitable nature, private will is overpowered, and, maugre our efforts or our imperfections, your genius will speak from you, and mine from me. That which we are, we shall teach, not voluntarily but involuntarily. Thoughts come into our minds by avenues which we never left open, and thoughts go out of our minds through avenues which we never voluntarily opened. Character teaches over our head. The infallible index of true progress is found in the tone the man takes. Neither his age, nor his breeding, nor company, nor books, nor actions, nor talents, nor all together can hinder him from being deferential to a higher spirit than his own. If he have not found his home in God, his manner, his forms of speech, the turn of his sentences, the build, shall I say, of all his opinions will involuntarily confess it, let him brave it out how he will. If he have found his centre, the Deity will shine through him, through all the disguises of ignorance, of ungenial temperament, of unfavorable circumstance. The tone of seeking is one, and the tone of having is another.

The great distinction between teachers sacred or literary,— between poets like Herbert, and poets like Pope,—between philosophers like Spinoza, Kant and Coleridge, and philosophers like Locke, Paley, Mackintosh and Stewart,—between men of the world who are reckoned accomplished talkers, and here and there a fervent mystic, prophesying half insane under the infinitude of his thought,—is that one class speak *from within*, or from experience, as parties and possessors of the fact; and the other class *from without*, as spectators merely, or perhaps as acquainted with the fact on the evidence of third persons. It is of no use to preach to me from without. I can do that too easily myself. Jesus speaks always from within, and in a degree that transcends all others. In that is the miracle. I believe beforehand that it ought so to be. All men stand continually in the expectation of the appearance of such a teacher. But if a man do not speak from within the veil, where the word is one with that it tells of, let him lowly confess it.

The same Omniscience flows into the intellect and makes what we call genius. Much of the wisdom of the world is not wisdom, and the most illuminated class of men are no doubt superior to literary fame, and are not writers. Among the multitude of scholars and authors we feel no hallowing presence; we are sensible of a knack and skill rather than of inspiration; they have a light and know not whence it comes and call it their own; their talent is some exaggerated faculty, some overgrown member, so that their strength is a disease. In these instances the intellectual gifts do not make the impression of virtue, but almost of vice; and we feel that a man's talents stand in the way of his advancement in truth. But genius is religious. It is a larger imbibing of the common heart. It is not anomalous, but more like and not less like other men. There is in all great poets a wisdom of humanity which is superior to any talents they exercise. The author, the wit, the partisan, the fine gentleman, does not take place of the man. Humanity shines in Homer, in Chaucer, in Spenser, in Shakspeare, in

Milton. They are content with truth. They use the positive degree. They seem frigid and phlegmatic to those who have been spiced with the frantic passion and violent coloring of inferior but popular writers. For they are poets by the free course which they allow to the informing soul, which through their eyes beholds again and blesses the things which it hath made. The soul is superior to its knowledge, wiser than any of its works. The great poet makes us feel our own wealth, and then we think less of his compositions. His best communication to our mind is to teach us to despise all he has done. Shakspeare carries us to such a lofty strain of intelligent activity as to suggest a wealth which beggars his own; and we then feel that the splendid works which he has created, and which in other hours we extol as a sort of self-existent poetry, take no stronger hold of real nature than the shadow of a passing traveller on the rock. The inspiration which uttered itself in Hamlet and Lear could utter things as good from day to day for ever. Why then should I make account of Hamlet and Lear, as if we had not the soul from which they fell as syllables from the tongue?

This energy does not descend into individual life on any other condition than entire possession. It comes to the lowly and simple; it comes to whomsoever will put off what is foreign and proud; it comes as insight; it comes as serenity and grandeur. When we see those whom it inhabits, we are apprised of new degrees of greatness. From that inspiration the man comes back with a changed tone. He does not talk with men with an eye to their opinion. He tries them. It requires of us to be plain and true. The vain traveller attempts to embellish his life by quoting my lord and the prince and the countess, who thus said or did to *him*. The ambitious vulgar show you their spoons and brooches and rings, and preserve their cards and compliments. The more cultivated, in their account of their own experience, cull out the pleasing, poetic circumstance,—the visit to Rome, the man of genius they saw, the brilliant friend they know; still further on perhaps the gorgeous landscape, the mountain lights, the mountain thoughts they enjoyed yesterday,—and so seek to throw a romantic color over their life. But the soul that ascends to worship the great God is plain and true; has no rose-color, no fine friends, no chivalry, no adventures; does not want admiration; dwells in the hour that now is, in the earnest experience of the common day,—by reason of the present moment and the mere trifle having become porous to thought and bibulous of the sea of light.

Converse with a mind that is grandly simple, and literature looks like word-catching. The simplest utterances are worthiest to be written, yet are they so cheap and so things of course, that in the infinite riches of the soul it is like gathering a few pebbles off the ground, or bottling a little air in a phial, when the whole earth and the whole atmosphere are ours. Nothing can pass there, or make you one of the circle, but the casting aside your trappings and dealing man to man in naked truth, plain confession and omniscient affirmation.

Souls such as these treat you as gods would, walk as gods in the earth, accepting without any admiration your wit, your bounty, your virtue even,—say rather your act of duty, for your virtue they own as their proper blood, royal as themselves, and over-royal, and the father of the gods. But what rebuke their plain fraternal bearing casts on the mutual flattery with which authors solace each other and wound themselves! These flatter not. I do not wonder that these men go to see Cromwell and Christina and Charles the Second and James the First and the Grand Turk. For they are, in their own elevation, the fellows of kings, and must feel the servile tone of conversation in the world. They must always be a godsend to princes, for they confront them, a king to a king, without ducking or concession, and give a high nature the refreshment and satisfaction of resistance, of plain humanity, of even companionship and of new ideas. They leave them wiser and superior men. Souls like these make us feel that sincerity is more excellent than flattery. Deal so plainly with man and woman as to constrain the utmost sincerity and destroy all hope of trifling with you. It is the highest compliment you can pay. Their "highest praising," said Milton, "is not flattery, and their plainest advice is a kind of praising."

Ineffable is the union of man and God in every act of the soul. The simplest person who in his integrity worships God, becomes God; yet for ever and ever the influx of this better and universal self is new and unsearchable. It inspires awe and astonishment. How dear, how soothing to man, arises the idea of God, peopling the lonely place, effacing the scars of our mistakes and disappointments! When we have broken our god of tradition and ceased from our god of rhetoric, then may God fire the heart with his presence. It is the doubling of the heart itself, nay, the infinite enlargement of the heart with a power of growth to a new infinity on every side. It inspires in man an infallible trust. He has not the conviction, but the sight, that the best is the true, and may in that thought easily dismiss all particular uncertainties and fears, and adjourn to the sure revelation of time the solution of his private riddles. He is sure that his welfare is dear to the heart of being. In the presence of law to his mind he is overflowed with a reliance so universal that it sweeps away all cherished hopes and the most stable projects of mortal condition in its flood. He believes that he cannot escape from his good. The things that are really for thee gravitate to thee. You are running to seek your friend. Let your feet run, but your mind need not. If you do not find him, will you not acquiesce that it is best you should not find him? for there is a power, which, as it is in you, is in him also, and could therefore very well bring you together, if it were for the best. You are preparing with eagerness to go and render a service to which your talent and your taste invite you, the love of men and the hope of fame. Has it not occurred to you that you have no right to go, unless you are equally willing to be prevented from going? O, believe, as thou livest, that every sound that is spoken over the round world, which thou oughtest to hear, will vibrate on thine ear! Every proverb, every book, every byword that belongs to thee for aid or comfort, shall surely come home through open or winding passages. Every friend whom not thy fantastic will but the great and tender heart in thee craveth, shall lock thee in his embrace. And this because the heart in thee is the heart of all; not a valve, not a wall, not an intersection is there anywhere in nature, but one blood rolls uninterruptedly an endless circulation through all men, as the water of the globe is all one sea, and, truly seen, its tide is one.

Let man then learn the revelation of all nature and all thought to his heart; this, namely; that the Highest dwells with him; that the sources of nature are in his own mind, if the sentiment of duty is there. But if he would know what the great God speaketh, he must 'go into his closet and shut the door,' as Jesus said. God will not make himself manifest to cowards. He must greatly listen to himself, withdrawing himself from all the accents of other men's devotion. Even their prayers are hurtful to him, until he have made his own. Our religion vulgarly stands on numbers of believers. Whenever the appeal is made,—no matter how indirectly,— to numbers, proclamation is then and there made that religion is not. He that finds God a sweet enveloping thought to him never counts his company. When I sit in that presence, who shall dare to come in? When I rest in perfect humility, when I burn with pure love, what can Calvin or Swedenborg say?

It makes no difference whether the appeal is to numbers or to one. The faith that stands on authority is not faith. The reliance on authority measures the decline of religion, the withdrawal of the soul. The position men have given to Jesus, now for many centuries of history, is a position of authority. It characterizes themselves. It cannot alter the eternal facts. Great is the soul, and plain. It is no flatterer, it is no follower; it never appeals from itself. It believes in itself. Before the immense possibilities of man all mere experience, all past biography, however spotless and sainted, shrinks away. Before that heaven which our presentiments foreshow us, we cannot easily praise any form of life we have seen or read of. We not only affirm that we have few great men, but, absolutely speaking, that we have none; that we have no history, no record of any character or mode of living that entirely contents us. The saints and demigods whom history worships we are constrained to accept with a grain of allowance. Though in our lonely hours we draw a new strength out of their memory, yet, pressed on our attention, as they are by the thoughtless and customary, they fatigue and invade. The soul gives itself, alone, original and pure, to the Lonely, Original and Pure, who, on that condition, gladly inhabits, leads and speaks through it. Then is it glad, young and nimble. It is not wise, but it sees through all things. It is not called religious, but it is innocent. It calls the light its own, and feels that the grass grows and the stone falls by a law inferior to, and dependent on, its nature. Behold, it saith, I am born into the great, the universal mind. I, the imperfect, adore my own Perfect. I am somehow receptive of the great soul, and thereby I do overlook the sun and the stars and feel them to be the fair accidents and effects which change and pass. More and more the surges of everlasting nature enter into me, and I become public and human in my regards and actions. So come I to live in thoughts and act with energies which are immortal. Thus revering the soul, and learning, as the ancient said, that "its beauty is immense," man will come to see that the world is the perennial miracle which the soul worketh, and be less astonished at particular wonders; he will learn that there is no profane history; that all history is sacred; that the universe is represented in an atom, in a moment of time. He will weave no longer a spotted life of shreds and patches, but he will live with a divine unity. He will cease from what is base and frivolous in his life and be content with all places and with any service he can render. He will calmly front the morrow in the negligency of that trust which carries God with it and so hath already the whole future in the bottom of the heart.

CIRCLES

Nature centres into balls,
And her proud ephemerals,
Fast to surface and outside,
Scan the profile of the sphere;
Knew they what that signified,
A new genesis were here.

The eye is the first circle; the horizon which it forms is the second; and throughout nature this primary figure is repeated without end. It is the highest emblem in the cipher of the world. St. Augustine described the nature of God as a circle whose centre was everywhere and its circumference nowhere. We are all our lifetime reading the copious sense of this first of forms. One moral we have already deduced in considering the circular or compensatory character of every human action. Another analogy we shall now trace, that every action admits of being outdone. Our life is an apprenticeship to the truth that around every circle another can be drawn; that there is no end in nature, but every end is a beginning; that there is always another dawn risen on mid-noon, and under every deep a lower deep opens.

This fact, as far as it symbolizes the moral fact of the Unattainable, the flying Perfect, around which the hands of man can never meet, at once the inspirer and the condemner of every success, may conveniently serve us to connect many illustrations of human power in every department.

There are no fixtures in nature. The universe is fluid and volatile. Permanence is but a word of degrees. Our globe seen by God is a transparent law, not a mass of facts. The law dissolves the fact and holds it fluid. Our culture is the predominance of an idea which draws after it this train of cities and institutions. Let us rise into another idea; they will disappear. The Greek sculpture is all melted away, as if it had been statues of ice; here and there a solitary figure or fragment remaining, as we see flecks and scraps of snow left in cold dells and mountain clefts in June and July. For the genius that created it creates now somewhat else. The Greek letters last a little longer, but are already passing under the same sentence and tumbling into the inevitable pit which the creation of new thought opens for all that is old. The new continents are built out of the ruins of an old planet; the new races fed out of the decomposition of the foregoing. New arts destroy the old. See the investment of capital in aqueducts, made useless by hydraulics; fortifications, by gun-powder; roads and canals, by railways; sails, by steam; steam by electricity.

You admire this tower of granite, weathering the hurts of so many ages. Yet a little waving hand built this huge wall, and that which builds is better than that which is built. The hand that built can topple it down much faster. Better than the hand and nimbler was the invisible thought which wrought through it; and thus ever, behind the coarse effect, is a fine cause, which, being narrowly seen, is itself the effect of a finer cause. Everything looks permanent until its secret is known. A rich estate appears to women a firm and lasting fact; to a merchant, one easily created out of any materials, and easily lost. An orchard, good tillage, good grounds, seem a fixture, like a gold mine, or a river, to a citizen; but to a large farmer, not much more fixed than the state of the crop. Nature looks provokingly stable and secular, but it has a cause like all the rest; and when once I comprehend that, will these fields stretch so immovably wide, these leaves hang so individually considerable? Permanence is a word of degrees. Every thing is medial. Moons are no more bounds to spiritual power than bat-balls.

The key to every man is his thought. Sturdy and defying though he look, he has a helm which he obeys, which is the idea after which all his facts are classified. He can only be reformed by showing him a new idea which commands his own. The life of man is a self-evolving circle, which, from a ring imperceptibly small, rushes on all sides outwards to new and larger circles, and that without end. The extent to which this generation of circles, wheel without wheel, will go, depends on the force or truth of the individual soul. For it is the inert effort of each thought, having formed itself into a circular wave of circumstance,—as for instance an empire, rules of an art, a local usage, a religious rite,—to heap itself on that ridge and to solidify and hem in the life. But if the soul is quick and strong it bursts over that boundary on all sides and expands another orbit on the great deep, which also runs up into a high wave, with attempt again to stop and to bind. But the heart refuses to be imprisoned; in its first and narrowest pulses it already tends outward with a vast force and to immense and innumerable expansions.

Every ultimate fact is only the first of a new series. Every general law only a particular fact of some more general law presently to disclose itself. There is no outside, no inclosing wall, no circumference to us. The man finishes his story,—how good! how final! how it puts a new face on all things! He fills the sky. Lo! on the other side rises also a man and draws a circle around the circle we had just pronounced the outline of the sphere. Then already is our first speaker not man, but only a first speaker. His only redress is forthwith to draw a circle outside of his antagonist. And so men do by themselves. The result of to-day, which haunts the mind and cannot be escaped, will presently be abridged into a word, and the principle that seemed to explain nature will itself be included as one example of a bolder generalization. In the thought of to-morrow there is a power to upheave all thy creed, all the creeds, all the literatures of the nations, and marshal thee to a heaven which no epic dream has yet depicted. Every man is not so much a workman in the world as he is a suggestion of that he should be. Men walk as prophecies of the next age.

Step by step we scale this mysterious ladder; the steps are actions, the new prospect is power. Every several result is threatened and judged by that which follows. Every one seems to be contradicted by the new; it is only limited by the new. The new statement is always hated by the old, and, to those dwelling in the old, comes like an abyss of scepticism. But the eye soon gets wonted to it, for the eye and it are effects of one cause; then its innocency and benefit appear, and presently, all its energy spent, it pales and dwindles before the revelation of the new hour.

Fear not the new generalization. Does the fact look crass and material, threatening to degrade thy theory of spirit? Resist it not; it goes to refine and raise thy theory of matter just as much.

There are no fixtures to men, if we appeal to consciousness. Every man supposes himself not to be fully understood; and if there is any truth in him, if he rests at last on the divine soul, I see not how it can be otherwise. The last chamber, the last closet, he must feel was never opened; there is always a residuum unknown, unanalyzable. That is, every man believes that he has a greater possibility.

Our moods do not believe in each other. To-day I am full of thoughts and can write what I please. I see no reason why I should not have the same thought, the same power of expression, to-morrow. What I write, whilst I write it, seems the most natural thing in the world; but yesterday I saw a dreary vacuity in this direction in which now I see so much; and a month hence, I doubt not, I shall wonder who he was that wrote so many continuous pages. Alas for this infirm faith, this will not strenuous, this vast ebb of a vast flow! I am God in nature; I am a weed by the wall.

The continual effort to raise himself above himself, to work a pitch above his last height, betrays itself in a man's relations. We thirst for approbation, yet cannot forgive the approver. The sweet of nature is love; yet if I have a friend I am tormented by my imperfections. The love of me accuses the other party. If he were high enough to slight me, then could I love him, and rise by my affection to new heights. A man's growth is seen in the successive choirs of his friends. For every friend whom he loses for truth, he gains a better. I thought as I walked in the woods and mused on my friends, why should I play with them this game of idolatry? I know and see too well, when not voluntarily blind, the speedy limits of persons called high and worthy. Rich, noble and great they are by the liberality of our speech, but truth is sad. O blessed Spirit, whom I forsake for these, they are not thou! Every personal consideration that we allow costs us heavenly state. We sell the thrones of angels for a short and turbulent pleasure.

How often must we learn this lesson? Men cease to interest us when we find their limitations. The only sin is limitation. As soon as you once come up with a man's limitations, it is all over with him. Has he talents? has he enterprise? has he knowledge? It boots not. Infinitely alluring and attractive was he to you yesterday, a great hope, a sea to swim in; now, you have found his shores, found it a pond, and you care not if you never see it again.

Each new step we take in thought reconciles twenty seemingly discordant facts, as expressions of one law. Aristotle and Plato are reckoned the respective heads of two schools. A wise man will see that Aristotle platonizes. By going one step farther back in thought, discordant opinions are reconciled by being seen to be two extremes of one principle, and we can never go so far back as to preclude a still higher vision.

Beware when the great God lets loose a thinker on this planet. Then all things are at risk. It is as when a conflagration has broken out in a great city, and no man knows what is safe, or where it will end. There is not a piece of science but its flank may be turned to-morrow; there is not any literary reputation, not the so-called eternal names of fame, that may not be revised and condemned. The very hopes of man, the thoughts of his heart, the religion of nations, the manners and morals of mankind are all at the mercy of a new generalization. Generalization is always a new influx of the divinity into the mind. Hence the thrill that attends it.

Valor consists in the power of self-recovery, so that a man cannot have his flank turned, cannot be out-generalled, but put him where you will, he stands. This can only be by his preferring truth to his past apprehension of truth, and his alert acceptance of it from whatever quarter; the intrepid conviction that his laws, his relations to society, his Christianity, his world, may at any time be superseded and decease.

There are degrees in idealism. We learn first to play with it academically, as the magnet was once a toy. Then we see in the heyday of youth and poetry that it may be true, that it is true in gleams and fragments. Then its countenance waxes stern and grand, and we see that it must be true. It now shows itself ethical and practical. We learn that God is; that he is in me; and that all things are shadows of him. The idealism of Berkeley is only a crude statement of the idealism of Jesus and that again is a crude statement of the fact that nature is the rapid efflux of goodness executing and organizing itself. Much more obviously is history and the state of the world at any one time directly dependent on the intellectual classification then existing in the minds of men. The things which are dear to men at this hour are so on account of the ideas which have emerged on their mental horizon, and which cause the present order of things, as a tree bears its apples. A new degree of culture would instantly revolutionize the entire system of human pursuits.

Conversation is a game of circles. In conversation we pluck up the *termini* which bound the common of silence on every side. The parties are not to be judged by the spirit they partake and even express under this Pentecost. To-morrow they will have receded from this high-water mark. To-morrow you shall find them stooping under the old pack-saddles. Yet let us enjoy the cloven flame whilst it glows on our walls. When each new speaker strikes a new light, emancipates us from the oppression of the last speaker to oppress us with the greatness and exclusiveness of his own thought, then yields us to another redeemer, we seem to recover our rights, to become men. O, what truths profound and executable only in ages and orbs, are supposed in the announcement of every truth! In common hours, society sits cold and statuesque. We all stand waiting, empty,—knowing, possibly, that we can be full, surrounded by mighty symbols which are not symbols to us, but prose and trivial toys. Then cometh the god and converts the statues into fiery men, and by a flash of his eye burns up the veil which shrouded all things, and the meaning of the very furniture, of cup and saucer, of chair and clock and tester, is manifest. The facts which loomed so large in the fogs of yesterday,— property, climate, breeding, personal beauty and the like, have strangely changed their proportions. All that we reckoned settled shakes and rattles; and literatures, cities, climates, religions, leave their foundations and dance before our eyes. And yet here again see the swift circumscription! Good as is discourse, silence is better, and shames it. The length of the discourse indicates the distance of thought betwixt the speaker and the hearer. If they were at a perfect understanding in any part, no words would be necessary thereon. If at one in all parts, no words would be suffered.

Literature is a point outside of our hodiernal circle through which a new one may be described. The use of literature is to afford us a platform whence we may command a view of our present life, a purchase by which we may move it. We fill ourselves with ancient learning, install ourselves the best we can in Greek, in Punic, in Roman houses, only that we may wiselier see French, English and American houses and modes of living. In like manner we see literature best from the midst of wild nature, or from the din of affairs, or from a high religion. The field cannot be well seen from within the field. The astronomer must have his diameter of the earth's orbit as a base to find the parallax of any star.

Therefore we value the poet. All the argument and all the wisdom is not in the encyclopædia, or the treatise on metaphysics, or the Body of Divinity, but in the sonnet or the play. In my daily work I incline to repeat my old steps, and do not believe in remedial force, in the power of change and reform. But some Petrarch or Ariosto, filled with the new wine of his imagination, writes me an ode or a brisk romance, full of daring thought and action. He smites and arouses me with his shrill tones, breaks up my whole chain of habits, and I open my eye on my own possibilities. He claps wings to the sides of all the solid old lumber of the world, and I am capable once more of choosing a straight path in theory and practice.

We have the same need to command a view of the religion of the world. We can never see Christianity from the catechism:— from the pastures, from a boat in the pond, from amidst the songs of wood-birds we possibly may. Cleansed by the elemental light and wind, steeped in the sea of beautiful forms which the field offers us, we may chance to cast a right glance back upon biography. Christianity is rightly dear to the best of mankind; yet was there never a young philosopher whose breeding had fallen into the Christian church by whom that brave text of Paul's was not specially prized: "Then shall also the Son be subject unto Him who put all things under him, that God may be all in all." Let the claims and virtues of persons be never so great and welcome, the instinct of man presses eagerly onward to the impersonal and illimitable, and gladly arms itself against the dogmatism of bigots with this generous word out of the book itself.

The natural world may be conceived of as a system of concentric circles, and we now and then detect in nature slight dislocations which apprise us that this surface on which we now stand is not fixed, but sliding. These manifold tenacious qualities, this chemistry and vegetation, these metals and animals, which seem to stand there for their own sake, are means and methods only,— are words of God, and as fugitive as other words. Has the naturalist or chemist learned his craft, who has explored the gravity of atoms and the elective affinities, who has not yet discerned the deeper law whereof this is only a partial or approximate statement, namely that like draws to like, and that the goods which belong to you gravitate to you and need not be pursued with pains and cost? Yet is that statement approximate also, and not final. Omnipresence is a higher fact. Not through subtle subterranean channels need friend and fact be drawn to their counterpart, but, rightly considered, these things proceed from the eternal generation of the soul. Cause and effect are two sides of one fact.

The same law of eternal procession ranges all that we call the virtues, and extinguishes each in the light of a better. The great man will not be prudent in the popular sense; all his prudence will be so much deduction from his grandeur. But it behooves each to see, when he sacrifices prudence, to what god he devotes it; if to ease and pleasure, he had better be prudent still; if to a great trust, he can well spare his mule and panniers who has a winged chariot instead. Geoffrey draws on his boots to go through the woods, that his feet may be safer from the bite of snakes; Aaron never thinks of such a peril. In many years neither is harmed by such an accident. Yet it seems to me that with every precaution you take against such an evil you put yourself into the power of the evil. I suppose that the highest prudence is the lowest prudence. Is this too sudden a rushing from the centre to the verge of our orbit? Think how many times we shall fall back into pitiful calculations before we take up our rest in the great sentiment, or make the verge of to-day the new centre. Besides, your bravest sentiment is familiar to the humblest men. The poor and the low have their way of expressing the last facts of philosophy as well as you. "Blessed be nothing" and "The worse things are, the better they are" are proverbs which express the transcendentalism of common life.

One man's justice is another's injustice; one man's beauty another's ugliness; one man's wisdom another's folly; as one beholds the same objects from a higher point. One man thinks justice consists in paying debts, and has no measure in his abhorrence of another who is very remiss in this duty and makes the creditor wait tediously. But that second man has his own way of looking at things; asks himself Which debt must I pay first, the debt to the rich, or the debt to the poor? the debt of money, or the debt of thought to mankind, of genius to nature? For you, O broker, there is no other principle but arithmetic. For me, commerce is of trivial import; love, faith, truth of character, the aspiration of man, these are sacred; nor can I detach one duty, like you, from all other duties, and concentrate my forces mechanically on the payment of moneys. Let me live onward; you shall find that, though slower, the progress of my character will liquidate all these debts without injustice to higher claims. If a man should dedicate himself to the payment of notes, would not this be injustice? Does he owe no debt but money? And are all claims on him to be postponed to a landlord's or a banker's?

There is no virtue which is final; all are initial. The virtues of society are vices of the saint. The terror of reform is the discovery that we must cast away our virtues, or what we have always esteemed such, into the same pit that has consumed our grosser vices:—

> "Forgive his crimes, forgive his virtues too,
>   Those smaller faults, half converts to the right."[1]

It is the highest power of divine moments that they abolish our contritions also. I accuse myself of sloth and unprofitableness day by day; but when these waves of God flow into me I no longer reckon lost time. I no longer poorly compute my possible achievement by what remains to me of the month or the year; for these moments confer a sort of omnipresence and omnipotence which asks nothing of duration, but sees that the energy of the mind is commensurate with the work to be done, without time.

And thus, O circular philosopher, I hear some reader exclaim, you have arrived at a fine Pyrrhonism, at an equivalence and indifferency of all actions, and would fain teach us that *if we are true*, forsooth, our crimes may be lively stones out of which we shall construct the temple of the true God!

I am not careful to justify myself. I own I am gladdened by seeing the predominance of the saccharine principle throughout vegetable nature, and not less by beholding in morals that unrestrained inundation of the principle of good into every chink and hole that selfishness has left open, yea into selfishness and sin itself; so that no evil is pure, nor hell itself without its extreme satisfactions. But lest I should mislead any when I have my own head and obey my whims, let me remind the reader that I am only an experimenter. Do not set the least value on what I do, or the least discredit on what I do not, as if I pretended to settle any thing as true or false. I unsettle all things. No facts are to me sacred; none are profane; I simply experiment, an endless seeker with no Past at my back.

Yet this incessant movement and progression which all things partake could never become sensible to us but by contrast to some principle of fixture or stability in the soul. Whilst the eternal generation of circles proceeds, the eternal generator abides. That central life is somewhat superior to creation, superior to knowledge and thought, and contains all its circles. Forever it labors to create a life and thought as large and excellent as itself, but in vain, for that which is made instructs how to make a better.

Thus there is no sleep, no pause, no preservation, but all things renew, germinate and spring. Why should we import rags and relics into the new hour? Nature abhors the old, and old age seems the only disease; all others run into this one. We call it by many names,—fever, intemperance, insanity, stupidity and crime; they are all forms of old age; they are rest, conservatism, appropriation, inertia; not newness, not the way onward. We grizzle every day. I see no need of it. Whilst we converse with what is above us, we do not grow old, but grow young. Infancy, youth, receptive, aspiring, with religious eye looking upward, counts itself nothing and abandons itself to the instruction flowing from all sides. But the man and woman of seventy assume to know all, they have outlived their hope, they renounce aspiration, accept the actual for the necessary and talk down to the young. Let them then become organs of the Holy Ghost; let them be lovers; let them behold truth; and their eyes are uplifted, their wrinkles smoothed, they are perfumed again with hope and power. This old age ought not to creep on a human mind. In nature every moment is new; the past is always swallowed and forgotten; the coming only is sacred. Nothing is secure but life, transition, the energizing spirit. No love can be bound by oath or covenant to secure it against a higher love. No truth so sublime but it may be trivial tomorrow in the light of new thoughts. People wish to be settled; only as far as they are unsettled is there any hope for them.

Life is a series of surprises. We do not guess to-day the mood, the pleasure, the power of to-morrow, when we are building up our being. Of lower states, of acts of routine and sense, we can tell somewhat; but the masterpieces of God, the total growths and universal movements of the soul, he hideth; they are incalculable. I can know that truth is divine and helpful; but how it shall help me I can have no guess, for *so to be* is the sole inlet of *so to know*. The new position of the advancing man has all the powers of the old, yet has them all new. It carries in its bosom all the energies of the past, yet is itself an exhalation of the morning. I cast away in this new moment all my once hoarded knowledge, as vacant and vain. Now for the first time seem I to know any thing rightly. The simplest words,—we do not know what they mean except when we love and aspire.

The difference between talents and character is adroitness to keep the old and trodden round, and power and courage to make a new road to new and better goals. Character makes an over-powering present; a cheerful, determined hour, which fortifies all the company by making them see that much is possible and excellent that was not thought of. Character dulls the impression of particular events. When we see the conqueror we do not think much of any one battle or success. We see that we had exaggerated the difficulty. It was easy to him. The great man is not convulsible or tormentable; events pass over him without much impression. People say sometimes, 'See what I have overcome; see how cheerful I am; see how completely I have triumphed over these black events.' Not if they still remind me of the black event. True conquest is the causing the calamity to fade and disappear as an early cloud of insignificant result in a history so large and advancing.

The one thing which we seek with insatiable desire is to forget ourselves, to be surprised out of our propriety, to lose our sempiternal memory and to do something without knowing how or why; in short to draw a new circle. Nothing great was ever achieved without enthusiasm. The way of life is wonderful; it is by abandonment. The great moments of history are the facilities of performance through the strength of ideas, as the works of genius and religion. "A man," said Oliver Cromwell, "never rises so high as when he knows not whither he is going." Dreams and drunkenness, the use of opium and alcohol are the semblance and counterfeit of this oracular genius, and hence their dangerous attraction for men. For the like reason they ask the aid of wild passions, as in gaming and war, to ape in some manner these flames and generosities of the heart.

NOTES

1. Edward Young, *Night Thoughts*.

THE TRANSCENDENTALIST

A LECTURE READ AT THE MASONIC
TEMPLE, BOSTON, JANUARY, 1842.

The first thing we have to say respecting what are called *new views* here in New England, at the present time, is, that they are not new, but the very oldest of thoughts cast into the mould of these new times. The light is always identical in its composition, but it falls on a great variety of objects, and by so falling is first revealed to us, not in its own form, for it is formless, but in theirs; in like manner, thought only appears in the objects it classifies. What is popularly called Transcendentalism among us, is Idealism; Idealism as it appears in 1842. As thinkers, mankind have ever divided into two sects, Materialists and Idealists; the first class founding on experience, the second on consciousness; the first class beginning to think from the data of the senses, the second class perceive that the senses are not final, and say, The senses give us representations of things, but what are the things themselves, they cannot tell. The materialist insists on facts, on history, on the force of circumstances and the animal wants of man; the idealist on the power of Thought and of Will, on inspiration, on miracle, on individual culture. These two modes of thinking are both natural, but the idealist contends that his way of thinking is in higher nature. He concedes all that the other affirms, admits the impressions of sense, admits their coherency, their use and beauty, and then asks the materialist for his grounds of assurance that things are as his senses represent them. But I, he says, affirm facts not affected by the illusions of sense, facts which are of the same nature as the faculty which reports them, and not liable to doubt; facts which in their first appearance to us assume a native superiority to material facts, degrading these into a language by which the first are to be spoken; facts which it only needs a retirement from the senses to discern. Every materialist will be an idealist; but an idealist can never go backward to be a materialist.

The idealist, in speaking of events, sees them as spirits. He does not deny the sensuous fact: by no means; but he will not see that alone. He does not deny the presence of this table, this chair, and the walls of this room, but he looks at these things as the reverse side of the tapestry, as the *other end*, each being a sequel or completion of a spiritual fact which nearly concerns him. This manner of looking at things transfers every object in nature from an independent and anomalous position without there, into the consciousness. Even the materialist Condillac, perhaps the most logical expounder of materialism, was constrained to say, "Though we should soar into the heavens, though we should sink into the abyss, we never go out of ourselves; it is always our own thought that we perceive." What more could an idealist say?

The materialist, secure in the certainty of sensation, mocks at fine-spun theories, at star-gazers and dreamers, and believes that his life is solid, that he at least takes nothing for granted, but knows where he stands, and what he does. Yet how easy it is to show him that he also is a phantom walking and working amid phantoms, and that he need only ask a question or two beyond his daily questions to find his solid universe growing dim and impalpable before his sense. The sturdy capitalist, no matter how deep and square on blocks of Quincy granite he lays the foundations of his banking-house or Exchange, must set it, at last, not on a cube corresponding to the angles of his structure, but on a mass of unknown materials and solidity, red-hot or white-hot perhaps at the core, which rounds off to an almost perfect sphericity, and lies floating in soft air, and goes spinning away, dragging bank and banker with it at a rate of thousands of miles the hour, he knows not whither,—a bit of bullet, now glimmering, now darkling through a small cubic space on the edge of an unimaginable pit of emptiness. And this wild balloon, in which his whole venture is embarked, is a just symbol of his whole state and faculty. One thing at least, he says, is certain, and does not give me the headache, that figures do not lie; the multiplication table has been hitherto found unimpeachable truth; and, moreover, if I put a gold eagle in my safe, I find it again to-morrow;—but for these thoughts, I know not whence they are. They change and pass away. But ask him why he believes that an uniform experience will continue uniform, or on what grounds he founds his faith in his figures, and he will perceive that his mental fabric is built up on just as strange and quaking foundations as his proud edifice of stone.

In the order of thought, the materialist takes his departure from the external world, and esteems a man as one product of that. The idealist takes his departure from his consciousness, and reckons the world an appearance. The materialist respects sensible masses, Society, Government, social art and luxury, every establishment, every mass, whether majority of numbers, or extent of space, or amount of objects, every social action. The idealist has another measure, which is metaphysical, namely the *rank* which things themselves take in his consciousness; not at all the size or appearance. Mind is the only reality, of which men and all other natures are better or worse reflectors. Nature, literature, history, are only subjective phenomena. Although in his action overpowered by the laws of action, and so, warmly co-operating with men, even preferring them to himself, yet when he speaks scientifically, or after the order of thought, he is constrained to degrade persons into representatives of truths. He does not respect labor, or the products of labor, namely property, otherwise than as a manifold symbol, illustrating with wonderful fidelity of details the laws of being; he does not respect government, except as far as it reiterates the law of his mind; nor the church, nor charities, nor arts, for themselves; but hears, as at a vast distance, what they say, as if his consciousness would speak to him through a pantomimic scene. His thought,—that is the Universe. His experience inclines him to behold the procession of facts you call the world, as flowing perpetually outward from an invisible, unsounded centre in himself, centre alike of him and of them, and necessitating him to regard all things as having a subjective or relative existence, relative to that aforesaid Unknown Centre of him.

From this transfer of the world into the consciousness, this beholding of all things in the mind, follow easily his whole ethics. It is simpler to be self-dependent. The height, the deity of man is to be self-sustained, to need no gift, no foreign force. Society is good when it does not violate me, but best when it is likest to solitude. Everything real is self-existent. Everything divine shares the self-existence of Deity. All that you call the world is the shadow of that substance which you are, the perpetual creation of the powers of thought, of those that are dependent and of those that are independent of your will. Do not cumber yourself with fruitless pains to mend and remedy remote effects; let the soul be erect, and all things will go well. You think me the child of my circumstances: I make my circumstance. Let any thought or motive of mine be different from that they are, the difference will transform my condition and economy. I—this thought which is called I—is the mould into which the world is poured like melted wax. The mould is invisible, but the world betrays the shape of the mould. You call it the power of circumstance, but it is the power of me. Am I in harmony with myself? my position will seem to you just and commanding. Am I vicious and insane? my fortunes will seem to you obscure and descending. As I am, so shall I associate, and so shall I act; Cæsar's history will paint out Cæsar. Jesus acted so, because he thought so. I do not wish to overlook or to gainsay any reality; I say I make my circumstance; but if you ask me, Whence am I? I feel like other men my relation to that Fact which cannot be spoken, or defined, nor even thought, but which exists, and will exist.

The Transcendentalist adopts the whole connection of spiritual doctrine. He believes in miracle, in the perpetual openness of the human mind to new influx of light and power; he believes in inspiration, and in ecstasy. He wishes that the spiritual principle should be suffered to demonstrate itself to the end, in all possible applications to the state of man, without the admission of anything unspiritual; that is, anything positive, dogmatic, personal. Thus the spiritual measure of inspiration is the depth of the thought, and never, who said it? And so he resists all attempts to palm other rules and measures on the spirit than its own.

In action he easily incurs the charge of antinomianism by his avowal that he, who has the Law-giver, may with safety not only neglect, but even contravene every written commandment. In the play of Othello, the expiring Desdemona absolves her husband of the murder, to her attendant Emilia, Afterwards, when Emilia charges him with the crime, Othello exclaims,

> "You heard her say herself it was not I."

Emilia replies,

> "The more angel she, and thou the blacker devil."

Of this fine incident, Jacobi, the Transcendental moralist, makes use, with other parallel instances, in his reply to Fichte. Jacobi, refusing all measure of right and wrong except the determinations of the private spirit, remarks that there is no crime but has sometimes been a virtue. "I," he says, "am that atheist, that godless person who, in opposition to an imaginary doctrine of calculation, would lie as the dying Desdemona lied; would lie and deceive, as Pylades when he personated Orestes; would assassinate like Timoleon; would perjure myself like Epaminondas and John de Witt; I would resolve on suicide like Cato; I would commit sacrilege with David; yea, and pluck ears of corn on the Sabbath, for no other reason than that I was fainting for lack of food. For I have assurance in myself that in pardoning these faults according to the letter, man exerts the sovereign right which the majesty of his being confers on him; he sets the seal of his divine nature to the grace he accords."

In like manner, if there is anything grand and daring in human thought or virtue, any reliance on the vast, the unknown; any presentiment, any extravagance of faith, the spiritualist adopts it as most in nature. The oriental mind has always tended to this largeness. Buddhism is an expression of it. The Buddhist, who thanks no man, who says, "Do not flatter your benefactors," but who, in his conviction that every good deed can by no possibility escape its reward, will not deceive the benefactor by pretending that he has done more than he should, is a Transcendentalist.

You will see by this sketch that there is no such thing as a Transcendental *party*; that there is no pure Transcendentalist; that we know of none but prophets and heralds of such a philosophy; that all who by strong bias of nature have leaned to the spiritual side in doctrine, have stopped short of their goal. We have had many harbingers and forerunners; but of a purely spiritual life, history has afforded no example. I mean we have yet no man who has leaned entirely on his character, and eaten angels' food; who, trusting to his sentiments, found life made of miracles; who, working for universal aims, found himself fed, he knew not how; clothed, sheltered, and weaponed, he knew not how, and yet it was done by his own hands. Only in the instinct of the lower animals we find the suggestion of the methods of it, and something higher than our understanding. The squirrel hoards nuts and the bee gathers honey, without knowing what they do, and they are thus provided for without selfishness or disgrace.

Shall we say then that Transcendentalism is the Saturnalia or excess of Faith; the presentiment of a faith proper to man in his integrity, excessive only when his imperfect obedience hinders the satisfaction of his wish? Nature is transcendental, exists primarily, necessarily, ever works and advances, yet takes no thought for the morrow. Man owns the dignity of the life which throbs around him, in chemistry, and tree, and animal, and in the involuntary functions of his own body; yet he is balked when he tries to fling himself into this enchanted circle, where all is done without degradation. Yet genius and virtue predict in man the same absence of private ends and of condescension to circumstances, united with every trait and talent of beauty and power.

This way of thinking, falling on Roman times, made Stoic philosophers; falling on despotic times, made patriot Catos and Brutuses; falling on superstitious times, made prophets and apostles; on popish times, made protestants and ascetic monks, preachers of Faith against the preachers of Works; on prelatical times, made Puritans and Quakers; and falling on Unitarian and commercial times, makes the peculiar shades of Idealism which we know.

It is well known to most of my audience that the Idealism of the present day acquired the name of Transcendental from the use of that term by Immanuel Kant, of Königsberg, who replied to the skeptical philosophy of Locke, which insisted that there was nothing in the intellect which was not previously in the experience of the senses, by showing that there was a very important class of ideas or imperative forms, which did not come by experience, but through which experience was acquired; that these were intuitions of the mind itself; and he denominated them *Transcendental* forms. The extraordinary profoundness and precision of that man's thinking have given vogue to his nomenclature, in Europe and America, to that extent that whatever belongs to the class of intuitive thought is popularly called at the present day *Transcendental*.

Although, as we have said, there is no pure Transcendentalist, yet the tendency to respect the intuitions and to give them, at least in our creed, all authority over our experience, has deeply colored the conversation and poetry of the present day; and the history of genius and of religion in these times, though impure, and as yet not incarnated in any powerful individual, will be the history of this tendency.

It is a sign of our times, conspicuous to the coarsest observer, that many intelligent and religious persons withdraw themselves from the common labors and competitions of the market and the caucus, and betake themselves to a certain solitary and critical way of living, from which no solid fruit has yet appeared to justify their separation. They hold themselves aloof: they feel the disproportion between their faculties and the work offered them, and they prefer to ramble in the country and perish of ennui, to the degradation of such charities and such ambitions as the city can propose to them. They are striking work, and crying out for somewhat worthy to do! What they do is done only because they are overpowered by the humanities that speak on all sides; and they consent to such labor as is open to them, though to their lofty dream the writing of Iliads or Hamlets, or the building of cities or empires seems drudgery.

Now every one must do after his kind, be he asp or angel, and these must. The question which a wise man and a student of modern history will ask, is, what that kind is? And truly, as in ecclesiastical history we take so much pains to know what the Gnostics, what the Essenes, what the Manichees, and what the Reformers believed, it would not misbecome us to inquire nearer home, what these companions and contemporaries of ours think and do, at least so far as these thoughts and actions appear to be not accidental and personal, but common to many, and the inevitable flower of the Tree of Time. Our American literature and spiritual history are, we confess, in the optative mood; but whoso knows these seething brains, these admirable radicals, these unsocial worshippers, these talkers who talk the sun and moon away, will believe that this heresy cannot pass away without leaving its mark.

They are lonely; the spirit of their writing and conversation is lonely; they repel influences; they shun general society; they incline to shut themselves in their chamber in the house, to live in the country rather than in the town, and to find their tasks and amusements in solitude. Society, to be sure, does not like this very well; it saith, Whoso goes to walk alone, accuses the whole world; he declares all to be unfit to be his companions; it is very uncivil, nay, insulting; Society will retaliate. Meantime, this retirement does not proceed from any whim on the part of these separators; but if any one will take pains to talk with them, he will find that this part is chosen both from temperament and from principle; with some unwillingness too, and as a choice of the less of two evils; for these persons are not by nature melancholy, sour, and unsocial,—they are not stockish or brute,—but joyous, susceptible, affectionate; they have even more than others a great wish to be loved. Like the young Mozart, they are rather ready to cry ten times a day, "But are you sure you love me?" Nay, if they tell you their whole thought, they will own that love seems to them the last and highest gift of nature; that there are persons whom in their hearts they daily thank for existing,—persons whose faces are perhaps unknown to them, but whose fame and spirit have penetrated their solitude,—and for whose sake they wish to exist. To behold the beauty of another character, which inspires a new interest in our own; to behold the beauty lodged in a human being, with such vivacity of apprehension that I am instantly forced home to inquire if I am not deformity itself; to behold in another the expression of a love so high that it assures itself,— assures itself also to me against every possible casualty except my unworthiness;—these are degrees on the scale of human happiness to which they have ascended; and it is a fidelity to this sentiment which has made common association distasteful to them.

They wish a just and even fellowship, or none. They cannot gossip with you, and they do not wish, as they are sincere and religious, to gratify any mere curiosity which you may entertain. Like fairies, they do not wish to be spoken of. Love me, they say, but do not ask who is my cousin and my uncle. If you do not need to hear my thought, because you can read it in my face and behavior, then I will tell you from sunrise to sunset. If you cannot divine it, you would not understand what I say. I will not molest myself for you. I do not wish to be profaned.

And yet, it seems as if this loneliness, and not this love, would prevail in their circumstances, because of the extravagant demand they make on human nature. That, indeed, constitutes a new feature in their portrait, that they are the most exacting and extortionate critics. Their quarrel with every man they meet is not with his kind, but with his degree. There is not enough of him,—that is the only fault. They prolong their privilege of childhood in this wise; of doing nothing, but making immense demands on all the gladiators in the lists of action and fame. They make us feel the strange disappointment which overcasts every human youth. So many promising youths, and never a finished man! The profound nature will have a savage rudeness; the delicate one will be shallow, or the victim of sensibility; the richly accomplished will have some capital absurdity; and so every piece has a crack. 'T is strange, but this masterpiece is the result of such an extreme delicacy that the most unobserved flaw in the boy will neutralize the most aspiring genius, and spoil the work. Talk with a seaman of the hazards to life in his profession and he will ask you, 'Where are the old sailors? Do you not see that all are young men?' And we, on this sea of human thought, in like manner inquire, Where are the old idealists? where are they who represented to the last generation that extravagant hope which a few happy aspirants suggest to ours? In looking at the class of counsel, and power, and wealth, and at the matronage of the land, amidst all the prudence and all the triviality, one asks, Where are they who represented genius, virtue, the invisible and heavenly world, to these? Are they dead,—taken in early ripeness to the gods,—as ancient wisdom foretold their fate? Or did the high idea die out of them, and leave their unperfumed body as its tomb and tablet, announcing to all that the celestial inhabitant, who once gave them beauty, had departed? Will it be better with the new generation? We easily predict a fair future to each new candidate who enters the lists, but we are frivolous and volatile, and by low aims and ill example do what we can to defeat this hope. Then these youths bring us a rough but effectual aid. By their unconcealed dissatisfaction they expose our poverty and the insignificance of man to man. A man is a poor limitary benefactor. He ought to be a shower of benefits— a great influence, which should never let his brother go, but should refresh old merits continually with new ones; so that though absent he should never be out of my mind, his name never far from my lips; but if the earth should open at my side, or my last hour were come, his name should be the prayer I should utter to the Universe. But in our experience, man is cheap and friendship wants its deep sense. We affect to dwell with our friends in their absence, but we do not; when deed, word, or letter comes not, they let us go. These exacting children advertise us of our wants. There is no compliment, no smooth speech with them; they pay you only this one compliment, of insatiable expectation; they aspire, they severely exact, and if they only stand fast in this watch-tower, and persist in demanding unto the end, and without end, then are they terrible friends, whereof poet and priest cannot choose but stand in awe; and what if they eat clouds, and drink wind, they have not been without service to the race of man.

With this passion for what is great and extraordinary, it cannot be wondered at that they are repelled by vulgarity and frivolity in people. They say to themselves, It is better to be alone than in bad company. And it is really a wish to be met,—the wish to find society for their hope and religion,—which prompts them to shun what is called society. They feel that they are never so fit for friendship as when they have quitted mankind and taken themselves to friend. A picture, a book, a favorite spot in the hills or the woods which they can people with the fair and worthy creation of the fancy, can give them often forms so vivid that these for the time shall seem real, and society the illusion.

But their solitary and fastidious manners not only withdraw them from the conversation, but from the labors of the world; they are not good citizens, not good members of society; unwillingly they bear their part of the public and private burdens; they do not willingly share in the public charities, in the public religious rites, in the enterprises of education, of missions foreign and domestic, in the abolition of the slave-trade, or in the temperance society. They do not even like to vote. The philanthropists inquire whether Transcendentalism does not mean sloth: they had as lief hear that their friend is dead, as that he is a Transcendentalist; for then is he paralyzed, and can never do anything for humanity. What right, cries the good world, has the man of genius to retreat from work, and indulge himself? The popular literary creed seems to be, 'I am a sublime genius; I ought not therefore to labor.' But genius is the power to labor better and more availably. Deserve thy genius: exalt it. The good, the illuminated, sit apart from the rest, censuring their dulness and vices, as if they thought that by sitting very grand in their chairs, the very brokers, attorneys, and congressmen would see the error of their ways, and flock to them. But the good and wise must learn to act, and carry salvation to the combatants and demagogues in the dusty arena below.

On the part of these children it is replied that life and their faculty seem to them gifts too rich to be squandered on such trifles as you propose to them. What you call your fundamental institutions, your great and holy causes, seem to them great abuses, and, when nearly seen, paltry matters. Each 'cause' as it is called,—say Abolition, Temperance, say Calvinism, or Unitarianism,—becomes speedily a little shop, where the article, let it have been at first never so subtle and ethereal, is now made up into portable and convenient cakes, and retailed in small quantities to suit purchasers. You make very free use of these words 'great' and 'holy,' but few things appear to them such. Few persons have any magnificence of nature to inspire enthusiasm, and the philanthropies and charities have a certain air of quackery. As to the general course of living, and the daily employments of men, they cannot see much virtue in these, since they are parts of this vicious circle; and as no great ends are answered by the men, there is nothing noble in the arts by which they are maintained. Nay, they have made the experiment and found that from the liberal professions to the coarsest manual labor, and from the courtesies of the academy and the college to the conventions of the cotillon-room and the morning call, there is a spirit of cowardly compromise and seeming which intimates a frightful skepticism, a life without love, and an activity without an aim.

Unless the action is necessary, unless it is adequate, I do not wish to perform it. I do not wish to do one thing but once. I do not love routine. Once possessed of the principle, it is equally easy to make four or forty thousand applications of it. A great man will be content to have indicated in any the slightest manner his perception of the reigning Idea of his time, and will leave to those who like it the multiplication of examples. When he has hit the white, the rest may shatter the target. Every thing admonishes us how needlessly long life is. Every moment of a hero so raises and cheers us that a twelve-month is an age. All that the brave Xanthus brings home from his wars is the recollection that at the storming of Samos, "in the heat of the battle, Pericles smiled on me, and passed on to another detachment."[1] It is the quality of the moment, not the number of days, of events, or of actors, that imports.

New, we confess, and by no means happy, is our condition: if you want the aid of our labor, we ourselves stand in greater want of the labor. We are miserable with inaction. We perish of rest and rust: but we do not like your work.

'Then,' says the world, 'show me your own.'

'We have none.'

'What will you do, then?' cries the world.

'We will wait.'

'How long?'

'Until the Universe beckons and calls us to work.'

'But whilst you wait, you grow old and useless.'

'Be it so: I can sit in a corner and *perish* (as you call it), but I will not move until I have the highest command. If no call should come for years, for centuries, then I know that the want of the Universe is the attestation of faith by my abstinence. Your virtuous projects, so called, do not cheer me. I know that which shall come will cheer me. If I cannot work, at least I need not lie. All that is clearly due to-day is not to lie. In other places other men have encountered sharp trials, and have behaved themselves well.

The martyrs were sawn asunder, or hung alive on meat-hooks. Cannot we screw our courage to patience and truth, and without complaint, or even with good-humor, await our turn of action in the Infinite Counsels?'

But to come a little closer to the secret of these persons, we must say that to them it seems a very easy matter to answer the objections of the man of the world, but not so easy to dispose of the doubts and objections that occur to themselves. They are exercised in their own spirit with queries which acquaint them with all adversity, and with the trials of the bravest heroes. When I asked them concerning their private experience, they answered somewhat in this wise: It is not to be denied that there must be some wide difference between my faith and other faith; and mine is a certain brief experience, which surprised me in the highway or in the market, in some place, at some time,—whether in the body or out of the body, God knoweth,—and made me aware that I had played the fool with fools all this time, but that law existed for me and for all; that to me belonged trust, a child's trust and obedience, and the worship of ideas, and I should never be fool more. Well, in the space of an hour probably, I was let down from this height; I was at my old tricks, the selfish member of a selfish society. My life is superficial, takes no root in the deep world; I ask, When shall I die and be relieved of the responsibility of seeing an Universe which I do not use? I wish to exchange this flash-of-lightning faith for continuous daylight, this fever-glow for a benign climate.

These two states of thought diverge every moment, and stand in wild contrast. To him who looks at his life from these moments of illumination, it will seem that he skulks and plays a mean, shiftless and subaltern part in the world. That is to be done which he has not skill to do, or to be said which others can say better, and he lies by, or occupies his hands with some plaything, until his hour comes again. Much of our reading, much of our labor, seems mere waiting: it was not that we were born for. Any other could do it as well or better. So little skill enters into these works, so little do they mix with the divine life, that it really signifies little what we do, whether we turn a grindstone, or ride, or run, or make fortunes, or govern the state. The worst feature of this double consciousness is, that the two lives, of the understanding and of the soul, which we lead, really show very little relation to each other; never meet and measure each other: one prevails now, all buzz and din; and the other prevails then, all infinitude and paradise; and, with the progress of life, the two discover no greater disposition to reconcile themselves. Yet, what is my faith? What am I? What but a thought of serenity and independence, an abode in the deep blue sky? Presently the clouds shut down again; yet we retain the belief that this pretty web we weave will at last be over-shot and reticulated with veins of the blue, and that the moments will characterize the days. Patience, then, is for us, is it not? Patience, and still patience. When we pass, as presently we shall, into some new infinitude, out of this Iceland of negations, it will please us to reflect that though we had few virtues or consolations, we bore with our indigence, nor once strove to repair it with hypocrisy or false heat of any kind.

But this class are not sufficiently characterized if we omit to add that they are lovers and worshippers of Beauty. In the eternal trinity of Truth, Goodness, and Beauty, each in its perfection including the three, they prefer to make Beauty the sign and head. Something of the same taste is observable in all the moral movements of the time, in the religious and benevolent enterprises. They have a liberal, even an aesthetic spirit. A reference to Beauty in action sounds, to be sure, a little hollow and ridiculous in the ears of the old church. In politics, it has often sufficed, when they treated of justice, if they kept the bounds of selfish calculation. If they granted restitution, it was prudence which granted it. But the justice which is now claimed for the black, and the pauper, and the drunkard, is for Beauty,—is for a necessity to the soul of the agent, not of the beneficiary. I say this is the tendency, not yet the realization. Our virtue totters and trips, does not yet walk firmly. Its representatives are austere; they preach and denounce; their rectitude is not yet a grace. They are still liable to that slight taint of burlesque which in our strange world attaches to the zealot. A saint should be as dear as the apple of the eye. Yet we are tempted to smile, and we flee from the working to the speculative reformer, to escape that same slight ridicule. Alas for these days of derision and criticism! We call the Beautiful the highest, because it appears to us the golden mean, escaping the dowdiness of the good and the heartlessness of the true. They are lovers of nature also, and find an indemnity in the inviolable order of the world for the violated order and grace of man.

There is, no doubt, a great deal of well-founded objection to be spoken or felt against the sayings and doings of this class, some of whose traits we have selected; no doubt they will lay themselves open to criticism and to lampoons, and as ridiculous stories will be to be told of them as of any. There will be cant and pretension; there will be subtilty and moon-shine. These persons are of unequal strength, and do not all prosper. They complain that everything around them must be denied; and if feeble, it takes all their strength to deny, before they can begin to lead their own life. Grave seniors insist on their respect to this institution and that usage; to an obsolete history; to some vocation, or college, or etiquette, or beneficiary, or charity, or morning or evening call, which they resist as what does not concern them. But it costs such sleepless nights, alienations and misgivings,—they have so many moods about it; these old guardians never change *their* minds; they have but one mood on the subject, namely, that Antony is very perverse,—that it is quite as much as Antony can do to assert his rights, abstain from what he thinks foolish, and keep his temper. He cannot help the reaction of this injustice in his own mind. He is braced-up and stilted; all freedom and flowing genius, all sallies of wit and frolic nature are quite out of the question; it is well if he can keep from lying, injustice, and suicide. This is no time for gaiety and grace. His strength and spirits are wasted in rejection. But the strong spirits overpower those around them without effort. Their thought and emotion comes in like a flood, quite withdraws them from all notice of these carping critics; they surrender themselves with glad heart to the heavenly guide, and only by implication reject the clamorous nonsense of the hour. Grave seniors talk to the deaf,—church and old book mumble and ritualize to an unheeding, preoccupied and advancing mind, and thus they by happiness of greater momentum lose no time, but take the right road at first.

But all these of whom I speak are not proficients; they are novices; they only show the road in which man should travel, when the soul has greater health and prowess. Yet let them feel the dignity of their charge, and deserve a larger power. Their heart is the ark in which the fire is concealed which shall burn in a broader and universal flame. Let them obey the Genius then most when his impulse is wildest; then most when he seems to lead to uninhabitable deserts of thought and life; for the path which the hero travels alone is the highway of health and benefit to mankind. What is the privilege and nobility of our nature but its persistency, through its power to attach itself to what is permanent?

Society also has its duties in reference to this class, and must behold them with what charity it can. Possibly some benefit may yet accrue from them to the state. In our Mechanics' Fair, there must be not only bridges, ploughs, carpenters' planes, and baking troughs, but also some few finer instruments,—rain-gauges, thermometers, and telescopes; and in society, besides farmers, sailors, and weavers, there must be a few persons of purer fire kept specially as gauges and meters of character; persons of a fine, detecting instinct, who note the smallest accumulations of wit and feeling in the bystander. Perhaps too there might be room for the exciters and monitors; collectors of the heavenly spark, with power to convey the electricity to others. Or, as the storm-tossed vessel at sea speaks the frigate or 'line packet' to learn its longitude, so it may not be without its advantage that we should now and then encounter rare and gifted men, to compare the points of our spiritual compass, and verify our bearings from superior chronometers.

Amidst the downward tendency and proneness of things, when every voice is raised for a new road or another statute or a subscription of stock; for an improvement in dress, or in dentistry; for a new house or a larger business; for a political party, or the division of an estate;—will you not tolerate one or two solitary voices in the land, speaking for thoughts and principles not marketable or perishable? Soon these improvements and mechanical inventions will be superseded; these modes of living lost out of memory; these cities rotted, ruined by war, by new inventions, by new seats of trade, or the geologic changes:—all gone, like the shells which sprinkle the sea-beach with a white colony to-day, forever renewed to be forever destroyed. But the thoughts which these few hermits strove to proclaim by silence as well as by speech, not only by what they did, but by what they forbore to do, shall abide in beauty and strength, to reorganize themselves in nature, to invest themselves anew in other, perhaps higher endowed and happier mixed clay than ours, in fuller union with the surrounding system.

NOTES

1. Walter Savage Landor, *Pericles and Aspasia.*

THE POET

A moody child and wildly wise
Pursued the game with joyful eyes,
Which chose, like meteors, their way,
And rived the dark with private ray:
They overleapt the horizon's edge,
Searched with Apollo's privilege;
Through man, and woman, and sea, and star
Saw the dance of nature forward far;
Through worlds, and races, and terms, and times
Saw musical order, and pairing rhymes.

Olympian bards who sung
   Divine ideas below,
Which always find us young,
   And always keep us so.

Those who are esteemed umpires of taste are often persons who have acquired some knowledge of admired pictures or sculptures, and have an inclination for whatever is elegant; but if you inquire whether they are beautiful souls, and whether their own acts are like fair pictures, you learn that they are selfish and sensual. Their cultivation is local, as if you should rub a log of dry wood in one spot to produce fire, all the rest remaining cold. Their knowledge of the fine arts is some study of rules and particulars, or some limited judgment of color or form, which is exercised for amusement or for show. It is a proof of the shallowness of the doctrine of beauty as it lies in the minds of our amateurs, that men seem to have lost the perception of the instant dependence of form upon soul. There is no doctrine of forms in our philosophy. We were put into our bodies, as fire is put into a pan to be carried about; but there is no accurate adjustment between the spirit and the organ, much less is the latter the germination of the former. So in regard to other forms, the intellectual men do not believe in any essential dependence of the material world on thought and volition. Theologians think it a pretty air-castle to talk of the spiritual meaning of a ship or a cloud, of a city or a contract, but they prefer to come again to the solid ground of historical evidence; and even the poets are contented with a civil and conformed manner of living, and to write poems from the fancy, at a safe distance from their own experience. But the highest minds of the world have never ceased to explore the double meaning, or shall I say the quadruple or the centuple or much more manifold meaning, of every sensuous fact; Orpheus, Empedocles, Heraclitus, Plato, Plutarch, Dante, Swedenborg, and the masters of sculpture, picture and poetry. For we are not pans and barrows, nor even porters of the fire and torch-bearers, but children of the fire, made of it, and only the same divinity transmuted and at two or three removes, when we know least about it. And this hidden truth, that the fountains whence all this river of Time and its creatures floweth are intrinsically ideal and beautiful, draws us to the consideration of the nature and functions of the Poet, or the man of Beauty; to the means and materials he uses, and to the general aspect of the art in the present time.

The breadth of the problem is great, for the poet is representative. He stands among partial men for the complete man, and apprises us not of his wealth, but of the common wealth. The young man reveres men of genius, because, to speak truly, they are more himself than he is. They receive of the soul as he also receives, but they more. Nature enhances her beauty, to the eye of loving men, from their belief that the poet is beholding her shows at the same time. He is isolated among his contemporaries by truth and by his art, but with this consolation in his pursuits, that they will draw all men sooner or later. For all men live by truth and stand in need of expression. In love, in art, in avarice, in politics, in labor, in games, we study to utter our painful secret. The man is only half himself, the other half is his expression.

Notwithstanding this necessity to be published, adequate expression is rare. I know not how it is that we need an interpreter, but the great majority of men seem to be minors, who have not yet come into possession of their own, or mutes, who cannot report the conversation they have had with nature. There is no man who does not anticipate a supersensual utility in the sun and stars, earth and water. These stand and wait to render him a peculiar service. But there is some obstruction or some excess of phlegm in our constitution, which does not suffer them to yield the due effect. Too feeble fall the impressions of nature on us to make us artists. Every touch should thrill. Every man should be so much an artist that he could report in conversation what had befallen him. Yet, in our experience, the rays or appulses have sufficient force to arrive at the senses, but not enough to reach the quick and compel the reproduction of themselves in speech. The poet is the person in whom these powers are in balance, the man without impediment, who sees and handles that which others dream of, traverses the whole scale of experience, and is representative of man, in virtue of being the largest power to receive and to impart.

For the Universe has three children, born at one time, which reappear under different names in every system of thought, whether they be called cause, operation and effect; or, more poetically, Jove, Pluto, Neptune; or, theologically, the Father, the Spirit and the Son; but which we will call here the Knower, the Doer and the Sayer. These stand respectively for the love of truth, for the love of good, and for the love of beauty. These three are equal. Each is that which he is, essentially, so that he cannot be surmounted or analyzed, and each of these three has the power of the others latent in him and his own, patent.

The poet is the sayer, the namer, and represents beauty. He is a sovereign, and stands on the centre. For the world is not painted or adorned, but is from the beginning beautiful; and God has not made some beautiful things, but Beauty is the creator of the universe. Therefore the poet is not any permissive potentate, but is emperor in his own right. Criticism is infested with a cant of materialism, which assumes that manual skill and activity is the first merit of all men, and disparages such as say and do not, overlooking the fact that some men, namely poets, are natural sayers, sent into the world to the end of expression, and confounds them with those whose province is action but who quit it to imitate the sayers. But Homer's words are as costly and admirable to Homer as Agamemnon's victories are to Agamemnon. The poet does not wait for the hero or the sage, but, as they act and think primarily, so he writes primarily what will and must be spoken, reckoning the others, though primaries also, yet, in respect to him, secondaries and servants; as sitters or models in the studio of a painter, or as assistants who bring building-materials to an architect.

For poetry was all written before time was, and whenever we are so finely organized that we can penetrate into that region where the air is music, we hear those primal warblings and attempt to write them down, but we lose ever and anon a word or a verse and substitute something of our own, and thus miswrite the poem. The men of more delicate ear write down these cadences more faithfully, and these transcripts, though imperfect, become the songs of the nations. For nature is as truly beautiful as it is good, or as it is reasonable, and must as much appear as it must be done, or be known. Words and deeds are quite indifferent modes of the divine energy. Words are also actions, and actions are a kind of words.

The sign and credentials of the poet are that he announces that which no man foretold. He is the true and only doctor; he knows and tells; he is the only teller of news, for he was present and privy to the appearance which he describes. He is a beholder of ideas and an utterer of the necessary and causal. For we do not speak now of men of poetical talents, or of industry and skill in metre, but of the true poet. I took part in a conversation the other day concerning a recent writer of lyrics, a man of subtle mind, whose head appeared to be a music-box of delicate tunes and rhythms, and whose skill and command of language we could not sufficiently praise. But when the question arose whether he was not only a lyrist but a poet, we were obliged to confess that he is plainly a contemporary, not an eternal man. He does not stand out of our low limitations, like a Chimborazo under the line, running up from a torrid base through all the climates of the globe, with belts of the herbage of every latitude on its high and mottled sides; but this genius is the landscape-garden of a modern house, adorned with fountains and statues, with well-bred men and women standing and sitting in the walks and terraces. We hear, through all the varied music, the ground-tone of conventional life. Our poets are men of talents who sing, and not the children of music. The argument is secondary, the finish of the verses is primary.

For it is not metres, but a metre-making argument that makes a poem,—a thought so passionate and alive that like the spirit of a plant or an animal it has an architecture of its own, and adorns nature with a new thing. The thought and the form are equal in the order of time, but in the order of genesis the thought is prior to the form. The poet has a new thought; he has a whole new experience to unfold; he will tell us how it was with him, and all men will be the richer in his fortune. For the experience of each new age requires a new confession, and the world seems always waiting for its poet. I remember when I was young how much I was moved one morning by tidings that genius had appeared in a youth who sat near me at table. He had left his work and gone rambling none knew whither, and had written hundreds of lines, but could not tell whether that which was in him was therein told; he could tell nothing but that all was changed,—man, beast, heaven, earth and sea. How gladly we listened! how credulous! Society seemed to be compromised. We sat in the aurora of a sunrise which was to put out all the stars. Boston seemed to be at twice the distance it had the night before, or was much farther than that. Rome,—what was Rome? Plutarch and Shakspeare were in the yellow leaf, and Homer no more should be heard of. It is much to know that poetry has been written this very day, under this very roof, by your side. What! that wonderful spirit has not expired! These stony moments are still sparkling and animated! I had fancied that the oracles were all silent, and nature had spent her fires; and behold! all night, from every pore, these fine auroras have been streaming. Every one has some interest in the advent of the poet, and no one knows how much it may concern him. We know that the secret of the world is profound, but who or what shall be our interpreter, we know not. A mountain ramble, a new style of face, a new person, may put the key into our hands. Of course the value of genius to us is in the veracity of its report. Talent may frolic and juggle; genius realizes and adds. Mankind in good earnest have availed so far in understanding themselves and their work, that the foremost watchman on the peak announces his news. It is the truest word ever spoken, and the phrase will be the fittest, most musical, and the unerring voice of the world for that time.

All that we call sacred history attests that the birth of a poet is the principal event in chronology. Man, never so often deceived, still watches for the arrival of a brother who can hold him steady to a truth until he has made it his own. With what joy I begin to read a poem which I confide in as an inspiration! And now my chains are to be broken; I shall mount above these clouds and opaque airs in which I live,—opaque, though they seem transparent,—and from the heaven of truth I shall see and comprehend my relations. That will reconcile me to life and renovate nature, to see trifles animated by a tendency, and to know what I am doing. Life will no more be a noise; now I shall see men and women, and know the signs by which they may be discerned from fools and satans. This day shall be better than my birthday: then I became an animal; now I am invited into the science of the real. Such is the hope, but the fruition is postponed. Oftener it falls that this winged man, who will carry me into the heaven, whirls me into mists, then leaps and frisks about with me as it were from cloud to cloud, still affirming that he is bound heavenward; and I, being myself a novice, am slow in perceiving that he does not know the way into the heavens, and is merely bent that I should admire his skill to rise like a fowl or a flying fish, a little way from the ground or the water; but the all-piercing, all-feeding and ocular air of heaven that man shall never inhabit. I tumble down again soon into my old nooks, and lead the life of exaggerations as before, and have lost my faith in the possibility of any guide who can lead me thither where I would be.

But, leaving these victims of vanity, let us, with new hope, observe how nature, by worthier impulses, has insured the poet's fidelity to his office of announcement and affirming, namely by the beauty of things, which becomes a new and higher beauty when expressed. Nature offers all her creatures to him as a picture-language. Being used as a type, a second wonderful value appears in the object, far better than its old value; as the carpenter's stretched cord, if you hold your ear close enough, is musical in the breeze. "Things more excellent than every image," says Jamblichus, "are expressed through images." Things admit of being used as symbols because nature is a symbol, in the whole, and in every part. Every line we can draw in the sand has expression; and there is no body without its spirit or genius. All form is an effect of character; all condition, of the quality of the life; all harmony, of health; and for this reason a perception of beauty should be sympathetic, or proper only to the good. The beautiful rests on the foundations of the necessary. The soul makes the body, as the wise Spenser teaches:—

> "So every spirit, as it is more pure,
> And hath in it the more of heavenly light,
> So it the fairer body doth procure
> To habit in, and it more fairly dight,
> With cheerful grace and amiable sight.
> For, of the soul, the body form doth take,
> For soul is form, and doth the body make."[1]

Here we find ourselves suddenly not in a critical speculation but in a holy place, and should go very warily and reverently. We stand before the secret of the world, there where Being passes into Appearance and Unity into Variety.

The Universe is the externization of the soul. Wherever the life is, that bursts into appearance around it. Our science is sensual, and therefore superficial. The earth and the heavenly bodies, physics and chemistry, we sensually treat, as if they were self-existent; but these are the retinue of that Being we have. "The mighty heaven," said Proclus, "exhibits, in its transfigurations, clear images of the splendor of intellectual perceptions; being moved in conjunction with the unapparent periods of intellectual natures." Therefore science always goes abreast with the just elevation of the man, keeping step with religion and metaphysics; or the state of science is an index of our self-knowledge. Since every thing in nature answers to a moral power, if any phenomenon remains brute and dark it is because the corresponding faculty in the observer is not yet active.

No wonder then, if these waters be so deep, that we hover over them with a religious regard. The beauty of the fable proves the importance of the sense; to the poet, and to all others; or, if you please, every man is so far a poet as to be susceptible of these enchantments of nature; for all men have the thoughts whereof the universe is the celebration. I find that the fascination resides in the symbol. Who loves nature? Who does not? Is it only poets, and men of leisure and cultivation, who live with her? No; but also hunters, farmers, grooms and butchers, though they express their affection in their choice of life and not in their choice of words. The writer wonders what the coachman or the hunter values in riding, in horses and dogs. It is not superficial qualities. When you talk with him he holds these at as slight a rate as you. His worship is sympathetic; he has no definitions, but he is commanded in nature by the living power which he feels to be there present. No imitation or playing of these things would content him; he loves the earnest of the north wind, of rain, of stone and wood and iron. A beauty not explicable is dearer than a beauty which we can see to the end of. It is nature the symbol, nature certifying the supernatural, body overflowed by life which he worships with coarse but sincere rites.

The inwardness and mystery of this attachment drive men of every class to the use of emblems. The schools of poets and philosophers are not more intoxicated with their symbols than the populace with theirs. In our political parties, compute the power of badges and emblems. See the great ball which they roll from Baltimore to Bunker Hill![2] In the political processions, Lowell goes in a loom, and Lynn in a shoe, and Salem in a ship. Witness the cider-barrel, the log-cabin, the hickory-stick, the palmetto, and all the cognizances of party. See the power of national emblems. Some stars, lilies, leopards, a crescent, a lion, an eagle, or other figure which came into credit God knows how, on an old rag of bunting, blowing in the wind on a fort at the ends of the earth, shall make the blood tingle under the rudest or the most conventional exterior. The people fancy they hate poetry, and they are all poets and mystics!

Beyond this universality of the symbolic language, we are apprised of the divineness of this superior use of things, whereby the world is a temple whose walls are covered with emblems, pictures and commandments of the Deity,—in this, that there is no fact in nature which does not carry the whole sense of nature; and the distinctions which we make in events and in affairs, of low and high, honest and base, disappear when nature is used as a symbol. Thought makes everything fit for use. The vocabulary of an omniscient man would embrace words and images excluded from polite conversation. What would be base, or even obscene, to the obscene, becomes illustrious, spoken in a new connection of thought. The piety of the Hebrew prophets purges their grossness. The circumcision is an example of the power of poetry to raise the low and offensive. Small and mean things serve as well as great symbols. The meaner the type by which a law is expressed, the more pungent it is, and the more lasting in the memories of men; just as we choose the smallest box or case in which any needful utensil can be carried. Bare lists of words are found suggestive to an imaginative and excited mind, as it is related of Lord Chatham that he was accustomed to read in Bailey's Dictionary when he was preparing to speak in Parliament. The poorest experience is rich enough for all the purposes of expressing thought. Why covet a knowledge of new facts? Day and night, house and garden, a few books, a few actions, serve us as well as would all trades and all spectacles. We are far from having exhausted the significance of the few symbols we use. We can come to use them yet with a terrible simplicity. It does not need that a poem should be long. Every word was once a poem. Every new relation is a new word. Also we use defects and deformities to a sacred purpose, so expressing our sense that the evils of the world are such only to the evil eye. In the old mythology, mythologists observe, defects are ascribed to divine natures, as lameness to Vulcan, blindness to Cupid, and the like,—to signify exuberances.

For as it is dislocation and detachment from the life of God that makes things ugly, the poet, who re-attaches things to nature and the Whole,—re-attaching even artificial things and violation of nature, to nature, by a deeper insight,—disposes very easily of the most disagreeable facts. Readers of poetry see the factory-village and the railway, and fancy that the poetry of the landscape is broken up by these; for these works of art are not yet consecrated in their reading; but the poet sees them fall within the great Order not less than the bee-hive or the spider's geometrical web. Nature adopts them very fast into her vital circles, and the gliding train of cars she loves like her own. Besides, in a centred mind, it signifies nothing how many mechanical inventions you exhibit. Though you add millions, and never so surprising, the fact of mechanics has not gained a grain's weight. The spiritual fact remains unalterable, by many or by few particulars; as no mountain is of any appreciable height to break the curve of the sphere. A shrewd country-boy goes to the city for the first time, and the complacent citizen is not satisfied with his little wonder. It is not that he does not see all the fine houses and know that he never saw such before, but he disposes of them as easily as the poet finds place for the railway. The chief value of the new fact is to enhance the great and constant fact of Life, which can dwarf any and every circumstance, and to which the belt of wampum and the commerce of America are alike.

The world being thus put under the mind for verb and noun, the poet is he who can articulate it. For though life is great, and fascinates and absorbs; and though all men are intelligent of the symbols through which it is named; yet they cannot originally use them. We are symbols and inhabit symbols; workmen, work, and tools, words and things, birth and death, all are emblems; but we sympathize with the symbols, and being infatuated with the economical uses of things, we do not know that they are thoughts. The poet, by an ulterior intellectual perception, gives them a power which makes their old use forgotten, and puts eyes and a tongue into every dumb and inanimate object. He perceives the independence of the thought on the symbol, the stability of the thought, the accidency and fugacity of the symbol. As the eyes of Lyncæus were said to see through the earth, so the poet turns the world to glass, and shows us all things in their right series and procession. For through that better perception he stands one step nearer to things, and sees the flowing or metamorphosis; perceives that thought is multiform; that within the form of every creature is a force impelling it to ascend into a higher form; and following with his eyes the life, uses the forms which express that life, and so his speech flows with the flowing of nature. All the facts of the animal economy, sex, nutriment, gestation, birth, growth, are symbols of the passage of the world into the soul of man, to suffer there a change and reappear a new and higher fact. He uses forms according to the life, and not according to the form. This is true science. The poet alone knows astronomy, chemistry, vegetation and animation, for he does not stop at these facts, but employs them as signs. He knows why the plain or meadow of space was strown with these flowers we call suns and moons and stars; why the great deep is adorned with animals, with men, and gods; for in every word he speaks he rides on them as the horses of thought.

By virtue of this science the poet is the Namer or Language-maker, naming things sometimes after their appearance, sometimes after their essence, and giving to every one its own name and not another's, thereby rejoicing the intellect, which delights in detachment or boundary. The poets made all the words, and therefore language is the archives of history, and, if we must say it, a sort of tomb of the muses. For though the origin of most of our words is forgotten, each word was at first a stroke of genius, and obtained currency because for the moment it symbolized the world to the first speaker and to the hearer. The etymologist finds the deadest word to have been once a brilliant picture. Language is fossil poetry. As the limestone of the continent consists of infinite masses of the shells of animalcules, so language is made up of images or tropes, which now, in their secondary use, have long ceased to remind us of their poetic origin. But the poet names the thing because he sees it, or comes one step nearer to it than any other. This expression or naming is not art, but a second nature, grown out of the first, as a leaf out of a tree. What we call nature is a certain self-regulated motion or change; and nature does all things by her own hands, and does not leave another to baptize her but baptizes herself; and this through the metamorphosis again. I remember that a certain poet described it to me thus:

Genius is the activity which repairs the decays of things, whether wholly or partly of a material and finite kind. Nature, through all her kingdoms, insures herself. Nobody cares for planting the poor fungus; so she shakes down from the gills of one agaric countless spores, any one of which, being preserved, transmits new billions of spores to-morrow or next day. The new agaric of this hour has a chance which the old one had not. This atom of seed is thrown into a new place, not subject to the accidents which destroyed its parent two rods off. She makes a man; and having brought him to ripe age, she will no longer run the risk of losing this wonder at a blow, but she detaches from him a new self, that the kind may be safe from accidents to which the individual is exposed. So when the soul of the poet has come to ripeness of thought, she detaches and sends away from it its poems or songs,—a fearless, sleepless, deathless progeny, which is not exposed to the accidents of the weary kingdom of time; a fearless, vivacious offspring, clad with wings (such was the virtue of the soul out of which they came) which carry them fast and far, and infix them irrecoverably into the hearts of men. These wings are the beauty of the poet's soul. The songs, thus flying immortal from their mortal parent, are pursued by clamorous flights of censures, which swarm in far greater numbers and threaten to devour them; but these last are not winged. At the end of a very short leap they fall plump down and rot, having received from the souls out of which they came no beautiful wings. But the melodies of the poet ascend and leap and pierce into the deeps of infinite time.

So far the bard taught me, using his freer speech. But nature has a higher end, in the production of new individuals, than security, namely *ascension*, or the passage of the soul into higher forms. I knew in my younger days the sculptor who made the statue of the youth which stands in the public garden. He was, as I remember, unable to tell directly what made him happy or unhappy, but by wonderful indirections he could tell. He rose one day, according to his habit, before the dawn, and saw the morning break, grand as the eternity out of which it came, and for many days after, he strove to express this tranquillity, and lo! his chisel had fashioned out of marble the form of a beautiful youth, Phosphorus, whose aspect is such that it is said all persons who look on it become silent. The poet also resigns himself to his mood, and that thought which agitated him is expressed, but *alter idem*, in a manner totally new. The expression is organic, or the new type which things themselves take when liberated. As, in the sun, objects paint their images on the retina of the eye, so they, sharing the aspiration of the whole universe, tend to paint a far more delicate copy of their essence in his mind. Like the metamorphosis of things into higher organic forms is their change into melodies. Over everything stands its dæmon or soul, and, as the form of the thing is reflected by the eye, so the soul of the thing is reflected by a melody. The sea, the mountain-ridge, Niagara, and every flower-bed, pre-exist, or super-exist, in pre-cantations, which sail like odors in the air, and when any man goes by with an ear sufficiently fine, he overhears them and endeavors to write down the notes without diluting or depraving them. And herein is the legitimation of criticism, in the mind's faith that the poems are a corrupt version of some text in nature with which they ought to be made to tally. A rhyme in one of our sonnets should not be less pleasing than the iterated nodes of a seashell, or the resembling difference of a group of flowers. The pairing of the birds is an idyl, not tedious as our idyls are; a tempest is a rough ode, without falsehood or rant; a summer, with its harvest sown, reaped and stored, is an epic song, subordinating how many admirably executed parts. Why should not the symmetry and truth that modulate these, glide into our spirits, and we participate the invention of nature?

This insight, which expresses itself by what is called Imagination, is a very high sort of seeing, which does not come by study, but by the intellect being where and what it sees; by sharing the path or circuit of things through forms, and so making them translucid to others. The path of things is silent. Will they suffer a speaker to go with them? A spy they will not suffer; a lover, a poet, is the transcendency of their own nature,—him they will suffer. The condition of true naming, on the poet's part, is his resigning himself to the divine *aura* which breathes through forms, and accompanying that.

It is a secret which every intellectual man quickly learns, that beyond the energy of his possessed and conscious intellect he is capable of a new energy (as of an intellect doubled on itself), by abandonment to the nature of things; that beside his privacy of power as an individual man, there is a great public power on which he can draw, by unlocking, at all risks, his human doors, and suffering the ethereal tides to roll and circulate through him; then he is caught up into the life of the Universe, his speech is thunder, his thought is law, and his words are universally intelligible as the plants and animals. The poet knows that he speaks adequately then only when he speaks somewhat wildly, or "with the flower of the mind;" not with the intellect used as an organ, but with the intellect released from all service and suffered to take its direction from its celestial life; or as the ancients were wont to express themselves, not with intellect alone but with the intellect inebriated by nectar. As the traveller who has lost his way throws his reins on his horse's neck and trusts to the instinct of the animal to find his road, so must we do with the divine animal who carries us through this world. For if in any manner we can stimulate this instinct, new passages are opened for us into nature; the mind flows into and through things hardest and highest, and the metamorphosis is possible.

This is the reason why bards love wine, mead, narcotics, coffee, tea, opium, the fumes of sandalwood and tobacco, or whatever other procurers of animal exhilaration. All men avail themselves of such means as they can, to add this extraordinary power to their normal powers; and to this end they prize conversation, music, pictures, sculpture, dancing, theatres, travelling, war, mobs, fires, gaming, politics, or love, or science, or animal intoxication,—which are several coarser or finer *quasi*-mechanical substitutes for the true nectar, which is the ravishment of the intellect by coming nearer to the fact. These are auxiliaries to the centrifugal tendency of a man, to his passage out into free space, and they help him to escape the custody of that body in which he is pent up, and of that jail-yard of individual relations in which he is enclosed.

Hence a great number of such as were professionally expressers of Beauty, as painters, poets, musicians and actors, have been more than others wont to lead a life of pleasure and indulgence; all but the few who received the true nectar; and, as it was a spurious mode of attaining freedom, as it was an emancipation not into the heavens but into the freedom of baser places, they were punished for that advantage they won, by a dissipation and deterioration. But never can any advantage be taken of nature by a trick. The spirit of the world, the great calm presence of the Creator, comes not forth to the sorceries of opium or of wine. The sublime vision comes to the pure and simple soul in a clean and chaste body. That is not an inspiration, which we owe to narcotics, but some counterfeit excitement and fury. Milton says that the lyric poet may drink wine and live generously, but the epic poet, he who shall sing of the gods and their descent unto men, must drink water out of a wooden bowl. For poetry is not 'Devil's wine,' but God's wine. It is with this as it is with toys. We fill the hands and nurseries of our children with all manner of dolls, drums and horses; withdrawing their eyes from the plain face and sufficing objects of nature, the sun and moon, the animals, the water and stones, which should be their toys. So the poet's habit of living should be set on a key so low that the common influences should delight him. His cheerfulness should be the gift of the sunlight; the air should suffice for his inspiration, and he should be tipsy with water. That spirit which suffices quiet hearts, which seems to come forth to such from every dry knoll of sere grass, from every pine stump and half-imbedded stone on which the dull March sun shines, comes forth to the poor and hungry, and such as are of simple taste. If thou fill thy brain with Boston and New York, with fashion and covetousness, and wilt stimulate thy jaded senses with wine and French coffee, thou shalt find no radiance of wisdom in the lonely waste of the pinewoods.

If the imagination intoxicates the poet, it is not inactive in other men. The metamorphosis excites in the beholder an emotion of joy. The use of symbols has a certain power of emancipation and exhilaration for all men. We seem to be touched by a wand which makes us dance and run about happily, like children. We are like persons who come out of a cave or cellar into the open air. This is the effect on us of tropes, fables, oracles and all poetic forms. Poets are thus liberating gods. Men have really got a new sense, and found within their world another world, or nest of worlds; for, the metamorphosis once seen, we divine that it does not stop. I will not now consider how much this makes the charm of algebra and the mathematics, which also have their tropes, but it is felt in every definition; as when Aristotle defines *space* to be an immovable vessel in which things are contained;—or when Plato defines a *line* to be a flowing point; or *figure* to be a bound of solid; and many the like. What a joyful sense of freedom we have when Vitruvius announces the old opinion of artists that no architect can build any house well who does not know something of anatomy. When Socrates, in Charmides, tells us that the soul is cured of its maladies by certain incantations, and that these incantations are beautiful reasons, from which temperance is generated in souls; when Plato calls the world an animal, and Timæus affirms that the plants also are animals; or affirms a man to be a heavenly tree, growing with his root, which is his head, upward; and, as George Chapman, following him, writes,

> "So in our tree of man, whose nervie root
> Springs in his top;"—[3]

when Orpheus speaks of hoariness as "that white flower which marks extreme old age;" when Proclus calls the universe the statue of the intellect; when Chaucer, in his praise of 'Gentilesse,' compares good blood in mean condition to fire, which, though carried to the darkest house betwixt this and the mount of Caucasus, will yet hold its natural office and burn as bright as if twenty thousand men did it behold; when John saw, in the Apocalypse, the ruin of the world through evil, and the stars fall from heaven as the fig tree casteth her untimely fruit; when Æsop reports the whole catalogue of common daily relations through the masquerade of birds and beasts;—we take the cheerful hint of the immortality of our essence and its versatile habit and escapes, as when the gypsies say of themselves "it is in vain to hang them, they cannot die."

The poets are thus liberating gods. The ancient British bards had for the title of their order, "Those who are free throughout the world." They are free, and they make free. An imaginative book renders us much more service at first, by stimulating us through its tropes, than afterward when we arrive at the precise sense of the author. I think nothing is of any value in books excepting the transcendental and extraordinary. If a man is inflamed and carried away by his thought, to that degree that he forgets the authors and the public and heeds only this one dream which holds him like an insanity, let me read his paper, and you may have all the arguments and histories and criticism. All the value which attaches to Pythagoras, Paracelsus, Cornelius Agrippa, Cardan, Kepler, Swedenborg, Schelling, Oken, or any other who introduces questionable facts into his cosmogony, as angels, devils, magic, astrology, palmistry, mesmerism, and so on, is the certificate we have of departure from routine, and that here is a new witness. That also is the best success in conversation, the magic of liberty, which puts the world like a ball in our hands. How cheap even the liberty then seems; how mean to study, when an emotion communicates to the intellect the power to sap and upheave nature; how great the perspective! nations, times, systems, enter and disappear like threads in tapestry of large figure and many colors; dream delivers us to dream, and while the drunkenness lasts we will sell our bed, our philosophy, our religion, in our opulence.

There is good reason why we should prize this liberation. The fate of the poor shepherd, who, blinded and lost in the snowstorm, perishes in a drift within a few feet of his cottage door, is an emblem of the state of man. On the brink of the waters of life and truth, we are miserably dying. The inaccessibleness of every thought but that we are in, is wonderful. What if you come near to it; you are as remote when you are nearest as when you are farthest. Every thought is also a prison; every heaven is also a prison. Therefore we love the poet, the inventor, who in any form, whether in an ode or in an action or in looks and behavior, has yielded us a new thought. He unlocks our chains and admits us to a new scene.

This emancipation is dear to all men, and the power to impart it, as it must come from greater depth and scope of thought, is a measure of intellect. Therefore all books of the imagination endure, all which ascend to that truth that the writer sees nature beneath him, and uses it as his exponent. Every verse or sentence possessing this virtue will take care of its own immortality. The religions of the world are the ejaculations of a few imaginative men.

But the quality of the imagination is to flow, and not to freeze. The poet did not stop at the color or the form, but read their meaning; neither may he rest in this meaning, but he makes the same objects exponents of his new thought. Here is the difference betwixt the poet and the mystic, that the last nails a symbol to one sense, which was a true sense for a moment, but soon becomes old and false. For all symbols are fluxional; all language is vehicular and transitive, and is good, as ferries and horses are, for conveyance, not as farms and houses are, for homestead. Mysticism consists in the mistake of an accidental and individual symbol for an universal one. The morning-redness happens to be the favorite meteor to the eyes of Jacob Behmen, and comes to stand to him for truth and faith; and, he believes, should stand for the same realities to every reader. But the first reader prefers as naturally the symbol of a mother and child, or a gardener and his bulb, or a jeweller polishing a gem. Either of these, or of a myriad more, are equally good to the person to whom they are significant. Only they must be held lightly, and be very willingly translated into the equivalent terms which others use. And the mystic must be steadily told,—All that you say is just as true without the tedious use of that symbol as with it. Let us have a little algebra, instead of this trite rhetoric,—universal signs, instead of these village symbols,— and we shall both be gainers. The history of hierarchies seems to show that all religious error consisted in making the symbol too stark and solid, and was at last nothing but an excess of the organ of language.

Swedenborg, of all men in the recent ages, stands eminently for the translator of nature into thought. I do not know the man in history to whom things stood so uniformly for words. Before him the metamorphosis continually plays. Everything on which his eye rests, obeys the impulses of moral nature. The figs become grapes whilst he eats them. When some of his angels affirmed a truth, the laurel twig which they held blossomed in their hands. The noise which at a distance appeared like gnashing and thumping, on coming nearer was found to be the voice of disputants. The men in one of his visions, seen in heavenly light, appeared like dragons, and seemed in darkness; but to each other they appeared as men, and when the light from heaven shone into their cabin, they complained of the darkness, and were compelled to shut the window that they might see.

There was this perception in him which makes the poet or seer an object of awe and terror, namely that the same man or society of men may wear one aspect to themselves and their companions, and a different aspect to higher intelligences. Certain priests, whom he describes as conversing very learnedly together, appeared to the children who were at some distance, like dead horses; and many the like misappearances. And instantly the mind inquires whether these fishes under the bridge, yonder oxen in the pasture, those dogs in the yard, are immutably fishes, oxen and dogs, or only so appear to me, and perchance to themselves appear upright men; and whether I appear as a man to all eyes. The Brahmins and Pythagoras propounded the same question, and if any poet has witnessed the transformation he doubtless found it in harmony with various experiences. We have all seen changes as considerable in wheat and caterpillars. He is the poet and shall draw us with love and terror, who sees through the flowing vest the firm nature, and can declare it.

I look in vain for the poet whom I describe. We do not with sufficient plainness or sufficient profoundness address ourselves to life, nor dare we chaunt our own times and social circumstance. If we filled the day with bravery, we should not shrink from celebrating it. Time and nature yield us many gifts, but not yet the timely man, the new religion, the reconciler, whom all things await. Dante's praise is that he dared to write his autobiography in colossal cipher, or into universality. We have yet had no genius in America, with tyrannous eye, which knew the value of our incomparable materials, and saw, in the barbarism and materialism of the times, another carnival of the same gods whose picture he so much admires in Homer; then in the Middle Age; then in Calvinism. Banks and tariffs, the newspaper and caucus, Methodism and

Unitarianism, are flat and dull to dull people, but rest on the same foundations of wonder as the town of Troy and the temple of Delphi, and are as swiftly passing away. Our log-rolling, our stumps and their politics, our fisheries, our Negroes and Indians, our boats and our repudiations, the wrath of rogues and the pusillanimity of honest men, the northern trade, the southern planting, the western clearing, Oregon and Texas, are yet unsung. Yet America is a poem in our eyes; its ample geography dazzles the imagination, and it will not wait long for metres. If I have not found that excellent combination of gifts in my countrymen which I seek, neither could I aid myself to fix the idea of the poet by reading now and then in Chalmers's collection of five centuries of English poets. These are wits more than poets, though there have been poets among them. But when we adhere to the ideal of the poet, we have our difficulties even with Milton and Homer. Milton is too literary, and Homer too literal and historical.

But I am not wise enough for a national criticism, and must use the old largeness a little longer, to discharge my errand from the muse to the poet concerning his art.

Art is the path of the creator to his work. The paths or methods are ideal and eternal, though few men ever see them; not the artist himself for years, or for a lifetime, unless he come into the conditions. The painter, the sculptor, the composer, the epic rhapsodist, the orator, all partake one desire, namely to express themselves symmetrically and abundantly, not dwarfishly and fragmentarily. They found or put themselves in certain conditions, as, the painter and sculptor before some impressive human figures; the orator into the assembly of the people; and the others in such scenes as each has found exciting to his intellect; and each presently feels the new desire. He hears a voice, he sees a beckoning. Then he is apprised, with wonder, what herds of dæmons hem him in. He can no more rest; he says, with the old painter, "By God it is in me and must go forth of me." He pursues a beauty, half seen, which flies before him. The poet pours out verses in every solitude. Most of the things he says are conventional, no doubt; but by and by he says something which is original and beautiful. That charms him. He would say nothing else but such things. In our way of talking we say 'That is yours, this is mine;' but the poet knows well that it is not his; that it is as strange and beautiful to him as to you; he would fain hear the like eloquence at length. Once having tasted this immortal ichor, he cannot have enough of it, and as an admirable creative power exists in these intellections, it is of the last importance that these things get spoken. What a little of all we know is said! What drops of all the sea of our science are baled up! and by what accident it is that these are exposed, when so many secrets sleep in nature! Hence the necessity of speech and song; hence these throbs and heart-beatings in the orator, at the door of the assembly, to the end namely that thought may be ejaculated as Logos, or Word.

Doubt not, O poet, but persist. Say 'It is in me, and shall out.' Stand there, balked and dumb, stuttering and stammering, hissed and hooted, stand and strive, until at last rage draw out of thee that *dream*-power which every night shows thee is thine own; a power transcending all limit and privacy, and by virtue of which a man is the conductor of the whole river of electricity. Nothing walks, or creeps, or grows, or exists, which must not in turn arise and walk before him as exponent of his meaning. Comes he to that power, his genius is no longer exhaustible. All the creatures by pairs and by tribes pour into his mind as into a Noah's ark, to come forth again to people a new world. This is like the stock of air for our respiration or for the combustion of our fireplace; not a measure of gallons, but the entire atmosphere if wanted. And therefore the rich poets, as Homer, Chaucer, Shakspeare, and Raphael, have obviously no limits to their works except the limits of their lifetime, and resemble a mirror carried through the street, ready to render an image of every created thing.

O poet! a new nobility is conferred in groves and pastures, and not in castles or by the sword-blade any longer. The conditions are hard, but equal. Thou shalt leave the world, and know the muse only. Thou shalt not know any longer the times, customs, graces, politics, or opinions of men, but shalt take all from the muse. For the time of towns is tolled from the world by funereal chimes, but in nature the universal hours are counted by succeeding tribes of animals and plants, and by growth of joy on joy. God wills also that thou abdicate a manifold and duplex life, and that thou be content that others speak for thee. Others shall be thy gentlemen and shall represent all courtesy and worldly life for thee; others shall do the great and resounding actions also. Thou shalt lie close hid with nature, and canst not be afforded to the Capitol or the Exchange. The world is full of renunciations and apprenticeships, and this is thine; thou must pass for a fool and a churl for a long season. This is the screen and sheath in which Pan has protected his well-beloved flower and thou shalt be known only to thine own, and they shall console thee with tenderest love. And thou shalt not be able to rehearse the names of thy friends in thy verse, for an old shame before the holy ideal. And this is the reward; that the ideal shall be real to thee, and the impressions of the actual world shall fall like summer rain, copious, but not troublesome to thy invulnerable essence. Thou shalt have the whole land for thy park and manor, the sea for thy bath and navigation, without tax and without envy; the woods and the rivers thou shalt own, and thou shalt possess that wherein others are only tenants and boarders. Thou true land-lord! sea-lord! air-lord! Wherever snow falls or water flows or birds fly, wherever day and night meet in twilight, wherever the blue heaven is hung by clouds or sown with stars, wherever are forms with transparent boundaries, wherever are outlets into celestial space, wherever is danger, and awe, and love,—there is Beauty, plenteous as rain, shed for thee, and though thou shouldst walk the world over, thou shalt not be able to find a condition inopportune or ignoble.

NOTES

1. "An Hymn in Honour of Beauty."
2. The supporters of President William Henry Harrison organized such a spectacle in 1840.
3. In the Dedication of Chapman's *Homer.*

stands at the door by which we enter, and gives us the lethe to drink, that we may tell no tales, mixed the cup too strongly, and we cannot shake off the lethargy now at noonday. Sleep lingers all our lifetime about our eyes, as night hovers all day in the boughs of the fir-tree. All things swim and glitter. Our life is not so much threatened as our perception. Ghostlike we glide through nature, and should not know our place again. Did our birth fall in some fit of indigence and frugality in nature, that she was so sparing of her fire and so liberal of her earth that it appears to us that we lack the affirmative principle, and though we have health and reason, yet we have no superfluity of spirit for new creation? We have enough to live and bring the year about, but not an ounce to impart or to invest. Ah that our Genius were a little more of a genius! We are like millers on the lower levels of a stream, when the factories above them have exhausted the water. We too fancy that the upper people must have raised their dams.

If any of us knew what we were doing, or where we are going, then when we think we best know! We do not know to-day whether we are busy or idle. In times when we thought ourselves indolent, we have afterwards discovered that much was accomplished and much was begun in us. All our days are so unprofitable while they pass, that 't is wonderful where or when we ever got anything of this which we call wisdom, poetry, virtue. We never got it on any dated calendar day. Some heavenly days must have been intercalated somewhere, like those that Hermes won with dice of the Moon, that Osiris might be born. It is said all martyrdoms looked mean when they were suffered. Every ship is a romantic object, except that we sail in. Embark, and the romance quits our vessel and hangs on every other sail in the horizon. Our life looks trivial, and we shun to record it. Men seem to have learned of the horizon the art of perpetual retreating and reference. 'Yonder uplands are rich pasturage, and my neighbor has fertile meadow, but my field,' says the querulous farmer, 'only holds the world together.' I quote another man's saying; unluckily that other withdraws himself in the same way, and quotes me. 'T is the trick of nature thus to degrade today; a good deal of buzz, and somewhere a result slipped magically in. Every roof is agreeable to the eye until it is lifted; then we find tragedy and moaning women and hard-eyed husbands and deluges of lethe, and the men ask, 'What's the news?' as if the old were so bad. How many individuals can we count in society? how many actions? how many opinions? So much of our time is preparation, so much is routine, and so much retrospect, that the pith of each man's genius contracts itself to a very few hours. The history of literature—take the net result of Tiraboschi, Warton, or Schlegel—is a sum of very few ideas and of very few original tales; all the rest being variation of these. So in this great society wide lying around us, a critical analysis would find very few spontaneous actions. It is almost all custom and gross sense. There are even few opinions, and these seem organic in the speakers, and do not disturb the universal necessity.

What opium is instilled into all disaster! It shows formidable as we approach it, but there is at last no rough rasping friction, but the most slippery sliding surfaces; we fall soft on a thought; *Ate Dea* is gentle,—

> "Over men's heads walking aloft,
> With tender feet treading so soft."

People grieve and bemoan themselves, but it is not half so bad with them as they say. There are moods in which we court suffering, in the hope that here at least we shall find reality, sharp peaks and edges of truth. But it turns out to be scene-painting and counterfeit. The only thing grief has taught me is to know how shallow it is. That, like all the rest, plays about the surface, and never introduces me into the reality, for contact with which we would even pay the costly price of sons and lovers. Was it Boscovich who found out that bodies never come in contact? Well, souls never touch their objects. An innavigable sea washes with silent waves between us and the things we aim at and converse with. Grief too will make us idealists. In the death of my son, now more than two years ago, I seem to have lost a beautiful estate,—no more. I cannot get it nearer to me. If tomorrow I should be informed of the bankruptcy of my principal debtors, the loss of my property would be a great inconvenience to me, perhaps, for many years; but it would leave me as it found me,—neither better nor worse.

So is it with this calamity; it does not touch me; something which I fancied was a part of me, which could not be torn away without tearing me nor enlarged without enriching me, falls off from me and leaves no scar. It was caducous. I grieve that grief can teach me nothing, nor carry me one step into real nature. The Indian who was laid under a curse that the wind should not blow on him, nor water flow to him, nor fire burn him, is a type of us all. The dearest events are summer-rain, and we the Para coats that shed every drop. Nothing is left us now but death. We look to that with a grim satisfaction, saying, There at least is reality that will not dodge us.

I take this evanescence and lubricity of all objects, which lets them slip through our fingers then when we clutch hardest, to be the most unhandsome part of our condition. Nature does not like to be observed, and likes that we should be her fools and play-mates. We may have the sphere for our cricket-ball, but not a berry for our philosophy. Direct strokes she never gave us power to make; all our blows glance, all our hits are accidents. Our relations to each other are oblique and casual.

Dream delivers us to dream, and there is no end to illusion. Life is a train of moods like a string of beads, and as we pass through them they prove to be many-colored lenses which paint the world their own hue, and each shows only what lies in its focus. From the mountain you see the mountain. We animate what we can, and we see only what we animate. Nature and books belong to the eyes that see them. It depends on the mood of the man whether he shall see the sunset or the fine poem. There are always sunsets, and there is always genius; but only a few hours so serene that we can relish nature or criticism. The more or less depends on structure or temperament. Temperament is the iron wire on which the beads are strung. Of what use is fortune or talent to a cold and defective nature? Who cares what sensibility or discrimination a man has at some time shown, if he falls asleep in his chair? or if he laugh and giggle? or if he apologize? or is infected with egotism? or thinks of his dollar? or cannot go by food? or has gotten a child in his boyhood? Of what use is genius, if the organ is too convex or too concave and cannot find a focal distance within the actual horizon of human life? Of what use, if the brain is too cold or too hot, and the man does not care enough for results to stimulate him to experiment, and hold him up in it? or if the web is too finely woven, too irritable by pleasure and pain, so that life stagnates from too much reception without due outlet? Of what use to make heroic vows of amendment, if the same old law-breaker is to keep them? What cheer can the religious sentiment yield, when that is suspected to be secretly dependent on the seasons of the year and the state of the blood? I knew a witty physician who found the creed in the biliary duct, and used to affirm that if there was disease in the liver, the man became a Calvinist, and if that organ was sound, he became a Unitarian. Very mortifying is the reluctant experience that some unfriendly excess or imbecility neutralizes the promise of genius. We see young men who owe us a new world, so readily and lavishly they promise, but they never acquit the debt; they die young and dodge the account; or if they live they lose themselves in the crowd.

Temperament also enters fully into the system of illusions and shuts us in a prison of glass which we cannot see. There is an optical illusion about every person we meet. In truth they are all creatures of given temperament, which will appear in a given character, whose boundaries they will never pass; but we look at them, they seem alive, and we presume there is impulse in them. In the moment it seems impulse; in the year, in the lifetime, it turns out to be a certain uniform tune which the revolving barrel of the music-box must play. Men resist the conclusion in the morning, but adopt it as the evening wears on, that temper prevails over everything of time, place, and condition, and is inconsumable in the flames of religion. Some modifications the moral sentiment avails to impose, but the individual texture holds its dominion, if not to bias the moral judgments, yet to fix the measure of activity and of enjoyment.

I thus express the law as it is read from the platform of ordinary life, but must not leave it without noticing the capital exception. For temperament is a power which no man willingly hears any one praise but himself. On the platform of physics we cannot resist the contracting influences of so-called science. Temperament puts all divinity to rout. I know the mental proclivity of physicians.

I hear the chuckle of the phrenologists. Theoretic kidnappers and slave-drivers, they esteem each man the victim of another, who winds him round his finger by knowing the law of his being; and, by such cheap signboards as the color of his beard or the slope of his occiput, reads the inventory of his fortunes and character. The grossest ignorance does not disgust like this impudent knowingness. The physicians say they are not materialists; but they are:— Spirit is matter reduced to an extreme thinness: O *so* thin!—But the definition of *spiritual* should be, *that which is its own evidence*. What notions do they attach to love! what to religion! One would not willingly pronounce these words in their hearing, and give them the occasion to profane them. I saw a gracious gentleman who adapts his conversation to the form of the head of the man he talks with! I had fancied that the value of life lay in its inscrutable possibilities; in the fact that I never know, in addressing myself to a new individual, what may befall me. I carry the keys of my castle in my hand, ready to throw them at the feet of my lord, whenever and in what disguise soever he shall appear. I know he is in the neighborhood, hidden among vagabonds. Shall I preclude my future by taking a high seat and kindly adapting my conversation to the shape of heads? When I come to that, the doctors shall buy me for a cent.—'But, sir, medical history; the report to the Institute; the proven facts!'—I distrust the facts and the inferences. Temperament is the veto or limitation-power in the constitution, very justly applied to restrain an opposite excess in the constitution, but absurdly offered as a bar to original equity. When virtue is in presence, all subordinate powers sleep. On its own level, or in view of nature, temperament is final. I see not, if one be once caught in this trap of so-called sciences, any escape for the man from the links of the chain of physical necessity. Given such an embryo, such a history must follow. On this platform one lives in a sty of sensualism, and would soon come to suicide. But it is impossible that the creative power should exclude itself. Into every intelligence there is a door which is never closed, through which the creator passes. The intellect, seeker of absolute truth, or the heart, lover of absolute good, intervenes for our succor, and at one whisper of these high powers we awake from ineffectual struggles with this nightmare. We hurl it into its own hell, and cannot again contract ourselves to so base a state.

The secret of the illusoriness is in the necessity of a succession of moods or objects. Gladly we would anchor, but the anchorage is quicksand. This onward trick of nature is too strong for us: *Pero si muove.*[1] When at night I look at the moon and stars, I seem stationary, and they to hurry. Our love of the real draws us to permanence, but health of body consists in circulation, and sanity of mind in variety or facility of association. We need change of objects. Dedication to one thought is quickly odious. We house with the insane, and must humor them; then conversation dies out. Once I took such delight in Montaigne that I thought I should not need any other book; before that, in Shakspeare; then in Plutarch; then in Plotinus; at one time in Bacon; afterwards in Goethe; even in Bettine; but now I turn the pages of either of them languidly, whilst I still cherish their genius. So with pictures; each will bear an emphasis of attention once, which it cannot retain, though we fain would continue to be pleased in that manner. How strongly I have felt of pictures that when you have seen one well, you must take your leave of it; you shall never see it again. I have had good lessons from pictures which I have since seen without emotion or remark. A deduction must be made from the opinion which even the wise express on a new book or occurrence. Their opinion gives me tidings of their mood, and some vague guess at the new fact, but is nowise to be trusted as the lasting relation between that intellect and that thing. The child asks, 'Mamma, why don't I like the story as well as when you told it me yesterday?' Alas! child, it is even so with the oldest cherubim of knowledge. But will it answer thy question to say, Because thou wert born to a whole and this story is a particular? The reason of the pain this discovery causes us (and we make it late in respect to works of art and intellect) is the plaint of tragedy which murmurs from it in regard to persons, to friendship and love.

That immobility and absence of elasticity which we find in the arts, we find with more pain in the artist. There is no power of expansion in men. Our friends early appear to us as representatives of certain ideas which they never pass or exceed. They stand on the brink of the ocean of thought and power, but they never take the single step that would bring them there. A man is like a bit of Labrador spar, which has no lustre as you turn it in your hand until you come to a particular angle; then it shows deep and beautiful colors. There is no adaptation or universal applicability in men, but each has his special talent, and the mastery of successful men consists in adroitly keeping themselves where and when that turn shall be oftenest to be practised. We do what we must, and call it by the best names we can, and would fain have the praise of having intended the result which ensues. I cannot recall any form of man who is not superfluous sometimes. But is not this pitiful? Life is not worth the taking, to do tricks in.

Of course it needs the whole society to give the symmetry we seek. The party-colored wheel must revolve very fast to appear white. Something is earned too by conversing with so much folly and defect. In fine, whoever loses, we are always of the gaining party. Divinity is behind our failures and follies also. The plays of children are nonsense, but very educative nonsense. So it is with the largest and solemnest things, with commerce, government, church, marriage, and so with the history of every man's bread, and the ways by which he is to come by it. Like a bird which alights nowhere, but hops perpetually from bough to bough, is the Power which abides in no man and in no woman, but for a moment speaks from this one, and for another moment from that one.

But what help from these fineries or pedantries? What help from thought? Life is not dialectics. We, I think, in these times, have had lessons enough of the futility of criticism. Our young people have thought and written much on labor and reform, and for all that they have written, neither the world nor themselves have got on a step. Intellectual tasting of life will not supersede muscular activity. If a man should consider the nicety of the passage of a piece of bread down his throat, he would starve. At Education Farm the noblest theory of life sat on the noblest figures of young men and maidens, quite powerless and melancholy. It would not rake or pitch a ton of hay; it would not rub down a horse; and the men and maidens it left pale and hungry. A political orator wittily

compared our party promises to western roads, which opened
stately enough, with planted trees on either side to tempt the traveller, but soon became narrow and narrower and ended in a
squirrel-track and ran up a tree. So does culture with us; it ends in
headache. Unspeakably sad and barren does life look to those
who a few months ago were dazzled with the splendor of the
promise of the times. "There is now no longer any right course of
action nor any self-devotion left among the Iranis." Objections
and criticism we have had our fill of. There are objections to every
course of life and action, and the practical wisdom infers an indifferency, from the omnipresence of objection. The whole frame of
things preaches indifferency. Do not craze yourself with thinking,
but go about your business anywhere. Life is not intellectual or
critical, but sturdy. Its chief good is for well-mixed people who
can enjoy what they find, without question. Nature hates peeping,
and our mothers speak her very sense when they say, "Children,
eat your victuals, and say no more of it." To fill the hour,—that is
happiness; to fill the hour and leave no crevice for a repentance or
an approval. We live amid surfaces, and the true art of life is to
skate well on them. Under the oldest mouldiest conventions a
man of native force prospers just as well as in the newest world,
and that by skill of handling and treatment. He can take hold
anywhere. Life itself is a mixture of power and form, and will not
bear the least excess of either. To finish the moment, to find the
journey's end in every step of the road, to live the greatest number
of good hours, is wisdom. It is not the part of men, but of fanat-
ics, or of mathematicians if you will, to say that, the shortness of
life considered, it is not worth caring whether for so short a duration we were sprawling in want or sitting high. Since our office is
with moments, let us husband them. Five minutes of today are
worth as much to me as five minutes in the next millennium. Let
us be poised, and wise, and our own, to-day. Let us treat the men
and women well; treat them as if they were real; perhaps they are.
Men live in their fancy, like drunkards whose hands are too soft
and tremulous for successful labor. It is a tempest of fancies, and
the only ballast I know is a respect to the present hour. Without any
shadow of doubt, amidst this vertigo of shows and politics, I settle myself ever the firmer in the creed that we should not postpone

and refer and wish, but do broad justice where we are, by whomsoever we deal with, accepting our actual companions and circumstances, however humble or odious, as the mystic officials to whom the universe has delegated its whole pleasure for us. If these are mean and malignant, their contentment, which is the last victory of justice, is a more satisfying echo to the heart than the voice of poets and the casual sympathy of admirable persons. I think that however a thoughtful man may suffer from the defects and absurdities of his company, he cannot without affectation deny to any set of men and women a sensibility to extraordinary merit. The coarse and frivolous have an instinct of superiority, if they have not a sympathy, and honor it in their blind capricious way with sincere homage.

The fine young people despise life, but in me, and in such as with me are free from dyspepsia, and to whom a day is a sound and solid good, it is a great excess of politeness to look scornful and to cry for company. I am grown by sympathy a little eager and sentimental, but leave me alone and I should relish every hour and what it brought me, the potluck of the day, as heartily as the oldest gossip in the bar-room. I am thankful for small mercies. I compared notes with one of my friends who expects everything of the universe and is disappointed when anything is less than the best, and I found that I begin at the other extreme, expecting nothing, and am always full of thanks for moderate goods. I accept the clangor and jangle of contrary tendencies. I find my account in sots and bores also. They give a reality to the circumjacent picture which such a vanishing meteorous appearance can ill spare. In the morning I awake and find the old world, wife, babes and mother, Concord and Boston, the dear old spiritual world and even the dear old devil not far off. If we will take the good we find, asking no questions, we shall have heaping measures. The great gifts are not got by analysis. Everything good is on the highway. The middle region of our being is the temperate zone. We may climb into the thin and cold realm of pure geometry and lifeless science, or sink into that of sensation. Between these extremes is the equator of life, of thought, of spirit, of poetry,—a narrow belt. Moreover, in popular experience everything good is on the highway. A collector peeps into all the picture-shops of Europe for a landscape of Poussin, a crayon-sketch of Salvator; but the Transfiguration, the Last Judgment, the Communion of Saint Jerome, and what are as transcendent as these, are on the walls of the Vatican, the Uffizi, or the Louvre, where every footman may see them; to say nothing of Nature's pictures in every street, of sunsets and sunrises every day, and the sculpture of the human body never absent. A collector recently bought at public auction, in London, for one hundred and fifty-seven guineas, an autograph of Shakspeare; but for nothing a school-boy can read Hamlet and can detect secrets of highest concernment yet unpublished therein. I think I will never read any but the commonest books,—the Bible, Homer, Dante, Shakspeare and Milton. Then we are impatient of so public a life and planet, and run hither and thither for nooks and secrets. The imagination delights in the woodcraft of Indians, trappers and bee-hunters. We fancy that we are strangers, and not so intimately domesticated in the planet as the wild man and the wild beast and bird. But the exclusion reaches them also; reaches the climbing, flying, gliding, feathered and four-footed man. Fox and wood-chuck, hawk and snipe and bittern, when nearly seen, have no more root in the deep world than man, and are just such superficial tenants of the globe. Then the new molecular philosophy shows astronomical interspaces betwixt atom and atom, shows that the world is all outside; it has no inside.

The mid-world is best. Nature, as we know her, is no saint. The lights of the church, the ascetics, Gentoos and corn-eaters, she does not distinguish by any favor. She comes eating and drinking and sinning. Her darlings, the great, the strong, the beautiful, are not children of our law; do not come out of the Sunday School, nor weigh their food, nor punctually keep the commandments. If we will be strong with her strength we must not harbor such disconsolate consciences, borrowed too from the consciences of other nations. We must set up the strong present tense against all the rumors of wrath, past or to come. So many things are unsettled which it is of the first importance to settle;—and, pending their settlement, we will do as we do. Whilst the debate goes forward on the equity of commerce, and will not be closed for a century or two, New and Old England may keep shop. Law of copyright and international copyright is to be discussed, and in the interim we will sell our books for the most we can. Expediency of literature, reason of literature, lawfulness of writing down a thought, is questioned; much is to say on both sides, and, while the fight waxes hot, thou, dearest scholar, stick to thy foolish task, add a line every hour, and between whiles add a line. Right to hold land, right of property, is disputed, and the conventions convene, and before the vote is taken, dig away in your garden, and spend your earnings as a waif or godsend to all serene and beautiful purposes. Life itself is a bubble and a scepticism, and a sleep within a sleep. Grant it, and as much more as they will,—but thou, God's darling! heed thy private dream; thou wilt not be missed in the scorning and scepticism; there are enough of them; stay there in thy closet and toil until the rest are agreed what to do about it. Thy sickness, they say, and thy puny habit require that thou do this or avoid that, but know that thy life is a flitting state, a tent for a night, and do thou, sick or well, finish that stint. Thou art sick, but shalt not be worse, and the universe, which holds thee dear, shall be the better.

Human life is made up of the two elements, power and form, and the proportion must be invariably kept if we would have it sweet and sound. Each of these elements in excess makes a mischief as hurtful as its defect. Everything runs to excess; every good quality is noxious if unmixed, and, to carry the danger to the edge of ruin, nature causes each man's peculiarity to superabound. Here, among the farms, we adduce the scholars as examples of this treachery. They are nature's victims of expression. You who see the artist, the orator, the poet, too near, and find their life no more excellent than that of mechanics or farmers, and themselves victims of partiality, very hollow and haggard, and pronounce them failures, not heroes, but quacks,—conclude very reasonably that these arts are not for man, but are disease. Yet nature will not bear you out. Irresistible nature made men such, and makes legions more of such, every day. You love the boy reading in a book, gazing at a drawing or a cast; yet what are these millions who read and behold, but incipient writers and sculptors? Add a little more of that quality which now reads and sees, and they will seize the pen and chisel. And if one remembers how innocently he began to be an artist, he perceives that nature joined with his enemy. A man is a golden impossibility. The line he must walk is a hair's breadth. The wise through excess of wisdom is made a fool.

How easily, if fate would suffer it, we might keep forever these beautiful limits, and adjust ourselves, once for all, to the perfect calculation of the kingdom of known cause and effect. In the street and in the newspapers, life appears so plain a business that manly resolution and adherence to the multiplication-table through all weathers will insure success. But ah! presently comes a day, or is it only a half-hour, with its angel-whispering,—which discomfits the conclusions of nations and of years! Tomorrow again every thing looks real and angular, the habitual standards are reinstated, common-sense is as rare as genius,—is the basis of genius, and experience is hands and feet to every enterprise;— and yet, he who should do his business on this understanding would be quickly bankrupt. Power keeps quite another road than the turnpikes of choice and will; namely the subterranean and invisible tunnels and channels of life. It is ridiculous that we are diplomatists, and doctors, and considerate people; there are no dupes like these. Life is a series of surprises, and would not be worth taking or keeping if it were not. God delights to isolate us every day, and hide from us the past and the future. We would look about us, but with grand politeness he draws down before us an impenetrable screen of purest sky, and another behind us of purest sky. 'You will not remember,' he seems to say, 'and you will not expect.' All good conversation, manners and action come from a spontaneity which forgets usages and makes the moment great. Nature hates calculators; her methods are saltatory and impulsive. Man lives by pulses; our organic movements are such; and the chemical and ethereal agents are undulatory and alternate; and the mind goes antagonizing on, and never prospers but by fits. We thrive by casualties. Our chief experiences have been casual. The most attractive class of people are those who are powerful obliquely and not by the direct stroke; men of genius, but not yet accredited; one gets the cheer of their light without paying too great a tax. Theirs is the beauty of the bird or the morning light, and not of art. In the thought of genius there is always a surprise;

and the moral sentiment is well called "the newness," for it is never other; as new to the oldest intelligence as to the young child;—"the kingdom that cometh without observation." In like manner, for practical success, there must not be too much design. A man will not be observed in doing that which he can do best. There is a certain magic about his properest action which stupefies your powers of observation, so that though it is done before you, you wist not of it. The art of life has a pudency, and will not be exposed. Every man is an impossibility until he is born; every thing impossible until we see a success. The ardors of piety agree at last with the coldest scepticism,—that nothing is of us or our works,—that all is of God. Nature will not spare us the smallest leaf of laurel. All writing comes by the grace of God, and all doing and having. I would gladly be moral and keep due metes and bounds, which I dearly love, and allow the most to the will of man; but I have set my heart on honesty in this chapter, and I can see nothing at last, in success or failure, than more or less of vital force supplied from the Eternal. The results of life are uncalculated and uncalculable. The years teach much which the days never know. The persons who compose our company converse, and come and go, and design and execute many things, and somewhat comes of it all, but an unlooked-for result. The individual is always mistaken. He designed many things, and drew in other persons as coadjutors, quarrelled with some or all, blundered much, and something is done; all are a little advanced, but the individual is always mistaken. It turns out somewhat new and very unlike what he promised himself.

The ancients, struck with this irreducibleness of the elements of human life to calculation, exalted Chance into a divinity; but that is to stay too long at the spark, which glitters truly at one point, but the universe is warm with the latency of the same fire. The miracle of life which will not be expounded but will remain a miracle, introduces a new element. In the growth of the embryo, Sir Everard Home I think noticed that the evolution was not from one central point, but coactive from three or more points. Life has no memory. That which proceeds in succession might be remembered, but that which is coexistent, or ejaculated from a deeper cause, as yet far from being conscious, knows not its own tendency. So is it with us, now sceptical or without unity, because immersed in forms and effects all seeming to be of equal yet hostile value, and now religious, whilst in the reception of spiritual law. Bear with these distractions, with this coetaneous growth of the parts; they will one day be *members*, and obey one will. On that one will, on that secret cause, they nail our attention and hope. Life is hereby melted into an expectation or a religion. Underneath the inharmonious and trivial particulars, is a musical perfection; the Ideal journeying always with us, the heaven without rent or seam. Do but observe the mode of our illumination. When I converse with a profound mind, or if at any time being alone I have good thoughts, I do not at once arrive at satisfactions, as when, being thirsty, I drink water; or go to the fire, being cold; no! but I am at first apprised of my vicinity to a new and excellent region of life. By persisting to read or to think, this region gives further sign of itself, as it were in flashes of light, in sudden discoveries of its profound beauty and repose, as if the clouds that covered it parted at intervals and showed the approaching traveller the inland mountains, with the tranquil eternal meadows spread at their base, whereon flocks graze and shepherds pipe and dance. But every insight from this realm of thought is felt as initial, and promises a sequel. I do not make it; I arrive there, and behold what was there already. I make! O no! I clap my hands in infantine joy and amazement before the first opening to me of this august magnificence, old with the love and homage of innumerable ages, young with the life of life, the sun-bright Mecca of the desert. And what a future it opens! I feel a new heart beating with the love of the new beauty. I am ready to die out of nature and be born again into this new yet unapproachable America I have found in the West:—

> "Since neither now nor yesterday began
> These thoughts, which have been ever, nor yet can
> A man be found who their first entrance knew."[2]

If I have described life as a flux of moods, I must now add that there is that in us which changes not and which ranks all sensations and states of mind. The consciousness in each man is a sliding scale, which identifies him now with the First Cause, and now with the flesh of his body; life above life, in infinite degrees. The sentiment from which it sprung determines the dignity of any deed, and the question ever is, not what you have done or forborne, but at whose command you have done or forborne it.

Fortune, Minerva, Muse, Holy Ghost,—these are quaint names, too narrow to cover this unbounded substance. The baffled intellect must still kneel before this cause, which refuses to be named,—ineffable cause, which every fine genius has essayed to represent by some emphatic symbol, as, Thales by water, Anaximenes by air, Anaxagoras by (*Noûs*) thought, Zoroaster by fire, Jesus and the moderns by love; and the metaphor of each has become a national religion. The Chinese Mencius has not been the least successful in his generalization. "I fully understand language," he said, "and nourish well my vast-flowing vigor."—"I beg to ask what you call vast-flowing vigor?" said his companion. "The explanation," replied Mencius, "is difficult. This vigor is supremely great, and in the highest degree unbending. Nourish it correctly and do it no injury, and it will fill up the vacancy between heaven and earth. This vigor accords with and assists justice and reason, and leaves no hunger."—In our more correct writing we give to this generalization the name of Being, and thereby confess that we have arrived as far as we can go. Suffice it for the joy of the universe that we have not arrived at a wall, but at interminable oceans. Our life seems not present so much as prospective; not for the affairs on which it is wasted, but as a hint of this vast-flowing vigor. Most of life seems to be mere advertisement of faculty; information is given us not to sell ourselves cheap; that we are very great. So, in particulars, our greatness is always in a tendency or direction, not in an action. It is for us to believe in the rule, not in the exception. The noble are thus known from the ignoble. So in accepting the leading of the sentiments, it is not what we believe concerning the immortality of the soul or the like, but *the universal impulse to believe*, that is the material circumstance and is the principal fact in the history of the globe. Shall we describe this cause as that which works directly? The spirit is not helpless or needful of mediate organs. It has plentiful powers and direct effects. I am explained without explaining, I am felt without acting, and where I am not. Therefore all just persons are satisfied with their own praise. They refuse to explain themselves, and are content that new actions should do them that office. They believe that we communicate without speech and above speech, and that no right action of ours is quite unaffecting to our friends, at whatever distance; for the influence of action is not to be measured by miles. Why should I fret myself because a circumstance has occurred which hinders my presence where I was expected? If I am not at the meeting, my presence where I am should be as useful to the commonwealth of friendship and wisdom, as would be my presence in that place. I exert the same quality of power in all places. Thus journeys the mighty Ideal before us; it never was known to fall into the rear. No man ever came to an experience which was satiating, but his good is tidings of a better. Onward and onward! In liberated moments we know that a new picture of life and duty is already possible; the elements already exist in many minds around you of a doctrine of life which shall transcend any written record we have. The new statement will comprise the scepticisms as well as the faiths of society, and out of unbeliefs a creed shall be formed. For scepticisms are not gratuitous or lawless, but are limitations of the affirmative statement, and the new philosophy must take them in and make affirmations outside of them, just as much as it must include the oldest beliefs.

It is very unhappy, but too late to be helped, the discovery we have made that we exist. That discovery is called the Fall of Man. Ever afterwards we suspect our instruments. We have learned that we do not see directly, but mediately, and that we have no means of correcting these colored and distorting lenses which we are, or of computing the amount of their errors. Perhaps these subject-lenses have a creative power; perhaps there are no objects. Once we lived in what we saw; now, the rapaciousness of this new power, which threatens to absorb all things, engages us. Nature, art, persons, letters, religions, objects, successively tumble in, and God is but one of its ideas. Nature and literature are subjective phenomena; every evil and every good thing is a shadow which we cast. The street is full of humiliations to the proud. As the fop contrived to dress his bailiffs in his livery and make them wait on his guests at table, so the chagrins which the bad heart gives off as bubbles, at once take form as ladies and gentlemen in the street, shopmen or bar-keepers in hotels, and threaten or insult whatever is threatenable and insultable in us. 'T is the same with our idolatries. People forget that it is the eye which makes the horizon, and the rounding mind's eye which makes this or that man a type or representative of humanity, with the name of hero or saint. Jesus, the "providential man," is a good man on whom many people are agreed that these optical laws shall take effect. By love on one part and by forbearance to press objection on the other part, it is for a time settled that we will look at him in the centre of the horizon, and ascribe to him the properties that will attach to any man so seen. But the longest love or aversion has a speedy term. The great and crescive self, rooted in absolute nature, supplants all relative existence and ruins the kingdom of mortal friendship and love. Marriage (in what is called the spiritual world) is impossible, because of the inequality between every subject and every object. The subject is the receiver of Godhead, and at every comparison must feel his being enhanced by that cryptic might. Though not in energy, yet by presence, this magazine of substance cannot be otherwise than felt; nor can any force of intellect attribute to the object the proper deity which sleeps or wakes forever in every subject. Never can love make consciousness and ascription equal in force. There will be the same gulf between every me and thee as between the original and the picture. The universe is the bride of the soul. All private sympathy is partial. Two human beings are like globes, which can touch only in a point, and whilst they remain in contact all other points of each of the spheres are inert; their turn must also come, and the longer a particular union lasts the more energy of appetency the parts not in union acquire.

Life will be imaged, but cannot be divided nor doubled. Any invasion of its unity would be chaos. The soul is not twin-born but the only begotten, and though revealing itself as child in time, child in appearance, is of a fatal and universal power, admitting no co-life. Every day, every act betrays the ill-concealed deity. We believe in ourselves as we do not believe in others. We permit all things to ourselves, and that which we call sin in others is experiment for us. It is an instance of our faith in ourselves that men never speak of crime as lightly as they think; or every man thinks a latitude safe for himself which is nowise to be indulged to another. The act looks very differently on the inside and on the outside; in its quality and in its consequences. Murder in the murderer is no such ruinous thought as poets and romancers will have it; it does not unsettle him or fright him from his ordinary notice of trifles; it is an act quite easy to be contemplated; but in its sequel it turns out to be a horrible jangle and confounding of all relations. Especially the crimes that spring from love seem right and fair from the actor's point of view, but when acted are found destructive of society. No man at last believes that he can be lost, or that the crime in him is as black as in the felon. Because the intellect qualifies in our own case the moral judgments. For there is no crime to the intellect. That is antinomian or hypernomian, and judges law as well as fact. "It is worse than a crime, it is a blunder," said Napoleon, speaking the language of the intellect. To it, the world is a problem in mathematics or the science of quantity, and it leaves out praise and blame and all weak emotions. All stealing is comparative. If you come to absolutes, pray who does not steal? Saints are sad, because they behold sin (even when they speculate) from the point of view of the conscience, and not of the intellect; a confusion of thought. Sin, seen from the thought, is a diminution, or *less*; seen from the conscience or will, it is pravity or *bad*. The intellect names it shade, absence of light, and no essence. The conscience must feel it as essence, essential evil. This it is not; it has an objective existence, but no subjective.

Thus inevitably does the universe wear our color, and every object fall successively into the subject itself. The subject exists, the subject enlarges; all things sooner or later fall into place. As I am, so I see; use what language we will, we can never say anything but what we are; Hermes, Cadmus, Columbus, Newton, Bonaparte, are the mind's ministers. Instead of feeling a poverty when we encounter a great man, let us treat the new-comer like a travelling geologist who passes through our estate and shows us good slate, or limestone, or anthracite, in our brush pasture. The partial action of each strong mind in one direction is a telescope for the objects on which it is pointed. But every other part of knowledge is to be pushed to the same extravagance, ere the soul attains her due sphericity. Do you see that kitten chasing so prettily her own tail? If you could look with her eyes you might see her surrounded with hundreds of figures performing complex dramas, with tragic and comic issues, long conversations, many characters, many ups and downs of fate,—and meantime it is only puss and her tail. How long before our masquerade will end its noise of tambourines, laughter and shouting, and we shall find it was a solitary performance? A subject and an object,—it takes so much to make the galvanic circuit complete, but magnitude adds nothing. What imports it whether it is Kepler and the sphere, Columbus and America, a reader and his book, or puss with her tail?

It is true that all the muses and love and religion hate these developments, and will find a way to punish the chemist who publishes in the parlor the secrets of the laboratory. And we cannot say too little of our constitutional necessity of seeing things under private aspects, or saturated with our humors. And yet is the God the native of these bleak rocks. That need makes in morals the capital virtue of self-trust. We must hold hard to this poverty, however scandalous, and by more vigorous self-recoveries, after the sallies of action, possess our axis more firmly. The life of truth is cold and so far mournful; but it is not the slave of tears, contritions and perturbations. It does not attempt another's work, nor adopt another's facts. It is a main lesson of wisdom to know your own from another's. I have learned that I cannot dispose of other people's facts; but I possess such a key to my own as persuades me, against all their denials, that they also have a key to theirs. A sympathetic person is placed in the dilemma of a swimmer among drowning men, who all catch at him, and if he give so much as a leg or a finger they will drown him. They wish to be saved from the mischiefs of their vices, but not from their vices. Charity would be wasted on this poor waiting on the symptoms. A wise and hardy physician will say, *Come out of that*, as the first condition of advice.

In this our talking America we are ruined by our good nature and listening on all sides. This compliance takes away the power of being greatly useful. A man should not be able to look other than directly and forthright. A preoccupied attention is the only answer to the importunate frivolity of other people; an attention, and to an aim which makes their wants frivolous. This is a divine answer, and leaves no appeal and no hard thoughts. In Flaxman's drawing of the Eumenides of Æschylus, Orestes supplicates Apollo, whilst the Furies sleep on the threshold. The face of the god expresses a shade of regret and compassion, but is calm with the conviction of the irreconcilableness of the two spheres. He is born into other politics, into the eternal and beautiful. The man at his feet asks for his interest in turmoils of the earth, into which his nature cannot enter. And the Eumenides there lying express pictorially this disparity. The god is surcharged with his divine destiny.

Illusion, Temperament, Succession, Surface, Surprise, Reality, Subjectiveness,—these are threads on the loom of time, these are the lords of life. I dare not assume to give their order, but I name them as I find them in my way. I know better than to claim any completeness for my picture. I am a fragment, and this is a fragment of me. I can very confidently announce one or another law, which throws itself into relief and form, but I am too young yet by some ages to compile a code. I gossip for my hour concerning the eternal politics. I have seen many fair pictures not in vain. A wonderful time I have lived in. I am not the novice I was fourteen, nor yet seven years ago. Let who will ask, Where is the fruit? I find a private fruit sufficient. This is a fruit,—that I should not ask for a rash effect from meditations, counsels and the hiving of truths. I should feel it pitiful to demand a result on this town and country, an overt effect on the instant month and year. The effect is deep and secular as the cause. It works on periods in which mortal lifetime is lost. All I know is reception; I am and I have: but I do not get, and when I have fancied I had gotten anything, I found I did not. I worship with wonder the great Fortune. My reception has been so large, that I am not annoyed by receiving this or that superabundantly. I say to the Genius, if he will pardon the proverb, *In for a mill, in for a million*. When I receive a new gift, I do not macerate my body to make the account square, for if I should die I could not make the account square. The benefit overran the merit the first day, and has overrun the merit ever since. The merit itself, so-called, I reckon part of the receiving.

Also that hankering after an overt or practical effect seems to me an apostasy. In good earnest I am willing to spare this most unnecessary deal of doing. Life wears to me a visionary face. Hardest roughest action is visionary also. It is but a choice between soft and turbulent dreams. People disparage knowing and the intellectual life, and urge doing. I am very content with knowing, if only I could know. That is an august entertainment, and would suffice me a great while. To know a little would be worth the expense of this world. I hear always the law of Adrastia, "that every soul which had acquired any truth, should be safe from harm until another period."

I know that the world I converse with in the city and in the farms, is not the world I *think*. I observe that difference, and shall observe it. One day I shall know the value and law of this discrepance. But I have not found that much was gained by manipular attempts to realize the world of thought. Many eager persons successively make an experiment in this way, and make themselves ridiculous. They acquire democratic manners, they foam at the mouth, they hate and deny. Worse, I observe that in the history of mankind there is never a solitary example of success,—taking their own tests of success. I say this polemically, or in reply to the inquiry, Why not realize your world? But far be from me the despair which prejudges the law by a paltry empiricism;—since there never was a right endeavor but it succeeded. Patience and patience, we shall win at the last. We must be very suspicious of the deceptions of the element of time. It takes a good deal of time to eat or to sleep, or to earn a hundred dollars, and a very little time to entertain a hope and an insight which becomes the light of our life. We dress our garden, eat our dinners, discuss the household with our wives, and these things make no impression, are forgotten next week; but, in the solitude to which every man is always returning, he has a sanity and revelations which in his passage into new worlds he will carry with him. Never mind the ridicule, never mind the defeat; up again, old heart!—it seems to say,—there is victory yet for all justice; and the true romance which the world exists to realize will be the transformation of genius into practical power.

NOTES

1. "Still it moves"; Galileo's remark after retracting, before the Court of the Inquisition, his theory that the earth was not fixed but revolved around the sun.
2. Adaptation of Antigone's words in Sophocles's tragedy.

MONTAIGNE;
OR, THE SKEPTIC

Every fact is related on one side to sensation, and on the other to morals. The game of thought is, on the appearance of one of these two sides, to find the other: given the upper, to find the under side. Nothing so thin but has these two faces, and when the observer has seen the obverse, he turns it over to see the reverse. Life is a pitching of this penny,—heads or tails. We never tire of this game, because there is still a slight shudder of astonishment at the exhibition of the other face, at the contrast of the two faces. A man is flushed with success, and bethinks himself what this good luck signifies. He drives his bargain in the street; but it occurs that he also is bought and sold. He sees the beauty of a human face, and searches the cause of that beauty, which must be more beautiful. He builds his fortunes, maintains the laws, cherishes his children; but he asks himself, Why? and whereto? This head and this tail are called, in the language of philosophy, Infinite and Finite; Relative and Absolute; Apparent and Real; and many fine names beside.

Each man is born with a predisposition to one or the other of these sides of nature; and it will easily happen that men will be found devoted to one or the other. One class has the perception of difference, and is conversant with facts and surfaces, cities and persons, and the bringing certain things to pass;—the men of talent and action. Another class have the perception of identity, and are men of faith and philosophy, men of genius.

Each of these riders drives too fast. Plotinus believes only in philosophers; Fenelon, in saints; Pindar and Byron, in poets. Read the haughty language in which Plato and the Platonists speak of all men who are not devoted to their own shining abstractions: other men are rats and mice. The literary class is usually proud and exclusive. The correspondence of Pope and Swift describes mankind around them as monsters; and that of Goethe and Schiller, in our own time, is scarcely more kind.

It is easy to see how this arrogance comes. The genius is a genius by the first look he casts on any object. Is his eye creative? Does he not rest in angles and colors, but beholds the design?—he will presently undervalue the actual object. In powerful moments, his thought has dissolved the works of art and nature into their causes, so that the works appear heavy and faulty. He has a conception of beauty which the sculptor cannot embody. Picture, statue, temple, railroad, steam-engine, existed first in an artist's mind, without flaw, mistake, or friction, which impair the executed models. So did the Church, the State, college, court, social circle, and all the institutions. It is not strange that these men, remembering what they have seen and hoped of ideas, should affirm disdainfully the superiority of ideas. Having at some time seen that the happy soul will carry all the arts in power, they say, Why cumber ourselves with superfluous realizations? and like dreaming beggars they assume to speak and act as if these values were already substantiated.

On the other part, the men of toil and trade and luxury,—the animal world, including the animal in the philosopher and poet also, and the practical world, including the painful drudgeries which are never excused to philosopher or poet any more than to the rest,—weigh heavily on the other side. The trade in our streets believes in no metaphysical cause, thinks nothing of the force which necessitated traders and a trading planet to exist: no, but sticks to cotton, sugar, wool and salt. The ward meetings, on election days, are not softened by any misgiving of the value of these ballotings. Hot life is streaming in a single direction. To the men of this world, to the animal strength and spirits, to the men of practical power, whilst immersed in it, the man of ideas appears out of his reason. They alone have reason.

Things always bring their own philosophy with them, that is, prudence. No man acquires property without acquiring with it a little arithmetic also. In England, the richest country that ever existed, property stands for more, compared with personal ability, than in any other. After dinner, a man believes less, denies more: verities have lost some charm. After dinner, arithmetic is the only science; ideas are disturbing, incendiary, follies of young men, repudiated by the solid portion of society: and a man comes to be valued by his athletic and animal qualities. Spence relates that Mr. Pope was with Sir Godfrey Kneller one day, when his nephew, a Guinea trader, came in. "Nephew," said Sir Godfrey, "you have the honor of seeing the two greatest men in the world." "I don't know how great men you may be," said the Guinea man, "but I don't like your looks. I have often bought a man much better than both of you, all muscles and bones, for ten guineas." Thus the men of the senses revenge themselves on the professors and repay scorn for scorn. The first had leaped to conclusions not yet ripe, and say more than is true; the others make themselves merry with the philosopher, and weigh man by the pound. They believe that mustard bites the tongue, that pepper is hot, friction-matches incendiary, revolvers are to be avoided, and suspenders hold up pantaloons; that there is much sentiment in a chest of tea; and a man will be eloquent, if you give him good wine. Are you tender and scrupulous,—you must eat more mince-pie. They hold that Luther had milk in him when he said,—

> "Wer nicht liebt Wein, Weiber, Gesang,
> Der bleibt ein Narr sein Leben lang;"—[1]

and when he advised a young scholar, perplexed with fore-ordination and free-will, to get well drunk. "The nerves," says Cabanis, "they are the man." My neighbor, a jolly farmer, in the tavern bar-room, thinks that the use of money is sure and speedy spending. For his part, he says, he puts his down his neck and gets the good of it.

The inconvenience of this way of thinking is that it runs into indifferentism and then into disgust. Life is eating us up. We shall be fables presently. Keep cool: it will be all one a hundred years hence. Life's well enough, but we shall be glad to get out of it, and they will all be glad to have us. Why should we fret and drudge?

Our meat will taste to-morrow as it did yesterday, and we may at last have had enough of it. "Ah," said my languid gentleman at Oxford, "there's nothing new or true,—and no matter."

With a little more bitterness, the cynic moans; our life is like an ass led to market by a bundle of hay being carried before him; he sees nothing but the bundle of hay. "There is so much trouble in coming into the world," said Lord Bolingbroke, "and so much more, as well as meanness, in going out of it, that 't is hardly worth while to be here at all." I knew a philosopher of this kidney who was accustomed briefly to sum up his experience of human nature in saying, "Mankind is a damned rascal:" and the natural corollary is pretty sure to follow,—'The world lives by humbug, and so will I.'

The abstractionist and the materialist thus mutually exasperating each other, and the scoffer expressing the worst of materialism, there arises a third party to occupy the middle ground between these two, the skeptic, namely. He finds both wrong by being in extremes. He labors to plant his feet, to be the beam of the balance. He will not go beyond his card. He sees the one-sidedness of these men of the street; he will not be a Gibeonite; he stands for the intellectual faculties, a cool head and whatever serves to keep it cool; no unadvised industry, no unrewarded self-devotion, no loss of the brains in toil. Am I an ox, or a dray?—You are both in extremes, he says. You that will have all solid, and a world of pig-lead, deceive yourselves grossly. You believe yourselves rooted and grounded on adamant; and yet, if we uncover the last facts of our knowledge, you are spinning like bubbles in a river, you know not whither or whence, and you are bottomed and capped and wrapped in delusions. Neither will he be betrayed to a book and wrapped in a gown. The studious class are their own victims; they are thin and pale, their feet are cold, their heads are hot, the night is without sleep, the day a fear of interruption,—pallor, squalor, hunger and egotism. If you come near them and see what conceits they entertain,—they are abstractionists, and spend their days and nights in dreaming some dream; in expecting the homage of society to some precious scheme, built on a truth, but destitute of proportion in its presentment, of justness in its application, and of all energy of will in the schemer to embody and vitalize it.

But I see plainly, he says, that I cannot see. I know that human strength is not in extremes, but in avoiding extremes. I, at least, will shun the weakness of philosophizing beyond my depth. What is the use of pretending to powers we have not? What is the use of pretending to assurances we have not, respecting the other life? Why exaggerate the power of virtue? Why be an angel before your time? These strings, wound up too high, will snap. If there is a wish for immortality, and no evidence, why not say just that? If there are conflicting evidences, why not state them? If there is not ground for a candid thinker to make up his mind, yea or nay,— why not suspend the judgment? I weary of these dogmatizers. I tire of these hacks of routine, who deny the dogmas. I neither affirm nor deny. I stand here to try the case. I am here to consider, σκοπεῖν,[2] to consider how it is. I will try to keep the balance true. Of what use to take the chair and glibly rattle off theories of society, religion and nature, when I know that practical objections lie in the way, insurmountable by me and by my mates? Why so talkative in public, when each of my neighbors can pin me to my seat by arguments I cannot refute? Why pretend that life is so simple a game, when we know how subtle and elusive the Proteus is? Why think to shut up all things in your narrow coop, when we know there are not one or two only, but ten, twenty, a thousand things, and unlike? Why fancy that you have all the truth in your keeping? There is much to say on all sides.

Who shall forbid a wise skepticism, seeing that there is no practical question on which any thing more than an approximate solution can be had? Is not marriage an open question, when it is alleged, from the beginning of the world, that such as are in the institution wish to get out, and such as are out wish to get in? And the reply of Socrates, to him who asked whether he should choose a wife, still remains reasonable, that "whether he should choose one or not, he would repent it," Is not the State a question? All society is divided in opinion on the subject of the State. Nobody loves it; great numbers dislike it and suffer conscientious scruples to allegiance; and the only defence set up, is the fear of doing worse in disorganizing. Is it otherwise with the Church? Or, to put any of the questions which touch mankind nearest,—shall the young man aim at a leading part in law, in politics, in trade? It will not be pretended that a success in either of these kinds is quite coincident with what is best and inmost in his mind. Shall he then, cutting the stays that hold him fast to the social state, put out to sea with no guidance but his genius? There is much to say on both sides. Remember the open question between the present order of "competition" and the friends of "attractive and associated labor." The generous minds embrace the proposition of labor shared by all; it is the only honesty; nothing else is safe. It is from the poor man's hut alone that strength and virtue come: and yet, on the other side, it is alleged that labor impairs the form and breaks the spirit of man, and the laborers cry unanimously, 'We have no thoughts.' Culture, how indispensable! I cannot forgive you the want of accomplishments; and yet culture will instantly impair that chiefest beauty of spontaneousness. Excellent is culture for a savage; but once let him read in the book, and he is no longer able not to think of Plutarch's heroes. In short, since true fortitude of understanding consists "in not letting what we know be embarrassed by what we do not know," we ought to secure those advantages which we can command, and not risk them by clutching after the airy and unattainable. Come, no chimeras! Let us go abroad; let us mix in affairs; let us learn and get and have and climb. "Men are a sort of moving plants, and, like trees, receive a great part of their nourishment from the air. If they keep too much at home, they pine." Let us have a robust, manly life; let us know what we know, for certain; what we have, let it be solid and seasonable and our own. A world in the hand is worth two in the bush. Let us have to do with real men and women, and not with skipping ghosts.

This then is the right ground of the skeptic,—this of consideration, of self-containing; not at all of unbelief; not at all of universal denying, nor of universal doubting,—doubting even that he doubts; least of all of scoffing and profligate jeering at all that is stable and good. These are no more his moods than are those of religion and philosophy. He is the considerer, the prudent, taking in sail, counting stock, husbanding his means, believing that a man has too many enemies than that he can afford to be his own foe; that we cannot give ourselves too many advantages in this unequal conflict, with powers so vast and unweariable ranged on one side, and this little conceited vulnerable popinjay that a man is, bobbing up and down into every danger, on the other. It is a position taken up for better defence, as of more safety, and one that can be maintained; and it is one of more opportunity and range: as, when we build a house, the rule is to set it not too high nor too low, under the wind, but out of the dirt.

The philosophy we want is one of fluxions and mobility. The Spartan and Stoic schemes are too stark and stiff for our occasion. A theory of Saint John, and of non-resistance, seems, on the other hand, too thin and aerial. We want some coat woven of elastic steel, stout as the first and limber as the second. We want a ship in these billows we inhabit. An angular, dogmatic house would be rent to chips and splinters in this storm of many elements. No, it must be tight, and fit to the form of man, to live at all; as a shell must dictate the architecture of a house founded on the sea. The soul of man must be the type of our scheme, just as the body of man is the type after which a dwelling-house is built. Adaptiveness is the peculiarity of human nature. We are golden averages, volitant stabilities, compensated or periodic errors, houses founded on the sea. The wise skeptic wishes to have a near view of the best game and the chief players; what is best in the planet; art and nature, places and events; but mainly men. Every thing that is excellent in mankind,—a form of grace, an arm of iron, lips of persuasion, a brain of resources, every one skilful to play and win,—he will see and judge.

The terms of admission to this spectacle are, that he have a certain solid and intelligible way of living of his own; some method of answering the inevitable needs of human life; proof that he has played with skill and success; that he has evinced the temper, stoutness and the range of qualities which, among his contemporaries and countrymen, entitle him to fellowship and trust. For the secrets of life are not shown except to sympathy and likeness. Men do not confide themselves to boys, or coxcombs, or pedants, but to their peers. Some wise limitation, as the modern phrase is; some condition between the extremes, and having, itself, a positive quality; some stark and sufficient man, who is not salt or sugar, but sufficiently related to the world to do justice to Paris or London, and, at the same time, a vigorous and original thinker, whom cities can not overawe, but who uses them,—is the fit person to occupy this ground of speculation.

These qualities meet in the character of Montaigne. And yet, since the personal regard which I entertain for Montaigne may be unduly great, I will, under the shield of this prince of egotists, offer, as an apology for electing him as the representative of skepticism, a word or two to explain how my love began and grew for this admirable gossip.

A single odd volume of Cotton's translation of the Essays remained to me from my father's library, when a boy. It lay long neglected, until, after many years, when I was newly escaped from college, I read the book, and procured the remaining volumes. I remember the delight and wonder in which I lived with it. It seemed to me as if I had myself written the book, in some former life, so sincerely it spoke to my thought and experience. It happened, when in Paris, in 1833, that, in the cemetery of Père Lachaise, I came to a tomb of Auguste Collignon, who died in 1830, aged sixty-eight years, and who, said the monument, "lived to do right, and had formed himself to virtue on the Essays of Montaigne." Some years later, I became acquainted with an accomplished English poet, John Sterling; and, in prosecuting my correspondence, I found that, from a love of Montaigne, he had made a pilgrimage to his chateau, still standing near Castellan, in Périgord, and, after two hundred and fifty years, had copied from the walls of his library the inscriptions which Montaigne had written there. That Journal of Mr. Sterling's, published in the Westminster Review, Mr. Hazlitt has reprinted in the *Prolegomena* to his edition of the Essays. I heard with pleasure that one of the newly-discovered autographs of William Shakspeare was in a copy of Florio's translation of Montaigne. It is the only book which we certainly know to have been in the poet's library. And, oddly enough, the duplicate copy of Florio, which the British Museum purchased with a view of protecting the Shakspeare autograph (as I was informed in the Museum), turned out to have the autograph of Ben Jonson in the fly-leaf. Leigh Hunt relates of Lord Byron, that Montaigne was the only great writer of past times whom he read with avowed satisfaction. Other coincidences, not needful to be mentioned here, concurred to make this old Gascon still new and immortal to me.

In 1571, on the death of his father, Montaigne, then thirty-eight years old, retired from the practice of law at Bordeaux, and settled himself on his estate. Though he had been a man of pleasure and sometimes a courtier, his studious habits now grew on him, and he loved the compass, staidness and independence of the country gentleman's life. He took up his economy in good earnest, and made his farms yield the most. Downright and plaindealing, and abhorring to be deceived or to deceive, he was esteemed in the country for his sense and probity. In the civil wars of the League, which converted every house into a fort, Montaigne kept his gates open and his house without defence. All parties freely came and went, his courage and honor being universally esteemed. The neighboring lords and gentry brought jewels and papers to him for safe-keeping. Gibbon reckons, in these bigoted times, but two men of liberality in France,—Henry IV. and Montaigne.

Montaigne is the frankest and honestest of all writers. His French freedom runs into grossness; but he has anticipated all censure by the bounty of his own confessions. In his times, books were written to one sex only, and almost all were written in Latin; so that in a humorist a certain nakedness of statement was permitted, which our manners, of a literature addressed equally to both sexes, do not allow. But though a biblical plainness coupled with a most uncanonical levity may shut his pages to many sensitive readers, yet the offence is superficial. He parades it: he makes the most of it: nobody can think or say worse of him than he does. He pretends to most of the vices; and, if there be any virtue in him, he says, it got in by stealth. There is no man, in his opinion, who has not deserved hanging five or six times; and he pretends no exception in his own behalf. "Five or six as ridiculous stories," too, he says, "can be told of me, as of any man living." But, with all this really superfluous frankness, the opinion of an invincible probity grows into every reader's mind. "When I the most strictly and religiously confess myself, I find that the best virtue I have has in it some tincture of vice; and I, who am as sincere and perfect a lover of virtue of that stamp as any other whatever, am afraid that Plato, in his purest virtue, if he had listened and laid his ear close to himself, would have heard some jarring sound of human mixture; but faint and remote and only to be perceived by himself."

Here is an impatience and fastidiousness at color or pretence of any kind. He has been in courts so long as to have conceived a furious disgust at appearances; he will indulge himself with a little cursing and swearing; he will talk with sailors and gipsies, use flash and street ballads; he has stayed in-doors till he is deadly sick; he will to the open air, though it rain bullets. He has seen too much of gentlemen of the long robe, until he wishes for cannibals; and is so nervous, by factitious life, that he thinks the more barbarous man is, the better he is. He likes his saddle. You may read theology, and grammar, and metaphysics elsewhere. Whatever you get here shall smack of the earth and of real life, sweet, or smart, or stinging. He makes no hesitation to entertain you with the records of his disease, and his journey to Italy is quite full of that matter. He took and kept this position of equilibrium. Over his name he drew an emblematic pair of scales, and wrote *Que sçais je?*³ under it. As I look at his effigy opposite the title-page, I seem to hear him say, 'You may play old Poz,⁴ if you will; you may rail and exaggerate,—I stand here for truth, and will not, for all the states and churches and revenues and personal reputations of Europe, overstate the dry fact, as I see it; I will rather mumble and prose about what I certainly know,—my house and barns; my father, my wife and my tenants; my old lean bald pate; my knives and forks; what meats I eat and what drinks I prefer, and a hundred straws just as ridiculous,—than I will write, with a fine crow-quill, a fine romance. I like gray days, and autumn and winter weather. I am gray and autumnal myself, and think an undress and old shoes that do not pinch my feet, and old friends who do not constrain me, and plain topics where I do not need to strain myself and pump my brains, the most suitable. Our condition as men is risky and ticklish enough. One cannot be sure of himself and his fortune an hour, but he may be whisked off into some pitiable or ridiculous plight. Why should I vapor and play the philosopher, instead of ballasting, the best I can, this dancing balloon? So, at least, I live within compass, keep myself ready for action, and can shoot the gulf at last with decency. If there be anything farcical in such a life, the blame is not mine; let it lie at fate's and nature's door.'

The Essays, therefore, are an entertaining soliloquy on every random topic that comes into his head; treating every thing without ceremony, yet with masculine sense. There have been men with deeper insight; but, one would say, never a man with such abundance of thoughts: he is never dull, never insincere, and has the genius to make the reader care for all that he cares for.

The sincerity and marrow of the man reaches to his sentences. I know not anywhere the book that seems less written. It is the language of conversation transferred to a book. Cut these words, and they would bleed; they are vascular and alive. One has the same pleasure in it that he feels in listening to the necessary speech of men about their work, when any unusual circumstance gives momentary importance to the dialogue. For blacksmiths and teamsters do not trip in their speech; it is a shower of bullets. It is Cambridge men who correct themselves and begin again at every half sentence, and, moreover, will pun, and refine too much, and swerve from the matter to the expression. Montaigne talks with shrewdness, knows the world and books and himself, and uses the positive degree; never shrieks, or protests, or prays: no weakness, no convulsion, no superlative: does not wish to jump out of his skin, or play any antics, or annihilate space or time, but is stout and solid; tastes every moment of the day; likes pain because it makes him feel himself and realize things; as we pinch ourselves to know that we are awake. He keeps the plain; he rarely mounts or sinks; likes to feel solid ground and the stones underneath. His writing has no enthusiasms, no aspiration; contented, self-respecting and keeping the middle of the road. There is but one exception,— in his love for Socrates. In speaking of him, for once his cheek flushes and his style rises to passion.

Montaigne died of a quinsy, at the age of sixty, in 1592. When he came to die he caused the mass to be celebrated in his chamber. At the age of thirty-three, he had been married. "But," he says, "might I have had my own will, I would not have married Wisdom herself, if she would have had me: but 't is to much purpose to evade it, the common custom and use of life will have it so. Most of my actions are guided by example, not choice." In the hour of death, he gave the same weight to custom. *Que sçais je?* What do I know?

This book of Montaigne the world has endorsed by translating it into all tongues and printing seventy-five editions of it in Europe; and that, too, a circulation somewhat chosen, namely among courtiers, soldiers, princes, men of the world and men of wit and generosity.

Shall we say that Montaigne has spoken wisely, and given the right and permanent expression of the human mind, on the conduct of life?

We are natural believers. Truth, or the connection between cause and effect, alone interests us. We are persuaded that a thread runs through all things: all worlds are strung on it, as beads; and men, and events, and life, come to us only because of that thread: they pass and repass only that we may know the direction and continuity of that line. A book or statement which goes to show that there is no line, but random and chaos, a calamity out of nothing, a prosperity and no account of it, a hero born from a fool, a fool from a hero,—dispirits us. Seen or unseen, we believe the tie exists. Talent makes counterfeit ties; genius finds the real ones. We hearken to the man of science, because we anticipate the sequence in natural phenomena which he uncovers. We love whatever affirms, connects, preserves; and dislike what scatters or pulls down. One man appears whose nature is to all men's eyes conserving and constructive; his presence supposes a well-ordered society, agriculture, trade, large institutions and empire. If these did not exist, they would begin to exist through his endeavors. Therefore he cheers and comforts men, who feel all this in him very readily. The nonconformist and the rebel say all manner of unanswerable things against the existing republic, but discover to our sense no plan of house or state of their own. Therefore, though the town and state and way of living, which our counsellor contemplated, might be a very modest or musty prosperity, yet men rightly go for him, and reject the reformer so long as he comes only with axe and crowbar.

But though we are natural conservers and causationists, and reject a sour, dumpish unbelief, the skeptical class, which Montaigne represents, have reason, and every man, at some time, belongs to it. Every superior mind will pass through this domain of equilibration,—I should rather say, will know how to avail himself of the checks and balances in nature, as a natural weapon against the exaggeration and formalism of bigots and blockheads.

Skepticism is the attitude assumed by the student in relation to the particulars which society adores, but which he sees to be reverend only in their tendency and spirit. The ground occupied by the skeptic is the vestibule of the temple. Society does not like to have any breath of question blown on the existing order. But the interrogation of custom at all points is an inevitable stage in the growth of every superior mind, and is the evidence of its perception of the flowing power which remains itself in all changes.

The superior mind will find itself equally at odds with the evils of society and with the projects that are offered to relieve them. The wise skeptic is a bad citizen; no conservative, he sees the selfishness of property and the drowsiness of institutions. But neither is he fit to work with any democratic party that ever was constituted; for parties wish every one committed, and he penetrates the popular patriotism. His politics are those of the "Soul's Errand" of Sir Walter Raleigh; or of Krishna, in the Bhagavat, "There is none who is worthy of my love or hatred;" whilst he sentences law, physic, divinity, commerce and custom. He is a reformer; yet he is no better member of the philanthropic association. It turns out that he is not the champion of the operative, the pauper, the prisoner, the slave. It stands in his mind that our life in this world is not of quite so easy interpretation as churches and school-books say. He does not wish to take ground against these benevolences, to play the part of devil's attorney, and blazon every doubt and sneer that darkens the sun for him. But he says, There are doubts.

I mean to use the occasion, and celebrate the calendar-day of our Saint Michel de Montaigne, by counting and describing these doubts or negations. I wish to ferret them out of their holes and

sun them a little. We must do with them as the police do with old
rogues, who are shown up to the public at the marshal's office.
They will never be so formidable when once they have been identified and registered. But I mean honestly by them,—that justice
shall be done to their terrors. I shall not take Sunday objections,
made up on purpose to be put down. I shall take the worst I can
find, whether I can dispose of them or they of me.

I do not press the skepticism of the materialist. I know the
quadruped opinion will not prevail. 'T is of no importance what
bats and oxen think. The first dangerous symptom I report is, the
levity of intellect; as if it were fatal to earnestness to know much.
Knowledge is the knowing that we can not know. The dull pray;
the geniuses are light mockers. How respectable is earnestness on
every platform! but intellect kills it. Nay, San Carlo,⁵ my subtle
and admirable friend, one of the most penetrating of men, finds
that all direct ascension, even of lofty piety, leads to this ghastly
insight and sends back the votary orphaned. My astonishing San
Carlo thought the lawgivers and saints infected. They found the
ark empty; saw, and would not tell; and tried to choke off their
approaching followers, by saying, 'Action, action, my dear fellows, is for you!' Bad as was to me this detection by San Carlo,
this frost in July, this blow from a bride, there was still a worse,
namely the cloy or satiety of the saints. In the mount of vision, ere
they have yet risen from their knees, they say, 'We discover that
this our homage and beatitude is partial and deformed: we must
fly for relief to the suspected and reviled Intellect, to the Understanding, the Mephistopheles, to the gymnastics of talent.'

This is hobgoblin the first; and though it has been the subject of
much elegy in our nineteenth century, from Byron, Goethe and
other poets of less fame, not to mention many distinguished private observers,—I confess it is not very affecting to my imagination; for it seems to concern the shattering of baby-houses and
crockery-shops. What flutters the Church of Rome, or of England, or of Geneva, or of Boston, may yet be very far from touching any principle of faith. I think that the intellect and moral
sentiment are unanimous; and that though philosophy extirpates
bugbears, yet it supplies the natural checks of vice, and polarity to
the soul. I think that the wiser a man is, the more stupendous he

finds the natural and moral economy, and lifts himself to a more absolute reliance.

There is the power of moods, each setting at nought all but its own tissue of facts and beliefs. There is the power of complexions, obviously modifying the dispositions and sentiments. The beliefs and unbeliefs appear to be structural; and as soon as each man attains the poise and vivacity which allow the whole machinery to play, he will not need extreme examples, but will rapidly alternate all opinions in his own life. Our life is March weather, savage and serene in one hour. We go forth austere, dedicated, believing in the iron links of Destiny, and will not turn on our heel to save our life: but a book, or a bust, or only the sound of a name, shoots a spark through the nerves, and we suddenly believe in will: my finger-ring shall be the seal of Solomon; fate is for imbeciles; all is possible to the resolved mind. Presently a new experience gives a new turn to our thoughts: common sense resumes its tyranny; we say, 'Well, the army, after all, is the gate to fame, manners and poetry: and, look you,—on the whole, selfishness plants best, prunes best, makes the best commerce and the best citizen.' Are the opinions of a man on right and wrong, on fate and causation, at the mercy of a broken sleep or an indigestion? Is his belief in God and Duty no deeper than a stomach evidence? And what guaranty for the permanence of his opinions? I like not the French celerity,—a new Church and State once a week. This is the second negation; and I shall let it pass for what it will. As far as it asserts rotation of states of mind, I suppose it suggests its own remedy, namely in the record of larger periods. What is the mean of many states; of all the states? Does the general voice of ages affirm any principle, or is no community of sentiment discoverable in distant times and places? And when it shows the power of self-interest, I accept that as part of the divine law and must reconcile it with aspiration the best I can.

The word Fate, or Destiny, expresses the sense of mankind, in all ages, that the laws of the world do not always befriend, but often hurt and crush us. Fate, in the shape of *Kinde* or nature, grows over us like grass. We paint Time with a scythe; Love and Fortune, blind; and Destiny, deaf. We have too little power of resistance against this ferocity which champs us up. What front can we make against these unavoidable, victorious, maleficent forces? What can I do against the influence of Race, in my history? What can I do against hereditary and constitutional habits; against scrofula, lymph, impotence? against climate, against barbarism, in my country? I can reason down or deny every thing, except this perpetual Belly: feed he must and will, and I cannot make him respectable.

But the main resistance which the affirmative impulse finds, and one including all others, is in the doctrine of the Illusionists. There is a painful rumor in circulation that we have been practised upon in all the principal performances of life, and free agency is the emptiest name. We have been sopped and drugged with the air, with food, with woman, with children, with sciences, with events, which leave us exactly where they found us. The mathematics, 't is complained, leave the mind where they find it: so do all sciences; and so do all events and actions. I find a man who has passed through all the sciences, the churl he was; and, through all the offices, learned, civil and social, can detect the child. We are not the less necessitated to dedicate life to them. In fact we may come to accept it as the fixed rule and theory of our state of education, that God is a substance, and his method is illusion. The Eastern sages owned the goddess Yoganidra, the great illusory energy of Vishnu, by whom, as utter ignorance, the whole world is beguiled.

Or shall I state it thus?—The astonishment of life is the absence of any appearance of reconciliation between the theory and practice of life. Reason, the prized reality, the Law, is apprehended, now and then, for a serene and profound moment amidst the hubbub of cares and works which have no direct bearing on it;—is then lost for months or years, and again found for an interval, to be lost again. If we compute it in time, we may, in fifty years, have half a dozen reasonable hours. But what are these cares and works the better? A method in the world we do not see, but this parallelism of great and little, which never react on each other, nor discover the smallest tendency to converge. Experiences, fortunes, governings, readings, writings, are nothing to the purpose; as when a man comes into the room it does not appear whether he has been fed on yams or buffalo,—he has contrived to get so much bone and fibre as he wants, out of rice or out of snow. So vast is the disproportion between the sky of law and the pismire of performance under it, that whether he is a man of worth or a sot is not so great a matter as we say. Shall I add, as one juggle of this enchantment, the stunning non-intercourse law which makes co-operation impossible? The young spirit pants to enter society. But all the ways of culture and greatness lead to solitary imprisonment. He has been often baulked. He did not expect a sympathy with his thought from the village, but he went with it to the chosen and intelligent, and found no entertainment for it, but mere misapprehension, distaste and scoffing. Men are strangely mistimed and misapplied; and the excellence of each is an inflamed individualism which separates him more.

There are these, and more than these diseases of thought, which our ordinary teachers do not attempt to remove. Now shall we, because a good nature inclines us to virtue's side, say, There are no doubts,—and lie for the right? Is life to be led in a brave or in a cowardly manner? and is not the satisfaction of the doubts essential to all manliness? Is the name of virtue to be a barrier to that which is virtue? Can you not believe that a man of earnest and burly habit may find small good in tea, essays and catechism, and want a rougher instruction, want men, labor, trade, farming, war, hunger, plenty, love, hatred, doubt and terror to make things plain to him; and has he not a right to insist on being convinced in his own way? When he is convinced, he will be worth the pains.

Belief consists in accepting the affirmations of the soul; unbelief, in denying them. Some minds are incapable of skepticism. The doubts they profess to entertain are rather a civility or accommodation to the common discourse of their company. They may well give themselves leave to speculate, for they are secure of a return. Once admitted to the heaven of thought, they see no relapse into night, but infinite invitation on the other side. Heaven is within heaven, and sky over sky, and they are encompassed with divinities. Others there are to whom the heaven is brass, and it shuts down to the surface of the earth. It is a question of temperament, or of more or less immersion in nature. The last class must needs have a reflex or parasite faith; not a sight of realities, but an instinctive reliance on the seers and believers of realities. The manners and thoughts of believers astonish them and convince them that these have seen something which is hid from themselves. But their sensual habit would fix the believer to his last position, whilst he as inevitably advances; and presently the unbeliever, for love of belief, burns the believer.

Great believers are always reckoned infidels, impracticable, fantastic, atheistic, and really men of no account. The spiritualist finds himself driven to express his faith by a series of skepticisms. Charitable souls come with their projects and ask his co-operation. How can he hesitate? It is the rule of mere comity and courtesy to agree where you can, and to turn your sentence with something auspicious, and not freezing and sinister. But he is forced to say, 'O, these things will be as they must be: what can you do? These particular griefs and crimes are the foliage and fruit of such trees as we see growing. It is vain to complain of the leaf or the berry; cut it off, it will bear another just as bad. You must begin your cure lower down.' The generosities of the day prove an intractable element for him. The people's questions are not his; their methods are not his; and against all the dictates of good nature he is driven to say he has no pleasure in them.

Even the doctrines dear to the hope of man, of the divine Providence and of the immortality of the soul, his neighbors can not put the statement so that he shall affirm it. But he denies out of more faith, and not less. He denies out of honesty. He had rather stand charged with the imbecility of skepticism, than with untruth. I believe, he says, in the moral design of the universe; it exists hospitably for the weal of souls; but your dogmas seem to me caricatures: why should I make believe them? Will any say, This is cold and infidel? The wise and magnanimous will not say so. They will exult in his far-sighted good-will that can abandon to the adversary all the ground of tradition and common belief, without losing a jot of strength. It sees to the end of all transgression. George Fox saw that there was "an ocean of darkness and death; but withal an infinite ocean of light and love which flowed over that of darkness."

The final solution in which skepticism is lost, is in the moral sentiment, which never forfeits its supremacy. All moods may be safely tried, and their weight allowed to all objections: the moral sentiment as easily outweighs them all, as any one. This is the drop which balances the sea. I play with the miscellany of facts, and take those superficial views which we call skepticism; but I know that they will presently appear to me in that order which makes skepticism impossible. A man of thought must feel the thought that is parent of the universe; that the masses of nature do undulate and flow.

This faith avails to the whole emergency of life and objects. The world is saturated with deity and with law. He is content with just and unjust, with sots and fools, with the triumph of folly and fraud. He can behold with serenity the yawning gulf between the ambition of man and his power of performance, between the demand and supply of power, which makes the tragedy of all souls.

Charles Fourier announced that "the attractions of man are proportioned to his destinies;" in other words, that every desire predicts its own satisfaction. Yet all experience exhibits the reverse of this; the incompetency of power is the universal grief of young and ardent minds. They accuse the divine Providence of a certain parsimony. It has shown the heaven and earth to every child and filled him with a desire for the whole; a desire raging, infinite; a hunger, as of space to be filled with planets; a cry of famine, as of devils for souls. Then for the satisfaction,—to each man is administered a single drop, a bead of dew of vital power, *per day*,—a cup as large as space, and one drop of the water of life in it. Each man woke in the morning with an appetite that could eat the solar system like a cake; a spirit for action and passion without bounds; he could lay his hand on the morning star; he could try conclusions with gravitation or chemistry; but, on the first motion to prove his strength,—hands, feet, senses, gave way and would not serve him. He was an emperor deserted by his states, and left to whistle by himself, or thrust into a mob of emperors, all whistling: and still the sirens sang, "The attractions are proportioned to the destinies." In every house, in the heart of each maiden and of each boy, in the soul of the soaring saint, this chasm is found,— between the largest promise of ideal power, and the shabby experience.

The expansive nature of truth comes to our succor, elastic, not to be surrounded. Man helps himself by larger generalizations. The lesson of life is practically to generalize; to believe what the years and the centuries say, against the hours; to resist the usurpation of particulars; to penetrate to their catholic sense. Things seem to say one thing, and say the reverse. The appearance is immoral; the result is moral. Things seem to tend downward, to justify despondency, to promote rogues, to defeat the just; and by knaves as by martyrs the just cause is carried forward. Although knaves win in every political struggle, although society seems to be delivered over from the hands of one set of criminals into the hands of another set of criminals, as fast as the government is changed, and the march of civilization is a train of felonies,—yet, general ends are somehow answered. We see, now, events forced on which seem to retard or retrograde the civility of ages. But the world-spirit is a good swimmer, and storms and waves cannot drown him. He snaps his finger at laws: and so, throughout history, heaven seems to affect low and poor means. Through the years and the centuries, through evil agents, through toys and atoms, a great and beneficent tendency irresistibly streams.

Let a man learn to look for the permanent in the mutable and fleeting; let him learn to bear the disappearance of things he was wont to reverence without losing his reverence; let him learn that he is here, not to work but to be worked upon; and that, though abyss open under abyss, and opinion displace opinion, all are at last contained in the Eternal Cause.—

"If my bark sink, 't is to another sea."[6]

NOTES

1. "Who does not love wine, women, song, Remains a fool his whole life long."
2. *Skopein*—to look out.
3. "What do I know?"

4. A character in Maria Edgeworth's stories for children who was positive about his knowledge of all matters.

5. Charles K. Newcomb, a mystic who published a few pieces in the *Dial*, but who showed Emerson his unpublished writings on his visits to him.

6. "A Poet's Hope," by William Ellery Channing, nephew of the great Unitarian minister of the same name.

NAPOLEON; OR,
THE MAN OF THE WORLD

Among the eminent persons of the nineteenth century, Bonaparte is far the best known and the most powerful; and owes his predominance to the fidelity with which he expresses the tone of thought and belief, the aims of the masses of active and cultivated men. It is Swedenborg's theory that every organ is made up of homogeneous particles; or as it is sometimes expressed, every whole is made of similars; that is, the lungs are composed of infinitely small lungs; the liver, of infinitely small livers; the kidney, of little kidneys, etc. Following this analogy, if any man is found to carry with him the power and affections of vast numbers, if Napoleon is France, if Napoleon is Europe, it is because the people whom he sways are little Napoleons.

In our society there is a standing antagonism between the conservative and the democratic classes; between those who have made their fortunes, and the young and the poor who have fortunes to make; between the interests of dead labor,—that is, the labor of hands long ago still in the grave, which labor is now entombed in money stocks, or in land and buildings owned by idle capitalists,—and the interests of living labor, which seeks to possess itself of land and buildings and money stocks. The first class is timid, selfish, illiberal, hating innovation, and continually losing numbers by death. The second class is selfish also, encroaching, bold, self-relying, always outnumbering the other and recruiting its numbers every hour by births. It desires to keep open every avenue to the competition of all, and to multiply avenues: the class of business men in America, in England, in France and throughout

Europe; the class of industry and skill. Napoleon is its representative. The instinct of active, brave, able men, throughout the middle class every where, has pointed out Napoleon as the incarnate Democrat. He had their virtues and their vices; above all, he had their spirit or aim. That tendency is material, pointing at a sensual success and employing the richest and most various means to that end; conversant with mechanical powers, highly intellectual, widely and accurately learned and skilful, but subordinating all intellectual and spiritual forces into means to a material success. To be the rich man, is the end. "God has granted," says the Koran, "to every people a prophet in its own tongue." Paris and London and New York, the spirit of commerce, of money and material power, were also to have their prophet; and Bonaparte was qualified and sent.

Every one of the million readers of anecdotes or memoirs or lives of Napoleon, delights in the page, because he studies in it his own history. Napoleon is thoroughly modern, and, at the highest point of his fortunes, has the very spirit of the newspapers. He is no saint,—to use his own word, "no capuchin," and he is no hero, in the high sense. The man in the street finds in him the qualities and powers of other men in the street. He finds him, like himself, by birth a citizen, who, by very intelligible merits, arrived at such a commanding position that he could indulge all those tastes which the common man possesses but is obliged to conceal and deny: good society, good books, fast travelling, dress, dinners, servants without number, personal weight, the execution of his ideas, the standing in the attitude of a benefactor to all persons about him, the refined enjoyments of pictures, statues, music, palaces and conventional honors,—precisely what is agreeable to the heart of every man in the nineteenth century, this powerful man possessed.

It is true that a man of Napoleon's truth of adaptation to the mind of the masses around him, becomes not merely representative but actually a monopolizer and usurper of other minds. Thus Mirabeau plagiarized every good thought, every good word that was spoken in France. Dumont relates that he sat in the gallery of the Convention and heard Mirabeau make a speech. It struck

Dumont that he could fit it with a peroration, which he wrote in pencil immediately, and showed it to Lord Elgin, who sat by him. Lord Elgin approved it, and Dumont, in the evening, showed it to Mirabeau. Mirabeau read it, pronounced it admirable, and declared he would incorporate it into his harangue to-morrow, to the Assembly. "It is impossible," said Dumont, "as, unfortunately, I have shown it to Lord Elgin." "If you have shown it to Lord Elgin and to fifty persons beside, I shall still speak it to-morrow:" and he did speak it, with much effect, at the next day's session. For Mirabeau, with his overpowering personality, felt that these things which his presence inspired were as much his own as if he had said them, and that his adoption of them gave them their weight. Much more absolute and centralizing was the successor to Mirabeau's popularity and to much more than his predominance in France. Indeed, a man of Napoleon's stamp almost ceases to have a private speech and opinion. He is so largely receptive, and is so placed, that he comes to be a bureau for all the intelligence, wit and power of the age and country. He gains the battle; he makes the code; he makes the system of weights and measures; he levels the Alps; he builds the road. All distinguished engineers, savans, statists, report to him: so likewise do all good heads in every kind: he adopts the best measures, sets his stamp on them, and not these alone, but on every happy and memorable expression. Every sentence spoken by Napoleon and every line of his writing, deserves reading, as it is the sense of France.

Bonaparte was the idol of common men because he had in transcendent degree the qualities and powers of common men. There is a certain satisfaction in coming down to the lowest ground of politics, for we get rid of cant and hypocrisy. Bonaparte wrought, in common with that great class he represented, for power and wealth,—but Bonaparte, specially, without any scruple as to the means. All the sentiments which embarrass men's pursuit of these objects, he set aside. The sentiments were for women and children. Fontanes, in 1804, expressed Napoleon's own sense, when in behalf of the Senate he addressed him,—"Sire, the desire of perfection is the worst disease that ever afflicted the human mind." The advocates of liberty and of progress are "ideologists;"—a word of contempt often in his mouth;—"Necker is an ideologist:" "Lafayette is an ideologist."

An Italian proverb, too well known, declares that "if you would succeed, you must not be too good." It is an advantage, within certain limits, to have renounced the dominion of the sentiments of piety, gratitude and generosity; since what was an impassable bar to us, and still is to others, becomes a convenient weapon for our purposes; just as the river which was a formidable barrier, winter transforms into the smoothest of roads.

Napoleon renounced, once for all, sentiments and affections, and would help himself with his hands and his head. With him is no miracle and no magic. He is a worker in brass, in iron, in wood, in earth, in roads, in buildings, in money and in troops, and a very consistent and wise master-workman. He is never weak and literary, but acts with the solidity and the precision of natural agents. He has not lost his native sense and sympathy with things. Men give way before such a man, as before natural events. To be sure there are men enough who are immersed in things, as farmers, smiths, sailors and mechanics generally; and we know how real and solid such men appear in the presence of scholars and grammarians: but these men ordinarily lack the power of arrangement, and are like hands without a head. But Bonaparte superadded to this mineral and animal force, insight and generalization, so that men saw in him combined the natural and the intellectual power, as if the sea and land had taken flesh and begun to cipher. Therefore the land and sea seem to presuppose him. He came unto his own and they received him. This ciphering operative knows what he is working with and what is the product. He knew the properties of gold and iron, of wheels and ships, of troops and diplomatists, and required that each should do after its kind.

The art of war was the game in which he exerted his arithmetic. It consisted, according to him, in having always more forces than the enemy, on the point where the enemy is attacked, or where he attacks: and his whole talent is strained by endless manœuvre and evolution, to march always on the enemy at an angle, and destroy his forces in detail. It is obvious that a very small force, skilfully and rapidly manoeuvring so as always to bring two men against one at the point of engagement, will be an overmatch for a much larger body of men.

The times, his constitution and his early circumstances combined to develop this pattern democrat. He had the virtues of his class and the conditions for their activity. That common-sense which no sooner respects any end than it finds the means to effect it; the delight in the use of means; in the choice, simplification and combining of means; the directness and thoroughness of his work; the prudence with which all was seen and the energy with which all was done, make him the natural organ and head of what I may almost call, from its extent, the *modern* party.

Nature must have far the greatest share in every success, and so in his. Such a man was wanted, and such a man was born; a man of stone and iron, capable of sitting on horseback sixteen or seventeen hours, of going many days together without rest or food except by snatches, and with the speed and spring of a tiger in action; a man not embarrassed by any scruples; compact, instant, selfish, prudent, and of a perception which did not suffer itself to be baulked or misled by any pretences of others, or any superstition or any heat or haste of his own. "My hand of iron," he said, "was not at the extremity of my arm, it was immediately connected with my head." He respected the power of nature and fortune, and ascribed to it his superiority, instead of valuing himself, like inferior men, on his opinionativeness, and waging war with nature. His favorite rhetoric lay in allusion to his star; and he pleased himself, as well as the people, when he styled himself the "Child of Destiny." "They charge me," he said, "with the commission of great crimes: men of my stamp do not commit crimes. Nothing has been more simple than my elevation, 't is in vain to ascribe it to intrigue or crime; it was owing to the peculiarity of the times and to my reputation of having fought well against the enemies of my country. I have always marched with the opinion of great masses and with events. Of what use then would crimes be to me?" Again he said, speaking of his son, "My son can not replace me; I could not replace myself. I am the creature of circumstances."

He had a directness of action never before combined with so much comprehension. He is a realist, terrific to all talkers and confused truth-obscuring persons. He sees where the matter hinges, throws himself on the precise point of resistance, and slights all other considerations. He is strong in the right manner, namely by insight. He never blundered into victory, but won his battles in his head before he won them on the field. His principal means are in himself. He asks counsel of no other. In 1796 he writes to the Directory: "I have conducted the campaign without consulting any one. I should have done no good if I had been under the necessity of conforming to the notions of another person. I have gained some advantages over superior forces and when totally destitute of every thing, because, in the persuasion that your confidence was reposed in me, my actions were as prompt as my thoughts."

History is full, down to this day, of the imbecility of kings and governors. They are a class of persons much to be pitied, for they know not what they should do. The weavers strike for bread, and the king and his ministers, knowing not what to do, meet them with bayonets. But Napoleon understood his business. Here was a man who in each moment and emergency knew what to do next. It is an immense comfort and refreshment to the spirits, not only of kings, but of citizens. Few men have any next; they live from hand to mouth, without plan, and are ever at the end of their line, and after each action wait for an impulse from abroad. Napoleon had been the first man of the world, if his ends had been purely public. As he is, he inspires confidence and vigor by the extraordinary unity of his action. He is firm, sure, self-denying, self-postponing, sacrificing every thing,—money, troops, generals, and his own safety also, to his aim; not misled, like common adventurers, by the splendor of his own means. "Incidents ought not to govern policy," he said, "but policy, incidents." "To be hurried away by every event is to have no political system at all." His victories were only so many doors, and he never for a moment lost sight of his way onward, in the dazzle and uproar of the present circumstance. He knew what to do, and he flew to his mark. He would shorten a straight line to come at his object. Horrible anecdotes may no doubt be collected from his history, of the price at which he bought his successes; but he must not therefore be set down as cruel, but only as one who knew no impediment to his will; not bloodthirsty, not cruel,—but wo to what thing or person

stood in his way! Not bloodthirsty, but not sparing of blood,—
and pitiless. He saw only the object: the obstacle must give way.
"Sire, General Clarke can not combine with General Junot, for
the dreadful fire of the Austrian battery."—"Let him carry the
battery."—"Sire, every regiment that approaches the heavy artillery is sacrificed: Sire, what orders?"—"Forward, forward!" Seru-
zier, a colonel of artillery, gives, in his "Military Memoirs," the
following sketch of a scene after the battle of Austerlitz.—"At the
moment in which the Russian army was making its retreat, painfully, but in good order, on the ice of the lake, the Emperor Napoleon came riding at full speed toward the artillery. 'You are losing
time,' he cried; 'fire upon those masses; they must be engulfed:
fire upon the ice!' The order remained unexecuted for ten minutes. In vain several officers and myself were placed on the slope
of a hill to produce the effect: their balls and mine rolled upon the
ice without breaking it up. Seeing that, I tried a simple method of
elevating light howitzers. The almost perpendicular fall of the
heavy projectiles produced the desired effect. My method was
immediately followed by the adjoining batteries, and in less than
no time we buried" some "thousands of Russians and Austrians
under the waters of the lake."

   In the plenitude of his resources, every obstacle seemed to vanish. "There shall be no Alps," he said; and he built his perfect
roads, climbing by graded galleries their steepest precipices, until
Italy was as open to Paris as any town in France. He laid his bones
to, and wrought for his crown. Having decided what was to be
done, he did that with might and main. He put out all his strength.
He risked every thing and spared nothing, neither ammunition,
nor money, nor troops, nor generals, nor himself.

   We like to see every thing to do its office after its kind, whether
it be a milch-cow or a rattlesnake; and if fighting be the best mode
of adjusting national differences, (as large majorities of men seem
to agree,) certainly Bonaparte was right in making it thorough.
The grand principle of war, he said, was that an army ought
always to be ready, by day and by night and at all hours, to make
all the resistance it is capable of making. He never economized his
ammunition, but, on a hostile position, rained a torrent of iron,—
shells, balls, grape-shot,—to annihilate all defence. On any point

of resistance he concentrated squadron on squadron in over-whelming numbers until it was swept out of existence. To a regiment of horse-chasseurs at Lobenstein, two days before the battle of Jena, Napoleon said, "My lads, you must not fear death; when soldiers brave death, they drive him into the enemy's ranks." In the fury of assault, he no more spared himself. He went to the edge of his possibility. It is plain that in Italy he did what he could, and all that he could. He came, several times, within an inch of ruin; and his own person was all but lost. He was flung into the marsh at Arcola. The Austrians were between him and his troops, in the *mêlée*, and he was brought off with desperate efforts. At Lonato, and at other places, he was on the point of being taken prisoner. He fought sixty battles. He had never enough. Each victory was a new weapon. "My power would fall, were I not to support it by new achievements. Conquest has made me what I am, and conquest must maintain me." He felt, with every wise man, that as much life is needed for conversation as for creation. We are always in peril, always in a bad plight, just on the edge of destruction and only to be saved by invention and courage.

This vigor was guarded and tempered by the coldest prudence and punctuality. A thunder-bolt in the attack, he was found invulnerable in his intrenchments. His very attack was never the inspiration of courage, but the result of calculation. His idea of the best defence consists in being still the attacking party. "My ambition," he says, "was great, but was of a cold nature." In one of his conversations with Las Casas, he remarked, "As to moral courage, I have rarely met with the two-o'clock-in-the-morning kind: I mean unprepared courage; that which is necessary on an unexpected occasion, and which, in spite of the most unforeseen events, leaves full freedom of judgment and decision:" and he did not hesitate to declare that he was himself eminently endowed with this two-o'clock-in-the-morning courage, and that he had met with few persons equal to himself in this respect.

Every thing depended on the nicety of his combinations, and the stars were not more punctual than his arithmetic. His personal attention descended to the smallest particulars. "At Montebello, I ordered Kellermann to attack with eight hundred horse, and with these he separated the six thousand Hungarian grenadiers, before the very eyes of the Austrian cavalry. This cavalry was half a league off and required a quarter of an hour to arrive on the field of action, and I have observed that it is always these quarters of an hour that decide the fate of a battle." "Before he fought a battle, Bonaparte thought little about what he should do in case of success, but a great deal about what he should do in case of a reverse of fortune." The same prudence and good sense mark all his behavior. His instructions to his secretary at the Tuileries are worth remembering. "During the night, enter my chamber as seldom as possible. Do not awake me when you have any good news to communicate; with that there is no hurry. But when you bring bad news, rouse me instantly, for then there is not a moment to be lost." It was a whimsical economy of the same kind which dictated his practice, when general in Italy, in regard to his burdensome correspondence. He directed Bourrienne to leave all letters unopened for three weeks, and then observed with satisfaction how large a part of the correspondence had thus disposed of itself and no longer required an answer. His achievement of business was immense, and enlarges the known powers of man. There have been many working kings, from Ulysses to William of Orange, but none who accomplished a tithe of this man's performance.

To these gifts of nature, Napoleon added the advantage of having been born to a private and humble fortune. In his later days he had the weakness of wishing to add to his crowns and badges the prescription of aristocracy; but he knew his debt to his austere education, and made no secret of his contempt for the born kings, and for "the hereditary asses," as he coarsely styled the Bourbons. He said that "in their exile they had learned nothing, and forgot nothing." Bonaparte had passed through all the degrees of military service, but also was citizen before he was emperor, and so has the key to citizenship. His remarks and estimates discover the information and justness of measurement of the middle class. Those who had to deal with him found that he was not to be imposed upon, but could cipher as well as another man. This appears in all parts of his Memoirs, dictated at St. Helena. When the expenses of the empress, of his household, of his palaces, had accumulated great debts, Napoleon examined the bills of the

creditors himself, detected overcharges and errors, and reduced
the claims by considerable sums.

His grand weapon, namely the millions whom he directed, he
owed to the representative character which clothed him. He interests us as he stands for France and for Europe; and he exists as
captain and king only as far as the Revolution, or the interest of
the industrious masses, found an organ and a leader in him. In the
social interests, he knew the meaning and value of labor, and
threw himself naturally on that side. I like an incident mentioned
by one of his biographers at St. Helena. "When walking with Mrs.
Balcombe, some servants, carrying heavy boxes, passed by on the
road, and Mrs. Balcombe desired them, in rather an angry tone,
to keep back. Napoleon interfered, saying 'Respect the burden,
Madam.'" In the time of the empire he directed attention to the
improvement and embellishment of the markets of the capital. "The
market-place," he said, "is the Louvre of the common people."
The principal works that have survived him are his magnificent
roads. He filled the troops with his spirit, and a sort of freedom
and companionship grew up between him and them, which the
forms of his court never permitted between the officers and himself. They performed, under his eye, that which no others could
do. The best document of his relation to his troops is the order of
the day on the morning of the battle of Austerlitz, in which Napoleon promises the troops that he will keep his person out of reach
of fire. This declaration, which is the reverse of that ordinarily
made by generals and sovereigns on the eve of a battle, sufficiently
explains the devotion of the army to their leader.

But though there is in particulars this identity between Napoleon and the mass of the people, his real strength lay in their conviction that he was their representative in his genius and aims, not
only when he courted, but when he controlled, and even when he
decimated them by his conscriptions. He knew, as well as any
Jacobin in France, how to philosophize on liberty and equality;
and when allusion was made to the precious blood of centuries,
which was spilled by the killing of the Duc d'Enghien, he suggested, "Neither is my blood ditch-water." The people felt that no
longer the throne was occupied and the land sucked of its nourishment, by a small class of legitimates, secluded from all commu-

nity with the children of the soil, and holding the ideas and superstitions of a long-forgotten state of society. Instead of that vampyre, a man of themselves held, in the Tuileries, knowledge and ideas like their own, opening of course to them and their children all places of power and trust. The day of sleepy, selfish policy, ever narrowing the means and opportunities of young men, was ended, and a day of expansion and demand was come. A market for all the powers and productions of man was opened; brilliant prizes glittered in the eyes of youth and talent. The old, iron-bound, feudal France was changed into a young Ohio or New York; and those who smarted under the immediate rigors of the new monarch, pardoned them as the necessary severities of the military system which had driven out the oppressor. And even when the majority of the people had begun to ask whether they had really gained any thing under the exhausting levies of men and money of the new master, the whole talent of the country, in every rank and kindred, took his part and defended him as its natural patron. In 1814, when advised to rely on the higher classes, Napoleon said to those around him, "Gentlemen, in the situation in which I stand, my only nobility is the rabble of the Faubourgs."

Napleon met this natural expectation. The necessity of his position required a hospitality to every sort of talent, and its appointment to trusts; and his feeling went along with this policy. Like every superior person, he undoubtedly felt a desire for men and compeers, and a wish to measure his power with other masters, and an impatience of fools and underlings. In Italy, he sought for men and found none. "Good God!" he said, "how rare men are! There are eighteen millions in Italy, and I have with difficulty found two,—Dandolo and Melzi." In later years, with larger experience, his respect for mankind was not increased. In a moment of bitterness he said to one of his oldest friends, "Men deserve the contempt with which they inspire me. I have only to put some gold-lace on the coat of my virtuous republicans and they immediately become just what I wish them." This impatience at levity was, however, an oblique tribute of respect to those able persons who commanded his regard not only when he found them friends and coadjutors but also when they resisted his will. He could not confound Fox and Pitt, Carnot, Lafayette and Bernadotte, with the danglers of his court; and in spite of the detraction which his systematic egotism dictated toward the great captains who conquered with and for him, ample acknowledgments are made by him to Lannes, Duroc, Kleber, Dessaix, Massena, Murat, Ney and Augereau. If he felt himself their patron and the founder of their fortunes, as when he said "I made my generals out of mud,"—he could not hide his satisfaction in receiving from them a seconding and support commensurate with the grandeur of his enterprise. In the Russian campaign he was so much impressed by the courage and resources of Marshal Ney, that he said, "I have two hundred millions in my coffers, and I would give them all for Ney." The characters which he has drawn of several of his marshals are discriminating, and though they did not content the insatiable vanity of French officers, are no doubt substantially just. And in fact every species of merit was sought and advanced under his government. "I know," he said, "the depth and draught of water of every one of my generals." Natural power was sure to be well received at his court. Seventeen men in his time were raised from common soldiers to the rank of king, marshal, duke, or general; and the crosses of his Legion of Honor were given to personal valor, and not to family connexion. "When soldiers have been baptized in the fire of a battlefield, they have all one rank in my eyes."

When a natural king becomes a titular king, every body is pleased and satisfied. The Revolution entitled the strong populace of the Faubourg St. Antoine, and every horse-boy and powder-monkey in the army, to look on Napoleon as flesh of his flesh and the creature of *his* party: but there is something in the success of grand talent which enlists an universal sympathy. For in the prevalence of sense and spirit over stupidity and malversation, all reasonable men have an interest; and as intellectual beings we feel the air purified by the electric shock, when material force is overthrown by intellectual energies. As soon as we are removed out of the reach of local and accidental partialities, Man feels that Napoleon fights for him; these are honest victories; this strong steam-engine does our work. Whatever appeals to the imagination, by transcending the ordinary limits of human ability, wonderfully encourages and liberates us. This capacious head, revolving and

disposing sovereignly trains of affairs, and animating such multitudes of agents; this eye, which looked through Europe; this
prompt invention; this inexhaustible resource:—what events! what
romantic pictures! what strange situations!—when spying the
Alps, by a sunset in the Sicilian sea; drawing up his army for battle in sight of the Pyramids, and saying to his troops, "From the
tops of those pyramids, forty centuries look down on you;" ford-
ing the Red Sea; wading in the gulf of the Isthmus of Suez. On the
shore of Ptolemais, gigantic projects agitated him. "Had Acre
fallen, I should have changed the face of the world." His army, on
the night of the battle of Austerlitz, which was the anniversary of
his inauguration as Emperor, presented him with a bouquet of
forty standards taken in the fight. Perhaps it is a little puerile, the
pleasure he took in making these contrasts glaring; as when he
pleased himself with making kings wait in his antechambers, at
Tilsit, at Paris and at Erfurt.

We cannot, in the universal imbecility, indecision and indolence of men, sufficiently congratulate ourselves on this strong
and ready actor, who took occasion by the beard, and showed us
how much may be accomplished by the mere force of such virtues
as all men possess in less degrees; namely, by punctuality, by personal attention, by courage and thoroughness. "The Austrians,"
he said, "do not know the value of time." I should cite him, in his
earlier years, as a model of prudence. His power does not consist
in any wild or extravagant force; in any enthusiasm like Mahomet's, or singular power of persuasion; but in the exercise of common-
sense on each emergency, instead of abiding by rules and customs.
The lesson he teaches is that which vigor always teaches;—that
there is always room for it. To what heaps of cowardly doubts is
not that man's life an answer. When he appeared it was the belief
of all military men that there could be nothing new in war; as it is
the belief of men to-day that nothing new can be undertaken in
politics, or in church, or in letters, or in trade, or in farming, or in
our social manners and customs; and as it is at all times the belief
of society that the world is used up. But Bonaparte knew better
than society; and moreover knew that he knew better. I think all
men know better than they do; know that the institutions we so
volubly commend are go-carts and baubles; but they dare not

trust their presentiments. Bonaparte relied on his own sense, and did not care a bean for other people's. The world treated his novelties just as it treats everybody's novelties,—made infinite objection, mustered all the impediments; but he snapped his finger at their objections. "What creates great difficulty," he remarks, "in the profession of the land-commander, is the necessity of feeding so many men and animals. If he allows himself to be guided by the commissaries he will never stir, and all his expeditions will fail." An example of his common-sense is what he says of the passage of the Alps in winter, which all writers, one repeating after the other, had described as impracticable. "The winter," says Napoleon, "is not the most unfavorable season for the passage of lofty mountains. The snow is then firm, the weather settled, and there is nothing to fear from avalanches, the real and only danger to be apprehended in the Alps. On these high mountains there are often very fine days in December, of a dry cold, with extreme calmness in the air." Read his account, too, of the way in which battles are gained. "In all battles a moment occurs when the bravest troops, after having made the greatest efforts, feel inclined to run. That terror proceeds from a want of confidence in their own courage, and it only requires a slight opportunity, a pretence, to restore confidence to them. The art is, to give rise to the opportunity and to invent the pretence. At Arcola I won the battle with twenty-five horsemen. I seized that moment of lassitude, gave every man a trumpet, and gained the day with this handful. You see that two armies are two bodies which meet and endeavor to frighten each other; a moment of panic occurs, and that moment must be turned to advantage. When a man has been present in many actions, he distinguishes that moment without difficulty: it is as easy as casting up an addition."

This deputy of the nineteenth century added to his gifts a capacity for speculation on general topics. He delighted in running through the range of practical, of literary and of abstract questions. His opinion is always original and to the purpose. On the voyage to Egypt he liked, after dinner, to fix on three or four persons to support a proposition, and as many to oppose it. He gave a subject, and the discussions turned on questions of religion, the different kinds of government, and the art of war. One day he asked whether the planets were inhabited? On another, what was the age of the world? Then he proposed to consider the probability of the destruction of the globe, either by water or by fire: at another time, the truth or fallacy of presentiments, and the interpretation of dreams. He was very fond of talking of religion. In 1806 he conversed with Fournier, bishop of Montpellier, on matters of theology. There were two points on which they could not agree, viz. that of hell, and that of salvation out of the pale of the church. The Emperor told Josephine that he disputed like a devil on these two points, on which the bishop was inexorable. To the philosophers he readily yielded all that was proved against religion as the work of men and time, but he would not hear of materialism. One fine night, on deck, amid a clatter of materialism, Bonaparte pointed to the stars, and said, "You may talk as long as you please, gentlemen, but who made all that?" He delighted in the conversation of men of science, particularly of Monge and Berthollet; but the men of letters he slighted; they were "manufacturers of phrases." Of medicine too he was fond of talking, and with those of its practitioners whom he most esteemed,—with Corvisart at Paris, and with Antonomarchi at St. Helena. "Believe me," he said to the last, "we had better leave off all these remedies: life is a fortress which neither you nor I know any thing about. Why throw obstacles in the way of its defence? Its own means are superior to all the apparatus of your laboratories. Corvisart candidly agreed with me that all your filthy mixtures are good for nothing. Medicine is a collection of uncertain prescriptions, the results of which, taken collectively, are more fatal than useful to mankind. Water, air and cleanliness are the chief articles in my pharmacopœia."

His memoirs, dictated to Count Montholon and General Gourgaud at St. Helena, have great value, after all the deduction that it seems is to be made from them on account of his known disingenuousness. He has the good-nature of strength and conscious superiority. I admire his simple, clear narrative of his battles;—good as Cæsar's; his good-natured and sufficiently respectful account of Marshal Wurmser and his other antagonists; and his own equality as a writer to his varying subject. The most agreeable portion is the Campaign in Egypt.

He had hours of thought and wisdom. In intervals of leisure, either in the camp or the palace, Napoleon appears as a man of genius directing on abstract questions the native appetite for truth and the impatience of words he was wont to show in war. He could enjoy every play of invention, a romance, a *bon mot*, as well as a stratagem in a campaign. He delighted to fascinate Josephine and her ladies, in a dim-lighted apartment, by the terrors of a fiction to which his voice and dramatic power lent every addition.

I call Napoleon the agent or attorney of the middle class of modern society; of the throng who fill the markets, shops, counting-houses, manufactories, ships, of the modern world, aiming to be rich. He was the agitator, the destroyer of prescription, the internal improver, the liberal, the radical, the inventor of means, the opener of doors and markets, the subverter of monopoly and abuse. Of course the rich and aristocratic did not like him. England, the centre of capital, and Rome and Austria, centres of tradition and genealogy, opposed him. The consternation of the dull and conservative classes, the terror of the foolish old men and old women of the Roman conclave, who in their despair took hold of any thing, and would cling to red-hot iron,—the vain attempts of statists to amuse and deceive him, of the emperor of Austria to bribe him; and the instinct of the young, ardent and active men every where, which pointed him out as the giant of the middle class, make his history bright and commanding. He had the virtues of the masses of his constituents: he had also their vices. I am sorry that the brilliant picture has its reverse. But that is the fatal quality which we discover in our pursuit of wealth, that it is treacherous, and is bought by the breaking or weakening of the sentiments; and it is inevitable that we should find the same fact in the history of this champion, who proposed to himself simply a brilliant career, without any stipulation or scruple concerning the means.

Bonaparte was singularly destitute of generous sentiments. The highest-placed individual in the most cultivated age and population of the world,—he has not the merit of common truth and honesty. He is unjust to his generals; egotistic and monopolizing;

meanly stealing the credit of their great actions from Kellermann, from Bernadotte; intriguing to involve his faithful Junot in hopeless bankruptcy, in order to drive him to a distance from Paris, because the familiarity of his manners offends the new pride of his throne. He is a boundless liar. The official paper, his "Moniteur," and all his bulletins, are proverbs for saying what he wished to be believed; and worse,—he sat, in his premature old age, in his lonely island, coldly falsifying facts and dates and characters, and giving to history a theatrical *éclat*. Like all Frenchmen he has a passion for stage effect. Every action that breathes of generosity is poisoned by this calculation. His star, his love of glory, his doctrine of the immortality of the soul, are all French. "I must dazzle and astonish. If I were to give the liberty of the press, my power could not last three days." To make a great noise is his favorite design. "A great reputation is a great noise: the more there is made, the farther off it is heard. Laws, institutions, monuments, nations, all fall; but the noise continues, and resounds in after ages." His doctrine of immortality is simply fame. His theory of influence is not flattering. "There are two levers for moving men,—interest and fear. Love is a silly infatuation, depend upon it. Friendship is but a name. I love nobody. I do not even love my brothers: perhaps Joseph a little, from habit, and because he is my elder; and Duroc, I love him too; but why?—because his character pleases me: he is stern and resolute, and I believe the fellow never shed a tear. For my part I know very well that I have no true friends. As long as I continue to be what I am, I may have as many pretended friends as I please. Leave sensibility to women; but men should be firm in heart and purpose, or they should have nothing to do with war and government." He was thoroughly unscrupulous. He would steal, slander, assassinate, drown and poison, as his interest dictated. He had no generosity, but mere vulgar hatred; he was intensely selfish; he was perfidious; he cheated at cards; he was a prodigious gossip, and opened letters, and delighted in his infamous police, and rubbed his hands with joy when he had intercepted some morsel of intelligence concerning the men and women about him, boasting that "he knew every thing;" and interfered with the cutting the dresses of the women; and listened after the hurrahs and the compliments of the street, incognito.

His manners were coarse. He treated women with low familiarity. He had the habit of pulling their ears and pinching their cheeks when he was in good humor, and of pulling the ears and whiskers of men, and of striking and horse-play with them, to his last days. It does not appear that he listened at key-holes, or at least that he was caught at it. In short, when you have penetrated through all the circles of power and splendor, you were not dealing with a gentleman, at last; but with an impostor and a rogue; and he fully deserves the epithet of *Jupiter Scapin*, or a sort of Scamp Jupiter.

In describing the two parties into which modern society divides itself,—the democrat and the conservative,—I said, Bonaparte represents the democrat, or the party of men of business, against the stationary or conservative party. I omitted then to say, what is material to the statement, namely that these two parties differ only as young and old. The democrat is a young conservative; the conservative is an old democrat. The aristocrat is the democrat ripe and gone to seed;—because both parties stand on the one ground of the supreme value of property, which one endeavors to get, and the other to keep. Bonaparte may be said to represent the whole history of this party, its youth and its age; yes, and with poetic justice its fate, in his own. The counter-revolution, the counter-party, still waits for its organ and representative, in a lover and a man of truly public and universal aims.

Here was an experiment, under the most favorable conditions, of the powers of intellect without conscience. Never was such a leader so endowed and so weaponed; never leader found such aids and followers. And what was the result of this vast talent and power, of these immense armies, burned cities, squandered treasures, immolated millions of men, of this demoralized Europe? It came to no result. All passed away like the smoke of his artillery, and left no trace. He left France smaller, poorer, feebler, than he found it; and the whole contest for freedom was to be begun again. The attempt was in principle suicidal. France served him with life and limb and estate, as long as it could identify its interest with him; but when men saw that after victory was another war; after the destruction of armies, new conscriptions; and they

who had toiled so desperately were never nearer to the reward,—
they could not spend what they had earned, nor repose on their
down-beds, nor strut in their châteaux,—they deserted him. Men
found that his absorbing egotism was deadly to all other men. It
resembled the torpedo, which inflicts a succession of shocks on
any one who takes hold of it, producing spasms which contract
the muscles of the hand, so that the man can not open his fingers;
and the animal in lets new and more violent shocks, until he paralyzes and kills his victim. So this exorbitant egotist narrowed,
impoverished and absorbed the power and existence of those who
served him; and the universal cry of France and of Europe in 1814
was, "Enough of him;" *"Assez de Bonaparte."*

It was not Bonaparte's fault. He did all that in him lay to live
and thrive without moral principle. It was the nature of things,
the eternal law of man and of the world which baulked and ruined
him; and the result, in a million experiments, will be the same.
Every experiment, by multitudes or by individuals, that has a sensual and selfish aim, will fail. The pacific Fourier will be as inef-
ficient as the pernicious Napoleon. As long as our civilization is
essentially one of property, of fences, or exclusiveness, it will be
mocked by delusions. Our riches will leave us sick; there will be
bitterness in our laughter, and our wine will burn our mouth.
Only that good profits which we can taste with all doors open,
and which serves all men.

FATE

Delicate omens traced in air,
To the lone bard true witness bare;
Birds with auguries on their wings
Chanted undeceiving things,
Him to beckon, him to warn;
Well might then the poet scorn
To learn of scribe or courier
Hints writ in vaster character;
And on his mind, at dawn of day,
Soft shadows of the evening lay.
For the prevision is allied
Unto the thing so signified;
Or say, the foresight that awaits
Is the same Genius that creates.

It chanced during one winter a few years ago, that our cities were bent on discussing the theory of the Age. By an odd coincidence, four or five noted men were each reading a discourse to the citizens of Boston or New York, on the Spirit of the Times. It so happened that the subject had the same prominence in some remarkable pamphlets and journals issued in London in the same season. To me, however, the question of the times resolved itself into a practical question of the conduct of life. How shall I live? We are incompetent to solve the times. Our geometry cannot span the huge orbits of the prevailing ideas, behold their return and reconcile their opposition. We can only obey our own polarity. 'T is fine for

us to speculate and elect our course, if we must accept an irresistible dictation.

In our first steps to gain our wishes we come upon immovable
limitations. We are fired with the hope to reform men. After many
experiments we find that we must begin earlier,—at school. But
the boys and girls are not docile; we can make nothing of them.
We decide that they are not of good stock. We must begin our
reform earlier still,—at generation: that is to say, there is Fate, or
laws of the world.

But if there be irresistible dictation, this dictation understands
itself. If we must accept Fate, we are not less compelled to affirm
liberty, the significance of the individual, the grandeur of duty,
the power of character. This is true, and that other is true. But
our geometry cannot span these extreme points and reconcile
them. What to do? By obeying each thought frankly, by harping,
or, if you will, pounding on each string, we learn at last its power.
By the same obedience to other thoughts we learn theirs, and then
comes some reasonable hope of harmonizing them. We are sure
that, though we know not how, necessity does comport with liberty, the individual with the world, my polarity with the spirit of
the times. The riddle of the age has for each a private solution. If
one would study his own time, it must be by this method of taking
up in turn each of the leading topics which belong to our scheme
of human life, and by firmly stating all that is agreeable to experience on one, and doing the same justice to the opposing facts in
the others, the true limitations will appear. Any excess of emphasis on one part would be corrected, and a just balance would be
made.

But let us honestly state the facts. Our America has a bad name
for superficialness. Great men, great nations, have not been boast-
ers and buffoons, but perceivers of the terror of life, and have
manned themselves to face it. The Spartan, embodying his religion in his country, dies before its majesty without a question.
The Turk, who believes his doom is written on the iron leaf in the
moment when he entered the world, rushes on the enemy's sabre
with undivided will. The Turk, the Arab, the Persian, accepts the
foreordained fate:—

The diseases, the elements, fortune, gravity, lightning, respect no persons. The way of Providence is a little rude. The habit of snake and spider, the snap of the tiger and other leapers and bloody jumpers, the crackle of the bones of his prey in the coil of the anaconda,—these are in the system, and our habits are like theirs. You have just dined, and however scrupulously the slaughterhouse is concealed in the graceful distance of miles, there is complicity, expensive races,—race living at the expense of race. The planet is liable to shocks from comets, perturbations from planets, rendings from earthquake and volcano, alterations of climate, precessions of equinoxes. Rivers dry up by opening of the forest. The sea changes its bed. Towns and counties fall into it. At Lisbon an earthquake killed men like flies. At Naples three years ago ten thousand persons were crushed in a few minutes. The scurvy at sea, the sword of the climate in the west of Africa, at Cayenne, at Panama, at New Orleans, cut off men like a massacre. Our western prairie shakes with fever and ague. The cholera, the small-pox, have proved as mortal to some tribes as a frost to the crickets, which, having filled the summer with noise, are silenced by a fall of the temperature of one night. Without uncovering what does not concern us, or counting how many species of parasites hang on a bombyx, or groping after intestinal parasites or infusory biters, or the obscurities of alternate generation,—the forms of the shark, the *labrus*, the jaw of the sea-wolf paved with crushing teeth, the weapons of the grampus, and other warriors hidden in the sea, are hints of ferocity in the interiors of nature. Let us not deny it up and down. Providence has a wild, rough, incalculable road to its end, and it is of no use to try to whitewash its huge, mixed instrumentalities, or to dress up that terrific benefactor in a clean shirt and white neckcloth of a student in divinity.

Will you say, the disasters which threaten mankind are exceptional, and one need not lay his account for cataclysms every day? Aye, but what happens once may happen again, and so long as these strokes are not to be parried by us they must be feared.

But these shocks and ruins are less destructive to us than the stealthy power of other laws which act on us daily. An expense of ends to means is fate;—organization tyrannizing over character. The menagerie, or forms and powers of the spine, is a book of

fate; the bill of the bird, the skull of the snake, determines tyran-
nically its limits. So is the scale of races, of temperaments; so is
sex; so is climate; so is the reaction of talents imprisoning the vital
power in certain directions. Every spirit makes its house; but
afterwards the house confines the spirit.

The gross lines are legible to the dull; the cab-man is phrenologist so far, he looks in your face to see if his shilling is sure. A
dome of brow denotes one thing, a pot-belly another; a squint, a
pug-nose, mats of hair, the pigment of the epidermis, betray character. People seem sheathed in their tough organization. Ask
Spurzheim, ask the doctors, ask Quetelet if temperaments decide
nothing?—or if there be anything they do not decide? Read the
description in medical books of the four temperaments and you
will think that you are reading your own thoughts which you had
not yet told. Find the part which black eyes and which blue eyes
play severally in the company. How shall a man escape from his
ancestors, or draw off from his veins the black drop which he
drew from his father's or his mother's life? It often appears in a
family as if all the qualities of the progenitors were potted in several jars,—some ruling quality in each son or daughter of the
house; and sometimes the unmixed temperament, the rank unmit-
igated elixir, the family vice is drawn off in a separate individual
and the others are proportionally relieved. We sometimes see a
change of expression in our companion and say his father or his
mother comes to the windows of his eyes, and sometimes a remote
relative. In different hours a man represents each of several of his
ancestors, as if there were seven or eight of us rolled up in each
man's skin,—seven or eight ancestors at least; and they constitute
the variety of notes for that new piece of music which his life is.
At the corner of the street you read the possibility of each passenger in the facial angle, in the complexion, in the depth of his eye.
His parentage determines it. Men are what their mothers made
them. You may as well ask a loom which weaves huckabuck why
it does not make cashmere, as expect poetry from this engineer,
or a chemical discovery from that jobber. Ask the digger in the
ditch to explain Newton's laws; the fine organs of his brain have
been pinched by overwork and squalid poverty from father to son
for a hundred years. When each comes forth from his mother's

womb, the gate of gifts closes behind him. Let him value his hands and feet, he has but one pair. So he has but one future, and that is already predetermined in his lobes and described in that little fatty face, pig-eye, and squat form. All the privilege and all the legislation of the world cannot meddle or help to make a poet or a prince of him.

Jesus said, "When he looketh on her, he hath committed adultery." But he is an adulterer before he has yet looked on the woman, by the superfluity of animal and the defect of thought in his constitution. Who meets him, or who meets her, in the street, sees that they are ripe to be each other's victim.

In certain men digestion and sex absorb the vital force, and the stronger these are, the individual is so much weaker. The more of these drones perish, the better for the hive. If, later, they give birth to some superior individual, with force enough to add to this animal a new aim and a complete apparatus to work it out, all the ancestors are gladly forgotten. Most men and most women are merely one couple more. Now and then one has a new cell or camarilla opened in his brain,—an architectural, a musical, or a philological knack; some stray taste or talent for flowers, or chemistry, or pigments, or story-telling; a good hand for drawing, a good foot for dancing, an athletic frame for wide journeying, etc.—which skill nowise alters rank in the scale of nature, but serves to pass the time; the life of sensation going on as before. At last these hints and tendencies are fixed in one or in a succession. Each absorbs so much food and force as to become itself a new centre. The new talent draws off so rapidly the vital force that not enough remains for the animal functions, hardly enough for health; so that in the second generation, if the like genius appear, the health is visibly deteriorated and the generative force impaired.

People are born with the moral or with the material bias;— uterine brothers with this diverging destination; and I suppose, with high magnifiers, Mr. Frauenhofer or Dr. Carpenter might come to distinguish in the embryo, at the fourth day,—this is a Whig, and that a Free-soiler.

It was a poetic attempt to lift this mountain of Fate, to reconcile this despotism of race with liberty, which led the Hindoos to say, "Fate is nothing but the deeds committed in a prior state of existence." I find the coincidence of the extremes of Eastern and Western speculation in the daring statement of Schelling, "There is in every man a certain feeling that he has been what he is from all eternity, and by no means became such in time." To say it less sublimely,—in the history of the individual is always an account of his condition, and he knows himself to be a party to his present estate.

A good deal of our politics is physiological. Now and then a man of wealth in the heyday of youth adopts the tenet of broadest freedom. In England there is always some man of wealth and large connection, planting himself, during all his years of health, on the side of progress, who, as soon as he begins to die, checks his forward play, calls in his troops and becomes conservative. All conservatives are such from personal defects. They have been effeminated by position or nature, born halt and blind, through luxury of their parents, and can only, like invalids, act on the defensive. But strong natures, backwoodsmen, New Hampshire giants, Napoleons, Burkes, Broughams, Websters, Kossuths, are inevitable patriots, until their life ebbs and their defects and gout, palsy and money, warp them.

The strongest idea incarnates itself in majorities and nations, in the healthiest and strongest. Probably the election goes by avoirdupois weight, and if you could weigh bodily the tonnage of any hundred of the Whig and the Democratic party in a town on the Dearborn balance, as they passed the hay-scales, you could predict with certainty which party would carry it. On the whole it would be rather the speediest way of deciding the vote, to put the selectmen or the mayor and aldermen at the hay-scales.

In science we have to consider two things: power and circumstance. All we know of the egg, from each successive discovery, is, *another vesicle*; and if, after five hundred years you get a better observer or a better glass, he finds, within the last observed, another. In vegetable and animal tissue it is just alike, and all that the primary power or spasm operates is still vesicles, vesicles. Yes,—but the tyrannical Circumstance! A vesicle in new circumstances, a vesicle lodged in darkness, Oken thought, became animal; in light, a plant. Lodged in the parent animal, it suffers changes which end in unsheathing miraculous capability in the unaltered vesicle, and it unlocks itself to fish, bird, or quadruped, head and foot, eye and claw. The Circumstance is Nature. Nature is what you may do. There is much you may not. We have two things,—the circumstance, and the life. Once we thought positive power was all. Now we learn that negative power, or circumstance, is half. Nature is the tyrannous circumstance, the thick skull, the sheathed snake, the ponderous, rock-like jaw; necessitated activity; violent direction; the conditions of a tool, like the locomotive, strong enough on its track, but which can do nothing but mischief off of it; or skates, which are wings on the ice but fetters on the ground.

The book of Nature is the book of Fate. She turns the gigantic pages,—leaf after leaf,—never re-turning one. One leaf she lays down, a floor of granite; then a thousand ages, and a bed of slate; a thousand ages, and a measure of coal; a thousand ages, and a layer of marl and mud: vegetable forms appear; her first misshapen animals, zoöphyte, trilobium, fish; then, saurians,—rude forms, in which she has only blocked her future statue, concealing under these unwieldy monsters the fine type of her coming king. The face of the planet cools and dries, the races meliorate, and man is born. But when a race has lived its term, it comes no more again.

The population of the world is a conditional population; not the best, but the best that could live now; and the scale of tribes, and the steadiness with which victory adheres to one tribe and defeat to another, is as uniform as the superposition of strata. We know in history what weight belongs to race. We see the English, French, and Germans planting themselves on every shore and market of America and Australia, and monopolizing the commerce of these countries. We like the nervous and victorious habit of our own branch of the family. We follow the step of the Jew, of the Indian, of the Negro. We see how much will has been expended to extinguish the Jew, in vain. Look at the unpalatable conclusions of Knox, in his "Fragment of Races";—a rash and unsatisfactory writer, but charged with pungent and unforgetable truths. "Nature respects race, and not hybrids." "Every race has its own *habitat*." "Detach a colony from the race, and it deteriorates to the crab." See the shades of the picture. The German and

Irish millions, like the Negro, have a great deal of guano in their destiny. They are ferried over the Atlantic and carted over America, to ditch and to drudge, to make corn cheap and then to lie down prematurely to make a spot of green grass on the prairie.

One more fagot of these adamantine bandages is the new science of Statistics. It is a rule that the most casual and extraordinary events, if the basis of population is broad enough, become matter of fixed calculation. It would not be safe to say when a captain like Bonaparte, a singer like Jenny Lind, or a navigator like Bowditch would be born in Boston; but, on a population of twenty or two hundred millions, something like accuracy may be had.

'T is frivolous to fix pedantically the date of particular inventions. They have all been invented over and over fifty times. Man is the arch machine of which all these shifts drawn from himself are toy models. He helps himself on each emergency by copying or duplicating his own structure, just so far as the need is. 'T is hard to find the right Homer, Zoroaster, or Menu; harder still to find the Tubal Cain, or Vulcan, or Cadmus, or Copernicus, or Fust, or Fulton; the indisputable inventor. There are scores and centuries of them. "The air is full of men." This kind of talent so abounds, this constructive tool-making efficiency, as if it adhered to the chemic atoms; as if the air he breathes were made of Vaucansons, Franklins, and Watts.

Doubtless in every million there will be an astronomer, a mathematician, a comic poet, a mystic. No one can read the history of astronomy without perceiving that Copernicus, Newton, Laplace, are not new men, or a new kind of men, but that Thales, Anaximenes, Hipparchus, Empedocles, Aristarchus, Pythagoras, Œnipodes, had anticipated them; each had the same tense geometrical brain, apt for the same vigorous computation and logic; a mind parallel to the movement of the world. The Roman mile probably rested on a measure of a degree of the meridian. Mahometan and Chinese know what we know of leap-year, of the Gregorian calendar, and of the precession of the equinoxes. As in every barrel of cowries brought to New Bedford there shall be one *orangia*, so there will, in a dozen millions of Malays and Mahometans, be one or two astronomical skulls. In a large city, the most casual things, and things whose beauty lies in their casuality, are produced as punctually and to order as the baker's muffin for breakfast. Punch makes exactly one capital joke a week; and the journals contrive to furnish one good piece of news every day.

And not less work the laws of repression, the penalties of violated functions. Famine, typhus, frost, war, suicide and effete races must be reckoned calculable parts of the system of the world.

These are pebbles from the mountain, hints of the terms by which our life is walled up, and which show a kind of mechanical exactness, as of a loom or mill in what we call casual or fortuitous events.

The force with which we resist these torrents of tendency looks so ridiculously inadequate that it amounts to little more than a criticism or protest made by a minority of one, under compulsion of millions. I seemed in the height of a tempest to see men overboard struggling in the waves, and driven about here and there. They glanced intelligently at each other, but 't was little they could do for one another; 't was much if each could keep afloat alone. Well, they had a right to their eye-beams, and all the rest was Fate.

We cannot trifle with this reality, this cropping-out in our planted gardens of the core of the world. No picture of life can have any veracity that does not admit the odious facts. A man's power is hooped in by a necessity which, by many experiments, he touches on every side until he learns its arc.

The element running through entire nature, which we popularly call Fate, is known to us as limitation. Whatever limits us we call Fate. If we are brute and barbarous, the fate takes a brute and dreadful shape. As we refine, our checks become finer. If we rise to spiritual culture, the antagonism takes a spiritual form. In the Hindoo fables, Vishnu follows Maya through all her ascending changes, from insect and crawfish up to elephant; whatever form she took, he took the male form of that kind, until she became at last woman and goddess, and he a man and a god. The limitations refine as the soul purifies, but the ring of necessity is always perched at the top.

When the gods in the Norse heaven were unable to bind the Fenris Wolf with steel or with weight of mountains,—the one he snapped and the other he spurned with his heel,—they put round his foot a limp band softer than silk or cobweb, and this held him; the more he spurned it the stiffer it drew. So soft and so stanch is the ring of Fate. Neither brandy, nor nectar, nor sulphuric ether, nor hell-fire, nor ichor, nor poetry, nor genius, can get rid of this limp band. For if we give it the high sense in which the poets use it, even thought itself is not above Fate; that too must act according to eternal laws, and all that is wilful and fantastic in it is in opposition to its fundamental essence.

And last of all, high over thought, in the world of morals, Fate appears as vindicator, levelling the high, lifting the low, requiring justice in man, and always striking soon or late when justice is not done. What is useful will last, what is hurtful will sink. "The doer must suffer," said the Greeks; "you would soothe a Deity not to be soothed." "God himself cannot procure good for the wicked," said the Welsh triad. "God may consent, but only for a time," said the bard of Spain. The limitation is impassable by any insight of man. In its last and loftiest ascensions, insight itself and the freedom of the will is one of its obedient members. But we must not run into generalizations too large, but show the natural bounds or essential distinctions, and seek to do justice to the other elements as well.

Thus we trace Fate in matter, mind, and morals; in race, in retardations of strata, and in thought and character as well. It is everywhere bound or limitation. But Fate has its lord; limitation its limit,—is different seen from above and from below, from within and from without. For though Fate is immense, so is Power, which is the other fact in the dual world, immense. If Fate follows and limits Power, Power attends and antagonizes Fate. We must respect Fate as natural history, but there is more than natural history. For who and what is this criticism that pries into the matter? Man is not order of nature, sack and sack, belly and members, link in a chain, nor any ignominious baggage; but a stupendous antagonism, a dragging together of the poles of the Universe. He betrays his relation to what is below him,—thick-skulled, small-brained,

fishy, quadrumanous, quadruped ill-disguised, hardly escaped
into biped,—and has paid for the new powers by loss of some of
the old ones. But the lightning which explodes and fashions planets, maker of planets and suns, is in him. On one side elemental
order, sandstone and granite, rock-ledges, peat-bog, forest, sea
and shore; and on the other part thought, the spirit which com-
poses and decomposes nature,—here they are, side by side, god
and devil, mind and matter, king and conspirator, belt and spasm,
riding peacefully together in the eye and brain of every man.

Nor can he blink the freewill. To hazard the contradiction,—
freedom is necessary. If you please to plant yourself on the side of
Fate, and say, Fate is all; then we say, a part of Fate is the freedom
of man. Forever wells up the impulse of choosing and acting in the
soul. Intellect annuls Fate. So far as a man thinks, he is free. And
though nothing is more disgusting than the crowing about liberty
by slaves, as most men are, and the flippant mistaking for freedom of some paper preamble like a "Declaration of Independence" or the statute right to vote, by those who have never dared
to think or to act,—yet it is wholesome to man to look not at Fate,
but the other way: the practical view is the other. His sound relation to these facts is to use and command, not to cringe to them.
"Look not on Nature, for her name is fatal," said the oracle. The
too much contemplation of these limits induces meanness. They
who talk much of destiny, their birth-star, etc., are in a lower dangerous plane, and invite the evils they fear.

I cited the instinctive and heroic races as proud believers in
Destiny. They conspire with it; a loving resignation is with the
event. But the dogma makes a different impression when it is held
by the weak and lazy. 'T is weak and vicious people who cast the
blame on Fate. The right use of Fate is to bring up our conduct to
the loftiness of nature. Rude and invincible except by themselves
are the elements. So let man be. Let him empty his breast of his
windy conceits, and show his lordship by manners and deeds on
the scale of nature. Let him hold his purpose as with the tug of
gravitation. No power, no persuasion, no bribe shall make him
give up his point. A man ought to compare advantageously with a
river, an oak or a mountain. He shall have not less the flow, the
expansion, and the resistance of these.

'T is the best use of Fate to teach a fatal courage. Go face the fire at sea, or the cholera in your friend's house, or the burglar in your own, or what danger lies in the way of duty,—knowing you are guarded by the cherubim of Destiny. If you believe in Fate to your harm, believe it at least for your good.

For if Fate is so prevailing, man also is part of it, and can confront fate with fate. If the Universe have these savage accidents, our atoms are as savage in resistance. We should be crushed by the atmosphere, but for the reaction of the air within the body. A tube made of a film of glass can resist the shock of the ocean if filled with the same water. If there be omnipotence in the stroke, there is omnipotence of recoil.

1. But Fate against Fate is only parrying and defence: there are also the noble creative forces. The revelation of Thought takes man out of servitude into freedom. We rightly say of ourselves, we were born and afterward we were born again, and many times. We have successive experiences so important that the new forgets the old, and hence the mythology of the seven or the nine heavens. The day of days, the great day of the feast of life, is that in which the inward eye opens to the Unity in things, to the omnipresence of law:—sees that what is must be and ought to be, or is the best. This beatitude dips from on high down on us and we see. It is not in us so much as we are in it. If the air come to our lungs, we breathe and live; if not, we die. If the light come to our eyes, we see; else not. And if truth come to our mind we suddenly expand to its dimensions, as if we grew to worlds. We are as lawgivers; we speak for Nature; we prophesy and divine.

This insight throws us on the party and interest of the Universe, against all and sundry; against ourselves as much as others. A man speaking from insight affirms of himself what is true of the mind: seeing its immortality, he says, I am immortal; seeing its invincibility, he says, I am strong. It is not in us, but we are in it. It is of the maker, not of what is made. All things are touched and changed by it. This uses and is not used. It distances those who share it from those who share it not. Those who share it not are flocks and herds. It dates from itself; not from former men or better men, gospel, or constitution, or college, or custom. Where it shines, Nature is no longer intrusive, but all things make a musical or pictorial impression. The world of men show like a comedy without laughter: populations, interests, government, history; 't is all toy figures in a toy house. It does not overvalue particular truths. We hear eagerly every thought and word quoted from an intellectual man. But in his presence our own mind is roused to activity, and we forget very fast what he says, much more interested in the new play of our own thought than in any thought of his. 'T is the majesty into which we have suddenly mounted, the impersonality, the scorn of egotisms, the sphere of laws, that engage us. Once we were stepping a little this way and a little that way; now we are as men in a balloon, and do not think so much of the point we have left, or the point we would make, as of the liberty and glory of the way.

Just as much intellect as you add, so much organic power. He who sees through the design, presides over it, and must will that which must be. We sit and rule, and, though we sleep, our dream will come to pass. Our thought, though it were only an hour old, affirms an oldest necessity, not to be separated from thought, and not to be separated from will. They must always have coexisted. It apprises us of its sovereignty and godhead, which refuse to be severed from it. It is not mine or thine, but the will of all mind. It is poured into the souls of all men, as the soul itself which constitutes them men. I know not whether there be, as is alleged, in the upper region of our atmosphere, a permanent westerly current which carries with it all atoms which rise to that height, but I see that when souls reach a certain clearness of perception they accept a knowledge and motive above selfishness. A breath of will blows eternally through the universe of souls in the direction of the Right and Necessary. It is the air which all intellects inhale and exhale, and it is the wind which blows the worlds into order and orbit.

Thought dissolves the material universe by carrying the mind up into a sphere where all is plastic. Of two men, each obeying his own thought, he whose thought is deepest will be the strongest character. Always one man more than another represents the will of Divine Providence to the period.

2. If thought makes free, so does the moral sentiment. The

mixtures of spiritual chemistry refuse to be analyzed. Yet we can see that with the perception of truth is joined the desire that it shall prevail; that affection is essential to will. Moreover, when a strong will appears, it usually results from a certain unity of organization, as if the whole energy of body and mind flowed in one direction. All great force is real and elemental. There is no manufacturing a strong will. There must be a pound to balance a pound. Where power is shown in will, it must rest on the universal force. Alaric and Bonaparte must believe they rest on a truth, or their will can be bought or bent. There is a bribe possible for any finite will. But the pure sympathy with universal ends is an infinite force, and cannot be bribed or bent. Whoever has had experience of the moral sentiment cannot choose but believe in unlimited power. Each pulse from that heart is an oath from the Most High. I know not what the word *sublime* means, if it be not the intimations, in this infant, of a terrific force. A text of heroism, a name and anecdote of courage, are not arguments bu sallies of freedom. One of these is the verse of the Persian Hafiz, "'T is written on the gate of Heaven, 'Woe unto him who suffers himself to be betrayed by Fate!'" Does the reading of history make us fatalists? What courage does not the opposite opinion show! A little whim of will to be free gallantly contending against the universe of chemistry.

But insight is not will, nor is affection will. Perception is cold, and goodness dies in wishes. As Voltaire said, 't is the misfortune of worthy people that they are cowards; "*un des plus grands malheurs des honnêtes gens c'est qu'ils sont des lâches.*" There must be a fusion of these two to generate the energy of will. There can be no driving force except through the conversion of the man into his will, making him the will, and the will him. And one may say boldly that no man has a right perception of any truth who has not been reacted on by it so as to be ready to be its martyr.

The one serious and formidable thing in nature is a will. Society is servile from want of will, and therefore the world wants saviours and religions. One way is right to go; the hero sees it, and moves on that aim, and has the world under him for root and support. He is to others as the world. His approbation is honor; his dissent, infamy. The glance of his eye has the force of sunbeams. A personal influence towers up in memory only worthy, and we gladly forget numbers, money, climate, gravitation, and the rest of Fate.

We can afford to allow the limitation, if we know it is the meter of the growing man. We stand against Fate, as children stand up against the wall in their father's house and notch their height from year to year. But when the boy grows to man, and is master of the house, he pulls down that wall and builds a new and bigger. 'T is only a question of time. Every brave youth is in training to ride and rule this dragon. His science is to make weapons and wings of these passions and retarding forces. Now whether, seeing these two things, fate and power, we are permitted to believe in unity? The bulk of mankind believe in two gods. They are under one dominion here in the house, as friend and parent, in social circles, in letters, in art, in love, in religion; but in mechanics, in dealing with steam and climate, in trade, in politics, they think they come under another; and that it would be a practical blunder to transfer the method and way of working of one sphere into the other. What good, honest, generous men at home, will be wolves and foxes on 'Change! What pious men in the parlor will vote for what reprobates at the polls! To a certain point, they believe themselves the care of a Providence. But in a steamboat, in an epidemic, in war, they believe a malignant energy rules.

But relation and connection are not somewhere and sometimes, but everywhere and always. The divine order does not stop where their sight stops. The friendly power works on the same rules in the next farm and the next planet. But where they have not experience they run against it and hurt themselves. Fate then is a name for facts not yet passed under the fire of thought; for causes which are unpenetrated.

But every jet of chaos which threatens to exterminate us is convertible by intellect into wholesome force. Fate is unpenetrated causes. The water drowns ship and sailor like a grain of dust. But learn to swim, trim your bark, and the wave which drowned it will be cloven by it and carry it like its own foam, a plume and a power. The cold is inconsiderate of persons, tingles your blood, freezes a man like a dew-drop. But learn to skate, and the ice will give you a graceful, sweet, and poetic motion. The cold will brace your limbs and brain to genius, and make you foremost men of time. Cold and sea will train an imperial Saxon race, which nature cannot bear to lose, and after cooping it up for a thousand years in yonder England, gives a hundred Englands, a hundred Mexicos. All the bloods it shall absorb and domineer: and more than Mexicos, the secrets of water and steam, the spasms of electricity, the ductility of metals, the chariot of the air, the ruddered balloon are awaiting you.

The annual slaughter from typhus far exceeds that of war; but right drainage destroys typhus. The plague in the sea-service from scurvy is healed by lemon juice and other diets portable or procurable; the depopulation by cholera and small-pox is ended by drainage and vaccination; and every other pest is not less in the chain of cause and effect, and may be fought off. And whilst art draws out the venom, it commonly extorts some benefit from the vanquished enemy. The mischievous torrent is taught to drudge for man; the wild beasts he makes useful for food, or dress, or labor; the chemic explosions are controlled like his watch. These are now the steeds on which he rides. Man moves in all modes, by legs of horses, by wings of wind, by steam, by gas of balloon, by electricity, and stands on tiptoe threatening to hunt the eagle in his own element. There's nothing he will not make his carrier.

Steam was till the other day the devil which we dreaded. Every pot made by any human potter or brazier had a hole in its cover, to let off the enemy, lest he should lift pot and roof and carry the house away. But the Marquis of Worcester, Watt, and Fulton bethought themselves that where was power was not devil, but was God; that it must be availed of, and not by any means let off and wasted. Could he lift pots and roofs and houses so handily? He was the workman they were in search of. He could be used to lift away, chain and compel other devils far more reluctant and dangerous, namely, cubic miles of earth, mountains, weight or resistance of water, machinery, and the labors of all men in the world; and time he shall lengthen, and shorten space.

It has not fared much otherwise with higher kinds of steam. The opinion of the million was the terror of the world, and it was attempted either to dissipate it, by amusing nations, or to pile it over with strata of society,—a layer of soldiers, over that a layer of lords, and a king on the top; with clamps and hoops of castles, garrisons, and police. But sometimes the religious principle would get in and burst the hoops and rive every mountain laid on top of it. The Fultons and Watts of politics, believing in unity, saw that it was a power, and by satisfying it (as justice satisfies everybody), through a different disposition of society,—grouping it on a level instead of piling it into a mountain,—they have contrived to make of this terror the most harmless and energetic form of a State.

Very odious, I confess, are the lessons of Fate. Who likes to have a dapper phrenologist pronouncing on his fortunes? Who likes to believe that he has, hidden in his skull, spine, and pelvis, all the vices of a Saxon or Celtic race, which will be sure to pull him down,—with what grandeur of hope and resolve he is fired,—into a selfish, huckstering, servile, dodging animal? A learned physician tells us the fact is invariable with the Neapolitan, that when mature he assumes the forms of the unmistakable scoundrel. That is a little overstated,—but may pass.

But these are magazines and arsenals. A man must thank his defects, and stand in some terror of his talents. A transcendent talent draws so largely on his forces as to lame him; a defect pays him revenues on the other side. The sufferance which is the badge of the Jew, has made him, in these days, the ruler of the rulers of the earth. If Fate is ore and quarry, if evil is good in the making, if limitation is power that shall be, if calamities, oppositions, and weights are wings and means,—we are reconciled.

Fate involves the melioration. No statement of the Universe can have any soundness which does not admit its ascending effort. The direction of the whole and of the parts is toward benefit, and in proportion to the health. Behind every individual closes organization; before him opens liberty,—the Better, the Best. The first and worse races are dead. The second and imperfect races are dying out, or remain for the maturing of higher. In the latest race, in man, every generosity, every new perception, the love and praise he extorts from his fellows, are certificates of advance out of fate into freedom. Liberation of the will from the sheaths and clogs of organization which he has outgrown, is the end and aim of this world. Every calamity is a spur and valuable hint; and where his endeavors do not yet fully avail, they tell as tendency. The whole circle of animal life—tooth against tooth, devouring war, war for food, a yelp of pain and a grunt of triumph, until at last the whole menagerie, the whole chemical mass is mellowed and refined for higher use—pleases at a sufficient perspective.

But to see how fate slides into freedom and freedom into fate, observe how far the roots of every creature run, or find if you can a point where there is no thread of connection. Our life is consentaneous and far-related. This knot of nature is so well tied that nobody was ever cunning enough to find the two ends. Nature is intricate, overlapped, interweaved and endless. Christopher Wren said of the beautiful King's College chapel, that "if anybody would tell him where to lay the first stone, he would build such another." But where shall we find the first atom in this house of man, which is all consent, inosculation and balance of parts?

The web of relation is shown in *habitat*, shown in hibernation. When hibernation was observed, it was found that whilst some animals became torpid in winter, others were torpid in summer: hibernation then was a false name. The *long sleep* is not an effect of cold, but is regulated by the supply of food proper to the animal. It becomes torpid when the fruit or prey it lives on is not in season, and regains its activity when its food is ready.

Eyes are found in light; ears in auricular air; feet on land; fins in water; wings in air; and each creature where it was meant to be, with a mutual fitness. Every zone has its own *Fauna*. There is adjustment between the animal and its food, its parasite, its enemy. Balances are kept. It is not allowed to diminish in numbers, nor to exceed. The like adjustments exist for man. His food is cooked when he arrives; his coal in the pit; the house ventilated; the mud of the deluge dried; his companions arrived at the same hour, and awaiting him with love, concert, laughter and tears. These are coarse adjustments, but the invisible are not less. There are more belongings to every creature than his air and his food. His instincts must be met, and he has predisposing power that bends and fits what is near him to his use. He is not possible until the invisible things are right for him, as well as the visible. Of what changes then in sky and earth, and in finer skies and earths, does the appearance of some Dante or Columbus apprise us!

How is this effected? Nature is no spendthrift, but takes the shortest way to her ends. As the general says to his soldiers, "If you want a fort, build a fort," so nature makes every creature do its own work and get its living,—is it planet, animal or tree. The planet makes itself. The animal cell makes itself;—then, what it wants. Every creature, wren or dragon, shall make its own lair. As soon as there is life, there is self-direction and absorbing and using of material. Life is freedom,—life in the direct ratio of its amount. You may be sure the new-born man is not inert. Life works both voluntarily and supernaturally in its neighborhood. Do you suppose he can be estimated by his weight in pounds, or that he is contained in his skin,—this reaching, radiating, jaculating fellow? The smallest candle fills a mile with its rays, and the papillæ of a man run out to every star.

When there is something to be done, the world knows how to get it done. The vegetable eye makes leaf, pericarp, root, bark, or thorn, as the need is; the first cell converts itself into stomach, mouth, nose, or nail, according to the want; the world throws its life into a hero or a shepherd, and puts him where he is wanted. Dante and Columbus were Italians, in their time; they would be Russians or Americans to-day. Things ripen, new men come. The adaptation is not capricious. The ulterior aim, the purpose beyond itself, the correlation by which planets subside and crystallize, then animate beasts and men,—will not stop but will work into finer particulars, and from finer to finest.

The secret of the world is the tie between person and event. Person makes event, and event person. The "times," "the age," what is that but a few profound persons and a few active persons who epitomize the times?—Goethe, Hegel, Metternich, Adams, Calhoun, Guizot, Peel, Cobden, Kossuth, Rothschild, Astor, Brunel, and the rest. The same fitness must be presumed between a man and the time and event, as between the sexes, or between a race of animals and the food it eats, or the inferior races it uses. He thinks his fate alien, because the copula is hidden. But the soul contains the event that shall befall it; for the event is only the actualization of its thoughts, and what we pray to ourselves for is always granted. The event is the print of your form. It fits you like your skin. What each does is proper to him. Events are the children of his body and mind. We learn that the soul of Fate is the soul of us, as Hafiz sings,—

> "Alas! till now I had not known,
> My guide and fortune's guide are one."

All the toys that infatuate men and which they play for,—houses, land, money, luxury, power, fame, are the selfsame thing, with a new gauze or two of illusion overlaid. And of all the drums and rattles by which men are made willing to have their heads broke, and are led out solemnly every morning to parade,—the most admirable is this by which we are brought to believe that events are arbitrary and independent of actions. At the conjuror's, we detect the hair by which he moves his puppet, but we have not eyes sharp enough to descry the thread that ties cause and effect.

Nature magically suits the man to his fortunes, by making these the fruit of his character. Ducks take to the water, eagles to the sky, waders to the sea margin, hunters to the forest, clerks to counting-rooms, soldiers to the frontier. Thus events grow on the same stem with persons; are sub-persons. The pleasure of life is according to the man that lives it, and not according to the work or the place. Life is an ecstasy. We know what madness belongs to love,—what power to paint a vile object in hues of heaven. As insane persons are indifferent to their dress, diet, and other accommodations, and as we do in dreams, with equanimity, the most absurd acts, so a drop more of wine in our cup of life will reconcile us to strange company and work. Each creature puts forth from itself its own condition and sphere, as the slug sweats out its slimy house on the pear-leaf, and the woolly aphides on the apple perspire their own bed, and the fish its shell. In youth we clothe ourselves with rainbows and go as brave as the zodiac. In age we put out another sort of perspiration,—gout, fever, rheumatism, caprice, doubt, fretting and avarice.

A man's fortunes are the fruit of his character. A man's friends

are his magnetisms. We go to Herodotus and Plutarch for examples of Fate; but we are examples. "*Quisque suos patimur manes.*"[2]
The tendency of every man to enact all that is in his constitution
is expressed in the old belief that the efforts which we make to
escape from our destiny only serve to lead us into it: and I have
noticed a man likes better to be complimented on his position, as
the proof of the last or total excellence, than on his merits.

A man will see his character emitted in the events that seem to
meet, but which exude from and accompany him. Events expand
with the character. As once he found himself among toys, so now
he plays a part in colossal systems, and his growth is declared in
his ambition, his companions and his performance. He looks like
a piece of luck, but is a piece of causation; the mosaic, angulated
and ground to fit into the gap he fills. Hence in each town there is
some man who is, in his brain and performance, an explanation
of the tillage, production, factories, banks, churches, ways of living and society of that town. If you do not chance to meet him, all
that you see will leave you a little puzzled; if you see him it will
become plain. We know in Massachusetts who built New Bedford, who built Lynn, Lowell, Lawrence, Clinton, Fitchburg,
Holyoke, Portland, and many another noisy mart. Each of these
men, if they were transparent, would seem to you not so much
men as walking cities, and wherever you put them they would
build one.

History is the action and reaction of these two,—Nature and
Thought; two boys pushing each other on the curbstone of the
pavement. Everything is pusher or pushed; and matter and mind
are in perpetual tilt and balance, so. Whilst the man is weak, the
earth takes up him. He plants his brain and affections. By and by
he will take up the earth, and have his gardens and vineyards in
the beautiful order and productiveness of his thought. Every solid
in the universe is ready to become fluid on the approach of the
mind, and the power to flux it is the measure of the mind. If the
wall remain adamant, it accuses the want of thought. To a subtle
force it will stream into new forms, expressive of the character of
the mind. What is the city in which we sit here, but an aggregate
of incongruous materials which have obeyed the will of some

man? The granite was reluctant, but his hands were stronger, and it came. Iron was deep in the ground and well combined with stone, but could not hide from his fires. Wood, lime, stuffs, fruits, gums, were dispersed over the earth and sea, in vain. Here they are, within reach of every man's day-labor,—what he wants of them. The whole world is the flux of matter over the wires of thought to the poles or points where it would build. The races of men rise out of the ground preoccupied with a thought which rules them, and divided into parties ready armed and angry to fight for this metaphysical abstraction. The quality of the thought differences the Egyptian and the Roman, the Austrian and the American. The men who come on the stage at one period are all found to be related to each other. Certain ideas are in the air. We are all impressionable, for we are made of them; all impressionable, but some more than others, and these first express them. This explains the curious contemporaneousness of inventions and discoveries. The truth is in the air, and the most impressionable brain will announce it first, but all will announce it a few minutes later. So women, as most susceptible, are the best index of the coming hour. So the great man, that is, the man most imbued with the spirit of the time, is the impressionable man;—of a fibre irritable and delicate, like iodine to light. He feels the infinitesimal attractions. His mind is righter than others because he yields to a current so feeble as can be felt only by a needle delicately poised.

The correlation is shown in defects. Möller, in his Essay on Architecture, taught that the building which was fitted accurately to answer its end would turn out to be beautiful though beauty had not been intended. I find the like unity in human structures rather virulent and pervasive; that a crudity in the blood will appear in the argument; a hump in the shoulder will appear in the speech and handiwork. If his mind could be seen, the hump would be seen. If a man has a see-saw in his voice, it will run into his sentences, into his poem, into the structure of his fable, into his speculation, into his charity. And as every man is hunted by his own dæmon, vexed by his own disease, this checks all his activity.

So each man, like each plant, has his parasites. A strong, astringent, bilious nature has more truculent enemies than the slugs and moths that fret my leaves. Such all one has curculios, borers, knife-worms; a swindler ate him first, then a client, then a quack, then smooth, plausible gentlemen, bitter and selfish as Moloch.

This correlation really existing can be divined. If the threads are there, thought can follow and show them. Especially when a soul is quick and docile, as Chaucer sings:—

> "Or if the soule of proper kind
> Be so parfite as men find,
> That it wot what is to come,
> And that he warneth all and some
> Of everiche of hir aventures,
> By avisions or figures;
> But that our flesh hath no might
> To understand it aright
> For it is warned too derkely."[3]

Some people are made up of rhyme, coincidence, omen, periodicity, and presage: they meet the person they seek; what their companion prepares to say to them, they first say to him; and a hundred signs apprise them of what is about to befall.

Wonderful intricacy in the web, wonderful constancy in the design this vagabond life admits. We wonder how the fly finds its mate, and yet year after year, we find two men, two women, without legal or carnal tie, spend a great part of their best time within a few feet of each other. And the moral is that what we seek we shall find; what we flee from flees from us; as Goethe said, "what we wish for in youth, comes in heaps on us in old age," too often cursed with the granting of our prayer: and hence the high caution, that since we are sure of having what we wish, we beware to ask only for high things.

One key, one solution to the mysteries of human condition, one solution to the old knots of fate, freedom, and foreknowledge, exists; the propounding, namely, of the double consciousness. A man must ride alternately on the horses of his private and his public nature, as the equestrians in the circus throw themselves nimbly from horse to horse, or plant one foot on the back of one and the other foot on the back of the other. So when a man is the victim of his fate, has sciatica in his loins and cramp in his mind; a club-foot and a club in his wit; a sour face and a selfish temper; a strut in his gait and a conceit in his affection; or is ground to powder by the vice of his race;—he is to rally on his relation to the Universe, which his ruin benefits. Leaving the dæmon who suffers, he is to take sides with the Deity who secures universal benefit by his pain.

To offset the drag of temperament and race, which pulls down, learn this lesson, namely, that by the cunning co-presence of two elements, which is throughout nature, whatever lames or paralyzes you draws in with it the divinity, in some form, to repay. A good intention clothes itself with sudden power. When a god wishes to ride, any chip or pebble will bud and shoot out winged feet and serve him for a horse.

Let us build altars to the Blessed Unity which holds nature and souls in perfect solution, and compels every atom to serve an universal end. I do not wonder at a snow-flake, a shell, a summer landscape, or the glory of the stars; but at the necessity of beauty under which the universe lies; that all is and must be pictorial; that the rainbow and the curve of the horizon and the arch of the blue vault are only results from the organism of the eye. There is no need for foolish amateurs to fetch me to admire a garden of flowers, or a sun-gilt cloud, or a waterfall, when I cannot look without seeing splendor and grace. How idle to choose a random sparkle here or there, when the indwelling necessity plants the rose of beauty on the brow of chaos, and discloses the central intention of Nature to be harmony and joy.

Let us build altars to the Beautiful Necessity. If we thought men were free in the sense that in a single exception one fantastical will could prevail over the law of things, it were all one as if a child's hand could pull down the sun. If in the least particular one could derange the order of nature,—who would accept the gift of life?

Let us build altars to the Beautiful Necessity, which secures that all is made of one piece; that plaintiff and defendant, friend and enemy, animal and planet, food and eater are of one kind. In astronomy is vast space but no foreign system; in geology, vast time but the same laws as to-day. Why should we be afraid of

Nature, which is no other than "philosophy and theology embodied"? Why should we fear to be crushed by savage elements, we who are made up of the same elements? Let us build to the Beautiful Necessity, which makes man brave in believing that he cannot shun a danger that is appointed, nor incur one that is not; to the Necessity which rudely or softly educates him to the perception that there are no contingencies; that Law rules throughout existence; a Law which is not intelligent but intelligence;—not personal nor impersonal—it disdains words and passes understanding; it dissolves persons; it vivifies nature; yet solicits the pure in heart to draw on all its omnipotence.

NOTES

1. Emerson's translation of a German version of a Persian poem by Ali ben Aba Toleb.
2. Virgil—"Each of us suffers his own spirit."
3. *The House of Fame.*

THOREAU

A queen rejoices in her peers,
And wary Nature knows her own,
By court and city, dale and down,
And like a lover volunteers,
And to her son will treasures more,
And more to purpose, freely pour
In one wood walk, than learned men
Will find with glass in ten times ten.

It seemed as if the breezes brought him,
It seemed as if the sparrows taught him,
As if by secret sign he knew
Where in far fields the orchis grew.

Henry David Thoreau was the last male descendant of a French
ancestor who came to this country from the Isle of Guernsey. His
character exhibited occasional traits drawn from this blood, in
singular combination with a very strong Saxon genius.

He was born in Concord, Massachusetts, on the 12th of July,
1817. He was graduated at Harvard College in 1837, but without
any literary distinction. An iconoclast in literature, he seldom
thanked colleges for their service to him, holding them in small
esteem, whilst yet his debt to them was important. After leaving
the University, he joined his brother in teaching a private school,
which he soon renounced. His father was a manufacturer of lead-
pencils, and Henry applied himself for a time to this craft, believing he could make a better pencil than was then in use. After

completing his experiments, he exhibited his work to chemists and artists in Boston, and having obtained their certificates to its excellence and to its equality with the best London manufacture, he returned home contented. His friends congratulated him that he had now opened his way to fortune. But he replied that he should never make another pencil. "Why should I? I would not do again what I have done once." He resumed his endless walks and miscellaneous studies, making every day some new acquaintance with Nature, though as yet never speaking of zoölogy or botany, since, though very studious of natural facts, he was incurious of technical and textual science.

At this time, a strong, healthy youth, fresh from college, whilst all his companions were choosing their profession, or eager to begin some lucrative employment, it was inevitable that his thoughts should be exercised on the same question, and it required rare decision to refuse all the accustomed paths and keep his solitary freedom at the cost of disappointing the natural expectations of his family and friends: all the more difficult that he had a perfect probity, was exact in securing his own independence, and in holding every man to the like duty. But Thoreau never faltered. He was a born protestant. He declined to give up his large ambition of knowledge and action for any narrow craft or profession, aiming at a much more comprehensive calling, the art of living well. If he slighted and defied the opinions of others, it was only that he was more intent to reconcile his practice with his own belief. Never idle or self-indulgent, he preferred, when he wanted money, earning it by some piece of manual labor agreeable to him, as building a boat or a fence, planting, grafting, surveying or other short work, to any long engagements. With his hardy habits and few wants, his skill in wood-craft, and his powerful arithmetic, he was very competent to live in any part of the world. It would cost him less time to supply his wants than another. He was therefore secure of his leisure.

A natural skill for mensuration, growing out of his mathematical knowledge and his habit of ascertaining the measures and distances of objects which interested him, the size of trees, the depth and extent of ponds and rivers, the height of mountains and the air-line distance of his favorite summits,—this, and his intimate knowledge of the territory about Concord, made him drift into the profession of land-surveyor. It had the advantage for him that it led him continually into new and secluded grounds, and helped his studies of Nature. His accuracy and skill in this work were readily appreciated, and he found all the employment he wanted.

He could easily solve the problems of the surveyor, but he was daily beset with graver questions, which he manfully confronted. He interrogated every custom, and wished to settle all his practice on an ideal foundation. He was a protestant *à outrance*,[1] and few lives contain so many renunciations. He was bred to no profession; he never married; he lived alone; he never went to church; he never voted; he refused to pay a tax to the State; he ate no flesh, he drank no wine, he never knew the use of tobacco; and, though a naturalist, he used neither trap nor gun. He chose, wisely no doubt for himself, to be the bachelor of thought and Nature. He had no talent for wealth, and knew how to be poor without the least hint of squalor or inelegance. Perhaps he fell into his way of living without forecasting it much, but approved it with later wisdom. "I am often reminded," he wrote in his journal, "that if I had bestowed on me the wealth of Crœsus, my aims must be still the same, and my means essentially the same." He had no temptations to fight against,—no appetites, no passions, no taste for elegant trifles. A fine house, dress, the manners and talk of highly cultivated people were all thrown away on him. He much preferred a good Indian, and considered these refinements as impediments to conversation, wishing to meet his companion on the simplest terms. He declined invitations to dinner-parties, because there each was in every one's way, and he could not meet the individuals to any purpose. "They make their pride," he said, "in making their dinner cost much; I make my pride in making my dinner cost little." When asked at table what dish he preferred, he answered, "The nearest." He did not like the taste of wine, and never had a vice in his life. He said,—"I have a faint recollection of pleasure derived from smoking dried lily-stems, before I was a man. I had commonly a supply of these. I have never smoked anything more noxious."

He chose to be rich by making his wants few, and supplying them himself. In his travels, he used the railroad only to get over so much country as was unimportant to the present purpose, walking hundreds of miles, avoiding taverns, buying a lodging in farmers' and fishermen's houses, as cheaper, and more agreeable to him, and because there he could better find the men and the information he wanted.

There was somewhat military in his nature, not to be subdued, always manly and able, but rarely tender, as if he did not feel himself except in opposition. He wanted a fallacy to expose, a blunder to pillory, I may say required a little sense of victory, a roll of the drum, to call his powers into full exercise. It cost him nothing to say No; indeed he found it much easier than to say Yes. It seemed as if his first instinct on hearing a proposition was to controvert it, so impatent was he of the limitations of our daily thought. This habit, of course, is a little chilling to the social affections; and though the companion would in the end acquit him of any malice or untruth, yet it mars conversation. Hence, no equal companion stood in affectionate relations with one so pure and guileless. "I love Henry," said one of his friends, "but I cannot like him; and as for taking his arm, I should as soon think of taking the arm of an elm-tree.'

Yet, hermit and stoic as he was, he was really fond of sympathy, and threw himself heartily and childlike into the company of young people whom he loved, and whom he delighted to entertain, as he only could, with the varied and endless anecdotes of his experiences by field and river: and he was always ready to lead a huckleberry-party or a search for chestnuts or grapes. Talking, one day, of a public discourse, Henry remarked that whatever succeeded with the audience was bad. I said, "Who would not like to write something which all can read, like Robinson Crusoe? and who does not see with regret that his page is not solid with a right materialistic treatment, which delights everybody?" Henry objected, of course, and vaunted the better lectures which reached only a few persons. But, at supper, a young girl, understanding that he was to lecture at the Lyceum, sharply asked him, "Whether his lecture would be a nice, interesting story, such as she wished to hear, or whether it was one of those old philosophical things that she did not care about." Henry turned to her, and bethought himself, and, I saw, was trying to believe that he had matter that might fit her and her brother, who were to sit up and go to the lecture, if it was a good one for them.

He was a speaker and actor of the truth, born such, and was ever running into dramatic situations from this cause. In any circumstance it interested all bystanders to know what part Henry would take, and what he would say; and he did not disappoint expectation, but used an original judgment on each emergency. In 1845 he built himself a small framed house on the shores of Walden Pond, and lived there two years alone, a life of labor and study. This action was quite native and fit for him. No one who knew him would tax him with affectation. He was more unlike his neighbors in his thought than in his action. As soon as he had exhausted the advantages of that solitude, he abandoned it. In 1847, not approving some uses to which the public expenditure was applied, he refused to pay his town tax, and was put in jail. A friend paid the tax for him, and he was released. The like annoyance was threatened the next year. But as his friends paid the tax, notwithstanding his protest, I believe he ceased to resist. No opposition or ridicule had any weight with him. He coldly and fully stated his opinion without affecting to believe that it was the opinion of the company. It was of no consequence if every one present held the opposite opinion. On one occasion he went to the University Library to procure some books. The librarian refused to lend them. Mr. Thoreau repaired to the President, who stated to him the rules and usages, which permitted the loan of books to resident graduates, to clergymen who were alumni, and to some others resident within a circle of ten miles' radius from the College. Mr. Thoreau explained to the President that the railroad had destroyed the old scale of distances,—that the library was useless, yes, and President and College useless, on the terms of his rules,— that the one benefit he owed to the College was its library,—that, at this moment, not only his want of books was imperative, but he wanted a large number of books, and assured him that he, Thoreau, and not the librarian, was the proper custodian of these. In short, the President found the petitioner so formidable, and the rules getting to look so ridiculous, that he ended by giving him a privilege which in his hands proved unlimited thereafter.

No truer American existed than Thoreau. His preference of his

country and condition was genuine, and his aversation from English and European manners and tastes almost reached contempt.
He listened impatiently to news or bonmots gleaned from London
circles; and though he tried to be civil, these anecdotes fatigued
him. The men were all imitating each other, and on a small
mould. Why can they not live as far apart as possible, and each be
a man by himself? What he sought was the most energetic nature;
and he wished to go to Oregon, not to London. "In every part of
Great Britain," he wrote in his diary, "are discovered traces of the
Romans, their funereal urns, their camps, their roads, their dwell-
ings. But New England, at least, is not based on any Roman ruins.
We have not to lay the foundations of our houses on the ashes of a
former civilization."

But idealist as he was, standing for abolition of slavery, abolition of tariffs, almost for abolition of government, it is needless to
say he found himself not only unrepresented in actual politics, but
almost equally opposed to every class of reformers. Yet he paid
the tribute of his uniform respect to the Anti-Slavery party. One
man, whose personal acquaintance he had formed, he honored
with exceptional regard. Before the first friendly word had been
spoken for Captain John Brown, he sent notices to most houses in
Concord that he would speak in a public hall on the condition
and character of John Brown, on Sunday evening, and invited all
people to come. The Republican Committee, the Abolitionist
Committee, sent him word that it was premature and not advis-
able. He replied,—"I did not send to you for advice, but to
announce that I am to speak." The hall was filled at an early hour
by people of all parties, and his earnest eulogy of the hero was
heard by all respectfully, by many with a sympathy that surprised
themselves.

It was said of Plotinus that he was ashamed of his body, and 't
is very likely he had good reason for it,—that his body was a bad
servant, and he had not skill in dealing with the material world,
as happens often to men of abstract intellect. But Mr. Thoreau
was equipped with a most adapted and serviceable body. He was
of short stature, firmly built, of light complexion, with strong,
serious blue eyes, and a grave aspect,—his face covered in the late
years with a becoming beard. His senses were acute, his frame

well-knit and hardy, his hands strong and skilful in the use of tools. And there was a wonderful fitness of body and mind. He could pace sixteen rods more accurately than another man could measure them with rod and chain. He could find his path in the woods at night, he said, better by his feet than his eyes. He could estimate the measure of a tree very well by his eye; he could estimate the weight of a calf or a pig, like a dealer. From a box containing a bushel or more of loose pencils, he could take up with his hands fast enough just a dozen pencils at every grasp. He was a good swimmer, runner, skater, boatman, and would probably outwalk most countrymen in a day's journey. And the relation of body to mind was still finer than we have indicated. He said he wanted every stride his legs made. The length of his walk uniformly made the length of his writing. If shut up in the house he did not write at all.

He had a strong common sense, like that which Rose Flammock, the weaver's daughter in Scott's romance, commends in her father, as resembling a yardstick, which, whilst it measures dowlas and diaper, can equally well measure tapestry and cloth of gold. He had always a new resource. When I was planting forest trees, and had procured half a peck of acorns, he said that only a small portion of them would be sound, and proceeded to examine them and select the sound ones. But finding this took time, he said, "I think if you put them all into water the good ones will sink;" which experiment we tried with success. He could plan a garden or a house or a barn; would have been competent to lead a "Pacific Exploring Expedition;" could give judicious counsel in the gravest private or public affairs.

He lived for the day, not cumbered and mortified by his memory. If he brought you yesterday a new proposition, he would bring you to-day another not less revolutionary. A very industrious man, and setting, like all highly organized men, a high value on his time, he seemed the only man of leisure in town, always ready for any excursion that promised well, or for conversation prolonged into late hours. His trenchant sense was never stopped by his rules of daily prudence, but was always up to the new occasion. He liked and used the simplest food, yet, when some one urged a vegetable diet, Thoreau thought all diets a very small matter, saying that "the man who shoots the buffalo lives better than the man who boards at the Graham House." He said,— "You can sleep near the railroad, and never be disturbed: Nature knows very well what sounds are worth attending to, and has made up her mind not to hear the railroad-whistle. But things respect the devout mind, and a mental ecstasy was never interrupted." He noted what repeatedly befell him, that, after receiving from a distance a rare plant, he would presently find the same in his own haunts. And those pieces of luck which happen only to good players happened to him. One day, walking with a stranger, who inquired where Indian arrowheads could be found, he replied, "Everywhere," and, stooping forward, picked one on the instant from the ground. At Mount Washington, in Tuckerman's Ravine, Thoreau had a bad fall, and sprained his foot. As he was in the act of getting up from his fall, he saw for the first time the leaves of the *Arnica mollis*.

His robust common sense, armed with stout hands, keen perceptions and strong will, cannot yet account for the superiority which shone in his simple and hidden life. I must add the cardinal fact, that there was an excellent wisdom in him, proper to a rare class of men, which showed him the material world as a means and symbol. This discovery, which sometimes yields to poets a certain casual and interrupted light, serving for the ornament of their writing, was in him an unsleeping insight; and whatever faults or obstructions of temperament might cloud it, he was not disobedient to the heavenly vision. In his youth, he said, one day, "The other world is all my art; my pencils will draw no other; my jack-knife will cut nothing else; I do not use it as a means." This was the muse and genius that ruled his opinions, conversation, studies, work and course of life. This made him a searching judge of men. At first glance he measured his companion, and, though insensible to some fine traits of culture, could very well report his weight and calibre. And this made the impression of genius which his conversation sometimes gave.

He understood the matter in hand at a glance, and saw the limitations and poverty of those he talked with, so that nothing seemed concealed from such terrible eyes. I have repeatedly known young men of sensibility converted in a moment to the belief that this was the man they were in search of, the man of men, who could tell them all they should do. His own dealing with them was never affectionate, but superior, didactic, scorning their petty ways,—very slowly conceding, or not conceding at all, the promise of his society at their houses, or even at his own. "Would he not walk with them?" "He did not know. There was nothing so important to him as his walk; he had no walks to throw away on company." Visits were offered him from respectful parties, but he declined them. Admiring friends offered to carry him at their own cost to the Yellowstone River,—to the West Indies,—to South America. But though nothing could be more grave or considered than his refusals, they remind one, in quite new relations, of that fop Brummel's reply to the gentleman who offered him his carriage in a shower, "But where will *you* ride, then?"—and what accusing silences, and what searching and irresistible speeches, battering down all defences, his companions can remember!

Mr. Thoreau dedicated his genius with such entire love to the fields, hills and waters of his native town, that he made them known and interesting to all reading Americans, and to people over the sea. The river on whose banks he was born and died he knew from its springs to its confluence with the Merrimack. He had made summer and winter observations on it for many years, and at every hour of the day and night. The result of the recent survey of the Water Commissioners appointed by the State of Massachusetts he had reached by his private experiments, several years earlier. Every fact which occurs in the bed, on the banks or in the air over it; the fishes, and their spawning and nests, their manners, their food; the shad-flies which fill the air on a certain evening once a year, and which are snapped at by the fishes so ravenously that many of these die of repletion; the conical heaps of small stones on the river-shallows, the huge nests of small fishes, one of which will sometimes overfill a cart; the birds which frequent the stream, heron, duck, sheldrake, loon, osprey; the snake, muskrat, otter, woodchuck and fox, on the banks; the turtle, frog, hyla and cricket, which make the banks vocal,—were all known to him, and, as it were, townsmen and fellow creatures; so that he felt an absurdity or violence in any narrative of one of these by itself apart, and still more of its dimensions on an inch-rule, or in the exhibition of its skeleton, or the specimen of a squirrel or a bird in brandy. He liked to speak of the manners of the river, as itself a lawful creature, yet with exactness, and always to an observed fact. As he knew the river, so the ponds in this region.

One of the weapons he used, more important to him than microscope or alcohol-receiver to other investigators, was a whim which grew on hin by indulgence, yet appeared in gravest statement, namely, of extolling his own town and neighborhood as the most favored centre for natural observation. He remarked that the Flora of Massachusetts embraced almost all the important plants of America,—most of the oaks, most of the willows, the best pines, the ash, the maple, the beech, the nuts. He returned Kane's "Arctic Voyage" to a friend of whom he had borrowed it, with the remark, that "Most of the phenomena noted might be observed in Concord." He seemed a little envious of the Pole, for the coincident sunrise and sunset, or five minutes' day after six months: a splendid fact, which Annursnuc had never afforded him. He found red snow in one of his walks, and told me that he expected to find yet the *Victoria regia* in Concord. He was the attorney of the indigenous plants, and owned to a preference of the weeds to the imported plants, as of the Indian to the civilized man, and noticed, with pleasure, that the willow bean-poles of his neighbor had grown more than his beans. "See these weeds," he said, "which have been hoed at by a million farmers all spring and summer, and yet have prevailed, and just now come out triumphant over all lanes, pastures, fields and gardens, such is their vigor. We have insulted them with low names, too,—as Pigweed, Wormwood, Chick-weed, Shad-blossom." He says, "They have brave names, too,—Ambrosia, Stellaria, Amelanchier, Amarantn, etc."

I think his fancy for referring everything to the meridian of Concord did not grow out of any ignorance or depreciation of other longitudes or latitudes, but was rather a playful expression of his conviction of the indifference of all places, and that the best place for each is where he stands. He expressed it once in this wise: "I think nothing is to be hoped from you, if this bit of mould under your feet is not sweeter to you to eat than any other in this world, or in any world."

The other weapon with which he conquered all obstacles in science was patience. He knew how to sit immovable a part of the rock he rested on, until the bird, the reptile, the fish, which had retired from him, should come back and resume its habits, nay, moved by curiosity, should come to him and watch him.

It was a pleasure and a privilege to walk with him. He knew the country like a fox or a bird, and passed through it as freely by paths of his own. He knew every track in the snow or on the ground, and what creature had taken this path before him. One must submit abjectly to such a guide, and the reward was great. Under his arm he carried an old music-book to press plants; in his pocket, his diary and pencil, a spy-glass for birds, microscope, jack-knife and twine. He wore a straw hat, stout shoes, strong gray trousers, to brave scrub-oaks and smilax, and to climb a tree for a hawk's or a squirrel's nest. He waded into the pool for the water-plants, and his strong legs were no insignificant part of his armor. On the day I speak of he looked for the Menyanthes, detected it across the wide pool, and, on examination of the florets, decided that it had been in flower five days. He drew out of his breast-pocket his diary, and read the names of all the plants that should bloom on this day, whereof he kept account as a banker when his notes fall due. The Cypripedium not due till to-morrow. He thought that, if waked up from a trance, in this swamp, he could tell by the plants what time of the year it was within two days. The redstart was flying about, and presently the fine grosbeaks, whose brilliant scarlet "makes the rash gazer wipe his eye," and whose fine clear note Thoreau compared to that of a tanager which has got rid of its hoarseness. Presently he heard a note which he called that of the night-warbler, a bird he had never identified, had been in search of twelve years, which always, when he saw it, was in the act of diving down into a tree or bush, and which it was vain to seek; the only bird which sings indifferently by night and by day. I told him he must beware of finding and booking it, lest life should have nothing more to show him. He said, "What you seek in vain for, half your life, one day you come full upon, all the family at dinner. You seek it like a dream, and as soon as you find it you become its prey."

His interest in the flower or the bird lay very deep in his mind, was connected with Nature,—and the meaning of Nature was never attempted to be defined by him. He would not offer a memoir of his observations to the Natural History Society. "Why should I? To detach the description from its connections in my mind would make it no longer true or valuable to me: and they do not wish what belongs to it." His power of observation seemed to indicate additional senses. He saw as with microscope, heard as with ear-trumpet, and his memory was a photographic register of all he saw and heard. And yet none knew better than he that it is not the fact that imports, but the impression or effect of the fact on your mind. Every fact lay in glory in his mind, a type of the order and beauty of the whole.

His determination on Natural History was organic. He confessed that he sometimes felt like a hound or a panther, and, if born among Indians, would have been a fell hunter. But, restrained by his Massachusetts culture, he played out the game in this mild form of botany and ichthyology. His intimacy with animals suggested what Thomas Fuller records of Butler the apiologist, that "either he had told the bees things or the bees had told him." Snakes coiled round his legs; the fishes swam into his hand, and he took them out of the water; he pulled the woodchuck out of its hole by the tail, and took the foxes under his protection from the hunters. Our naturalist had perfect magnanimity; he had no secrets: he would carry you to the heron's haunt, or even to his most prized botanical swamp,—possibly knowing that you could never find it again, yet willing to take his risks.

No college ever offered him a diploma, or a professor's chair; no academy made him its corresponding secretary, its discoverer or even its member. Perhaps these learned bodies feared the satire of his presence. Yet so much knowledge of Nature's secret and genius few others possessed; none in a more large and religious synthesis. For not a particle of respect had he to the opinions of any man or body of men, but homage solely to the truth itself; and as he discovered everywhere among doctors some leaning of courtesy, it discredited them. He grew to be revered and admired by his townsmen, who had at first known him only as an oddity. The farmers who employed him as a surveyor soon discovered his rare accuracy and skill, his knowledge of their lands, of trees, of birds, of Indian remains and the like, which enabled him to tell every farmer more than he knew before of his own farm; so that he began to feel a little as if Mr. Thoreau had better rights in his land than he. They felt, too, the superiority of character which addressed all men with a native authority.

Indian relics abound in Concord,—arrow-heads, stone chisels, pestles and fragments of pottery; and on the river-bank, large heaps of clam-shells and ashes mark spots which the savages frequented. These, and every circumstance touching the Indian, were important in his eyes. His visits to Maine were chiefly for love of the Indian. He had the satisfaction of seeing the manufacture of the bark canoe, as well as of trying his hand in its management on the rapids. He was inquisitive about the making of the stone arrow-head, and in his last days charged a youth setting out for the Rocky Mountains to find an Indian who could tell him that: "It was well worth a visit to California to learn it." Occasionally, a small party of Penobscot Indians would visit Concord, and pitch their tents for a few weeks in summer on the river-bank. He failed not to make acquaintance with the best of them; though he well knew that asking questions of Indians is like catechizing beavers and rabbits. In his last visit to Maine he had great satisfaction from Joseph Polis, an intelligent Indian of Oldtown, who was his guide for some weeks.

He was equally interested in every natural fact. The depth of his perception found likeness of law throughout Nature, and I know not any genius who so swiftly inferred universal law from the single fact. He was no pedant of a department. His eye was open to beauty, and his ear to music. He found these, not in rare conditions, but wheresoever he went. He thought the best of music was in single strains; and he found poetic suggestion in the humming of the telegraph-wire.

His poetry might be bad or good; he no doubt wanted a lyric facility and technical skill, but he had the source of poetry in his spiritual perception. He was a good reader and critic, and his judgment on poetry was to the ground of it. He could not be deceived as to the presence or absence of the poetic element in any composition, and his thirst for this made him negligent and perhaps scornful of superficial graces. He would pass by many delicate rhythms, but he would have detected every live stanza or line in a volume and knew very well where to find an equal poetic charm in prose. He was so enamoured of the spiritual beauty that he held all actual written poems in very light esteem in the comparison. He admired Æschylus and Pindar; but when some one was commending them, he said that Æschylus and the Greeks, in describing Apollo and Orpheus, had given no song, or no good one. "They ought not to have moved trees, but to have chanted to the gods such a hymn as would have sung all their old ideas out of their heads, and new ones in." His own verses are often rude and defective. The gold does not yet run pure, is drossy and crude. The thyme and marjoram are not yet honey. But if he want lyric fineness and technical merits, if he have not the poetic temperament, he never lacks the causal thought, showing that his genius was better than his talent. He knew the worth of the Imagination for the uplifting and consolation of human life, and liked to throw every thought into a symbol. The fact you tell is of no value, but only the impression. For this reason his presence was poetic, always piqued the curiosity to know more deeply the secrets of his mind. He had many reserves, an unwillingness to exhibit to profane eyes what was still sacred in his own, and knew well how to throw a poetic veil over his experience. All readers of "Walden" will remember his mythical record of his disappointments:—

"I long ago lost a hound, a bay horse and a turtledove, and am still on their trail. Many are the travellers I have spoken concerning them, describing their tracks, and what calls they answered to. I have met one or two who have heard the hound, and the tramp of the horse, and even seen the dove disappear behind a cloud; and they seemed as anxious to recover them as if they had lost them themselves."

His riddles were worth the reading, and I confide that if at any time I do not understand the expression, it is yet just. Such was the wealth of his truth that it was not worth his while to use words in vain. His poem entitled "Sympathy" reveals the tenderness under that triple steel of stoicism, and the intellectual subtility it could animate. His classic poem on "Smoke" suggests Simonides, but is better than any poem of Simonides. His biography is in his verses. His habitual thought makes all his poetry a hymn to the Cause of causes, the Spirit which vivifies and controls his own:—

> "I hearing get, who had but ears,
> And sight, who had but eyes before;
> I moments live, who lived but years,
> And truth discern, who knew but learning's lore."

And still more in these religious lines:—

> "Now chiefly is my natal hour,
> And only now my prime of life;
> I will not doubt the love untold,
> Which not my worth nor want have bought,
> Which wooed me young, and wooes me old,
> And to this evening hath me brought."

Whilst he used in his writings a certain petulance of remark in reference to churches or churchmen, he was a person of a rare, tender and absolute religion, a person incapable of any profanation, by act or by thought. Of course, the same isolation which belonged to his original thinking and living detached him from the social religious forms. This is neither to be censured nor regretted. Aristotle long ago explained it, when he said, "One who surpasses his fellow citizens in virtue is no longer a part of the city. Their law is not for him, since he is a law to himself."

Thoreau was sincerity itself, and might fortify the convictions of prophets in the ethical laws by his holy living. It was an affirmative experience which refused to be set aside. A truth-speaker he, capable of the most deep and strict conversation; a physician to the wounds of any soul; a friend, knowing not only the secret of friendship, but almost worshipped by those few persons who resorted to him as their confessor and prophet, and knew the deep value of his mind and great heart. He thought that without religion or devotion of some kind nothing great was ever accomplished: and he thought that the bigoted sectarian had better bear this in mind.

His virtues, of course, sometimes ran into extremes. It was easy to trace to the inexorable demand on all for exact truth that austerity which made this willing hermit more solitary even than he wished. Himself of a perfect probity, he required not less of others. He had a disgust at crime, and no worldly success would cover it. He detected paltering as readily in dignified and prosperous persons as in beggars, and with equal scorn. Such dangerous frankness was in his dealing that his admirers called him "that terrible Thoreau," as if he spoke when silent, and was still present when he had departed. I think the severity of his ideal interfered to deprive him of a healthy sufficiency of human society.

The habit of a realist to find things the reverse of their appearance inclined him to put every statement in a paradox. A certain habit of antagonism defaced his earlier writings,—a trick of rhetoric not quite outgrown in his later, of substituting for the obvious word and thought its diametrical opposite. He praised wild mountains and winter forests for their domestic air, in snow and ice he would find sultriness, and commended the wilderness for resembling Rome and Paris. "It was so dry, that you might call it wet."

The tendency to magnify the moment, to read all the laws of Nature in the one object or one combination under your eye, is of course comic to those who do not share the philosopher's perception of identity. To him there was no such thing as size. The pond was a small ocean; the Atlantic, a large Walden Pond. He referred every minute fact to cosmical laws. Though he meant to be just, he seemed haunted by a certain chronic assumption that the science of the day pretended completeness, and he had just found out that the *savans* had neglected to discriminate a particular botanical variety, had failed to describe the seeds or count the sepals. "That is to say," we replied, "the blockheads were not born in Concord; but who said they were? It was their unspeakable misfortune to be born in London, or Paris, or Rome; but, poor fellows, they did what they could, considering that they never saw Bateman's Pond, or Nine-Acre Corner, or Becky Stow's Swamp; besides, what were you sent into the world for, but to add this observation?"

Had his genius been only contemplative, he had been fitted to his life, but with his energy and practical ability he seemed born for great enterprise and for command; and I so much regret the loss of his rare powers of action, that I cannot help counting it a fault in him that he had no ambition. Wanting this, instead of engineering for all America, he was the captain of a huckleberry-party. Pounding beans is good to the end of pounding empires one of these days; but if, at the end of years, it is still only beans!

But these foibles, real or apparent, were fast vanishing in the incessant growth of a spirit so robust and wise, and which effaced its defeats with new triumphs. His study of Nature was a perpetual ornament to him, and inspired his friends with curiosity to see the world through his eyes, and to hear his adventures. They possessed every kind of interest.

He had many elegancies of his own, whilst he scoffed at conventional elegance. Thus, he could not bear to hear the sound of his own steps, the grit of gravel; and therefore never willingly walked in the road, but in the grass, on mountains and in woods. His senses were acute, and he remarked that by night every dwelling-house gives out bad air, like a slaughter-house. He liked the pure fragrance of melilot. He honored certain plants with special regard, and, over all, the pond-lily,—then, the gentian, and the *Mikania scandens*, and "life-everlasting," and a bass-tree which he visited every year when it bloomed, in the middle of July. He thought the scent a more oracular inquisition than the sight,—more oracular and trustworthy. The scent, of course, reveals what is concealed from the other senses. By it he detected earthiness. He delighted in echoes, and said they were almost the only kind of kindred voices that he heard. He loved Nature so well, was so happy in her solitude, that he became very jealous of cities and the sad work which their refinements and artifices made with man and his dwelling. The axe was always destroying his forest. "Thank God," he said, "they cannot cut down the clouds!" "All kinds of figures are drawn on the blue ground with this fibrous white paint."

I subjoin a few sentences taken from his unpublished manuscripts, not only as records of his thought and feeling, but for their power of description and literary excellence:—

"Some circumstantial evidence is very strong, as when you find a trout in the milk."

"The chub is a soft fish, and tastes like boiled brown paper salted."

"The youth gets together his materials to build a bridge to the moon, or, perchance, a palace or temple on the earth, and, at length the middle-aged man concludes to build a wood-shed with them."

"The locust z-ing."

"Devil's-needles zigzagging along the Nut-Meadow brook."

"Sugar is not so sweet to the palate as sound to the healthy ear."

"I put on some hemlock-boughs, and the rich salt crackling of their leaves was like mustard to the ear, the crackling of uncountable regiments. Dead trees love the fire."

"The bluebird carries the sky on his back."

"The tanager flies through the green foliage as if it would ignite the leaves."

"If I wish for a horse-hair for my compass-sight I must go to the stable; but the hair-bird, with her sharp eyes, goes to the road."

"Immortal water, alive even to the superficies."

"Fire is the most tolerable third party."

"Nature made ferns for pure leaves, to show what she could do in that line."

"No tree has so fair a bole and so handsome an instep as the beech."

"How did these beautiful rainbow-tints get into the shell of the fresh-water clam, buried in the mud at the bottom of our dark river?"

"Hard are the times when the infant's shoes are second-foot."

"We are strictly confined to our men to whom we give liberty."

"Nothing is so much to be feared as fear. Atheism may comparatively be popular with God himself."

"Of what significance the things you can forget? A little thought is sexton to all the world."

"How can we expect a harvest of thought who have not had a seed-time of character?"

"Only he can be trusted with gifts who can present a face of bronze to expectations."

"I ask to be melted. You can only ask of the metals that they be tender to the fire that melts them. To nought else can they be tender."

There is a flower known to botanists, one of the same genus with our summer plant called "Life-Everlasting," a *Gnaphalium* like that, which grows on the most inaccessible cliffs of the Tyrolese mountains, where the chamois dare hardly venture, and which the hunter, tempted by its beauty, and by his love (for it is immensely valued by the Swiss maidens), climbs the cliffs to gather, and is sometimes found dead at the foot, with the flower in his hand. It is called by botanists the *Gnaphalium leontopodium*, but by the Swiss *Edelweisse*, which signifies *Noble Purity*. Thoreau seemed to me living in the hope to gather this plant, which belonged to him of right. The scale on which his studies proceeded was so large as to require longevity, and we were the less prepared for his sudden disappearance. The country knows not yet, or in the least part, how great a son it has lost. It seems an injury that he should leave in the midst his broken task which none else can finish, a kind of indignity to so noble a soul that he should depart out of Nature before yet he has been really shown to his peers for what he is. But he, at least, is content. His soul was made for the noblest society; he had in a short life exhausted the capabilities of this world; wherever there is knowledge, wherever there is virtue, wherever there is beauty, he will find a home.

NOTES

1. "To the limit."

The Portable Emerson

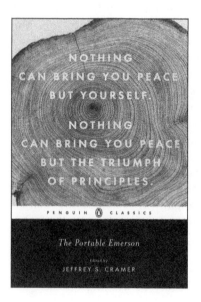

Ralph Waldo Emerson's body of work has done more than perhaps any other thinker to shape and define the American mind. His central text, *Nature*, engendered an entire spiritual and intellectual movement in transcendentalism. The first in more than thirty years, this update presents the core of his writings, including *Nature* and *The American Scholar*, along with revelatory journal entries, letters, poetry, and a sermon.